D. D. Boateng is a London-based MD. He is a member of the Royal College of General Practitioners who has contributed to several international publications including The *Lancet*, *British Journal of Surgery* and *Epilepsy & Behaviour Journal*. He has presented in multiple national and international conferences in the field of neurology and behaviour. *Morten: The Xahlia Tale* is his first fantasy novel.

For Nana

D. D. Boateng

MORTEN: THE XAHLIA TALE

AUSTIN MACAULEY PUBLISHERS™
LONDON • CAMBRIDGE • NEW YORK • SHARJAH

Copyright © D.D. Boateng 2023

The right of D.D. Boateng to be identified as author of this work has been asserted by the author in accordance with sections 77 and 78 of the Copyright, Designs and Patents Act 1988.

All rights reserved. No part of this publication may be reproduced, stored in a retrieval system, or transmitted in any form or by any means, electronic, mechanical, photocopying, recording, or otherwise, without the prior permission of the publishers.

Any person who commits any unauthorized act in relation to this publication may be liable to criminal prosecution and civil claims for damages.

This is a work of fiction. Names, characters, businesses, places, events, locales, and incidents are either the products of the author's imagination or used in a fictitious manner. Any resemblance to actual persons, living or dead, or actual events is purely coincidental.

A CIP catalogue record for this title is available from the British Library.

ISBN 9781398421592 (Paperback)
ISBN 9781398421608 (ePub e-book)

www.austinmacauley.com

First Published 2023
Austin Macauley Publishers Ltd®
1 Canada Square
Canary Wharf
London
E14 5AA

20230110

Thank you to everyone at Austin Macauley who believed in this book. I owe my friends and family a great debt of gratitude. Thank you to Nana, for your support, guidance and faith over the years. Without your genius and wisdom this book would not exist. NMYK – the unit.

Thank you to SEK, for spending copious amounts of time editing and shaping this book, without your honesty and devotion this book would not be what it is today. Thank you PAM, for instilling the idea and creating the spark. Thank you LJC, for your faith and seeing this novel through from start to finish. To Alanna Jones for your support.

Prologue

Morten was a land filled with vast masses of beautiful vegetation from the deep red of the poppy plants to the violet of the Mecular marshes. Each dawn, the birds would chirp their daybreak hymns and alert the populace it was time for another pleasant morning. The trees stood tall and protective, using their broad arms to shelter the inhabitants of the settlements below.

But there was something peculiar about Morten and the people who called this place home. Each family within its walls had a connection to a particular ancestry. The two main lineages were of Xanthari and Dahlia descent, perhaps the most presiding of all the bloodlines. Each had its own unique distinguishing ability, held only by those of that lineage. It was thus that the creative minds and exceptional gifts possessed by this remarkable population had allowed Morten to become self-sustainable.

This interesting, yet unfathomable, land had maintained thousands of years of peaceful civilisation. However, the ageing Emperor D'Xav had bore no child and therefore gave rise to no heir. His death brought about an uproar. The emperor's only sibling had undertaken an excursion to the Nanavic Empire for peace talks, in order to improve trading between the two regions. Thus, no substantial figurehead was present to stop Morten's slow and painful demise into anarchy.

Lurking beneath the facade of an unperturbed realm, an underlying tension between the Xanthari and Dahlia bloodlines had been humming. The death of the emperor (born of Xanthari father and Dahlia mother) severed all relationships between the two races. Following D'Xav's passing, the lack of order and hierarchy intensified the humming discord; now it was a monosyllabic drum.

Inevitably, the task of choosing D'Xav's successor was passed to congress. After weeks of intense and strenuous decision-making, the final electives were filed down to two: the eldest and most astute Xanthari – Xaioth and Daeth – a Dahlian politician, who held a high position in congress.

Come Election Day, Morten was on edge. Most, if not all, of its residents had taken to the streets in parade and celebration. Their dark and diminishing land was soon to be illuminated by the light of a new leader. The morning of this momentous day was brilliant and the wind was calm. Townspeople dressed in their finest garments to mark the special occasion, and the military were deployed to ensure the historic event went without a hitch.

The votes were counted.

They were neck and neck.

Morten was back to square one.

A coalition was suggested to the congressional committee but was swiftly rejected. Over the following days, friction between the two major ethnicities grew immensely, forcing the smaller, less populated groups to keep to themselves and avoid being caught in the crossfire.

Weeks quickly became months and the animosity between the two races continued to grate, each day gradually peeling away new layers and opening fresh wounds. Occasionally, there would be public brawls, theft, and – in the worse cases – murder, as Morten slowly declined into sheer mobocracy.

On the 8th of March 1791, Xaioth passed away. Immediately, an inquest was held to establish the cause of death. Undoubtedly, the Xantharis had already decided the Dahlias were the culprits. However, the lack of physical evidence meant the inquiry was closed and a death of natural causes was declared. A few days later, Daeth was found dead in his bed, again showing all the signs of a natural death…

The streets were now hostile and brooding, and the partition between bloodlines became fixed. The once multicultural society was no more. Roaming the streets alone was no longer wise.

Lineages moved farther away from the centre of Morten to finer, more enclosed areas where they would build their own intimate fortifications. Soon, the former nation was divided into six smaller states: Dahlia, Xanthari, Chantrieri, Danq, Nanavic and Yaw tribes – each sector protected by their own, arcane religious and ordained gift.

…this is the Xanthari-Dahlia tale.

Chapter I

She couldn't believe what was happening. How had he found out? Or was she just overthinking the situation?

"OK, Xander, I'll play along, but please calm down; you're scaring me. OK, who are you?"

"Xander Xictorus. Born of Xanthari father and mother, Xasteria and Xani. Now, your turn. Who are you?"

"Xander, what is going on, baby? I don't understand this game, and I'm not in the mood for games, so can you just tell me what's wrong?" she attempted to caress his face but he pushed her hand away.

"Seriously. You bore my child. I almost had myself killed for you, and you won't answer me this one question, and for what? To save face? Your face is already tainted! Or if you really don't want to answer this simple question, you can show me your Xanthari birthmark."

It was over. Her double life had now come to a bitter, confrontational end. Her mouth quivered as her eyes searched his face for any sign of warmth. Within seconds, she was reduced to tears. She opened and closed her mouth several times trying to find any words.

"Xander… I'm so, so sorry…" Her words merged into one as she drowned in her emotions. "I didn't know how to tell you. I don't know where to start."

Xander was as cold as ice, immune to her pleas.

"How about your name?"

"My birth name is Iilera Asherdimer."

Iilera Asherdimer approached Xander with caution; at this moment, in all the time she had known him, he had never seemed so volatile.

"Xander, I never intended things to turn out this way; you know what we feel for each other is genuine. I love you and I know you still love me… I hope."

Xander stared, unhinged. His face was unintelligible, she couldn't read his emotions or tell if he was even feeling any. She continued,

"Yes, I am not a Xanthari by birth, but I am a Xanthari by heart. That is why I am still here, that is why I have risked my life for you and for this Xanthari war!" sadness flushed Iilera's body – her voice became a diapason of crying, screaming and shouting.

Xander looked away. "Xander! Look at me!" she was furious with him, both for not believing how she felt and for the fact that it seemed as if he was questioning her intentions. He followed her command and looked up – his eyes a monstrous red, the veins in his temples pulsating like he was trying to cage his inner beast.

"I love you!" her voice now resembled a mourning widow. "Do you believe me when I say that? You bloody Xanthari!" His head snapped up at the word. He broke his silence after what felt like an hour of emotional warfare.

"*Iilera*... any other names you go by, huh? You deceitful, manipulative, evil, scheming, cantankerous, homeless... alien!" he pressed his knuckles against his temples to stop his head from exploding. "You tricked me, you made me fall for you, you made me forsake my first love for you. I told you everything! You made me feel sorry for you and your imaginary story! 'After the war I ran out to the battlefield and spent hours crawling over dead Xanthari carcasses searching for my parents.' You made a mockery of my history. And now you tell me you love me and expect me to believe you? Has anything you have told me actually been true and not some fabrication conjured in your sick, twisted mind?"

"Yes."

"What?"

"That I'm sorry, and I wish that I was truly one of you. This life is all I know, I don't have a real life anywhere except here, with you."

"Oh really?"

"Really."

"Were you ever going to tell me? I mean, honestly, if I had never found out like this, would you have told me?"

"I don't know, Xander. Life like this has been so perfect I don't think I would have wanted to have done something, anything to jeopardise that."

"So, no?"

She was speechless. Of course the easy way out would have been to say she would have come clean one day. But after all this time she had had enough of lies and deceit.

"So what happens now, do you seriously think that things can go back to the way they were? Christ, *Iilera*, you bore my child! Don't you think before that would have been a better time to tell me? Just something like, Oh Xander, just before we decide to start a family together, there's something you should know, I'm not really who I say I am and everything we have has been built on a lie!"

"I am sorry."

"Well, guess what? Sorry isn't enough. So I guess I'm the one that's sorry."

"So what happens now, do we say goodbye? If you want me to leave the Fortress I will. But I'll be damned if I leave without my child."

"Our child is a *Xanthari* – you are not. If you leave, our child stays with his kind. As for you, you will go to your kind."

"No, if I leave he leaves with me." She stared at him defiantly.

It seemed as if they had hit a brick wall in the conversation. Deep down, Xander knew he was ignoring his true feelings; he wasn't sure if he could live without her, or his child. His head was just so packed with fury that he simply wanted to emotionally scar her as she did him.

The arguing duo froze for a moment, thinking of what should come next in this deep meaningful conversation. Both of them were flabbergasted and fatigued by the intensity of it. Xander was panting heavily, his hands resting upon his head, his eyes fixated on the ground. Iilera was hunched over, sweaty and clammy, the heart-wrenching words expelled from her lover's lips echoing in her ears.

"Look, *Iilera,* this isn't the time to discuss this."

"God, Xander, will there ever be a good time? This isn't one of those let's wait and let things blow over moments."

"I know, I know, I just need time. If I decide now I think my decision will be too rash."

"I just really don't want to lose this, or us."

At this point the tempo finally slowed down.

"I need to go for a walk, clear my head, mull things over." Xander left, leaving Iilera heartbroken, fragile and emotionally distraught. She was left to counsel herself and the baby, who was now wailing frantically.

Out of the blue, there were three loud knocks on Xianni's door. To her utter surprise and delight, Xander stood at the doorway, one hand resting on the frame, his head bowed down. When he looked up at her, her eyes lit up like fireworks on a dark night. At this moment, Xander was now a desperate man: desperate for answers, desperate for reassurance, desperate for closure. Vengeance was his merciless fuel. When wronged, even the most humble of hearts seek revenge of some sort, as subtle as it may be. And this was Xander's plight, his turn to create some form of mental and emotional stability.

They both sat quietly in the living area, looking at each other, Xander trying his hardest to piece back the features of the woman he used to admire so fervently.

"Drink?" suggested Xianni, in a ploy to shatter the icy tension.

"Sure."

"I haven't got your favourite, 'Noire D'afrique', but I have your second, I hope that will do; you look like you need something a bit stronger anyway."

Xianni ran her fingers through her hair and shook her head seductively, like a lioness flicking her mane. She exaggerated the movements of her hips as she cruised over to the kitchen. Xander watched his first love with fascination. Granted, time had healed the majority of her scars and blemishes, but something was missing. It just wasn't the same.

They sat and enjoyed each other's company, recalling anecdotes of a happier history. The pair had an extensive past, and Xander drew upon these in order to re-establish the flame he had allowed to die out.

Before they knew it, they had drunk three bottles of wine and were laughing hysterically about one particular memory. It occurred fifteen years ago and they were both in a training session. During the spar, Xander's trousers had slowly loosened and eventually fell down to his ankles – unfortunately the day was cold and not at all flattering. Xander promised her that it had grown a lot since then and that it was no longer afraid of the cold.

Before long, it began to feel like they had never parted. Despite this, one person stayed at the forefront of both their minds – Iilera. Xander's thoughts were unsteady. He felt the only way to regain what he had lost in Iilera was to give Xianni a go.

"Just going to freshen up." Xianni smiled playfully and left the room, making her way up the croaky wooden staircase. For some reason, she felt whole again – a feeling she had long missed. Tonight was the night – the night she had waited for all those months. The one person she lived for had come back to her, her tolerance was no longer in vain. His previous relationship was no longer of importance. What mattered was that he had finally chosen her. Her jigsaw was now complete, and the picture was a happy one.

As she was away, Xander checked himself in the reflection of the window, running his fingers through his hair and washing his face and neck in the sink. He hurriedly went to sit down when he heard the staircase begin to creak, of course he never got up to check himself out; he was sitting there all along.

Xianni entered not as she had left. For one, she was no longer wearing her cloak, but a silk, lilac knee-length nightdress, which revealed her beautiful hourglass figure. She had rosied her cheeks and let her hair fall sexily over her shoulders. She felt seductive, an enjoyment that had been stripped from her until now. She felt sexy. She felt wanted. Xander ogled her, almost having to wipe the dribble from the corners of his mouth.

"Sorry I took so long; I figured I'd just get ready for bed. But you can stay as long as you like, that wasn't a ploy to get you out." She decided to shut her mouth before her tongue became even more knotted. She floated over to the sofa where Xander was sitting, forgetting that the alcohol had complete control over her being.

"Oh that's fine, it has been so long since I've seen you in your nightgown, I guess I was slightly too naive or young to appreciate how lucky I was!"

Enough talk. Xander placed his glass onto the table ahead of him and turned to face her. Pheromones surrounded them like an invisible magnet pulling them closer and closer… They connected. Their lips gently pressed against each other's; their humble noses side by side. Gradually, the kiss grew more passionate. Hands were trusted to their faces, tongues were swirling like worms out of moist soil.

Xianni willingly reclined further into the chair, almost supine. Xander removed his garments one by one.

Xianni watched him strip, her heart rate quickening as she felt herself moistening at the labia. Her nipples were red, hot and hard. Xander began to help her undress, gently kissing and caressing every part of her body.

With her back bare, all the scars from the torture she had endured were visible and covered the entirety of her dorsum. The extent of the damage was severe; her back resembled a Jackson Pollock canvas. His fingers traced every scar as he pulled her closer to his chest. At long last, what Xianni had waited for and clung on to had finally happened. She was happier than she could have ever imagined. She was finally fulfilled. Her life now had meaning.

There they lay, bare on the couch with a strip of cloth covering them both. She stared imploringly at him but couldn't help but notice the fact that his mind seemed to be elsewhere. She raised her hand and stroked his face delicately. He looked down at her and smiled.

"I've waited for this moment from even before I left the Fortress. For me, Xander my love, it has always been you and always will be as long as I am on this earth." Guilt took hold of Xander and shook him vigorously. He had been no different to those men who had taken advantage of her and stolen her innocence. He smiled awkwardly –

"I have missed you, Xianni." He chose his words carefully. After all, he did miss her.

A great wave of regret washed over him. How could he have been so heartless and foolish?

"I'm sorry, this shouldn't have happened. Not like this."

Her face changed instantly.

"What do you mean, why?"

"It just shouldn't have been like this, it should have never happened, I should go." He began to dress himself.

"What was it? My body? My face? My hands? I know they have done a lot to me. But I thought what we had was deeper than that…Xander. I loved you even before I knew what love was…even before I could spell the word! Please don't do this to me."

"Forgive me, I truly am sorry. But I can't help that my heart lies elsewhere. As much as I wish that it lay here with you, it doesn't; it lies with the mother of my son."

"So why did you just sleep with me?" Xander knew this question was coming but had no immediate justification other than malevolence.

"I was hurting, I needed somebody with me, you were the one person that I knew I could come to, to clear my mind and get my head straight. I never meant for it to go this far."

"Oh, that's great, Xander. I'm the one person you can come to, fuck, and then go home with a clear head back to your woman."

"No, ahh, I didn't mean it like that, Xi, please. I thought that Iilera and I were done for good and I thought that I could move on and come back to you, my first love. But I still can't help feeling guilty."

"Get out! You are no different to those Dincans who just used me as a relief. You are the last person in the world I would have expected to use me like a whore." Her voice was cracking. A deep, hoarse, demonic tone had possessed her.

"God damn you, Xander. May the Xanthari gods forsake you! Now get out! I don't ever want to see you again." Her cry was now weak and feeble. She sobbed silently into her arms, her hair covering her entire face. A few moments later, she stood up and stared at her lover, her eyes enraged. Xander no longer had a reason or the will to justify his actions. He was violently shoved, poked and kicked to the door, which hit him on the way out. Xander's quest for truth and security had failed. Xianni collapsed behind the door and wept, like a used, betrayed mistress. The one thing she lived for had abused, used, and left her.

She didn't know what to do with herself. Surely things couldn't get any worse? But on the other hand they couldn't get any better. The worst thing fathomable had just happened. Who was she living for now? The simple answer to that was nobody.

She cried until her eyes were red and sore. She was dehydrated and had lost her voice. There was no more cry left inside her. She lay unmoving, sprawled out on the wooden floor; eyes peeled back like something had taken control of her, her chest rising and falling rhythmically.

Every now and again she would scream, shout, cry her tearless sobs. Everything now seemed futile. She began to regret her decision to live through the torture in order to return home. She wished that she had just told the Dincans what they wanted or that they had just killed her. She had endured so much pain, clinging onto dear life for something that had now become nothing.

She remained on the floor in the very same spot for days, motionless, shackled by the pain, unable to move. She replayed that night in her mind continuously, and as she did her emotions fluctuated with each scene. She had long lost hope of any kind; she wanted to die, to be free of pain, disappointment and thought. Free, like the gods had made them to be.

Chapter II

It was a still night, and the sky was inky black. The full moon cast an eerie light onto a small, untroubled settlement named The Pars. Somewhere behind the village walls, a small figure ran down a cobbled street, unseen by the inhabitants of the crooked houses that lined the road. The only sounds were his ragged uneven breath and the damp, echoing thuds of his tired footsteps.

A single, flickering street lantern lit the cobbles. The silhouetted figure emerged, stumbling onto a narrow, meandering street from an alleyway, gasping and wheezing. Ramming himself into a wooden door, he collapsed inside. He staggered to his feet and slammed the door behind him – bolting all the locks. He looked around; the dwelling was derelict.

He could feel death lurking surreptitiously in the corners and corridors. The fireplace was dancing – but the air was still bleak and bitter. The shadow plumped his tired body onto a dark oak chair. His tongue hung from his mouth. After taking a moment's rest to compose himself, he bathed a feather quill onto the tip of his tongue, then repeatedly stabbed the quill into a dark ink pot.

He began to write. His quill scratched a frantic melody that complemented the spitting of the ebbing candles. There was a sickening bang at the door and his stomach lurched. They were here. Immediately, he snatched up the parchment and concealed it behind a portrait of a forlorn looking woman. *Crash…* splinters of wood flew across the room as the door burst open. The very hinges ruptured. The man turned to face the intruders and grinned derisively. They could kill him now; the key to the Xanthari secret was protected… at least for a while.

The intruders filed into the abode obnoxiously, each one's eyes fixated on him as if to penetrate his soul. They stood in silence. No questions asked, thus no excuses needed to be given. The wind whipped and murmured as it forced itself against the fragile windows. First they began to rattle, followed by the agitated glassware on the top shelves.

Inside the house, a woman began to make her way through the corridors to the main room where the intruders had allowed themselves entry. From behind the golden archway stepped forth this dark, distressed figure. Her nimble feet allowed her to glide to the centre of the archway; she faced south and glared at the intricate design on her dark silky cloak, her fingers intertwined in a longitudinal weave.

The breathless man attempted to arise; and without looking up the woman signalled elegantly with her arm, a sign of patience. The man slumped back into the chair, drowning his face in his palms. The intruders looked between them.

They wanted her, not him. For her mind was not like his. His mind was an impenetrable establishment built from years upon years of vigorous training; they would have to kill him. Cold hands stretched out to grip her arms. She twitched ever so slightly and the men cowered backwards – they knew what she was capable of.

As they marched her through the door, she passed the man and whispered "Preservation, Xanthe." He followed her with his probing eyes, her demeanour chilling his soul. She would be able to hold out, but for how long was the question.

The intruders escorted the hooded mistress out of the inn and surrounded her as they led her down the cobbled street where the chase had begun. Back inside, Xanthe dropped to all fours and began to peel back a pale rug that lay in the centre of the room.

Underneath the rug was a false mahogany floorboard. He pushed down on one end and the other creaked up. From the opening he retrieved a sack. Hastily, he untied the knot and removed a bow and arrow and marched towards the doorway of the house. They were still visible in the distance; he set up an arrow to the nocking point and stretched the string, firing into the pitch sky.

The arrow cawed as it disappeared into the tranquil atmosphere, before descending at a tremendous speed emitting a high-pitched whistle. It rushed straight through the cloaked woman and penetrated her torso, sending her crashing to the floor. With great effort she flipped herself over and looked at Xanthe, her face impassive. The struggle was over; she allowed herself the ease of eternal sleep.

Xanthe stared at her limp body for a moment; she was his most valued pupil – a protégé. The men looked at their prisoner sprawled across the cobble.

The clique advanced towards Xanthe, who casually set up a succession of three more arrows and fired once again. He waited. The arrows hissed like snakes, "Silence in numbers," muttered Xanthe. Simultaneously, the arrows tore through the soldiers. He returned to the cabin and made as if to close the door, forgetting that it had been removed from the hinges a few moments earlier.

He ran. His heart pounded with each footfall as he resumed his flight. There was no question as to whether he could fight off his pursuers, yet his instinct told him to flee. He reached the end of the passage and swiftly cut down the lantern causing the curtains to ignite, creating an inferno.

He allowed the flames to hungrily devour the building whilst he climbed up the stairs, slipped out of the window and was lost into the night. He descended down the rooftops as nimbly as a feather in free-fall, leaping off the roofs onto solid ground. He looked right then left. His arms arched for stability. With another quick glance to the right he made for the forest.

He could sense something peculiar, uncertain in his mind. He decided to play it down to the thick, chilly air clouding his judgement and continued his race to the forest, forbidding his heels to touch the ground; this was a delicate task, designated to the toes. He managed to clear the houses; it was now the open stretch of land that separated him from freedom and bondage.

He stopped abruptly as he approached the front line of trees leading into the forest. Lining the edge of the wood were hundreds of soldiers on their horses; he need not look up, he could sense them now.

They surrounded him. Their movements were as quiet as the mist that clung to the ground. The moonlight extended their shadows, making it seem as if Xanthe was besieged by contorted figures of monstrous proportions.

A cold, rasping voice pierced the tense silence, "Secure him." Two of the figures advanced towards Xanthe, and he did not defend himself. He suffered a sickening blow to the back of his skull. Slump. He fell to the floor. The smell of the earth filled his nostrils before he was dragged down into the black muggy oblivion of unconsciousness.

Through Xanthe's closed eyes the world was painted in reddish-purple. Slowly, he came to and was greeted by a dust laden bar striking him right across the face. He sat upright and found himself locked in a cage. Hours passed, and before he knew it darkness had swallowed him and his captors once again. Heavy manacles bound his wrists; they had already cut deep welts into his flesh. The cage opened and a harsh voice commanded him to march. He arose, head throbbing, shuffling like a slave in the wake of his captors.

As Xanthe trotted amongst the soldiers, he devised a multitude of plans to escape, running through each complex manoeuvre meticulously. Night had fallen and his eyes were clouded by black mist; the humidity of the forest gave his mouth a peculiar taste. Two of his captors fanned off from the sides as if to inspect the forest. Could it be them? Xanthe listened intently to his surroundings and heard a distant murmur, "Silence in numbers." His people were coming. He was saved.

Xanthe could sense their approach. He remained inconspicuous yet poised, careful not to relay any hint of their coming to his kidnappers. The soldiers sent out as scouts had not returned from the forest – a promising sign.

Men continued to vanish into the trees until Xanthe was alone. The darkness pressed in on him. His heart was in override and could be felt in every inch of his being. Two fingers were placed on Xanthe's shoulder. A Xanthari gesture. At this moment, he knew that his kind were here to reclaim him.

The pack gave him a sense of safety. "*I audire, ergo I vivere – I hear, therefore I live*," whispered the friend into his ear. Recognition.

"*I erit audire, et sequi – I will listen and follow*," replied Xanthe. It was pitch dark, but they both knew they each had smiled.

As Xanthe pinned back his ears, he now heard the many who had come to save him. One of the figures bent gracefully and relieved his wrists and ankles of the iron shackles. They dropped onto the crispy leaves with a muted clang. The figure rose and looked Xanthe in the eyes. The two embraced warmly, laughing into each other's shoulders. Both had doubted this reunion could have occurred after all this time, least of all as fugitives in the heart of the forest.

They released each other and sighed – one of gratitude and one of duty. The hidden rescuers remained as a part of the abiotic environment. Xanthe and his saviour delved into the dense forest, finally en route home to the Xanthari Fortress.

***

After hours of trickling through the woods like raindrops, Xanthe and his men arrived at a massive clearing immediately beyond a dense wall of trees. There it was. The beautiful, sui generis Xanthari Fortress.

Xanthe had only been away from the fortress for a year, but it had felt like a lifetime. Thoughts that had never crossed his mind until now came by the dozen. *What will I say to my people? Can I tell them the truth about my absence? How will I explain Xianni's death?* As they drew nearer to the gate, Xanthe thought it best to enter the Fortress through the underground tunnel to avoid any impromptu encounters.

Whispers and spiritual murmurs escaped through the cracks around the archaic architecture. Complex sequences of symbols had been carved into the stone walls. Xanthe gazed at these symbols, reminiscent of the past and what he had helped create. His rescuer retrieved a string leather necklace with a circular pendant. The pendant had an intricate braille illustration, familiar albeit indistinguishable.

He inserted the pendant into a slot between the legs of one of the illustrations. As the pendant was slotted into the carving, the character stood up and walked across the stone wall like a live cartoon. She pushed into the wall and created a real, tangible opening in the stone that Xanthe placed his hand into to pull the secret door open.

Inside the tunnel, vegetation consumed the cylindrical structure. A gothic stone construction loomed out of the trees. It was decrepit; ivy-throttled statues of Xanthari gods lined the walkway, judging each soul who dared to walk among them, like leering gargoyles. To an untrained eye it appeared to be a ruin, but as Xanthe crossed the threshold he sensed the watchful gazes amongst the shadows, protecting him.

Xanthe and his companion entered the annex; it was musty, cold and crypt-like. They sat at a small, claw-footed table. Settled, the companion took out a handsome ivory pipe and lit it. The cavern was quickly filled with heady smoke that made Xanthe feel light-headed.

"Now to business, my friend." They both stared at each other and burst out into a frenzy of laughter.

"Business?" shouted Xanthe.

"Yes, like the days where you would say, 'if you can sense me from ten metres I'll give you two silver pieces!' How young and naive I was." The companion looked at Xanthe in a way that a son looks at a father.

"I've missed you, we could have lost you tonight – for good!"

Xanthe interrupted, "It's OK, Xander; I know what I'm doing. And of course I could have escaped, but I see it best that the opposition knows not of my disposition. My time away has been an eye opener. My son, as our Elders predicted, war is close and even perhaps imminent… But that is a conversation for the morning. Christ, it has been so long since I have heard a familiar voice, except for Xianni's of course—" Xanthe paused, his sentence ripped roughly from his lips.

"What's wrong?"

"Xianni…was taken. In order to preserve the aim of our mission, I had to ensure that they could not break her. Xander, my son, I did what had to be done, before they did it to her." Xander's expression quickly turned into that of pure anguish.

"No… You killed her?" Xander whispered hoarsely; he was shaking. Xanthe extended a hand and squeezed Xander's shoulder by way of comfort.

"It was necessary—"

Xander became furious, "Necessary? You should have protected her but instead you murdered her!" he stood up, overturning the small table in the process. Xander's breathing was heavy, his eyes wild. There was a very pregnant pause. Finally, Xanthe broke the silence – "I had to, you should understand. You have become weak; emotion should not conquer rational action." Slowly, Xander slumped back in his chair. In an empty voice he uttered, "Master, I am sorry."

"It is fathomable, son: as much as you both tried to hide it, you were in love; however, your feelings must not, and will not, determine rationality. If anything, the death of one of us should hold us closer together. Time, son; time will heal your heart and renew your mind." Xanthe attempted to regain eye contact but Xander's were lost in mourning.

"You are right. I did love her, and I was only just beginning to realise how much she meant to me – and now she's gone, forever." Tears fell from Xander's wrinkled eyes as he buried his head in his palms and began to whimper.

"Son, what was the *septimo mensura*? Do not let emotions cloud your senses. I cannot deny, in your position I would feel exactly the same, but the key is to not allow it to take precedence."

The rest of the Xanthari clan had returned from the forest after slaughtering Xanthe's captors, unnoticed but sensed.

"They have returned. Perhaps you should get some rest. We know what they're after, and what battle waits. Anyway, you have a personal battle you need to triumph over." Xanthe stood tall, towering above his companion, before slowly turning and walking away – leaving Xander lost in his own thoughts.

Chapter III

Xander lay amidst the lush grass of a meadow, gazing at the brilliant blue azure. It was a scene of tranquillity. Xianni approached from a distance and dazzled him with that smile. She settled next to him, pressed her lips to his mouth and knotted her fingers through his. They lay there together; so close and entangled they could have been one.

The unexpressed love felt through a chemical signal so strong they could not only sense, but they could taste the pheromones. Xianni turned on her side to face him. Her intense blue eyes locking onto Xander's face like a missile on its target. She mouthed a few indecipherable words. Xander was in such bliss that listening to her wasn't important. The fact that she was there with him was sufficient satisfaction.

She raised her hand to stroke his face and Xander awoke with a start. He was in bed, cold and alone.

Chapter IV

The morning after Xanthe's return. Xander and the rest of the Xantharis congregated in the theatre. It was an ancient structure bedecked with intricate carvings, and lined with ivory-trimmed stalls. The air was musty and stale from neglect.

Xanthe, now fully recovered from his ordeal, stood on the gilded podium and cleared his throat. The crowd silenced. Xanthe aligned his spine and rotated his head 180 degrees, fanning the room with his eyes. He saw Xander's overcast appearance but decided to ignore him. Nothing could erase the great feeling of unity and oneness that Xanthe felt.

He missed these days; the days where he would teach, counsel and lead his people. His absence had been as hard on him as it had been on his people. He slowly exhaled and launched into speech.

"I must admit, it is the greatest feeling to be here once again in the presence of the ones who are so close to my heart. Once more, this emotion is amplified by the knowledge that I am here because of your bravery and your unwavering courage. It is reassuring to realise that what the elders and I have taught you is still alive and real inside each one of you. My sons, daughters, brothers and sisters…" the crowd burst into a succession of applause and merriment. Xanthe's head fanned the room once again, this time slower as he absorbed the atmosphere. He raised his palm to soothe the crowd.

"As you know, my time away has been to study the foreign enemies that have travelled across water to our shores with a purpose I do not yet know. What I do know is that they want something we have. And something that is ours is something we will never be prepared to give up. As for us, we prepare. We must sever our emotional attachments in light of the greater good. We must refine our physical abilities until they are as fluid as water yet powerful as fire." Xanthe stared fleetingly at Xander, their eyes connecting for a split second.

Unable to bear it any longer, Xander turned and shoved his way through the sea of subservient people and charged out of the hall.

The fresh air was revitalising. He ran his fingers through his dark, silky hair and kicked at the dirt. A girl sitting alone in the courtyard looked up at him, bewildered. He grunted something that sounded like an apology. So wrapped up in his own thoughts, he failed to recognise her familiar face.

The girl sat on the edge of a square wall surrounding lush, colourful plantation. She stared at him inquisitively, but feared to approach. From inside the auditorium, a rupture of another applause. Xander shielded his ears with trembling hands; he swayed from side to side attempting to drown out the unjustified admiration. The young girl observed his ridiculous display of immaturity and giggled to herself. Having heard enough, Xander ran out of the courtyard and headed for the perilous forest.

He fled, permitting the action of his legs to absorb his focus. He concentrated on moving, each footstep pounded the earth, creating little clouds of dust. He could hear his blood roaring in his ears, his lungs burned from the cold air but he couldn't stop – not yet. Not until he was out of reach. Finally, he approached a secluded clearing and dropped heavily to the ground, exhausted and empty – but free.

He closed his eyes and relaxed; reminiscent of the times Xianni and himself had shared. He stumbled upon a particular memory from their youth that he swore to himself he would never forget…

The sun was brilliant and the Xanthari warriors were away at battle; the children had been instructed to stay with the elderly and mothers to help prepare the Fortress to cater for injured fighters on their return home.

Xander and Xianni had managed to escape the confines of the Fortress to play a game of Find the Intruder. It was Xander's turn to hide. He ran as fast as his legs would carry him, while Xianni listened intently to his lissome feet. She was always better than him at sensing and listening to patterns from afar; Xander often wondered if it was perhaps for this reason that they favoured her over the rest of the Xanthari youth.

After counting to thirty, she began to sprint into the forest. On entering, she slowed right down to a crawl as she listened for cracking twigs and crunching leaves. Xander could see her from up in the tree he was hiding in. He limited his breathing in order to perplex her senses, and shuffled, sending a leaf spiralling to the ground. On the slight impact, Xianni's ears pinned back and her head fell to an angle. She turned. Xander held his breath.

Unexpectedly, a black panther cub approached her from behind. She sensed this too. She fell to all fours in order to confuse the beast... "Help" she whispered, which Xander heard.

The panther approached stealthily, like an inky shadow prowling towards the helpless girl. Xander's nerves were on fire; he was desperate to intervene yet terrified of disrupting the tension. The cat emitted a soft growl and suddenly pounced, knocking Xianni back onto the base of the very tree where Xander was perched. Petrified, Xianni could neither scream nor struggle. Xander came to his senses and leaped down from the tree, kicking the beast in the head on his descent. It yowled angrily and changed its focus. Xander glimpsed the three neat scratches across Xianni's cheek oozing crimson beads of blood, and his stomach plummeted.

The fearless creature exposed its gleaming, pearl-white teeth and licked the corners of its mouth. The cat stretched, folding its hind legs. For a short moment, it closed its emerald eyes. It said grace. Xander recited the Xanthari Mensuras, cataloguing them in order. From behind him, Xianni arose, stumbling slightly. She raised her hand to her face and smeared the crimson beads across her sweaty cheek. She remained meters away from Xander and the cub.

He began to feel at his waist, slowly and carefully removing his calf leather belt while maintaining eye contact with the creature. The cat glanced down at the belt and flashed its teeth again, warning him to stop. Xander mimicked in an attempt to divert the attention from his agenda. The belt was now unbuckled, and ready. The cat looked up at the sky, and boy Xander followed suit. Then suddenly the cat pounced, catching him of guard. Just in time, Xander freed his belt and delivered a powerful strike across the eyes of the beast, sending it crashing to the ground. It struggled to get up. But when it did, its right eye was protruding from its face and the emerald pigment had now merged with blood to produce a murky muddy hue.

The cat shuddered with pain; it's once graceful face was now a grotesque, matted mess. It whimpered and ambled away. Xander felt a strange mixture of relief and guilt; Xianni took his hand and tugged him away. Xander didn't blink, walking hand-in-hand with Xianni, not saying a word, shocked at his disposition...

As grown Xander lay in the forest reminiscing, he heard crunching leaves and snapping twigs in the far distance. He immediately sat upright, scanning his surroundings, but nothing was yet visible. He took to the trees, settling on a long branch, whose leaves shielded him from view. A group of soldiers came trudging through the forest. Xander recognised them immediately; they were the same soldiers who had kept Xanthe captive. It seemed they were still in pursuit of their ex-prisoner.

He observed them as they rallied past. They walked in perfect unison, the pitter-patter of their steps against the ground almost forming a melody. Amongst them, Xander noticed two soldiers carrying what appeared to be a corpse; shrouded in a black cloth – identical to the one Xianni would religiously wear. The cloth swung between them from side to side as they walked on unbothered by the weight they carried. It must be her. He would give anything just to see her face once more, to feel her gentle touch. Yearning and anger boiled up inside him. Their marching came to a halt, and they dropped the body onto the ground. The cloth gave, revealing long, dark brown hair. Now, he was certain.

She deserves a true Xanthari burial, he thought to himself.

Xander gazed down at the figure's pale face; if it wasn't for her ghostly complexion she might have been asleep. A single desire formed in his head: retribution. He fingered the blade of his weapon and began his pursuit.

He descended the mighty oak, hot blood coursing through his veins. He drew parallel to the thirsty soil, the sun beating a tiresome melody on the burrow of his back. He edged forward slightly, ready to pick them off one by one. A few soldiers were given orders to canvass the woods, leaving the main force with the beloved carcass.

Xander stalked his first victim like a famished wildcat, prowling silently over the bracken. The soldier was slow and arrogant, strolling carelessly and whistling tunelessly. Xander lurched forward without warning, severing the man's hamstrings, causing him to fall into the mud, howling like a lost wolf. Xander watched in disgust for a few seconds before finishing the job with one last, bone-shattering blow. Blood splattered leaves.

The remaining soldiers dispersed towards the source of the cry. It was now that Xander realised that he had once again disobeyed the seventh principle, *septimo mensura*, yet again his emotion had dictated to him.

Another soldier spotted him and grunted like a curious boar. His foolishness began to fill him; how could he try to gain revenge single-handedly against the entire force, without drawing attention? He walked away to minimise suspicion. The observant soldier followed him. A quick and sharp slice across the throat was sufficient.

Once again, he took to the trees to set back to the fortress. When he arrived he saw that Xanthe had finished his speech and people were leaving the hall, cheering and rejoicing at the long-awaited return of their leader. He locked eyes with the young girl who had witnessed his pathetic display of anger earlier. It was Xana – Xianni's best friend. He quickly threw his eyes elsewhere in embarrassment.

He joined the tide of jabbering people, hastily wiping his shaking, blood stained hands on the insides of his robe. His nerves were blazing, soon the alarm would sound signalling enemy presence. Lost in his troubled thoughts, he failed to notice Xana following him.

He twisted and turned amongst the ocean of people, discombobulated – looking for refuge or a friendly face. He stumbled into a gap between two walls. With his spine pressed against the wall he slid down onto his bottom with his knees bent. The young girl followed him into the gap and imitated Xander, sliding down by his side.

"There's blood on your robe," she said, hoping to enlighten him. He didn't respond.

"I know why you're upset," she declared. "I know you and Xianni used to be inseparable."

"You know nothing! Don't you dare talk about her as if she's dead!" his quivering, blood stained palms were now tugging the hair from his scalp. "She was the best, the most skilled, the most beautiful. How could she be gone…the best…" Xana hesitated before perching her arm over his shoulder.

"I know how you feel. As you know, when my parents were killed during the war she took me in and looked after me. Now she's gone, I don't really have any family left. You see that wall in the courtyard you saw me sitting on earlier… that's where I've been sitting since I heard of her death." Xander turned and looked at her face intently for the first time.

"Xana, I am sorry. How could I have forgotten you of all people? I've been too wrapped up in my own sorrow, if anyone understands it's you."

As they hugged, Xander gripped her tightly, relishing the feeling he felt as if now his emotional burden had been divided.

"This is wrong." He declared, nodding towards the crowd. "We are noted as the most honourable organisation in the whole Land of Morten, but now look at us: our leader sees it fit to kill his own to save the secrecy of our race – a secrecy which cannot even be deciphered by a non-Xanthari! We've become heartless, devoid of feeling." Xana looked on awkwardly. She agreed to an extent, but she did not dispute the fact that Xanthe's actions, although hasty, were necessary. "Something must be done."

"I know; as they are rejoicing we are mourning, but we must not dwell on their actions, we must not dwell on our loss. We must get on with our lives."

Xander's eyes widened. "That's the exact thing Xianni would say."

"I know; even more the reason why we should get on with things. It's not the family that caused her death – it's them. Xanthe believes they are still after the parchment. And they will not stop until they find it. It has even gone as far as discussions about a merger with the Dahlias in order to defeat their forces! I mean come on, after hundreds of years of discontent – really?"

Xander intervened, "I need to talk to Xanthe, to smooth things over. He still doubts me and thinks I am a slave to my emotions. I need to find out what's going on."

They stepped out of the gap into the main walkway where the townspeople paced, gossiping. They walked through the double doors and waded through the empty stalls.

They caught Xanthe, still on the podium but now without an audience. He seemed to be deep in thought, his mind drowning in a river of introspection. He muttered a few incoherent words in his deep, wise voice.

"Xander, Xana, why did I not receive your full attendance this morning?" they both looked at each other, willing the other to answer. Xander started,

"Sorry, I did attend but I felt slightly nauseous so I left to go and get some fresh air. Luckily, Xana was running late and caught me on the way out. She saw how ill I was looking and decided to make sure I was okay. If it wasn't for her, there would probably be regurgitation all over the courtyard." Xana was impressed by Xander's quick thinking.

Xanthe gave him a long thoughtful look. "Very well. Are you feeling any better?"

"Yes, thank you. How are you, master? You seem to be deep in contemplation, the assembly finished some time ago, so I wonder what has been going through your mind that has made you lose track of time?"

"A lot, my boy; far more than I care to think about. I will brief you both tonight at dinner if you will join me. Now I must go and sort out more of these toilsome official matters."

***

Bells rang from the Fortress towers. Xana let out a gasp and Xander's mouth fell open.

"Could it be them?" breathed Xana.

"Yes, it is them. It must be. And I led them here. The blood on my hands belongs to two of them," Xander admitted, his heart rate quickening at the realisation of what he had just caused.

"They are nearing, we must assemble!" bellowed a voice from outside the auditorium.

"It is time. They shall be forced to redeem themselves." They all scurried out of the auditorium and into the courtyard. Outside was the scene of a very organised clan. Each and every person knew their role, and what was expected of them. By the time Xander and Xana had reached the courtyard, the majority of the archers were already in place and the Elders, elderly and children were nowhere to be seen.

"Come, we must prepare. We shall take from them what they took from us."

Xander snatched a dark, matted robe. On the back was the symbolic Xanthari crest: a labyrinth with an *X* in its centre. He fastened the rope around his waist and flicked the hood up so it covered down to his eyebrows. A young boy climbed over the gate and announced that there were around a hundred soldiers marching towards the Fortress approximately half a kilometre away. Not long now.

They aligned themselves in a formation that appeared disjointed but was impeccably structured. The elites were the most advanced and skilled fighters, trained to perfection, headed by Xanthe's second-in-command Xander and Xianni. Given her relationship with Xianni, Xander had asked Xana to act in her place until a replacement was found. They disappeared into canals along the sides of the main gates, ready to emerge from underground tunnels outside the Fortress.

Xanthari warfare was an art; they were as dexterous as they were dangerous, with the gift of animal-like auscultation. The key to their ability stemmed from their arcane connection to music. Everything about the Xanthari people involved a melody. Their syntax and their movements were all in time, to the beat of the drum or to the tune of strings.

Xanthe approached Xander and whispered, "My son, I must apologise for what I have said over the last two days. But you must understand I did what was best for us all. I couldn't just consider you at the expense of the entire Xanthari race. Now you gain revenge. And after this you must be free of your attachment." The two warriors nodded in agreement, both with the same look of expectant retribution in their eyes.

Bundles of golden arrows were transported to the walls of the Fortress, and two-by-two the archers perched the arrows through sly slots in the walls. The children, Elders and elderly were stationed in the underground cabins for safety; if worst came to worst it would be down to them to raise a new generation, with the same principles and abilities as the old one. The enemies were now yards away from the Fortress walls. The drummers began to beat their drums. Simple common time:

Crochet, quaver, quaver, crochet, crochet, crochet, quaver, quaver, crochet, crochet

It was time to release the elites into the wilderness they called home. They dissolved furtively into the surrounding forest, the sound of their movements indiscernible to the average being, and hidden by the beat of the drum. This battle was a silent one. No charging or racing, they simply listened – then struck.

The soldiers were a few metres away from the gate. They knew of the unique Xanthari tactic, but had never come to visit them at home. The silence was disturbed for a second as the primary archer sent the first single arrow to flight; his accuracy was flawless – striking the smallest enemy in the centre of his forehead. On impact there was a forte in the drum beat. Then silence. Then the beat started up again… *Crochet, quaver, quaver, crochet, crochet…*

The remaining warriors drew their swords. Xana eyeballed the furthest soldier from the pack and stalked him; she waltzed around the trees with two other elites flanking her. She gained on the lone figure with lightning speed but suddenly stopped, standing half a metre behind him, thinking. He was totally oblivious to her presence and remained poised; the primary archer saw Xana's intentions and fired a single second arrow in a perfect parabola at the same time as she beheaded her prey, reconnecting the head to the body so the others did not hear it thud to the ground. Xana's flankers quietly ushered the enemy's body to the ground. Before the enemy knew it, their force was being dismantled piece by piece.

In the distance, Xander spotted eight soldiers surrounding a pile of cloth spread over a makeshift stretcher – it was Xianni's body. Xander quickly disposed of the guards and carried the carcass stealthily to the entrance of the underground tunnel where Xanthe was waiting. They unveiled the body and revealed a pale, ghostly woman. Despite slight differences in how he remembered her beautiful features, the resemblance was striking. Xanthe turned away, unable to lay eyes upon his victim, the silence weighing heavily between them. He stood, one hand leaning heavily on the crumbling stone wall supporting his frail frame. In this moment his age was truly highlighted; he suddenly seemed no more than a frail old man. Xander had fallen to his knees, his eyes transfixed to the ground, his face morbid and his jaw clenched.

One lonely element of Xianni remained. One aspect connecting this gory sight to the girl he still loved. She seemed to be at peace. Her eyelashes remaining the only poised detail of her limp being. Still engulfed in an emotional vacuum, Xander extended a quivering hand. He lightly brushed the tips of his fingers across her face. The impact of this was overwhelming. A ruthless desire for revenge seized him. He got up and stormed out of the tunnel, his strides wide and his fists clasped like mallets.

Xander ran towards the fray, darting nimbly between the masses. The ground was quickly stained red. It was times like these, thought Xander, that emotion was the most dangerous poison. He was hunting. Hunting for a figure of authority, one with the power to give orders. He did not concern himself with battling trivial, lower ranking soldiers.

He approached the top of the knoll from which the commanding officers were surveying the onslaught. He had adopted a predatory mindset, and lurked amongst a thicket of bushes, observing. It took him a few moments to assess the situation.

There were three of them. Two seem to be nothing more than cronies, their brawny physiques presumably intended to intimidate and deter attackers. This presented no challenge. Their bulk would make them slow, no match for his rapid style of combat. The third, however, posed a genuine threat; his very aura emanated a deadly menace. But Xander's machismo didn't falter, not for a moment. An image of Xianni's face surfaced in his mind. Overcome with anger, he darted out from the underbrush.

He took advantage of the element of surprise to slay the largest of them. Three quick slashes and the beast of a man was but a dark mass on the earth. As predicted, the other large soldier advanced in a bodyguard-like position. The third stood observing with interest, unfazed by his attack. The large man attempted to seize Xander's throat, his hands ready to crush his windpipe. Extending his arm made it simple for Xander to amputate it. The rest was easy. Throwing his sword to the ground, Xander stood silent and ready to take on the third.

The third man stared at Xander. He raised his hands and clapped three times… slowly. Xander glanced around, anxious that this was a method of summoning more soldiers. When no one arrived, Xander had the uncomfortable realisation that the man was applauding him sarcastically. Xander reassessed him. The daylight highlighted certain angles of his face, making his expression appear cruel, worsened by the twisted smile.

"Well done," his voice was high and full of contempt. "You are undoubtedly skilled and cherished by Xanthe. Pity… pity. It is such a waste for me to have to eliminate you. I do so admire skilled warriors, however I have reason to believe that you took the lives of some of my men and that is unforgivable." Xander dropped his head slightly and rotated his neck, releasing a sequence of clicks. The man continued: "She was beautiful, wasn't she? Her sleek brown hair and piercing blue eyes complimented her luscious figure, wouldn't you agree?" Xander's eyes opened abruptly, but the man hadn't finished, "Her death didn't go to waste. My men have made as much use of her as possible. Of course she couldn't protest, but we made sure we treated her like one of the family. Meat is meat, warm or cold, dry or wet… Did he really think it better to kill her over a little piece of parchment? Some hero you serve…" He began to laugh slowly; a cold, harrowing laugh.

Xander couldn't take another word. Only three thoughts trawled through his delicate psyche. Murder. Mutilation. Rape. His body was paralysed; did all this really happen to her?

If he were able to win this battle mentally and physically, he would then be ready for the war. The man began to laugh hysterically, throwing his hands upon his knees and gasping for oxygen; this interval gave Xander the time he needed to reform his mentality – the Xanthari mentality.

He drew closer to the hysterical man. Closer and closer. He placed two fingers on the handle of his sword. The man, still laughing, began to stumble around. Suddenly, in one quick, drunken stumble towards Xander the man launched at his waist, forcing his sword from its sheath.

Instantly the laughter ceased, and Xander stood weaponless. Xander portrayed an unhinged facade and walked closer to the enemy, unarmed.

The enemy's swing was gracefully dodged; Xander was now only a metre away from the cackling commissioner and seemed to be waltzing around him as the man continued to swing and jab the air in a foolish frenzy. The enemy swiped and Xander swerved his spine in the opposite direction, reaching into his attacker's belt and retrieving his dagger. *Now who's laughing?* Xander thought to himself.

The man's jaw dropped mid-smirk as the life was forcefully driven out of him. His mouth, now a gaping leer, seemed to mock Xander even in death. The air was heavy; the sounds of the battle were distant and unimportant. For Xander, this victory felt empty and meaningless. The man had not suffered. He had not done Xianni justice.

The compulsion for revenge that infiltrated his blood hadn't been satiated. With a strangled cry, he raised his blade and drove it into the cadaver repeatedly. His face was quickly wet with a concoction of blood and tears. His anger started to ebb and the force of his blows weakened.

Finally, exhausted both emotionally and physically, he dropped to his knees. The sword slipped from his grasp and hit the grass, and his whole body was wracked with violent sobs. Holding out his trembling hands he stared at the blood that coated them, physical evidence of his pursuit for retribution.

A hand gripped his shoulder tightly in reassurance. In his horrified state he did not care if it was a friend or foe. Craning his neck upwards, he saw Xanthe scrutinising him. He opened his mouth to explain, to justify himself. "I… I…" he stammered, his throat seemed constricted.

"Come," Xanthe pulled him to his feet. They turned and headed back to the Fortress. Xanthe demanded no explanation and Xander was grateful. As the thicket of trees began to thin, Xander glimpsed an eerie, red glow. The acrid smell of smoke filled his nostrils.

"The battle is over for now," Xanthe explained. "We are burning their dead bodies. Here." He offered Xander a pewter hip flask emblazoned with the Xanthari crest. Xander gladly accepted, relieved to see that his hands no longer trembled. He took a generous swig; the liquid burned his chapped lips. It sharpened yet dulled his senses at the same time. Thoughts appeared more lucid, and rationality returned.

Xanthe watched him closely. Still incapable of speech, Xander nodded curtly and they headed towards the dancing lights of the little fires. The smog from the burning bodies hung low over the battlefield, death was in the air. Xander tore away the bottom of his undergarment, fastening the material over his nose and mouth to protect him from the fumes.

His eyes scanned the throng of people in desperation as he hunted for Xana. People stared at him with empty, drawn expressions. Then he realised how strange he must have looked, coated in blood. Someone called his name, and his heart lifted as he saw Xana running towards him, fighting through the sea of people.

"What happened to you? You're covered in blood," she questioned.

"Not here," Xander muttered, relieved that the ability of speech appeared to have returned to him. They headed off towards the Fortress, seeking shelter, sanctity and explanations.

Chapter V

"I killed Commander Aditz. He and his men were behind the capture," confessed Xander, his face stark and unemotional.

"Well, then revenge is ours. I'm proud of you." She pulled her face closer to his as they sat side by side. Xander appeared almost lost, staring at the wall, she stroked his hand in order to relocate him, but it was of no use.

"So then why do I feel so empty? When I drove the dagger into his neck I was hoping to feel closure, but instead I feel... well that's just the problem – I don't feel, anything."

He ran his fingers through his thick, brown locks of hair and sighed. Xana stared at him, lost for words and no idea how to comfort her companion. She continued to stroke his hand in hope that maybe that was all he needed – for her to be there with him.

Night crept into the Fortress and engulfed it. The lit torches and ceremonial candles threw rays of flickering light onto the walls of the burial chamber. The burial chamber was the most treasured cavity in the fortress, where the fallen soldiers were cremated, blessed and given to the Xanthari gods. The room was bathed in gold and marble – sanctimonious elements.

The room was in the shape of an *X*; with the mineral encrusted alter positioned facing north. Giant stone sculptures of the four gods loomed over each apex of its structure. At its heart was a globular arrangement of stalls where the families of the lost ones sat.

Quietly, a cloaked man began to extinguish the torches and candles one-by-one.

It was black, utter darkness.

It was time for the ceremony to begin.

The children had ceased their petty conversations at the experience of feeling blind. At each point of the chamber's *X* were tall double wooden doors. Behind these doors, the Xanthari warriors awaited their cue to enter the burial chamber.

Xander and Xana stood in the same row, Xander following directly behind her. The other male warriors in the adjacent row frequently turned to glance at Xana, some even exchanged mocking comments. She turned momentarily and they quickly aligned their heads and ceased their banter.

Watching her silently, it was then that Xander began to appreciate her beauty. Her white chocolate skin emphasised her magnetic, light blue eyes; her salty red cheeks were like puffy pillows; her angel-given dimples fed into her face like waterfalls bordering luscious, strawberry-red full lips. Her hair fell to her shoulders, full of volume and reflecting the flickering lights. Her humble breasts lay concealed by her cloak but were still visible; as she walked her hips swayed like a Nubian goddess possessing the ability to enchant men. Tantalisingly attractive... beautiful in fact.

A few moments later, the four pinnacle doors opened, the wood creaking against the marble floors and cold air filling the chamber. Simultaneously, the warriors filed in through the four points, each shrouded in a black and bullion cloak with the Xanthari Crest engraved on their backs. Each warrior held a tall wax candle as they graduated to the centre of the chamber step-by-step in perfect synchrony. The aisles were now fully occupied with double-filed Xanthari warriors.

A long silk curtain encrusted with blue dusk jewels was drawn, revealing the bodies of the fallen Xantharis. The mothers set about blessing the bodies of their children, nephews and nieces. They wept, and mourned. At first feebly, then their cries became more belligerent until the chamber was filled with sorrow.

Each body was placed on a golden table. The mothers weaved their ways through the tables, twisting and winding, throwing their hands up to their wet, salty faces. The rest of them watched this dramatic display in a respectful silence. As the mothers shed their tears they reached into scarlet vases that sat on the floor at the corner of each table and drew out herbs and spices, sprinkling them over the cadavers. This part of the ceremony lasted for two hours but the audience watched without flinching. Finally, a sermon was delivered by Xanthe.

"Tonight, my beloved family, we gather in mourning of these who have sacrificed their own precious lives for our sakes and so that we may live another day. These courageous individuals knew the true definition of what it is to be a Xanthari. They will forever be with us, and us with them – let us begin the ritual." The cloaked warriors removed their hoods and placed their candles closer to their chins. In chorus they began:

> *As they enter the Valley of the Fallen Kin,*
> *no craft or evil shall hinder,*
> *you are with them,*
>
> *your voices, the crest of the Xantharis shall guide*
> *their minds – labyrinths they behold,*
> *Xanthari Gods,*
>
> *guide them through the labyrinths safely to your realm.*

The ritual was recited for each perished soul. The mothers had now left the podium and filed back into the central seating area. The cloaked individuals then mounted the altar, lighting the stage candles with their own. All the bodies lay naked except for pieces of cloth covering the groin and chest, if necessary. Xander and Xana glanced over the corpses, both silently looking for Xianni's body.

As they examined the corpses, they observed the generic labyrinth tattoos they all possessed imprinted around their umbilicus; memories of the sharp needle still vivid in their minds. Both Xander and Xana split up in order to find the right corpse.

Xana found her first and gave Xander a piercing stare; he soon felt the burning sensation at the back of his head. He slowly made his way over to her, lighting candles carelessly in order to divert his intentions. They walked around the corpse, analysing it for the very last time.

Suddenly, Xander noticed something peculiar about the cadaver: the Xanthari brand was missing. He thought intently, although his memories were hazy he was certain that he and Xianni had undergone the formal procedure together. He took a risk and opened his mouth.

"Where's the Xanthari birthmark?" he mouthed to Xana.

"I don't know… this can't be her." They gawked at each other, mystified. If this wasn't Xianni then who was it? Under scrutiny, the face, though remarkably blemished, still looked like hers; the jaw line, the eyes… Xander stared again at her exposed stomach in disbelief. The pale skin bore no mark; it had never been stained. He trailed his fingers over the place it should have been expecting the crest to appear. "It can't be her," he murmured to Xana, "what does this mean? Could it be that she is –" he stopped, interrupted by a sharp prod in the small of his back; he whipped around to face a surly looking Elder. "Attend in silence if you please, or not at all," his superior hissed.

Irritated, Xander nodded and grabbed Xana by the hand, pulling her towards the exit. They hurried across the flagstones, throwing shifty glances over their shoulders.

Xander tugged open the door to a small storage room in which cloths and candles were stacked in orderly rows. He struck a match whilst Xana pulled the door shut and bolted it. The match fizzed into life and he ignited the tapers, casting a comfortable light over the little chamber. Xana perched on a pile of blankets and Xander started to pace, a difficult feat in the restricted space.

"What does this mean?" he demanded. "Do you reckon they know about the Xanthari birthmark and expect us to realise it's a fake? Or do you think she tricked them? Maybe… maybe she's not dead. She could have outsmarted them. After all we are talking about Xianni," the excitement at this prospect was evident in his face and he couldn't help but grin.

"I don't know but I think it unwise to elevate our hopes when we have just begun to accept her demise. As for their knowledge of the crest, nobody knows about the Xanthari birthmark. They may have viewed it as an individual tattoo, I daresay they would have noticed the disfigurement regardless of its significance and tried to mimic it. We have no clue who switched the bodies, all we can be certain of is that the corpse lying in there does not belong to Xianni."

"When I saw them leave the corpse in the woods I was unable to glimpse her face clearly…"

A sharp rapping on the door cut him off.

"Now look, whoever's in there please vacate immediately. I've had enough. I know what it's like to be young and fiery but I have a job to do, you know, don't think I don't know what you're up to!"

Xana grinned and caught Xander's eye, she wiggled her eyebrows suggestively and he smiled in spite of himself. Reluctantly, she opened the door.

"Really, you two should be ashamed of yourselves," scolded the old woman, shaking her head. Choking out apologies they hurried around the corner where they doubled up laughing and for a moment – they forgot their troubles.

A few moments later, they hovered anxiously outside of Xanthe's office. From the window, they saw that the ceremony had come to an end. The crowds were notably subdued as they filed out, the majority of them undoubtedly headed to drown their sorrows in the local inn; taking comfort in cheap mead and mediocre barmaids.

As they patrolled, their footsteps echoed eerily. Down the corridor, the sounds of muffled chatter reached their ears from behind a closed door. Xander glanced at Xana who had already made her way towards the distant whispers. She raised her fist and delivered two neat knocks. The voices behind the door abruptly stopped. A few moments later, the door opened with a crack and a wrinkled but curious eye peeped out. "Yes?"

"We, er, we were wondering if we could speak with Xanthe. It is a matter of the utmost importance," Xana asked brightly.

"He has gone, you're out of luck," the man made to shut the door –

"Would you mind informing us of his whereabouts?" Xander interjected smoothly.

"Can't, don't know myself and I wouldn't tell *you* if I did. Goodbye." The door slammed and they heard the muted curse of "bloody kids".

Xana smiled, "Charming. What now?"

"I suppose we should wait. But Xanthe may have left the Fortress. For all we know, he may already be aware of the doppelgänger. Drink?" they headed out of the gloomy building towards the inn. Already, the sounds of raucous behaviour filled the evening's atmosphere. The small bar was well lit, a merry fire casted a yellow light across the room. It was heaving with people, all jabbering loudly or singing discordantly.

Xander ordered them two large pitchers of mead as they meandered through the boisterous crowd to a more secluded table. As they sipped their drinks, they observed the crowd for entertainment. The majority of people were simple, drunk and idiotic which made them hilarious to watch. Xander amused himself by watching the progress of a young lad attempting to flirt with the barmaid, seemingly oblivious to the fact that her boyfriend was also watching him with mounting anger.

Xander spotted a rather shady looking pair in a booth to their left. Both figures wore hooded cloaks despite the heat and appeared to be immersed in conversation. At the bar, the boyfriend had cracked and pounced on the young boy. A scuffle ensued, and the customers crowded around jeering at the fight. The shady pair looked up and noticed Xander watching; Xander dropped his gaze quickly. When he raised his eyes again, the pair had vanished.

***

Night crawled away, allowing the sun to rise up and bathe the earth. Xander peeled away the bed sheets and stretched, releasing a mighty yawn in the process. As he opened his mouth, his nose was greeted with the pleasant aroma of roasted meat. He held his hand to his stomach and felt it begin to rumble.

He walked haphazardly out of his bedroom and into the kitchen where Xana had prepared a glorious meal.

"Wow, where have you been all my life?" Xander enquired light-heartedly; she smiled and continued to flip the pancakes from the pan and onto plates.

"OK let's dig in. We've got a busy day ahead of us." She brought the last plate to the table and sat down opposite Xander, realising that he had already demolished three pancakes and begun to wage war on the sausages.

"These sausages must be the most delicious, tender sausages I have ever had. Ten out of ten!" she laughed a cute and modest laugh, and stared down at her plate, her cheeks rosied with embarrassment.

"Why thank you. The recipe was my mother's." Suddenly, she adopted a more solemn tone and began to fiddle with the food on her plate. Xander felt the need to change the subject, but his curiosity about her family's fate got the better of him.

"Well, she was a very talented woman! How did she pass, if… er… if you don't mind me asking?" he stopped posting food to his lips and looked at her intently.

"The Dahlias." Her eyes constricted to a squint at the sound of the name. Xander understood immediately and remembered how many of his loved ones died at the hands of the bloodiest battle in Xanthari history. She continued, "After the battle, the injured and dead were brought back to the Fortress, but Ma and Pa were not with them. I ran to the field to look for them; I screamed their names as loud as my lungs would allow me, but nobody answered. I trawled over the bodies of dead Dahlias and disfigured Xantharis. I can still smell the awful stench of blood and intestines burning my nostrils. But I never gave up. Without my parents I had nobody; no siblings, no aunts or uncles, I needed to find them, but I never did. Then Xianni took me in, although she wasn't that much older than I; she became my mother and my sister until I was stable enough to get on my own two feet. Of course I moved out and found my way, but if it wasn't for her there's no telling where I would be. She's always remained my big sister, and she will continue to play that role when we find her." And on that triumphant bravado she plunged into the remaining pancake. Xander looked on and agreed, "Yes, we will find her." They smiled at each other, both incredibly grateful for the other's company.

Chapter VI

Xana mounted the marble staircase that led to one of the oldest buildings in the Xanthari settlement: the library. It was a grand, ancient and airy building that contained works of historical literature written by famous Xanthari storytellers. Xana spent much of her time here. She had agreed to meet Xander at midday in the training arena. Since the ensuing threat of war had reared its head, defence preparations were in full swing. For now, however, she must search.

She passed the wizened pair of librarians who smiled at her in familiarity. Inside, she approached a random shelf in an attempt to hide her real intention, which was to sneak into an area of restricted access where records on all Xantharis were logged and filed. She waited for the librarian covering the entrance to busy herself… Surreptitiously, she breezed into the forbidden area. Once inside, she stood astounded by the multitude of scrolls and parchments. Some individual files were notably larger than others. She quickly deciphered the complex coding system and located Xianni's file; it was thick and heavy, a promising sign. If there were any legitimate reasons to explain Xianni's lack of birthmark, it would be here.

She took the file to a more secluded area. At her desk, she smoothed the scrolls across the plain of the table and dipped her head to read. Xianni's history was extensive. Her birth records were normal and the date of her marking was present. There was now no doubt in Xana's mind that the body did not belong to her beloved friend and sister.

The more recent entries in Xianni's records were a list of the books she had taken out or read from the Xanthari athenaeum. It seemed that most books she consulted were of little significance, merely fiction or instructive texts, no doubt related to education. However, the last few months' worth of loans were of far greater interest.

It appeared that Xianni had been extensively researching bloodlines. She had taken out various books on sects, cults, ancient religions and magic. Xana removed a quill and parchment from her satchel and hastily jotted down some of the more provocative titles in her spidery handwriting. One name in particular attracted her attention, a single rune 'X'.

She found it easily, for it stood out from the other volumes. It was thick and leather-bound, with a cover of emerald green. The gilded pages were fragile and yellow with age. She flicked through it and was somewhat disturbed by the illustrations and phrases that caught her attention. Wondering whether the book was really that important, she went to replace it, when a small scrawling drew her attention hidden perfectly at the end of the prologue. Her stomach lurched as she recognised Xianni's handwriting, a single word: 'Re-join'. On further, more detailed examination Xana discovered many more annotations of similar ambiguity.

Deciding that the book was indeed vital to their search for Xianni, Xana slipped it into her bag and quickly exited the library to find Xander and share the news of her breakthrough.

The midday sun was sitting directly on top of the Fortress's populace. The training arena was a battered implanted platform with groups of sand-filled bags to dictate the edges of the wrestling halos.

Xana walked around the dusty edges of the ring. She dropped her bag and perched on a stall, grinning as she observed the splendour of the Xanthari tactile. The choir was positioned on a balcony high above the wrestling halos. Their song dictated the start, finish, and tempo of training. She gawked at Xander as he flowed around his opponent, in and out, closing and drawing; admiring his skill and precision.

As his body gracefully bent and swerved, he soon realised that he now had an audience worthy of seeing him in flamboyancy. Egotistically, he offered his sword to his opponent and signalled to continue unarmed. The opponent advanced performing a balestra and then flèche. Xander was on form; side stepping whilst laughing subtly. His opponent continued to pursue him, but with one quick blow to the back of the knee, Xander sent his rival spiralling to the ground in a heap of dust. Xana arose and cheered humorously, "Woohoo! Winner!"

"Oh, Xana! When did you get back from the library?" questioned Xander credulously.

"Just now, and was fortunate enough to have caught the demise of your unworthy opponent!" the opponent shot them both a filthy look and then walked off.

"Right, well I'm just finishing up here so we can be on our way… if you don't want to show me what you're made of that is…" he laughed, and began to unwrap the cotton tape from around his knuckles.

"Okay then – let's have a quick tussle." Her remark startled him slightly as he questioned her seriousness.

"Really?" his voice went up a few octaves.

"Really." She dabbed the chalk bar onto her palms and removed her hairband.

"Not that I'm going to use your hair as a tool, but why do you remove your hairband?" questioned an increasingly puzzled Xander.

"With my hair in a ponytail, once you gain control of it, you gain control of the direction of my whole head. However, if you gain a section of my hair, my head is still comfortably free to move in any direction." She winked and without any further words stepped into the halo and greeted Xander. She placed two fingers from each hand on the tips of her ears and bowed. Xander hesitantly did the same. Just as he was about to rebuke his offer to duel, Xana delivered a mighty strike to his abdomen, forcing him back a few paces. His jaw dropped, "Did that really just happen?" he gasped to himself.

He gained back the steps he had lost and assumed the position for defence, knowing she was no longer the person he woke up to this morning. She ventured to catch him off guard by raising her arm, but instead attempting to swipe his legs from underneath him – Xianni's signature move. But he was accustomed to such trickery and counter-swiped her as she was in motion; she fell off-balance and Xander caught her just as she was about to hit the floor.

Seemingly unimpressed by his considerate heroism she wrestled herself from his grasp. Slapping her hands on her robe to remove the accumulated dust. Xander felt a false sense of superiority. She giggled at her naivety. Although she had learnt from the best, she had forgotten that he had also spent most of his training life with Xianni, thus he should be more advanced if anything. She assumed a position of defence, ready to take him on as an equal.

Given his false sense of security the next move sent Xander to the ground with a mighty thud. He choked as he lay on the dirt inhaling the sand and dust; Xana offered him a hand in retaliation for his previous act of selflessness. They both now acknowledged that they were equals and adopted a stance of offence. Their eyes locked as they stared at each other, expressions glazed and cold; for an isolated moment they were nothing but opponents. Then simultaneously they relaxed, smiling.

***

After having discovered Xianni's apparent obsessive fascination with some of the more ancient and obscure Xanthari traditions, Xana succeeded in persuading Xander to seek answers by delving deeper into their history. Then, just by chance, they remembered a place – a disused shrine to the ancient Gods – that seemed a promising place to commence their search.

Forgotten by this generation of Xantharis, the shrine lay amongst the ruins of the older settlement a short distance out of the main town, which bore the burden of a poignant history. It had been devastated by siege. The enemy had infiltrated under the heady cover of darkness, appearing like deadly shadows and gutting the very heart of the Xantharis. Assailed whilst lost in the innocence of sleep, there was no glimmer of survival. Most men, women and children were brutally slaughtered at the hands of the Dahlias.

Xander and Xana trekked through a shimmering meadow, heading to the woods. It was alive with activity; birds crooned luxuriously, insects droned and the high grass whipped their ankles. The late afternoon sun was warm and baked their exposed skin, creating little jewels of perspiration. They were grateful to enter the cool shade of the trees. When their eyes had adjusted to the gloom they headed across a forgotten path; once so worn and utilised, it was barely distinguishable now, since the forest had reclaimed it.

The ancient buildings, now crumbling shadows of their former grandeur, bared little hint at majesty. The grey, crumbling rocks stood still; seeped with solemnity. The forest had grown deeply silent, as if in a show of respect. Xander shivered unconsciously; the shade he had welcomed a short while ago had grown cold and uncanny in light of his new surroundings. He felt an uncomfortable sensation that compelled him to liken this village to a cadaver: dissected, cold and devoid of life. A ghostly tribute to what it once was.

Houses stood sorry and beaten, their windows and doors dark, gaping holes like the orbits of a skull. The church tower was a skeletal pile of rocks, precariously balanced and covered in veins of deep green ivy, cocklebur and honeysuckle. The church bell lay fallen amongst the dirt, rusted a deep crusty orange, never to tone again. Most unnerving were the welts in the stonework, a physical reminder of the sheer force that tore through the peaceful little village.

They approached the centre with caution. A large, paved area infiltrated by vegetation. Weeds and wild plants had thrust their way forcefully through the flagstones. Ruins, with their subtle menace, were on all sides.

A shrine stood on a small, circular podium. It was the statue of a striking woman – the goddess Xena – and the beautiful child peering cautiously from behind her leg was her son, Xi. According to legend, Xena had desired a child more than anything else. Eager to obtain the perfect son, she searched the earth and became enchanted by a small boy she found – Xi. Out of fear, the mortal family offered their son to Xena. When the other gods discovered what she had done, they condemned her. Her punishment was to return the child, be stripped of her godly title and cursed with infertility so she could never bear a child of her own. To escape punishment, Xena had thrown herself and Xi into the heart of a mighty tempest where they could live forever amongst the chaos, unreachable in their sanctuary, suspended together in the peaceful eye of the storm. Legend held that through the medium of water Xena and Xi watched over all mothers and children.

The statue stood in a pool of marble, which was miraculously, after so many years, still full of pearlescent water, its surface as still as glass. To Xander, the stone cherubs in the base seemed grotesque and monstrous, leering rather than preening. The woman's face was beautiful but terrible. Her blank eyes seemed to bore into him, her lips curled into a snide smile. The child, with its curly locks, seemed pitiful and desperate. Xander felt an inexplicable compulsion to reach up and snatch him away from the deranged goddess.

Shaken, he looked for Xana, who was intently searching the podium, drawing correlations with the literature that Xianni had been reading. The tension in the still air was unbearable. Xander was anxious to leave this silent, terrible place for reasons he could not explain. He felt disconcerted and irritated. He snapped at Xana, "Hurry!"

She looked at him in surprise, annoyance flashed across her face. She dipped her head and continued her work.

Xander turned his back on the shrine and wandered absently towards the church building. He needed a distraction; at least the eyes he felt probing him would have a moving target. The desire to leave was mounting. His neck prickled uncomfortably. The sun was setting and the shadow of the church tower casted a dark oblong across the shrine. It elongated and distorted Xena's facial features; her eyes seemed gaping and menacing. Xander looked away and stared back at the church.

He snapped his head quickly to the left, suddenly aware of a minute movement in the shadowy alley created between the wall of the church and the next building. Heart pounding, he edged back to gain a better view. His nerves were hypersensitive. It looked deserted. Unconvinced, he whipped around, intent on leaving immediately. He opened his mouth "Xana…" His voice died in his throat and his stomach somersaulted. The courtyard was empty.

Chapter VII

After spending a few days with his wife and family, Xanthe decided to return to his duties as a leader. His office felt estranged to him. The tapers around the room had been replaced and the chair was now so spotless it was difficult to rest his arms on the armrests without them gliding off.

He inhaled deeply, closing his eyes. Slowly, he allowed the air to escape his lungs. His heart rate diminished to the point where his pulse was barely palpable. Pleasure spelled across his face, deep meditation.

After one hour of cleansing, he opened his eyes, feeling and looking almost like a new man. He reached for his drawer, inserting his index finger into the slot to unlock it. He pulled out a wedge of paper and plumped it down onto his desk. From the drawer beneath it, he pulled out three long scrolls. On the front page of the wedged file read: *Xaxialemar Xanthe, Will and Distribution of Property*. Slowly and carefully he began to turn the pages, ensuring everything was as he had intended it to be. His wife Xari and their two children had their names detailed on almost every page of the document. Xander and Xianni were also to receive a portion of his estate. After spending the best part of the day meticulously ploughing through the official paper, he soon arrived at the last page. Headed:

In the unfortunate Demise of Xaxialemar Xanthe IV, he shall leave in charge of the Xanthari Fortress and name his successor to be:

1) Xean
2) Xianni
3) Xander

After pondering on the decision of his successor, Xanthe hesitated a moment, his eyes lingering on Xianni's name for a few seconds before signing the document and closing it with a loud clap. Something within him prevented him from taking her name out of his will, despite the prod of logic. It seemed that like Xander and Xana, he too was unconvinced of her death.

Next on his agenda were the scrolls. He laid out each one onto the table and kept them in position with heavy crystal paperweights. Detailed on two of these scrolls were maps of the Xanthari Fortress, Land of Morten and The Pars, with notes of the dense underground networks.

Xanthe looked at these and sighed. War. Xanthe never truly understood the concept of war. After all, what was the point of sending your friends and kinfolk to their deaths? To him, death was the worst thing to condemn a free-living man to, so why wish it on those who looked up to you? For the sake of acquiring land, land which belongs to no man, but the gods.

Nevertheless, as anybody would, it was his duty to defend his territory, and if that meant risking the lives of some, or even many, then so be it. He imbibed the plans thoroughly, from the river to the forest lining, to each open spread of land.

There had been certain events and information that Xanthe had chosen to keep secret. Only the Elders were fully aware of the foreign army closing in on their lands. An army so large it could easily consume the Xanthari force.

After examining the maps, he turned to the last scroll. It was smaller and had a black velvet ribbon tied around its centre. He untied the ribbon and unwound the parchment. It was a contract, which had already been signed by one party: Darshik Daveer – Leader of the Dahlias.

The relationship between the two divisions was volatile to say the least. Every battle or war up until this point was fought in alliance against the Dahlias. Across the generations both sides had lost thousands at the hands of the other. The contract was a proposition for a merger between the two tribes. The imminent threat had forced both Xanthe and Daveer to put aside their personal disdain in the best interest of their nations.

He stared long and hard at the contract. Thoughts raced through his mind. First and foremost was always: "Is this merger what is best for the preservation of the Xanthari race?"

The ink-tipped quill stained the parchment. Connection.

Chapter VIII

"Xana... This isn't funny!" Xander remonstrated, hoping she was hiding. He looked around desperately, hoping she would reappear bearing that mischievous smile he had grown accustomed to.

However, it soon dawned on him that this was no practical joke. He inspected the exact point Xana had been investigating in the courtyard. Fresh footsteps were scarcely imprinted in the sand, pointing in the direction of the podium. Strangely, there were no footsteps indicating that she had walked away from it.

She must be near, but where? Xander frenetically searched the podium for clues. After a few minutes he gave up and slumped down beside the statue, rubbing his forehead in bewilderment. Then, there was a noise. Grinding. He stood up and looked at the wall he had been slumped against... it had begun to give way.

He scoured the space made at the base of the statue. A steep, narrow spiralling staircase led up towards the head of the statue and continued down to an underground cavity beneath it. Realising that this must be where Xana had gone, he crouched down onto his hands and knees and crawled into the quadrangle opening, with every bone in his body trembling.

Once inside there was enough room – just – for him to stand up hunched over. As he delved further and further into the cavity, it became darker and darker, until he could no longer see his own feet. He continued to descend by molesting the walls and prodding each foot into the ground before deciding whether to trust the step or not.

His discombobulated mind was wrought with scepticism. Had Xana really come down the staircase, and if so, where did it end? He used his sonar-like hearing to build himself a mental image of his surrounding structures. The stairs began to increase in depth, which Xander assumed meant that he was almost at the foundation.

Foolishly, he let down his guard and picked up the pace in anticipation. Without warning, he lost his footing and his hand flung from the wall as he slithered down, rolling and coiling down the steps. The final ontological connection to the tangible realm was lost when his face slapped the concrete slab, sending him into the indistinct realm of Lethe.

The cavity was vast, and its architecture antiquated. The room was rectangular and had an intricate moulded design on its ceiling. Lining the floor, were hundreds of waxed candles, some used in entirety. Xana had lighted a few, just enough to have rays of light messily thrown to the corners of the chamber. She loomed over Xander's comatose body. His infrequent chest expansion was an indication that he was still alive. Whether he would wake up was what she was dubious about.

She had managed to tear a linen strip from her skirt and knot it around his forehead, which had been bleeding profusely. She stroked his bruised face and drew close to him. Feeling his central pulse she whispered, "It's not time yet, find your way back. You know the way; I'm here."

She walked over to the far wall and continued to admire the beautiful illustrations, full of vibrancy and colour. The scale of the piece was massive; the kind of work that would take an artist a lifetime to create. But it appeared somewhat incomplete. She gauged the area of the stone canvas and estimated it to be fifty-by-ten metres. It seemed as if the artist had been forced to abandon it mid-creation.

Along the bottom of the mural were a series of dates in chronological order from left to right. Initially, Xana thought that the artist may have died or been involved in a war many generations ago. To the bottom far right of the piece was a face, half-painted and half-outlined, Xana knelt down to inspect the unfinished portrait.

She could recognise the visage but its incompleteness jumbled her memory. After careful inspection, she stood up. To her astonishment, in front of her was an image of the utmost recognition. There, standing in the artwork she saw herself, Xianni and Xander. In the image, Xander and herself stood side by side with an unfamiliar infant between them. Xianni remained just behind them. Xianni's eyes transpired from the painting onto Xana's bare skin. She felt utterly uncomfortable. Behind her, Xander began to groan his way back to life, rendering her momentarily skittish.

Xander opened his eyes blearily and attempted to sit up. The effort made his limbs ache as they protested against his movements. Beaten, he slumped back to the ground; a searing pain in his head sent an appalling wave of nausea through him, he groaned and winced.

On reopening his eyes he was aware of the pale face amidst the gloom, hovering over him, just inches away from his nose. Struggling to focus, he heard someone speaking but the sound was faint – muted as if from far away. He shook his head in an attempt to clear it. Xana snapped into focus, talking urgently.

"Xander, can you hear me now? Xander?"

"Mm, yeah," his voice was thick and heavy.

"Finally!" Xana exclaimed, sounding exasperated but relieved. "How is your head? Do you feel able to move?" Xander nodded and instantly regretted it as the room began to spin before him. He gripped Xana's hand and heaved himself up. Lethargy overcame him. Leaning heavily on Xana, they left the secret room. The passageway was constricted and difficult. Xana muttered to him continuously, trying to guide him safely through the space. His senses felt dull and diminished. Exhaustion threatened to take over. For the first time in his life, he felt defenceless and vulnerable.

By the time they made it out into the open, night had seized the village; the ruins were concealed in the gloom. The darkness reached out and grabbed them, enveloping the two lonely figures in the velvety blackness. The cold night air was refreshing and heightened Xander's senses, puncturing his feeling of numbness. They hurried out of the silent village and back into the familiar atmosphere of the forest. They made slow progress due to Xander's newly inflicted lack of proprioception.

They paused in a clearing to enable Xana to regain her strength after keeping Xander upright for so long. Xander plumped himself down at the foot of a tree. He was shivering uncontrollably. The forest was menacing in the dark. Xana was growing anxious. His face was frighteningly pale in the moonlight and a sheen of sweat coated his features. Sunken and bloodshot eyes gave him a gauntly appearance.

The wound was still exsanguinating. In the dark it looked black and tar-like. She ripped off another length of material and bound it around his head in an attempt to stem the flow, apologising as he flinched. Fear for the amount of blood he was losing was not her only concern; the scent of it was perfect bait to hungry predators that ruled the forest by night. This thought inspired urgency in her and they trekked on.

Eventually, the Fortress loomed into view. The craggy turrets and high walls stood proud amongst the trees, promising a haven from their ordeal. They quickened their pace and approached wooden gates. Xana extended a fist and tapped the wood in a complex but precise rhythm producing a clean, purposeful sound that resonated through the still forest. After a brief but pregnant pause, a small window opened, exposing a narrow rectangle of tinted flesh, and a centre of white for the eyeball. Beady eyes peered suspiciously at them, scrutinising them momentarily, and then the window snapped shut, casting them once more in darkness. Set within the mighty gate, a small door creaked open to the left of them. They hurried through, relieved to be within the safety of the Fortress confines.

Despite his protest, Xana escorted Xander to the infirmary, frogmarching him up the stone steps into the examination room. She deposited him onto the single chair, a rather sinister looking item. He couldn't help but notice the ominous buckles tangled around the arms. He flicked one apprehensively and folded his arms in his lap. Xana returned with the nurse.

She was an old and disagreeable woman with locks of wiry grey hair pinned back in an immaculate little knot. Upon arrival, she pushed him back into the chair and began to probe at his sore head. The seat reclined until it was horizontal.

"Hmm, doesn't seem to be a fracture of the cranium; but undoubtedly caused by a single, heavy but blunt blow. How did you say he did this?"

"He fell down three flights of stairs."

Xander noticed, with some irritation, the suppressed humour in Xana's voice. He sent her a smouldering look of contempt. She grinned and winked. The nurse had started to remove the makeshift bandages, which were now entirely soaked in blood; the lapse in pressure caused a swooping sensation, and he sunk deeper into the reclined chair; gripping the arms so tightly that his knuckles stood out, white and gnarled.

To his surprise, the nurse brought out a razor – he flinched. Xana giggled and explained that she was not about to perform any miniature form of brain surgery, but simply needed to shave the hair from around the laceration.

Taking him into a side room, the nurse applied cool ointment to his head, which stung and burned. She tilted his head back with one cold hand and produced a needle and thread. Xander felt the uncomfortable tug of the fibres through his skin as the nurse stitched in five neat reef knots. On completion, she bandaged his skull and gave him a smile of approval and a tender but thoughtless pat on the head.

Xander left the room with a distinct sense of dislike for the woman. He trudged into the waiting room where Xana was waiting, absorbed in a heavy book.

She stared up at him and smiled, "We'll tell everyone you were ambushed by a pack of wolves?"

Xander smiled sarcastically and sat next to her, nodding towards the book.

"It was a fruitless effort though, wasn't it? We found nothing there."

"That's not strictly true." Xana murmured, looking both pensive and disturbed, she traced the intricate pattern on the silk cover of the book with one elegant finger. Lost in her pursuit of the pattern she failed to offer expansion. Xander's patience faltered.

"How so?" he prompted.

The sound of the nurse's flat little footsteps interrupted them. Xana rose from her seat, "Not here, back at the house."

The scent of fried sausages and pancakes had long escaped the lodging and they were greeted by the warm smell of pine instead. Once inside, Xana forgot herself and slammed the door shut. Xander cried out as he threw his hands over his ears in agony. Pulling an apologetic face, she lit two lanterns and went to sit next to him.

"How are you holding up?" she said, rubbing his back.

"I'm fine, it was just a little stumble really – nothing serious." They smiled at Xander's attempt to play down the gravity of an almost brain contusion.

"So tell me, what exactly did you find?"

Xana took out the book with the intricate engraving and sat it next to her. "Have you ever heard of a Xanthari artist, or a Xanthari portrait before?"

His face was blank. "No I can't say I have, why? I'm guessing you found a piece of work down there?"

"Yes I did, but it was incomplete. Nevertheless, it was the most enthralling piece of work my eyes have ever laid eyes on." Xana's gaze fixated in mid air; Xander could see she was reconstructing a mental image of the work.

"Right, that's incredibly helpful to finding Xianni, and possibly now Xanthe –"

"Don't be ridiculous, that obviously wasn't all. The illustration spanned the whole area of the far wall, however it wasn't finished, and there were illustrations of many familiar faces… for example, mine, yours and Xianni's."

Xander frowned, wrinkling his forehead to resemble a trio of waves crashing ashore.

"What? Are you sure they were really us?"

Xana shot Xander a cynical look. "I think I'm pretty sure what we look like. I'm guessing your common sense poured out with all that blood huh?" Xander glanced at her, unimpressed.

"In the image, the first thing which caught my eye was the bloodshed. Xanthari warriors with severed limbs and headless bodies, swimming in an ocean of tears and blood. Now, this is to the far left of the wall thus it was one of the first things to have been drawn. I figured this must symbolise the Great Xanthari, Dahlia War. Every section of the mural is dated, so it's possible to tell at which point each part had been drawn. Interestingly, there is a section on the image that shows the recent battle between us and the Acanthus soldiers on our Fortress just days ago, making me more inclined to think that the artist is amongst us. But then how was he or she able to depict the image of the Great War? Clearly nobody of our generation participated in that war. Even Xanthe was too young. How could one person be able to capture everything – past and present?" Xana paused, and released a frustrated groan. Xander sat there in silence for a few moments as he took it all in. Finally, he brought himself to repel his gums and mumble a combination of words.

"Where were we in this painting?"

"Just a few inches away from where the painter failed to complete it. You and I were stood side by side with Xianni in the background, but something really peculiar was portrayed on her face, her emotion seemed to transgress through the image and I felt her eyes crawl over my skin." Just saying it made her shiver.

"I must see it. Please, will you take me to it tomorrow morning?"

"Okay, if you are feeling better by then." Xana knew this wasn't the best idea but felt obligated given that he was as involved in the image as she was.

"Good. Now what about the book?"

"Just as ambiguous. But I feel the content alone is not important, I have a suspicion that Xianni may have left some kind of cryptic message within it. I have searched it for any of the standard codes, but so far nothing," she huffed. "You should get some sleep, especially if you want to go back tomorrow."

Chapter IX

By dawn, Xander was awake. It was a cold morning. His head was throbbing but the stinging of the wound had subsided notably. Clumsily, he clambered out of bed and performed his typical morning routine with particular care.

As expected, Xana had let herself in and was perched on a stool in the kitchen, alert and ready to leave. They had an estimated two hours before their absences would be noticed. Her head snapped up as he entered and she peered at him suspiciously.

"How's your head?"

"Fine," he lied. Her nimble fingers were drumming a relentless rhythm onto the table, each tap sending pulsatile pain through his head. He grimaced and then quickly exposed the white of his teeth in an attempt to pass it off as a smile.

"Let's get going?"

"Hmm," Xana got up from her chair and strode out of the room. "We'll have to be fast."

They left the house and hurried through the quiet streets. At the gate, they were relieved to find there had been a change of guards, making it easier to slip out.

The morning had coated the grass in the paddock in crystalline gems of dew. The disruption caused little clouds of vapour to rise, making rainbows in the weak sunlight. The cover of the forest caused the temperature to rise once they were inside the woodland; mist hugged the trees and the air smelt of moist soil. They followed their meandering footsteps from the previous night, leaping lightly over the twigs and bracken.

They approached the ruined village and quickly reached the centre. Xana swiftly located the mechanism that unlocked the entrance to the underground chamber. Again, they descended the stairs. Xana led the way and appeared to be walking extra slowly as if to labour the suspense.

At the foot of the staircase, Xana struck a match and the little light illuminated the dusty cavity. She lit two candles, handing one to Xander. They took tentative steps towards the mural. Xander lifted his flame to illuminate the details of the image. His stomach lurched as if somebody had started a fire inside him, a fire originating from his torso and spreading violently up his neck and into his head. He started sweating. There they were, a depiction he had never seen before, exactly as Xana had described it.

Xana sat cross-legged on the dusty floor, a small black book leant on her knee. Her hand gripped a piece of charcoal, which flurried across the page as she sketched the painting. He took a quick peek at her sketchbook – her skill was impressive.

He turned his attention back to the rest of the room. It appeared quite unremarkable. Bric-a-brac and memorabilia cluttered the corners. A blanket of cobwebs, like shrouds of lace, silently covered the disarrayed heap of relics.

A small chest caught his attention. He lifted it up and swiped away the surface layer of dust. He flicked the clasp and opened the lid. Inside, was a paint palette with an array of colours: deep blue, magenta, red with dabbles of yellow ochre. An ivory paintbrush was placed in the centre. He picked up the paintbrush and examined the instruments. On the underside of the palette there was an engraving:

Beloved daughter,
In order to endure, you must combine a gift you hate with one you love.

He replaced the palette, managing to dip his fingers into three colours.

"Xana, the paint is still wet. This was done recently… and there's something you should read." She glanced over the message. The levels of confusion had now quadrupled.

After a short time, Xana broke the silence by closing her sketchbook with a snap. Swiftly, she stood up and shoved her work into a shoulder bag. "Right, I think that's enough research, let's go back."

They ascended the staircase and immediately noticed that the mist had thickened. The sky was a mass of grey and purple clouds. As they stood in the courtyard, raindrops began to fall, spattering the cobbles. They hurried to the shelter of a nearby ruin that had managed to retain enough of its structure to provide a cover.

Sitting on a length of fallen timber, they listened to the sound of the rain pounding the forest. It was a calming milieu; nature's tears forcing the land into complete silence.

After ten minutes of unremitting rainfall, nature was disturbed. Something not quite right was happening. Xana and Xander exchanged startled looks as they heard the distinctive bass rumbling of male voices.

They crept around the wall and through an alleyway, now oblivious to the rain that was seeping through their clothes and coating their skin. They reached the ruined church and froze. Three cloaked figures stood in a triangle in the centre of the building's skeleton. They murmured to each other in low, serious voices, disguised by the percussion of the rain.

Two of the figures knelt down to the ground synchronously. The third drew a long, slivery dagger from the folds of his cloak. He offered it to the first man who took it and drew it across his wrist. Life's juice began to seep from the cut, dribbling down the man's arm in a tangled river. The second man repeated the act of the first. Xana and Xander looked on in shock at this blood binding ritual, wondering what sacred vow had just been agreed before their eyes.

The two men gripped each other's hands, their arms held high above their heads exposing the white of their flesh, now streaked with watery blood. They pressed their bleeding wrists together, hands intertwined. The bond between them could now only be broken by death.

Xana gripped Xander's hand questioningly. Blood-binding rituals were forgotten amongst the Xantharis a long, long time ago. In part, due to the mysticism of the ritual, but more so because of the fatal aftermath which inevitably ensued.

The men arose. The second nodded at the first and then began to clean his wound. Turning on his heel, he left the church through the fallen archway. The first man was left alone. He had made no effort to tend to his wound, allowing the blood to drip off his fingertips in little ruby beads. They splashed onto the cobbles and could have been as innocent as the rain if it were not for their telling tint.

A rumble of thunder growled across the sky, shaking the foundations of the ancient church. The man turned his head, apparently startled by the loud noise. As he did so, his hood fell softly from around his head. His face was exposed to the elements. Xana and Xander stared in horror at Xanthe.

"Traitor." The words fell from Xander's lips like lava, each letter tumbling from the corners of his mouth. Xana was speechless. How could the man she had trusted like a father do this to her, to them?

Xanthe glanced around and replaced his hood; in the corner of his eye he could vaguely see two figures watching him. Peering through the waterfall, he recognised his most favoured pupils. He could tell that they had witnessed the whole ceremony. With his head parallel to the floor he walked out from underneath the shelter and began to trudge through the perpetual rain.

The rain beat down on his cloak as he walked towards them; the crystal beads deflecting off his head and shoulders. Xander and Xana stood like two porous sponges in the rain, their minds overloaded with perplexing questions and speculations; their muscles were petrified and their facial expressions were stunned with trepidation.

He stopped and removed his hood, allowing nature's tears to molest his perfidious face. Blood was still flowing from his arm. He could not bring himself to look them in the eyes. Regiments of tears began to rally down Xana's throbbing red cheeks. Her anger was coupled with the feeling of shame and embarrassment, partly for Xanthe.

Xanthe slowly raised his head and looked at Xana first, whose tears had camouflaged with the rain, then Xander. Xana realised that the impenetrable facade that the almighty Xanthe had adopted was nothing but a way to disguise his true intentions. He had bound himself, and by default, the Xanthari people to another clan – without seeking approval.

She stepped one step closer to Xanthe and looked him squarely in the eye. Her breath was heavy and could be heard through the pitter-patter of the raindrops. Her shoulders rose slightly. She outstretched her palm and propelled it towards Xanthe's face. The slap echoed. Xanthe dropped his face once again. The red palm print on his face indicated the force behind Xana's blow. After a few moments of silence, she repeated with the other hand. His face was flung to the opposite side. The palmar imprint was now symmetrical.

"Go on, say something for yourself, you bastard!" Xana's crackling tone broke her cover and exposed her emotions; slowly she picked herself up and continued.

"You're a snake! You killed Xianni and for what? Did she find out about your disloyalty to your people, your 'fellow Xantharis'?" Xanthe raised his head and began to speak when Xander interrupted:

"How dare you. You treat us like your own and then you go and betray us like this. Going against your own people to form an outside alliance." Xander's tone took on a much more subtle and grave approach. Xanthe was finally given the chance to talk, taking a gasp of air he attempted to explain himself.

"Xander, Xana – I know you have reason to be infuriated, but you must understand, I have built this family to what it is today and I would never do anything to jeopardise the unity of it; I truly have what is in the best interest of the family at heart. If you don't believe anything else I say, then please believe this. I have done what any other honourable leader would do." He looked searchingly into their eyes but failed to find refuge in either one.

"I thought I could wait to deal with this by myself but it seems that I can't. I didn't know how to break it to you – or anyone for that matter. I cannot tell you out here in this abysmal weather. Come into the church and you will be enlightened to the revelations of our possible future. Now you shall know, whether you like it or not. Follow me." He turned away, walking back towards the church. After a moment's thought, they decide to follow him, Xana leading the way, her fists clenched.

The dullness of the sky seemed to have penetrated inside the church. The stools were derelict and the cobwebs had bridged the partition between the aisles. The dishevelled group began to break the bridges as they made their way to the altar.

"The Acanthus are going to declare war on the Dahlias; and it is only logical that we are next." The tone in his voice was empty, as though he had already been defeated.

"We suspect they intend to sweep through the North West in a circular motion, and then reach us at the South East. What's more is that we have reason to believe that they are in alliance with the Dinnoxias and have renamed themselves as the Dincans. Now, if this speculation is true they will not only want to annihilate the Xantharis and Dahlias, but they will want to capture and engulf the whole area as far as The Pars." Xander and Xana forgot their differences for a moment and absorbed the revelation.

"We suspect? Who do you mean 'we'?" questioned a rather sceptical Xander.

"The Dahlias have been in contact with us. Although they are… or shall I say were, our enemies, we should not forget that we were all once a part of Morten. The ceremony you just witnessed was the covenant agreement between

Daveer – the Dahlia leader – and I. We have sworn to fight side-by-side until the defeat of the Dincans." There was silence.

"Wait, the Dahlias, are you kidding? Do you seriously think anyone will agree to fight by their side? You have needlessly bound yourself into something that will never come to pass! How did the Elders agree to this?" Xander remonstrated, thoughts of what had happened to Xana's family at the forefront of his mind.

"You have sworn blood with another tribe. If by some miracle you do manage to get the Xantharis behind you to fight alongside those savage beasts, come the end of this war there is no way we will want to remain bound to them. So at the end of this ordeal, if both of you are alive, one of you will have to abdicate, and we all know that really means that one of you will have to die." Xana quite pointed out.

"I know this, my child," Xanthe faltered at the last word. "When word gets out about my dealings I will be counting on the both of you to head the Xantharis if need be." Xanthe placed his hand on Xander's shoulder, as if to physically pass on the pending responsibility. Xander shrugged his hand off; understandably, Xanthe did not dispute the action.

Xander couldn't bring himself to trust him again. Furious thoughts rose in his mind. Xanthe: the *great leader*, always acting for the *greater good*, without regard for his own life. His gaze met Xanthe's, who looked imploringly at him. Turning his back on him, Xander strode out of the ruined church and into the rain.

Through the murky light Xana looked at her master. He stood, shoulders hunched against the many burdens he carried, shivering very slightly from his drenched attire. A figure not of power, but of pity. She gave him a wry smile and whispered, "I understand," before she turned and ran in pursuit of Xander. She found him quickly, treading the now familiar path back to the fortress. She could tell from his disposition that he was emotionally dented. His feet pounded the soil, leaving thick depressions. She knew him well enough now to conclude that for the time being he would be unable to forgive the betrayal.

Silently, she joined him and looped her arm through his. They continued along the trail. The rain had subsided considerably; the drops fell tenderly through the trees, nourishing the woodland. The sound was comforting. As they both focused on their surroundings, their frantic heartbeats slowed to mimic the steady percussion of the raindrops. Each was wrapped in their own thick blanket of thought.

Xana's hair was dripping. She impatiently pushed the wet strands off her face. Xander's head was bleeding slightly, the recent conflict having aggravated the wound. They were exhausted before the day had even begun.

Once back inside, they defrosted by dousing themselves in hot water and changing into dry clothes. Xana scooped her sodden hair into a knot releasing a puddle of rainwater onto the ground before tying it loosely, whilst Xander attempted to tweak at his stitches to tighten them. They both relished the routine and absorption of the task. It seemed neither wanted to break the tranquil silence that had settled with discussion of the horrific torrent of information they now had to come to terms with. They left for the morning congregation without uttering a single word to one other.

They approached the intimidating building and entered the coolness of its interior, joining the mass of people filtering from the spacious antechamber into the central arena. The bustling crowd chatted animatedly; their babbling filled the cavernous space. Amongst the sea of black, a face appeared. An old man fought against the tide of people, face furrowed in concentration as he battled the current.

Xander smirked as he observed the figure's arduous progress. To his surprise, the little man reached out and gripped Xana's wrist with a single wizened hand. Xana turned to face him, startled. "Xana, Xander," he panted. "You will lead today's lecture. Xanthe is… absent. He has appointed you to lead today. He said that you would understand your duty."

Xana screwed up her face. With squinted eyes she declared firmly, "Sir, we cannot."

"Nonsense." The man dismissed and proceeded to drag her into the crowd, his grip alarmingly strong considering his obvious maturity. Panicked, Xana grabbed Xander and pulled him with her into the ocean of people. Over the excited chatter they conducted a frantic argument.

"Xana, we can't do it. Let go of his hand. Come on!"

The irritation was paramount in her voice as she replied, somewhat hysterically, "Do you really think *I* am holding onto *him?*"

"*Talk to him then, explain... explain* to him that we can't."

Exasperated, she shouted at the back of the man's head, "Sir, please, we cannot do the lecture. We have made no preparation. Think rationally, announce that there has been an unfortunate cancellation."

However, the man appeared oblivious to her pleas; she suspected that he was feigning deafness so as to avoid confronting her. They reached the base of the podium. The man parked them at the edge, instructed them to be silent and walked onto the podium. The chatter died away as he began an introduction in his slow and monotonous voice. Five feet to his left, Xana and Xander hissed angrily at each other.

"We can still run. He wouldn't be able to catch us. Look at him."

"No Xander! We can't, it's totally irresponsible."

"We are going to make fools of ourselves. Come on."

"No."

"Xana!"

"Xander, please."

"I'm going."

"No, do *not* leave me or I swear tomorrow you will wake up without any eyebrows."

"What?"

"What?"

The man slid over and murmured, "You have as long as you need," and shoved them roughly onto the podium.

A sea of faces greeted them, expectant, waiting, anticipating what they believed would be priceless words. The many eyes, dark and accusatory, drank in the two awkward figures hungrily. There was silence. And then some more silence. Followed by yet more silence. It almost seemed as if the speech was carried out in some form of telepathy.

An audible cough broke the stunned reverie; the discourteous old man made frantic gestures at them. Xana turned her attention back to the crowd and apprehensively cleared her throat.

"Good morning, we apologise for the alteration." Her voice was quiet and weak, nevertheless she pressed on.

"The task of today's lecture has befallen upon Xander and I and we hope we can deliver some meaningful words. As you know, Xander and myself head the Elites, and Xanthe has asked us to deliver this lecture in his absence. We hope we can relay something of his valuable teachings to you in this brief session." She faltered, and her voice died; it dawned on her that they had nothing to say.

Her mind was blank. She searched her memories for a stimulus from Xanthe's many speeches she had heard before, but all she could think of was their last conversation. As the silence elongated, the crowd began to stir, impatient murmuring broke out. Xana looked imploringly at Xander. Suddenly, inspiration struck him and he stepped forward.

"It has come to our attention that brutal conflict is imminent. The menace of battle threatens our mighty establishment once again." His words stunned the crowd into silence.

"Foreign enemies threaten our land, an alliance between the Dinnoxias and Acanthus has formed a new organisation, calling themselves the Dincans. Reliable sources claim that war will soon be declared on the Dahlias. So logic supports that we are next on their agenda. It is therefore vital that we remain united and strong. Make use of the coming weeks for scrupulous preparation. We must refine our skills in warfare. In the capacity of war there is no room for weakness.

"In the frenzy of battle, remember yourself; war can make animals of us all. You stand now amongst your brothers and sisters. Do not underestimate the power of unity. The lives of your comrades are as valuable as your own. Every one of you is a vital iota of this mechanism. We are the essence of Xanthari and without us the word is empty. Our blood is sacred. We shall not let it stain the ground."

A baffled hush followed. Faces looked around at each other, eyebrows furrowed for a second before the crowd erupted into applause, and cheering filled the auditorium. Relieved, Xander let out a sigh and grinned at Xana, who smiled back, albeit a little apprehensively. Hesitantly, they bowed and exited the stage.

Backstage the little old man eyed him furiously. "What have you *done,* boy? Do you realise the implications of your actions? The greater good is to protect our history, our culture, our arcane. Oh, when Xanthe hears of this…" He scurried onto the stage, shaking his head furiously and attempted to quiet the rallied crowd.

Xana beamed at Xander. "That was really beautiful."

Xander smirked, "I know."

"No really, I didn't know you had it in you," she nudged him teasingly.

"Ah yes, well you know me, always liking the element of surprise."

They walked quietly for a while, savouring the achievement.

"You were quite full-on though, Xander."

"They deserve to know the truth," he responded coolly.

"Xander, are you sure you understand the truth? Xanthe has always had our best interests at heart. You should not willingly cast away all respect for him."

Xander stared at Xana incredulously. "You still defend him? After what he did?"

"No, not entirely, but I can empathise with him. I think you are being irrational in your attacks. You are allowing your emotions to cloud the truth not because it is right but because it is easier."

"Said like the traitor himself." His voice dripped with venom as he turned and stormed off. Xana's arms flopped down to her thighs; she understood Xander's point, but she also appreciated Xanthe's motive, and knew such a ceremony was vital for the survival of the race. She was irresolute.

Then, it hit her. The single word Xianni had secretly scribed in the book – "Re-join". Xana's eyes widened as the word infiltrated her mind's eye, clear as day. Xianni had left clues. She knew. She already knew that the Dahlias and Xantharis would have to *re-join* and form an alliance similar to that of their past, Morten.

***

A few days passed and the Fortress was in the full swing of preparation. Their ammunition was more than sufficient, but they continued to produce. The mothers and children were taught combat; the ones showing the most potential were to be drafted. Xander and Xana were appointed head of the first and second regiments, which also included the task of preparing the forest for battle.

They deposited a multitude of surreptitious gauntlets, staged under the cover of the trees and leaves. Fine silk wires were used as triggers; the enemy would incur casualties even before the Fortress was in their sights. Prototypical weapons and traps were created to heighten enemy fear.

In amongst all this vigorous preparation, Xanthe was nowhere to be seen. Often, Xana would go to the Xanthari ruin to visit him where he rested in a solitary chamber with nothing but a mat and a map of the forest. He would relay ideas and tactics to her. Although she no longer had complete trust for him, she dared not challenge his meticulously developed strategies.

He suggested that they build a scale model of the Xanthari crest (a labyrinth) made of mud and sand, coated in vegetation, with the Fortress at its core. At first, she thought this was too ambitious, however Xanthe assured her that with the help of Daveer and his men his vision could be accomplished within a matter of weeks.

In sum, Xanthe and Daveer had 20,000 men and women ready for battle, and around 5000 youths to be drafted. If the Acanthus and Dinnoxias had merged, they would be up against at least 200,000 men sweeping in from the North West, meeting another 100,000 ready to receive them from the South West. The figures were overwhelming but Xanthe had no choice but to reveal the truth to Xana, as any more surprises and he would be risking losing her trust in entirety.

At first, Xander remained a quiet and distant figure amongst the crowd. But with time, his overwhelming desire to protect his people saw him paying a visit to Xanthe – of course in a very matter-of-fact capacity – to discuss tactics. Nevertheless, Xanthe was grateful.

It was an enlivening morning for the Fortress's populace; they were ready for another arduous day full of laborious tasks. As usual, all the Xantharis congregated in the main auditorium, their banter ceasing as Xana and Xander mounted the podium once again. They now commanded the respect that once belonged to Xanthe. As Xana began her motivational rhetoric, she noticed Xanthe sitting in the front stalls. He had managed a very successful disguise. In actual fact there was no real disguise – he had allowed his beard to grow down to his clavicles and hadn't trimmed his hair, which was now equal to his shoulders, wild and grey.

The sight of him threw her confidence. She began to stutter and her usual flow of elocution became fragmented.

Realising that his presence was impinging on her delivery, Xanthe rose from his seat, apologising as he waded through the stalls, knowing deep down he was apologising for much more than this ephemeral disturbance. He staggered into the aisle and made his way towards the podium; Xana's tongue froze as he swayed towards her. Her eyes followed him and so did the rest of the heads in the audience, wondering who this strange man was. Whispers ensued throughout the auditorium. Xanthe clambered up the podium and whispered to Xana, "Well done, my child, it is okay. They must know what is to come – and what I have done." She stepped aside, and Xanthe took centre stage. A voice yelled from the crowd "It's Xanthe!" and the audience erupted into a chorus of wonder and gasps.

"Yes, it is I." The crowd continued to erupt.

"Where have you been?" one voice shouted accusatorily.

"What happened to you?" said another. Heads all around nodded in unison.

"Who was it? The Dahlias or Acanthus? We will avenge your tormenters!" declared one more.

Xana and Xander glanced at each other nervously, unsure of what was to come.

"Please listen. They have done nothing to me, but for us one party has made a great and noble sacrifice, as have we. I am very aware that what I am about to tell you may turn you against me, but I hope those of you who have the interest of our race at heart will stand with me and alongside the collective of Morten and unite…" The exclamation "Morten?" was thrown into the air by one sceptical voice and bounced around the auditorium from one corner to the other.

"Let me finish. My beloved family, as you have already been enlightened, we will soon be experiencing another decisive moment in our history. But alone with our army, even at its peak, we will not be able to defeat the 200,000 strong alliance of the Dincan army. Thus, I – and only I – after much trepidation, but in complete resolution that it is for the best of our people – have agreed to unite with the Dahlias in order for us to win this war." The crowd erupted. Never before had Xanthe experienced such an outrage, turmoil was flowing through the stalls like poison; everyone was screaming and shouting, people were rising from their seats and hurling abuse.

"Wait…wait!" shouted a deep voice from the mid stalls. Xanthe recognised it as the same one who had blindly promised vengeance a few moments prior. "The Dahlias? Those demonic bastards are the ones who killed and almost annihilated our race. I was only a five-year-old boy when those heartless bastards tied me up and forced me to watch as they raped my mother and sister. They beheaded my father! I think I speak for all of us when I say death to all Dahlias!" A chorus of Death to the Dahlias echoed throughout the auditorium as others shouted out their own harrowing memories.

"What is your name, young man?" questioned Xanthe, still looking at the man in the stalls.

"My name is Xi, named after the child of the beautiful goddess Xena," declared the young man proudly.

"Am I speaking with Xi, Son of Xenon?"

"Yes! You knew my father?" his tone had mellowed, assuming a slither of hope as he rose from his stool.

"Yes I did, and I still do – he lives through you; you both share the same inclination for loyalty and justice. Your father and I fought side-by-side and a worthy warrior he was. Let us not forget that this war was of two races, and we were one of them. Equally as they almost annihilated us, we did them. I am not justifying their actions, I am not forgiving their atrocities – as I am sure you all know that my parents died as a result of the Dahlian barbarity. However, let us not lose sight of the fact that we were all once Morten, a force that withstood any attack. This new threat is not here to attack us – it is here to eradicate us. We must protect ourselves with any precaution necessary to stop yet another near-extinction disaster from occurring." Xi sat down with an empty look on his face.

The crowd was silent for a few moments, speechless. Absorbing the gravity of the situation – either be exterminated, or ally with the enemy. A few heads nodded slowly, their eyes grave with the reality of what they were agreeing to. Xanthe's eyes met theirs with sorrow. Whether they liked it or not, they had to fight alongside the children of the beasts that ruined their nation years ago.

Chapter X

A sense of bitter umbrage descended on the settlement as their sacred walls were infiltrated by foreign blood. Xanthe had decreed that in order to remain unified, the forces should train, live, and work together in the coming weeks in order to encourage a sense of cohesion between the ranks.

The Dahlias were a mysterious people, unaccustomed to the routine way of life adopted by the Xantharis. Their art was in dark magic, a power given to them by the dark spirits. Whereas the Xantharis art was a gift given unto them by deities – extreme dexterity with supernatural auscultation and perception.

Xander found them fascinating. They approached battle with a raw passion, a feat condemned by the Xantharis. He had taken to sitting on the veranda of the new combat academy and observing them in practice, enchanted by the frenzied choreography of their clashes.

On this particular occasion, he observed a fiery-haired woman sparring with a teenage boy. She was ruthless, despite the boy's apparent youth and inexperience. The woman darted about him, twirling with expert flexibility, avoiding every blow with ease. As she taunted him in dance, the boy's attacks became impatient and futile. The woman took advantage of his sluggishness, and snatched his fist from the air and twisted. With his arm acting as a pivot, she propelled him onto his knees. He howled in pain and she relinquished her hold. The boy stood up, massaging his hand, only to be reduced to a heap again with one clean sweep. They nodded stiffly but courteously at one other. The boy stormed off grumbling curses under his breath.

The woman looked up, apparently annoyed by the boy's lack of respect, and caught Xander's watchful eye. She flicked her chin up indicating the ground before her and Xander accepted the challenge with relish.

They stood a foot apart, assessing each other predatorily. Xander took in the woman, pinpointing her weaknesses. She was tall and agile, meaning she was probably quick; Xander figured he would need to use power to his advantage, being the stockier of the two. The woman regarded him lazily, standing nonchalant and slightly amused by his apparent commitment. She waited.

Xander stepped forward, aiming for her left side. As anticipated, she swerved to the right. She countered. He blocked. She grinned and retaliated with alarming force. Xander returned her blow. She took advantage of his apparent weakness, attempting to strike him with a sidekick. Again ready, he was able to seize her ankle and tip her balance. She pirouetted, commendably managing to maintain her stance.

The tempo quickened. She struck again. He misjudged her speed and received a blow to the ear that caused a sharp, tinny ringing which disorientated him. He seized her throat. Her strength was no match for his. She could not free herself. They stared at each other, two pairs of eyes locked; one triumphant, the other livid. Gradually her livid face began to calm, eventually to the point where she was no longer resisting Xander's hold. She smiled at him. Her teeth were perfect. She winked at him. Not invitingly, but mischievously. Xander's curiosity rose and he squinted his eyes. She was definitely planning something, or was she just bluffing? Then, without warning, and to Xander's astonishment, she began to thin out. Within seconds, she was gone. Vanished.

Xander knew that the Dahlias had a talent, one that easily rivalled the Xanthari. But never had he seen a person disband and thin into nothingness. He was lost in his own awe.

"Impressive," he said aloud, certain she could still hear him wherever she was. Xander was completely incognisant of his enemy. She reformed behind him, chopping him behind the knee. Xander fell to his knees. "Oh come on! How can you fight something you cannot see?" he heard a faint giggle, but could not pinpoint the location. She reappeared and wrapped her arm tightly around Xander's neck.

The feeling of fighting an invisible enemy made him feel ultimately vulnerable. He used the last of his energy to put his arms around her to toss her over his head. Just before she made contact with the ground her entity scattered once again.

Xander had a plan. He had noticed that before each one of her reappearances the wind changed in direction, ever so slightly. He slyly grabbed two handfuls of sand as he rose from his knees. Allowing the sand to slowly leak through his fingers, he stood waiting.

The sand in his left hand was blown, skewing the leakage towards the right. She was back. He turned just as she showed herself and blocked her attack. They fought for a while. Then she was gone again. They fought more, then she was gone. All the time, Xander was quickly picking up on ways to mark her presence. In one last rally, he grabbed her so tightly that she could not move a muscle. Both exhausted, they decided to call it a day.

They nodded curtly at each other. "You're talented, kid." Her voice was low, mysterious and deadly. Not what he was expecting. Xander smiled courteously and inclined his head, "As are you."

She did not smile. She stared at him for a brief moment, then turned and sauntered away, casting back over her shoulder a single instruction, "Come."

Intrigued, Xander followed.

They walked briskly into a skeleton of a building and climbed the stairs. On the top floor, the woman led him onto a balcony decorated with an intricate trellis. She seized the wooden framework and climbed onto what Xander could only guess to be the roof. He followed suit and deftly hoisted himself to join her on the secluded space at the top of the building. They stood, hidden and out of sight on the roof terrace.

They leaned on the single stone parapet, regarding the sprawling urban mess. The complicated network of the labyrinth looked tiny and unimposing from their lofty height.

The woman took out a small silver case and offered Xander a cigarette, he accepted and she extracted one for herself, twirling it between her nimble fingers. She took out a small wooden case of matches and sparked a yellow flame into life. Surrounded by the comforting cloud of rich smoke they observed the life of the city, far above the sparring duets. They watched the light bleed out of the sky, caught in deep contemplation.

"Look at them. Fully accepting their fate because they were instructed to do so."

The woman paused, taking a long drag on her cigarette. She exhaled, sending a ghostly white plume of smoke dissipating into the cold night air.

"Sheer proof that this whole establishment is corrupt at the very heart."

Xander regarded her warily, "That is an extremely heavy statement to make, and one that is open to serious contradiction."

"But not by you."

Xander was dumfounded. She returned her gaze to the city, sending shimmering flecks of ash dancing with a flick of her wrist.

"That may be so, but now we are striving for survival, I cannot fault that."

The woman said nothing. Xander felt irritation flair inexorably.

"Who are you?"

"Nothing. A tainted figure in the foible of this system. You should go by the way, Xander, they are looking for you."

"Who are you? How do you know?"

Xander attempted to draw more information from her but to no avail. She continued to survey the scene before her with a kind of aloof serenity as she inhaled on her cigarette. Dismayed, he headed back down to the ground floor where – strangely enough – Xana was standing, looking impatient and flustered.

As soon as he reached her, she immediately barraged him with questions about his strange companion, irritation evident on her face. Xander wondered if he could sense a hint of jealousy but thought it best not to probe. He answered her questions indifferently as they walked back, Xana a few steps in front of him, her jaw clenched and temples tense as she listened to his recounting of their duel.

It was time for Daveer and Xanthe to gather both ranks together in the main Xanthari auditorium for the first time. Although it was their home ground, the Xantharis still felt the immense tension present in the atmosphere.

Nobody had mounted the podium; nevertheless, the crowd remained unvoiced and unmoved. The auditorium was divided into two halves, with a longitudinal column of empty seats to symbolise the immiscibility. The air carried a repugnant odour of disdain and discontent.

Behind the podium in the prep room stood Xanthe, with Xander and Xana on either side of him; facing opposite them were Daveer and his two front warriors, one of whom was a strikingly beautiful young girl with thick, wet brown locks of precious silk flowing down to her hips like a frozen water fall. She was surprisingly petite to be a warrior of such eminence and value.

The other Dahlia was a man of equal height to Xander but with a sleeker physique, sculpted to perfection. The outline of his angular body and muscular limbs was visible even through his baggy attire. They both wore a deep blue cloak, to symbolise their status and ability. The two leagues weighed each other up. The differentiating characteristics were obvious: raw passion and hunger evident in the eyes of Daveer and his counsel, whilst a composed disposition and precision were present in the posture of Xanthe and his chosen aides.

The two leaders greeted each other with a short but firm handshake and stood side-by-side, their two chosen warriors paired behind them. They marched towards the back entrance towards the auditorium. In unison, Xanthe and Daveer banged on the door once, and it opened. As they emerged, the sea of expressionless faces in the crowd became transfixed by the vision of this antithetical union. They marched in lines onto the podium; the four soldiers fanned off to the sides behind their leaders, ordered Xanthari-Dahlia-Xanthari-Dahlia as an illustration of the unification.

Xanthe allowed Daveer to open:

"Today, my brothers and sisters, we are reunited as one, for the first time in far too long. First, I must thank the Xantharis for agreeing to fight alongside us in this war that sees the enemies trying to engulf the prehistoric land of Morten. I can see that it is too early in the stages of unification for us to fuse together, with the horrors partaken by both sides in the Great War still present in our minds. However, the existence of the descendants of Morten depends on it. Neither side has forgotten the atrocities we have endured, but we must allow the past to remain so. We cannot allow our pride and arrogance to get the better of us; we must show humility and the spirit of confederacy. For the sake of our own lives, for the lives of our children and for the innocent lives of our children's children, we must act together, as our great ancestors once did."

Next to the podium was Xanthe.

"My dear brother hath said all that need be said. Let the process of amalgamation commence with training, from dusk until dawn for the Elites and deuxieme regiment, and from dusk until the bell chime thrice for the rest. The quicker we can become accustomed to each other's techniques, the more undefeatable we will become and the shorter this inevitable war will be. Remember – we fight together, not each other. Let us begin."

Xander signalled to the Elites by tugging his earlobe; the first twenty rows arose and filed out of the auditorium. Daveer's front soldiers also signalled to the Dahlian Elites to follow on from the Xanthari.

Leading the way to the training field, Xander and Xana decided to make the acquaintance of their new joint leaders.

"Good day, I'm Xander and this is Xana. We head the Xanthari Elites." Xander waited for a reply but the two Dahlia heads did not utter a word.

"Well, to begin training we must know your names at least!" Xander chuckled and Xana smiled courteously.

"I'm Daena, nice to make your acquaintance," declared the girl, her eyes focused on the road ahead. The boy nudged her in annoyance.

"And who might you be, Mr Lemon-Sucker?" questioned a now rather irritated Xana. The young man looked at Xana and then to Xander; without saying a word he strode off. The small girl bobbed into vision, her expression now apologetic. "Don't mind him, he's finding it difficult to accept the alliance." Her voice was sweet and high to match her physique.

"We all are," replied Xana waspishly, "but at least some of us are making an effort."

Xander snorted and released a cough that sounded suspiciously like "lemon-sucker".

Daena cleared her throat, "I would be very glad to confer with the two of you. I will recount any information to my companion with great accuracy. In time, he will come round, I promise you." Xana noticed something about the way the two Dahlias were around each other, as if they were more than just comrades.

Xana and Xander smiled warmly at the girl; she was incredibly likeable and her wide, innocent eyes were trustful and inviting.

They walked through to the piazza and sat in the sunlight to discuss tactics; the innocent façade of the girl was soon shattered, reduced to dust in the conversation that ensued. She had an alarmingly vicious battle stance, quite contrary to the expectations of her physical appearance. She seemed to relish the idea of gore, pain, and brutality, depicting moves that were quite ruthless in nature. Xander sat wide-eyed, mouth slightly ajar as Daena recounted a particular anecdote: "…and then I gouged out his pretty green eyes…" she paused and sipped her tea daintily; Xander couldn't help but notice her neat fingernails, trimmed long and sharp.

"When they can't see you, they're not much of a threat," she remarked.

She gave a tinkling little laugh that sent shivers down Xana's spine. For the first time, they were grateful to be allied with the Dahlia kind rather than being their opposition.

Daveer's wife Darcie and their two sons had now formally moved into the Xanthari Fortress. Until this time, the two families had not been officially introduced. The Dahlia royals were greeted at the entrance of Xanthe's house. Xari linked arms with Darcie and took her on a tour of the house whilst the men sat in the study and talked about "important matters". The two women took an immediate shine to one another, as women do. They felt a sense of equality between them. Unlike their other halves, there was a lack of competition or superiority. The future of their nations didn't lie in their hands. Nor could they be a part of any counsel. First they were wives, second, they were mothers, and nothing else. In fact, their unifying feature was their shared inextinguishable fear for the future of their homes, families and their people.

They chitchatted whilst their children ran around in the play area. Xari found it intriguing to watch the two Dahlia infants use their gifts at such a young age. Whilst her children Xain and Xean simply thought it was cool.

The two men left the study after having heard enough official news. Soon after, they joined their wives in the lounge. The cook gladly announced that dinner was to be served. Xanthe sat opposite Darcie and Xari opposite Daveer, whilst the children were neatly tucked away at the end of the table.

Dinner went swimmingly. The four of them enjoyed the fact that they could discuss matters with each other in confidence. They were on the same level.

Under the table, Xari had felt something touch her leg. She put it down to an itch, and let it take its course. As expected, it wore off with time. Then again, the same tingly feeling worked its way around her shin.

Hours passed, and with bellies filled with rich food and wine, it was time to retire. Xanthe saw his guests off to the door. The Dahlia family stood in a line and touched the shoulder of the next and as a unit they shimmered into nothingness, frequently reappearing in the distance, until they were gone.

The success of the first dinner allowed for this to become a regular occurrence. Each week, the two families would unite at the house of Xanthe for an evening of conversation, indulgent food and expensive wine. The women would usually sit in the lounge, gossiping and laughing as they lazily kept an eye on their children whilst the men would spend the first hour in thoughtful discussion before allowing the effect of the alcohol to weaken their senses and lull their seriousness.

On one evening, as Xari made her way to the bathroom to relieve herself, she was caught by Daveer in the entrance to the study. He whispered her name hoarsely as she passed him with a short nod. Turning around and smiling warmly, she made to continue her quest for the bathroom, when he reached out and tapped her on the shoulder. He smelled overwhelmingly of liquor and cigars. "My dear friend, I request your aid," he slurred. He began to explain that it was soon to be Darcie's birthday and he was having some difficulty deciding how best to surprise her. "My wife is not one to be surprised – or pleased easily." He chuckled. Trying hard not to concentrate on her full bladder, Xari began to give a few suggestions. A moonlit dinner on the roof garden; a thousand roses and wildflowers in the bedroom; an expensive piece of jewellery – all were shot down as Daveer claimed them all cliché. After a few more minutes of thought, Xari suggested one last idea – a huge surprise party in the Great Hall – attended by the Xantharis and Dahlias plus royals from their allied nations with multiple live acts performing, and a dedicated sculpture of his beloved wife.

To her surprise, Daveer seemed half impressed by this proposal. He frowned for a few minutes, scratching at his beard before shaking his head vigorously. He then came up with a suggestion of his own: he would design garments of great luxury and elegance for his wife – but Xari would need to pair him with the best seamstress the Xantharis had to offer. Xari pondered why a woman in Darcie's position would need tailor-made garments – surely she owned them in abundance. Nonetheless, she agreed that it was a good idea, with a promise that she would find him a worthy seamstress.

For no reason in particular, Daveer suddenly became interested in Xari's cocoon cardigan. He complimented her on it and made it very clear that whoever had designed it for her would be the selected seamstress. Confused by this, she politely nodded. Still examining her very ordinary piece of clothing, he asked if he could have a better look at it. Xari offered it to him. To her surprise, his eyes lay transfixed upon her chest, ignoring the cardigan in her outstretched hand entirely.

Noticing his unsettling behaviour, he apologised, quickly rubbed the material of the garment between his fingers and then helped her place it back over shoulders. Needlessly straightening out the lapels on her cover up, he gently ran his hands alongside the outer contours of her breast, so gently that it could have been an accident. He smiled patiently and thanked her for her help. Thrown by his motives, Xari took some paces back and made to the restroom, whilst he continued standing there, smirking.

On this particular occasion, Xari couldn't wait for dinner to be over. Unfortunately for her she sat opposite Daveer at the table. For the most part, she couldn't tell with certainty that his intentions were immoral. And if they were, it had only been this one time, under the influence.

The feast continued despite Xari's noticeable silence. At the end of the table the children continued to giggle and play with their food.

"Isn't that right, Ri?" Xanthe's boisterous statement startled her and she leaped at the remark. Smiling, she took another swig of wine.

Xari felt something touch her leg. Just like it did every time they sat to have dinner with them. And every time she had put it down to an itch that, with time, wore off.

But today this itch was different in nature. It seemed a lot more persistent than usual. She looked up and caught eyes with Daveer, who was already fixed on her, grinning. Disengaging with him she went to relieve the itch by scratching, only to find Daveer's foot caressing her leg. It dawned on her that it was never an itch; it was the perverted whim of a man she and her husband had come to trust. A man whom they had formed an alliance with for the sake of their entire population. In all the years the handmaiden had spent standing observing the happenings at the table it didn't take her long to figure out the clandestine conversation happening underneath it.

Thankfully, soon it would be time for the Dahlias to retire. As usual, for the final few minutes they sat in the living area finalising their evening with a few more drinks.

Darcie made a comment and stroked Xari's arm, who failed to respond in her vacant state.

Seemingly fixed onto something in the distance, Xari suddenly dropped her glass, her hands shaking. Her face dripped with sweat as if something had sucked the life from her. Beads of perspiration ran down her face and neck. Her skin turned grey. A respite in conversation caused the rest of the party to notice Xari and the troubled state she resided in.

Xanthe carelessly threw his glass onto the tray; it spilled over and stained the rug. He cupped her face and raised a hand to feel her forehead, which was cold as ice. He wiped the sweat from her petrified face. After a sharp shake of the shoulders, Xari was resurrected back to life.

She coughed and spluttered for a few moments before throwing her head over the side of the couch; retching until the evening's meal had been completely expelled.

The handmaiden approached and helped Xari to her room whilst Xanthe saw to the exit of their guests.

"You had another vision, didn't you?" said the handmaiden.

"It was terrible… The war, everyone, the Dahlias." Xari remained in her own world.

"Rest, my lady. I will arrange a meeting with the elders first thing tomorrow. And I will put Xanthe's mind at rest."

The handmaiden was accustomed to such occurrences. In fact, Xari had been dependent on the kindness of the handmaiden since she was a young child.

In addition to her Xanthari gift, Xari also had a gift of her own. She was a *Wua hu*; the name given to those who possessed the ability to see future events. In Morten, this prestigious group of individuals remained silent amongst the masses to avoid exploitation. Playing down their gift as fortune telling, each lineage from Morten had a secret select few *Wua hus* who went unidentified to all, except the Elders of their line. Even their leaders did not know of their identities. They answered only to the Elders, who made sure their abilities were not used to modify or reverse current affairs in order to amend the future.

It was a gift but by no means a privilege.

The following morning, Xanthe sat on the armchair in the corner of the room waiting for Xari to awaken. The handmaiden was sat on a stool at the end of the bed. Peacefully, Xari blinked, accommodating the light that filled the room. Xanthe arose and made his way over to perch on the edge of the bed.

To Xanthe, these episodes were nothing but panic attacks. He knew not of the harsh realities underlying these spells. At first, Xari had found it difficult to keep such a secret from her husband. But with time and guidance from the elders, she realised that it would undoubtedly cause more harm than good. From her own experience she had found that nature had a way of restoring balance. No matter how much she had tried in the past to prevent one event from coming into existence, another would arise in its place.

At the tender age of seven, she had experienced her first vision – and a bitter image it was. It occurred one evening before bedtime. Her mother had just finished brushing her lanugo-thin hair ready for a fishtail plait. Without warning, Xari glazed over and her mind took her away from reality and into the realm of omniscience. That evening, as her mother sat behind her plaiting her hair, Xari witnessed the death of her father. She knew exactly how, when, and how much pain he felt in his final moments.

So young, she did not comprehend the weight of her gift, or burden. Despite her lack of understanding, she tried as best she could to explain to her mother what she had foreseen. When her father returned home, her mother asked her to explain her vision. Xari would never forget the look on both their faces when she told them. Later that night, peeping through the door, she saw her mother weeping on her father's shoulder: *She's a Wua hu... She's still so young. The things she will see will damage her... she doesn't deserve this.* Her father remained silent, stroking his wife's hair.

Then came the day. The day her father was supposed to die. Thinking they could cheat death, they stayed together in the house all day. Morning became night and it seemed that their plan had worked. The next morning, her father never woke up. Death took from them what it had intended, one way or another.

As commanded, she made herself known to the Elders, who would hear and catalogue the revelations.

Xanthe knelt down to her eye level.

"That was quite a panic attack yesterday, Ri; you haven't had one of those in a while. Is everything okay? Are you stressed? Is there something I can do?"

"No, thank you dear. I'm just going to go into town and get some fresh air, buy some goods for dinner if you don't mind."

"Breakfast is ready, Madam. And I will accompany you to town," nodded the handmaiden.

Xari always felt famished post-vision, such activity was not meant for humans, and her body's energy reserves were insufficient to handle the demand of an omnipotent task. After breakfast, they left the abode en route to their meeting with the Elders.

The Seven Elders sat evenly behind their marble table, whilst Xari the *Wua hu* stood before them on a level below. She told them what she had seen exactly as she had seen it. The Elders exchanged furtive glances with one another, surprised at the revelation and path the war would take.

Unexpectedly, one of them asked, "And what of Xanthe? Did he die like the rest of them?" the bluntness of the remark shook Xari. But the truth was she had no idea. She hadn't been given the knowledge. She could not see what she wanted to see, but rather what the gods had revealed to her. She had a funny feeling, a feeling that felt not quite right. This war was not going to be what she had expected.

As days went by, her urge to come clean to Xanthe became more intense. Although she knew that nature's course could not be redirected, a sense of duty and beneficence worked its way into her mind. The implications of revealing her secret were numerous. First, she would have to admit that all these years she had kept her true identity from him. Second, every time she would have a vision, he would be inclined to ask its details. And third, the moment she began to act differently around him he would know she had seen something terrible.

The war was drawing nearer, and to Xari's relief the weekly dinners had now become monthly events. She no longer had to put up with seeing Daveer's face every week at the dinner table. She cut all connection with him and only spoke to his wife whom she was not only fond of, but also felt guilty for. At their last meal, Xanthe noticed something peculiar about the way Xari shied away from partaking in conversation with Daveer. At first, it crossed his mind that she had felt guilty about something, something adulterous perhaps. So he confronted her. She was quick to deny anything of the sort. But claimed she felt uncomfortable with the look in his eye. She did not want to destroy their relationship, especially in such a crucial time as this.

Xari, with the weight of the world on her shoulders, escorted Xain and Xean to the auditorium where they would be taught the art of… Dance. Waltz and ballet were taught to the youth in order to loosen their movements, instil exactitude and precision as well as technical astuteness; the trademark features of a Xanthari warrior. Xain and Xean sat on the mat and tied up their ballet slippers. They were joined by another 200 youths, ranging from four to fourteen years of age. Lined up in a twenty-by-ten formation, they began their lesson. Three instructors lined the front of the stage of the auditorium, Xari being one of them.

Ballone-Bourree-cabriole-change-pirouette, and again, Ballone-Bourree Carbriole-change-pirouette, and again.

Xari found it increasingly difficult to concentrate. Her mind paused at the end of every sequence. The room began to swirl, then it stopped. Then it began to swirl again, and then it stopped. With each movement she made, the world around her seemed to contest her effort.

She soon realised that trying to keep a brave face was only hiding the obvious fact that not all was what it seemed; she took a step back and sat with her back straight against the wall. One of the other instructors appointed one of the more advanced pupils to mount the stage and teach alongside them. The end of the session couldn't have come sooner for Xari. Once the homework had been set, she dropped the children at home with the maid and went for walk outside the walls of the Fortress.

Chapter XI

Somewhere, a bell chimed; twelve tolls muffled by the stillness of the room. Midnight. Xana looked around for the first time in hours, stretching her shoulders and yawning widely. The library was entirely deserted, desks and aisles barren and unoccupied. Her lamp was the only light source in the cavernous hall; outside her little globe of illumination, the shelves stood quiet and dusty.

The air was eerily silent; dust particles were present like glitter floating in the moonlight that filtered through the archaic, high arched windows. With a damp thud, she overturned the cover of the volume she had been poring over and hastily shoved her notes away, parchment and quills joining the mess of memorabilia in her canvas bag. Tired, she swung the load over her shoulder. In one arm she scooped up her books, and with the other the little hurricane lamp.

Weaving her way down the aisles, she replaced the volumes. From a drawer in the front desk she extracted the heavy iron keys to the building. She blew out the lamp with a low whistle and fumbled in the darkness to the front door. She locked the heavy oak door behind her, listening to the satisfying clicks of the locking mechanism. As promised, she posted the keys back through the flap. Drawing her cloak around her she stepped out into the crisp night air.

Although the courtyard appeared completely deserted, Xana had an eerie feeling she was not alone. Exhausted and cold, she headed quickly down the steps and up a side alley towards the house. Her breath rose in a mist before her and her footsteps resounded in the empty street. The moonlight was patchy; clouds masked the light.

The nagging sensation that she was in company continued to heighten. Trying not to panic, she turned left and headed up the next narrow alley. It was long and windowless. She couldn't turn back – she could now sense her pursuer behind her. She quickened her pace. Heart pounding, adrenaline burning. She could hear the soft footfalls of her follower. After about twenty strides, she reached the halfway mark and considered turning to fight.

She took another hurried step forward, anxious not to stop with her back to her potential assailant. Without warning, a hand flew out from the wall and grabbed her arm, pulling her into a shady doorway. Another hand clamped firmly down over her lips, silencing the scream that had almost escaped her. She struggled furiously, but her attacker's grip was too strong. She attempted to bite down with no success. A low deep voice whispered in her ear, urgent, anxious: "Shh, do not be so foolish. They are coming." He softened his grip over her mouth.

"Who are you?" she whispered back angrily, keeping her voice low, sensing that this person was not the enemy. There was a pause.

"I am… Mr Lemon-Sucker." The man grinned dryly at her in the gloom and returned his gaze to the alley.

"And who is that?" she nodded at the figure advancing cautiously along the alley.

"An intruder. An impostor who appears to be intent on eradicating you."

"Intent on eradicating me? What do you mean? How is that even possible? Why? Answer me!"

"Be quiet, please," he urged her, his eyes fixed on the proceeding figure.

"How dare you! I have a right to kn –" he clamped a hand over her mouth again. The footsteps stopped.

They waited, hearts racing. The cloaked figure walked into view. They ogled the creature; it clearly wasn't of Xanthari or Dahlia lineage. It turned its head, peering into the shady doorway they were hiding in. She was looking right at him, hidden by the cover of darkness.

The cloaked figure approached. In this pitch it was impossible to see Xana, but oddly it seemed the figure could sense them. The figure stopped just inches away from Xana's face, smelling her. He raised his arm, brandishing a knife. Instinctively, Xana seized the figure's wrist, twisting the skin and sinew as he began to groan in pain. She continued to twist until she heard it snap. The knife clattered to the ground. Furious, the figure grabbed her neck; sharp, bony fingers squeezed her throat, lifting her into the air. Xana felt hot blood rush to her head as she gasped for breath. She kept her eyes focused on the figure as she struggled to loosen his grip from around her throat, her breath labouring by the second.

Then, miraculously, the grip was relinquished and she dropped to the ground. She watched as the Dahlia launched himself at her would-be assassin. He pinned the attacker to the ground with his knees. He rained blow after blow into the man's face, seeing the blood blossom from his mouth and nose. The figure sobbed, and finally lay limp and unconscious.

Mr Lemon-Sucker seized the figure's wrist and tore back the sleeve, exposing a white arm. The limb was covered in art: a symbolic '*A*' informed them this was a member of the Acanthus clan. He let it drop to the ground as he spat at the still figure. He offered her a bloody hand; she accepted and was pulled to her feet. "Are you well?"

"Fine. You?" her voice wavered slightly, as she tried to slow her breathing.

He said nothing; instead he picked up the lifeless body and began to walk away.

"What are you doing? Where are you taking him?"

"Evidence," *Mr Lemon-Sucker* grunted and headed off.

Xana found herself in an uncomfortable high backed wooden chair in Xanthe's office. Next to her sat *Mr Lemon-Sucker,* whose real name she still had not managed to learn. On the desk before her lay the unconscious form of the impostor, the light exposing his true features. Waxy skin and hollowed eyes; the man was almost the epitome of evil. On the other side of the desk sat Xanthe and Daveer. After listening to their story, a furious debate had been sparked. They had been arguing animatedly for the past half hour. The main question being, how on earth was the enemy able to penetrate their security and whose fault was it…?

Xana closed her eyes, allowing the angry voices to wash over her and be tuned out. Another fifteen minutes passed; fed up, she arose.

"May I request that I take my leave for tonight? I am very tired and I feel I can no longer be of any service here."

They barely acknowledged her, so absorbed in their fight. The lifeless body began to groan; a swift blow to the chest by Daveer was enough to send him back to sleep. She sighed and exited the room, followed swiftly by *Mr Lemon-Sucker*.

Xana could not stand it; she wanted answers and blurted out, "Thank you… for saving me."

"Do not flatter yourself, I was there simply to capture the impostor, the saving of your life was merely coincidental."

Anger and humiliation flared in Xana and she snapped, "Oh, then I am sorry for the inconvenience."

Silence.

"Tell me your name?"

He looked at her and opened his mouth but was interrupted, "Xana!"

Xander was pounding towards them. The elusive acquaintance nodded and strode away in the opposite direction. Xana watched his figure grow small and distant. Xander reached her and pulled her into a rough hug. "Some idiot messenger told me you had been attacked by an assassin, he made it sound like, well, you know, but you're not. I thought you were dead."

Xana smiled at him, "I'm not dead, I'm fine, come on let's go, I'm exhausted, I will explain everything on the way."

They arrived back at the cold, clammy lodging where they had now officially decided to cohabit; this decision gave them both a sense of security in a vulnerable period in both their lives, aside from the realisation that they both wildly enjoyed each other's company.

Xander came into the living area and stoked the fire, whilst Xana rested on the chair with her feeble hands trembling and her shoulders shuddering; it was clear that she had not entirely gotten over her ordeal.

Xander entered his bedroom, or what used to be his room as he had now donated it to Xana. He undressed hastily and threw on some night garments. As he changed Xana slowly crawled into the room stopping by the doorway.

"Don't mind me, carry on; I'm just going to try and get some shut eye." Xander looked at her for a moment and paused with his shirt tangled around his neck; he raised his head slightly to signal his approval.

She clambered on at the foot of the bed, dragging herself to the head. As she tugged at the quilt, she noticed Xander was about to dim the lantern and take up his usual position on the couch in the next room.

"Xander…" his head sprung around ready to cater for his distressed companion.

"Would you mind staying in here with me… just for tonight? I could do with the company." He walked back over to the bed where Xana had shuffled over leaving an area of welcoming bed space.

He sat on the edge of the bed at first. They talked for a while about the war and the soi-disant innovative alliance. The awkward barrier was shattered quickly enough and moments later they were lying side by side. Xander's lips were still moving as he blabbered about the discourteous nature of Daena's equal. He turned to face Xana and was surprised to see that her eyes were closed and her mouth hung open. Xander smiled to himself – glad to be of service.

Turning his whole body on his side, he glared at her. Xana's cheeks began to rise and lips tighten as she attempted to hold back her laughter. Realising she was only pretending to be asleep, Xander flung the pillow over her face.

"Do you often talk this much rubbish to unconscious people?" Xana enquired with a wide grin.

"*Tais-toi*, shut up!" exclaimed Xander, embarrassed. They lay there for a few moments just looking at each other; the chemistry between them was clear. Xander was hesitant but managed to move in ever so slightly to test the waters. Xana followed suit. Gradually, their faces met at the centre of the elongated pillow. Their noses just touching, Xander lifted up his chin slightly in an attempt to connect with her luscious lips. All of a sudden, a succession of bangs on the door drew them apart. Reluctantly, Xander got out of bed and asked whom the unwanted visitor was; Xanthe answered.

Xanthe entered, followed by Daveer and his two Elites. Xana emerged cautiously out of the bed once she heard the voices in the other room. The unannounced visit must have meant that it was important.

"We are extremely sorry for the intrusion, but we have calamitous news." Xana strolled into the main room to join the rest of them; her rescuer stared at her in her nightgown, and then at Xander with a curious look upon his face. His eyes engaged with Xander's; Xander delivered the *she's mine* scowl and Lemon Sucker's eyes fell to the floor. Xanthe continued,

"It has become apparent the allies have now become a permanent organisation and have renamed themselves the Dincans – a combination of the Dinnoxias and Acanthuses. They are recruiting other alliances to join them, and so far many have agreed. What's worse, they have already begun to attack; sweeping through via two regiments, they have already seized three-quarters of The Pars with The Resistance progressively becoming weaker. Spies have told us that they have two of the four Parchment pieces that hold the key to the Ancient Empire. Another one of the parchments remains hidden in The Pars. I managed to conceal it that same night that Xianni was… taken." Xana and Xander exchanged a look. "However, it's only a matter of time before they find it. We must retrieve it." Xanthe sighed and pressed his fingertips against his eyeballs. Daveer took the torch.

"We need to join The Pars resistance and find the parchments before it's too late. We cannot send an army as we do not want direct retaliation just yet; we've decided that just the four of you should go." The looks on their faces dropped;

they did not fear the challenge but the mere thought of four versus potentially 100,000 seemed slightly ambitious even by their standards.

"The resistance are expecting you. You shall leave tonight. You will enter armless and leave of the same accord. This is a mission of stealth. Daena and Daice, your translucence abilities will be vital. Xander and Xana, your auscultation skills will be just as instrumental. Xander knows where the parchment is concealed; he will enlighten you on the way. Is all understood?" Daveer looked each one of the charges in the eyes searchingly and concluded, "Good. If you're not back by dusk, the resistance link will inform us of your status, may it be dead or alive; only you decide on the success of this mission." Xander and Xana both smirked as *Mr Lemon-Sucker* had now been given a real name, Daice. On the other hand, the both of them were not accustomed to such raw and blunt statements made prior to conflict; they watched as Daena and Daice fed off the words dished out by Daveer. The two masters left the house without another word, leaving them to deliberate on their assignment.

"We need time to prepare," stated Xander in a flat unwelcoming tone.

"Oh sorry, were we interrupting something? Shall we let you finish off?" said Daice sarcastically, one eyebrow raised in amusement.

"Of course, we'll be waiting outside," declared Daena, neutralising the tension whilst dragging Daice by his arm.

Xander and Xana retreated into the reassuring confines of the bedroom, irritation flaring at the unwelcome interruption. The bed stood convivial and ready. Xana tugged the throw, up to the pillows, fighting the temptation to crawl within the cotton sheets. She plumped heavily onto the mattress.

Exhaustion clung to her like a shroud. Her limbs felt heavy and slow as she slipped her feet into her boots. Xander was desperate to break the silence that had expanded between them. She was hidden from him as he pulled a thick jumper over his head. On resurfacing he shot her another furtive look.

Unable to stand the tension he blurted out, "Talk about bad timing." Pathetic. She stared at him incredulously and then exhaled deeply, pushing herself from the bed, a definite smirk pasted on her face. She crossed to the mirror to hide her expression and fastened her hair into a small knot. Xander grinned and seized a pack, throwing a jumbled assortment of paraphernalia into the small compartment. He slung it over his shoulder and reached for the door, "Ready?"

"Ready."

There was a familiar moment of relaxation as the distance between them closed little by little. Daice and Daena were outside as promised. Daice lazed gracefully against the cobbled wall whilst Daena remained alert and unnaturally still.

"We will be making the first part of the journey on horseback, that is until the terrain proves too much of a challenge for the steeds. At that point we will continue on foot," asserted Xander.

They made their way to the stables on the other side of the Fortress. Daice dropped back behind the others, his pace falling in sync with Xana's. She smiled at him wryly. "What were you doing out so late anyway?" he asked.

She replied coolly, "I could ask the same of you."

"True, but I asked first, and personally I cannot deny my tendencies to operate under the obliging cover of darkness."

"I can appreciate that there are benefits of darkness."

"But are they not far outstripped by the advantages of light?" Xander interjected quite suddenly, his speech lilted with annoyance, his steps slowing to parallel theirs. He stationed himself between the pair, separating them.

"The advantages of sunlight are mediocre, associated only with leisure and aesthetics. Darkness is practical, necessary – a tool to be mastered."

They continued in such a way throughout the duration of the short walk. Daena raised an eyebrow at Xana.

By the time that they reached the stables, the air was wrought with tension. Daena addressed the keeper and selected four solemn, inky black stallions, built with powerful legs. The sturdy man led them out and started to saddle the beasts. Daena, being so tiny, couldn't reach the horse's spine, yet managed to expertly toss herself up a rather impressive height without assistance.

Xander decided to take advantage of the moment and smugly offered his hand to Xana; just before realising she had already mounted her steed independently.

They departed, sixteen hooves relentlessly pounding across the small bridge, which moaned at the impact. They were soon swallowed by the night.

The chilled breeze was refreshing and successfully banished any drowsiness. The cool temperature gradually became a burden however; their hands grew steadily numb. The weight of their task solidified in their minds as if a direct effect of the frozen air.

They reached the outskirts of The Pars quicker than expected, leaving them enough time to examine the position of the enemy camp. Xander suggested a period of allocating responsibilities, which was quickly debunked by Daice; however, after realising this task was greater than all of them combined, he set away his arrogance and listened in. The surreptitious quartet filed into the silent Pars through the south border.

The buildings were derelict and the streets bleached with blood. Carcasses lined the pavements and ditches leaked a dizzying, repugnant aroma. Xander followed Xanthe's instructions for how to locate the resistance; within a matter of moments they arrived on the corner of a street. The bodies had piled up, blocking the entrance to the door of an inn.

At the top of the mound of flesh lay a sword with a golden handle; the tip of its blade had been lodged into a skull. Underneath the skull lay corpses, each one with a black armband – symbolising that these were members of the resistance. It appeared that the entire resistance had all been slaughtered.

"You've got to be joking, right? There is no resistance… just the four of us to take on the Dincans?" remonstrated Daice rather sardonically.

"We're not taking on anybody," said Xander and Xana simultaneously; Xander continued, "Our assignment was to retrieve what's rightfully ours, not to fight."

Xana signalled for them to hush, she sensed something moving amongst the corpses; Xander sensed this too and they all back paced. Daena felt her waist to release her sword from its sheath – instinct to kill – but forgot they had made the expedition armless.

The rustling continued at the centre of the inert stack of flesh. An arm flopped off from the side of the pile and landed on the floor, followed by the twisting of a hip. Something alive was emerging from the mound of corpses. The quartet watched, whether it was resistance or Dincan they did not know. From the foundation of the mound a little opening was created, and a little trusting voice whispered,

"*Mors.*"

Daice and Daena answered, "*Vitam Nobiscum.*" At this, one of the carcasses sprung to life, shaking his limbs and throwing his neck from side to side. He signalled for them to follow him. They walked a few paces along the alley and stopped facing a large bricked wall spanning the length of the street. The newly found accomplice leaned with his back against wall and raised his foot behind him; delivering five quick, barely noticeable taps to the brickwork. After a few moments, a circular partition was made at the junction of the wall and the pavement. The man squatted and leaped into the crevice, followed by Xander, Xana, then Daena and finally the peculiar Daice. They emerged into a dark corridor and were greeted by another member of the resistance.

The corridor was littered with traps to cater for any unwanted guests. "Follow my feet and you will be fine," the second ally warned.

They continued trekking the subversive underground system until they arrived at a dead end. Ahead of them was a mouldy wall with an illustration on it – a morbidly obese man with a pint of ale in his hand. His eyes seem penetrative. They stood waiting. Then the eyes of the portrait blinked and the image began to roll up like a blind. Behind the image was a man. A real man. It was his eyes that were peering through the portrait. He welcomed them in and to their surprise they were greeted by dozens of resistance soldiers, all with the symbolic black armband tied around their bicep.

"Comrades, your hospitality is much appreciated. However, we must meet with the resistance leader urgently," Xander declared.

"'Course Xander, we know your task iz a heavy 'un. Me name iz Hatch, not hatch like a latch but hatch like a fine catch, kernal. Follow me scrawny ickle legs folks and I'll take you to where the fat bastard lives." The quartet looked at him in complete confusion, unable to decipher what he was saying.

They followed Hatch into a small, secluded room shielded by a single black curtain. A few moments later, a diminutive, round man entered, similar to the image on the wall.

"You must be Xander, and you Xana, and then you guys must be Daena and Daice…" the old man catalogued them consecutively. "Pleasure, I've been informed of your mission and we're here to make sure that all runs smoothly; even though we will not be accompanying you to the location of the parchment."

"So what exactly are you going to do?" Xander questioned.

"We're going to point you in the right direction. I am under strict orders not to help you more than necessary, Daveer and Xanthe have decided that this be a test of unity and humility on both your halves. This is a map of The Pars including the new trenches and forts." The man rolled out a map and used hemispherical stones to hold the corners flat. He spent the next hour dictating the best and most effective technique of infiltration.

It was time. The quartet were led by Hatch back out onto the street. He ushered them as far as he was able, "Alriaaaght, all of ya break ya legs, ex de de, n'oublie pas we are depending on ya, have fun." On that note, he waved cheerily before turning and walking away, flicking his neck from side-to-side, scanning for any strange activity.

From this point, the quartet no longer used words to convey thoughts, but eye contact and sign language. They divided into two groups; Xander and Daena took the west wing whilst Daice and Xana took the east.

The night was slightly comforting to them; the atmosphere was tense with a sense of vacuity. In their pairs, they carefully made their way to the rendezvous – the house where the parchment was hidden. Xander and Daena were the first to take to the rooftops in order to gain a better view of the village, in turn evading any unnecessary confrontations. Their feet graced the roof tiles; Xander was impressed by her ability to keep up, mostly because she was only a fraction of his size. Daice and Xana had decided to make their way to the rendezvous point via back roads and alleys.

The street lanterns flickered on and off, throwing bars of light onto Daice's face, which made him look as if he were shimmering. Xana felt like opening her mouth and asking him what it felt like to be able to shape shift into translucence, but managed to retain her inquisitiveness for a more appropriate occasion.

They reached the rendezvous a matter of seconds after Xander and Daena. It seemed that the house, which had once been burnt down, had been restored, and two soldiers guarded the heavy wooden door. For the meantime, the quartet ascended to the roof of the building for a clandestine entry. Xander and Xana both listened intently to the activities inside the house and estimated there were around sixteen men in the main room where the infiltration must take place and at least another dozen enemies in the side rooms – they had anticipated attack. The revised plan was to now pick them off, one-by-one, starting with the side rooms. Daena and Daice were to begin the task, with the remaining two joining them on the inside in exactly four minutes, through the main door.

It was clear from their performance that Daena and Daice were not coincidentally thrust into affiliation. Indeed, their interaction was so perfectly fluid that they appeared to merge seamlessly into one single, elastic entity.

They leaped nimbly from the rooftop and, at the zenith of the jump, vanished, simultaneously, their forms quivered and dissolved, their pale faces distorted as if through water and then they were gone.

Xander and Xana crawled beneath the shroud of heavy shadows to the periphery of the roof tiles, peering anxiously over the edge. The two soldiers stood alert, still and alone. Then, quite suddenly their forms crumpled, invisible blows shattering their postures and reducing them to dark heaps.

Their magenta robes were whipped from them to be donned by Xander and Xana upon their descent. The limp bodies were then dragged out of view as if on the strings of a perverse puppeteer. The newly appointed guards assumed their positions. The task of breaching the integrity of the house now fell to Daena and Daice. They had four minutes of security.

Xander and Xana listened for disturbance. All was silent amidst the gloom, aside from the chirruping of cicadas. Then there was a muffled cry of alarm: their cue. They turned in a sweeping movement and entered the domain of their enemy; the room leading on from the entrance was deserted, yet from upstairs rough cursing was heard and the definite sounds of a quarrel. A few men brushed roughly past Xander and Xana, unaware of their deception, to aid their companions on the upper floors.

The pressure was suffocating; there was very little time. With a curt nod they split up; Xana was to search the left chamber and Xander the right. Xander entered what appeared to be a kitchen and living area. A roughly hewn oak table filled the expanse of the hall, strewn with playing cards and tankards of ale and plates of half-devoured meals.

The stonework was newly placed; the sandy colour was not in keeping with the rustic theme of the original construction. The floor, too, was a mismatched jigsaw of flagstones. With no obvious evidence of a cavity or secret compartment, Xander condemned any effort of the search here as fruitless and left.

He met Xana in the hall; she had been equally unfortunate. The ground floor was deserted but violent sounds penetrated through the ceiling. They quickened their pace, ascending an ornate staircase, eyes roaming their surroundings for any sign of a secret.

Xana entered the stillness of what appeared to be a dormitory; rows of makeshift beds lined the walls, the linen crumpled and yellowing. The furthest wall was distinctly alluring; its comfortable hue connoted a distinct sense of age and promise. She approached it and ran her hand over the brickwork. It was quite unremarkable, and yet… An iron nail punctured the masonry discreetly; a sheen of coppery rust coated the pierced stone like blood from a wound. Xana stared blankly at the space, deducing.

A portrait or tapestry must have hung here – the perfect guise for a cavity. Her nails scrabbled desperately along the joints in the stone but it appeared to be solid. Her disappointment was punctuated by a strangled cry from above her. Panic. Their opportunity was running away like sand through their fingers.

She pounded a fist on the wall. She gasped as the skin, pulled taunt over her knuckles, split. Blood budded from the wound like little rose blossoms. She sucked her bleeding fist and grimaced as the salty taste slid across her tongue, she casted a resentful look at the wall… The stone had moved. One brick was further embedded in the wall than its fellows. In the inch exposed by the retreated rock there was a small, square cavity in which a scroll sat still and forgotten. She extended a quivering hand and snatched the parchment from its hiding place. A voice punctured her elation at success, "Oi! Who are you?"

She whirled around to see a hulking and formidable man blocking the doorway. Xana grinned, stealth was no longer required. She sprinted towards the man ready to attack when he slumped forward apparently of his own accord. Disgruntled, Xana entered the hall to see Xander brandishing a fire-stoker, "I've had to kill three of them already."

"With that?" raising one sceptic eyebrow at his choice of weapon.

"Nah, there were some more interesting things that proved too… bulky to carry around. Next floor? Think you'll need some form of weapon…"

"Oh! I have it, the parchment, look!" she waggled the scroll under his nose.

"Excellent. So time for action?"

"I believe so."

"Looks like we might have to take them all down."

"Shocking. But, if that's what is expected of us."

They felt a sense of superiority, euphoric at their success and eager to demonstrate their refined abilities in a fight. They took the stairs three at a time, so cocky that they failed to realise the silence, and what that silence symbolised.

The third floor was a single chamber, essentially the attic of the building. Roof struts compromised the capacity of the space and cast a cage of shadows over the occupants. A ring of people stood silent, an angry voice lashed the silence.

"How many are you?"

No answer.

"Answer me! How many?"

Their hearts plummeted at the irrefutable sound of Daice's strained voice, "It is but us two. No others."

"Liar."

There was a sharp intake of breath on Daice's part.

Still shrouded in their magenta robes, Xander and Xana joined the circle of about twenty men unnoticed. Daice was on his knees, his arms held fast in the vice like grip of two henchmen. His face was distorted, so was the extent of his injuries. His right eye was swollen and profusely bleeding, he was slumped slightly forward, clutching at his abdomen. Blood trickled beneath him onto the floor.

This was nothing to the scene that lay before him. Deana's tiny, pixie-like form lay sprawled across the floorboards. Her face, lifted towards the ceiling, was contorted in agony, her eyes wide and wild. For she had become the sacrifice, the incentive for answers. Every time Daice failed to supply a satisfactory response, the formidable ringleader appeared to drive the knife he bore into her flesh. Just as Xander and Xana joined the ring, he proceeded to plunge the silver knife into her thigh, withdrawing it slowly and luxuriously.

Daena had not uttered a sound, though she had become tachypnoeic, indicated by the rapid rise and fall of her chest. Daice, on the other hand, let out a low groan at witnessing his companion suffering. How did they get caught? They were skilled fighters and translucent to the naked eye. Something seemed inherently wrong with this situation.

"You two latecomers, what news from downstairs?" snapped the inflictor, a smirk tugging at his lips.

"None as of yet. It seems it may have only been these two," replied Xander, eyes transfixed on the knife held in the man's relaxed grip, stained with the blood of their friend.

"It appears you were telling the truth." The man advanced upon Daice. Delicately, he trailed the knifepoint across the contour of his cheek.

"Please," Daice hissed angrily, "leave her."

The man laughed a high, cruel chuckle. Daice interjected for a second time.

"And I would instruct the most recent entrants to reconsider their proclamation, why not skirt the terrain?"

Xander and Xana understood the hint; any attempt to rescue the two of them now would be futile. The pair had no chance of overcoming this many men without their weapons. However, they did not move. Their feet remained rooted to the ground.

"No one is to leave this room," barked the superior. "Tell me, what is your purpose here? With whom are you associated?"

Daice's face was agonised as he stared desperately at Daena, the colour draining from her by the second.

"Do not strike her again and I shall answer. Send someone to tend to her."

"You are in no position to bargain, cretin. Answer me!"

With an obvious effort, Daice stuttered.

"We were sent to assess the strength of the opposition; we are members of a small clan of the Aryes Mountains." His delivery was admirably convincing.

The tall man stared shrewdly at Daice. Xander and Xana mentally applauded his performance, especially under such conditions. There was a very tense silence, broken only by Daena's laboured breathing.

Then it struck Xana like a ton of bricks. They could not disband. If they did, it would be a clear infiltration of Dahlia forces. They couldn't risk publicising the fact they were Dahlias. The war would be brought straight to their gates.

"All of you, downstairs, assume your previous positions. I will require four."

The men filed smoothly out of the room. Xander and Xana stepped forward to remain. In the wake of the crowd, the tall man announced, "You will remain here, you may be of use to us later, if only as a token of our aggression." He turned to exit the room. Xander and Xana poised themselves for action; fortune had smiled upon them once more.

The revelry was broken in three fatal steps. The inflictor took three steps towards Daena's prone form. He leered down at her face, pale and drenched in sweat. In one unstoppable, unpredictable action he lifted the knife and plunged it in into her chest until it hit the wooden floor under her with a sickening crunch. Daena cried out a dry, wracking sob and shuddered against the impact as blood seeped about the knife handle and pooled on the floor.

Anticipating this action a millisecond too late, Xander lurched forward, attracting attention. Before he had time to comprehend, he was driven to the floor. Xana sprung nimbly to Daice's restrainers and managed to slit their throats with the very blades they held. In a moment of comic perversion, they grasped desperately at their empty scabbards and then dropped to the floor. Free, Daice lunged for the murderer in one swift motion. Two strong hands twisted the skin of the man's neck and he brutally wrenched the life out of him, drawing blood under his fingers with the intensity of his grip.

The dead face was even more grotesque due to the white bulging of its eyes and gaping cavern of his mouth. Daice dropped the figure roughly, and then turned to Daena. Her hands were curled into fists as she fought for her last breaths. Ripping his shirt, he attempted to stem the flow of blood with the wad of material.

"Come on, Daena. Come on, no!" he let out a sob.

In her last few words she muttered, "Daice, my darling," as she stroked his face with her bloodied hand. "Stay safe, I guess we will have to wait a while longer before we are wed. I'll see you on the other side…"

Xander and Xana could do nothing but watch in sorrow. Neither knew about the relationship between the two Dahlias. Daice watched desperately as Daena's eyes glazed over and the gentle lull of her breathing faded, his hand still pressed on her chest. She lay unmoving, and several minutes passed before he extended a trembling hand and allowed it to hover over her face momentarily, to close the whispery lids of her eyes.

Tears did not well or dwell in Daice's eyes; neither did he show respect for her dead carcass. His freshly stained hands crumpled into fists with his bulging knuckles trembling at the notion of revenge. He sat kneeling for moment, and then muttered his first words, "People will die brutal deaths and fall to their knees before begging me for forgiveness…" his voice was demonically structured, with a pause between each word; the threat in the scene was suffocating.

Xander and Xana could do nothing but look away in respect, avoiding eye contact. Slowly, Daice rose to his feet, as there was a clap of thunder from the tainted, convoluted sky. His form began to quiver and instantly he disbanded. Xander and Xana listened to his pulse as a means of tracking him, but found it difficult to keep up with his hurried, angered pace. The door was flung open by Daice's imperceptible form as he launched into the corridor, where he began to reformulate. The skirting of the corridors was soon littered with clueless victims.

The first fatality was oblivious to the wrath that was about to be unleashed upon him. Daice placed both hands back-to-back into the man's jaws and tore his hands apart, unfolding his victim's face. The man lay with his jaw unnaturally agape leaking life fuel. Succinct. Next please.

The next walking carcass paced towards him; on approach, Daice disbanded, sending the enemy into disarray. Suddenly a deafening crack echoed through the hallway. The Dincan looked down and saw the bone from his thigh protruding abnormally from his cloak. As the Dincan opened his trap to raise the alarm a dagger was flung straight into his mouth, slicing his tongue.

Daice's metaphysical form turned to look at where the dagger had come from – Xana. How dare she interrupt his vengeance? Remaining in his barely tangible form he continued his rally for justice. The next victim made no noise; he was dumfounded to see his arms cleanly severed from his shoulder blades.

Daice let him bellow for a few moments, allowing him to dwell in pain. Xana realised that the noises were bound to attract more Dincans and she drew another dagger. However, this time Xander held her arm, murmuring, "Allow his retribution." Just as she replaced her dagger back into its sheath, an army of Dincans came rushing out into the corridor from surrounding chambers; their mission of stealth had transformed into an open arena battle.

Xana and Xander sidestepped into opposite side rooms, which had now become butcher chambers; as long as they were not noticed, The Dincans would wait before bringing the war to the Fortress gates. Grunts and cries filled the air. Daice filed in and out of them, puncturing, amputating and disassembling… It was not long before his ability wore off and needed rejuvenation… slowly, he became more and more visible.

Xander and Xana faced each other as they stood in opposing doorways. Xander raised the hood over his head so his whole body was draped in cloth. Xana imitated. Synchronously they stepped out into the corridor and witnessed a floor caked with dead bodies and marinated in blood – but Daice was nowhere to be seen.

The dexterous duo stalked the corridor – fearless and faceless. From one of the rooms a body was flung out, slamming into the wall, the impact so great that the body was hoisted into the dent of the wall. It was Daice, no longer in his translucent form. He stared unwaveringly back into the room from where he had been mercilessly expelled. Shortly after, an enormous creature exited the room. Double the height and mass of him, the beast struck Daice, launching his hand into the wall to finish him off. Just before impact Daice thrust himself out of the cavity and casually re-entered the room as the beast attempted to pull his arm out of the wall.

The Dincan was massive. Someone this size could not be defeated by a mind clouded with anger and revenge. The room was also filled with other Dincans, however none were comparable to Daice's new charge.

As the mammoth and Daice took centre room, Xander and Xana fused with the others and watched the duel. They could see that Daice was exhausted. Xander and Xana went about the room, surreptitiously taking care of the spectators. Suddenly, the once bright room became pitch black, and the gargantuan mammal was lost to the darkness. The shearing sound of unsheathing swords filled the room. The floor absorbed the movement of toes, as Xander and Xana set about dismantling the creature. The lanterns were relit and flickered back to life. The duo stood one in front and one behind the Dincan, each with their swords pierced through his torso. The creature was legless and armless. Daice stood gory faced, and stormed out of the room.

"This is ridiculous, we never should have partnered with these savages. We could have done a perfect job by ourselves. They encompass too much pride and arrogance. Please. Let's leave. If he wishes to attempt to defeat an army of thousands, so be it," implored Xana. Xander concurred.

"Do you still have the parchment?"

"Yes. Now let's disappear before they discover that not only were the Dahlias involved, but the Xantharis too."

They fled the room and made to leave the abode the same way they entered. Glancing back down at the gloomy corridor they saw Daice pacing in the opposite direction. Slowly, he was absorbed by the blackness that filled the corridor before him. Xander and Xana left him to settle his feud. As Xander watched Daice's contour become one with the darkness, he recalled a scene watching Daveer and his soldiers in preparation for training.

"It's either kill or be killed; and if that individual threatens – destroy him, sever him, cut him so that he is immobile and if you feel it necessary let him keep his tongue to tell his family that it was the Dahlias who have punished him for his idiocy."

Daveer had implanted a one-track military psyche into the minds of his subjects. Granted, they had amazing skill, but what was the significance of this gift if it was not controlled by pragmatism?

"We should never have joined them," Xander mumbled.

"What?"

"I was just thinking."

"Through the window, we will avoid surplus contact. We will take the rooftops to the edge of the forest and cross the river, where hopefully the horses await our return."

"Sounds like a plan."

They stripped themselves from the demonic Dincan cloaks and made for the window.

The night air was chilly, yet refreshing. This opened the way for fresh thoughts and reflection on the night's events. Should they have left Daice? Would the alliance be able to function knowing that both Dahlias were dead and two Xantharis returned untouched? Xander was the first to crack the tension.

"I know we're both thinking the same thing right now. But the answers to our questions are that firstly, there was nothing we could do about the death of Daena. Secondly, he chose to seek revenge; we could not stop him without getting ourselves discovered in the process."

"Yes, I know. But I can't help but feel his anguish. I mean, if the situation were true with us, and I witnessed your merciless end, I would have taken on a whole army also, just for vengeance, and the thought of me not seeing you again…"

Her honesty surprised him. "And I the same; but we are sensible enough to make sure that we would never be put in such a predicament."

"We can't judge, we do not know how they were captured. I used to think that the Dahlias were callous, cold-blooded beings. Be that as it may, they still do feel for each other as a family…"

Xander placed his hand over Xana's mouth and drew her closer to him. He wrapped his arms around her. Everything was seemingly abiotic, but something strange was in action. Placing one foot behind him, he lowered them both over his body until they lay inert on the forest floor, Xana on top of him. They pinned their ears back, and listened for mysterious activity. From the distance, they heard two voices closing in.

"Listen, it is not my intention to kill you. We need you. You are our only strong connection to the opposition. All we need you to do is stay with them a little longer."

The first voice was grizzly, almost roar-like.

"Thank ya, sir, but what after ya have what ya want, will I join the Dincans? I 've shown me loyalty to ya, and proved it on many times – I can be trusted." The second voice was playful and juvenile. "Dey 'ave not a blue clue 'bout tomorra's ambush on the underground hide-out. After that there will be no more opposition and The Pars will be all ours! And…" the grizzly voice interrupted–

"What about tonight's infiltration? Do you call that smooth planning? That plan fucked up, and whose fault was that – yours! So don't give me all that righteous malarkey you stupid fuck-up. Listen to what I'm saying, and listen good, you hear? Just do what you're told and do not get ahead of yourself. More people will die, and it won't be you if you start playing your cards right."

"I beseech ya, master. But I did lead the Dahlias and Xantharis to ya. Plus, I also enlightened ya to the weakest one, I'd say that was job well done." The youthful voice giggled slightly, the second sound was a fist to face connection, and the third was a body collapsing to the floor.

"Don't you ever tell me what a 'job well done is', boy; you have no idea who I am. Now tell me, how many of the intruders got away?"

"Well errr, the Dahlia girl is definitely dead, killed, MIA, never to speak again, corpsified, mummified, decaying 100%. And her counterpart remains captured. He'll be tortured until we extract all za info we need. There were two Xantharis also but there iz no record of 'em being present in the retrieval of the parchment, however, a compartment was discovered unlocked, so they may 'ave been stealthier than we'd, er, anticipated."

"Fine, two out of a possible four is not too bad I suppose. Have the armour and weapons of the resistance hidden by the time we arrive tomorrow. I'll have a few of the men look for the Xantharis." One set of footsteps could be heard crunching the leaves when the grizzly voice bellowed one last time,

"Oh, Hatch! Try not to mess this one up. Your life depends on it." The footsteps graduated further and further away until there was only a pitter-patter.

Xander and Xana sat up to confirm that their trusted ally was the same seditious traitor. They watched him as he stood with one hand placed on his hip and the other running through his locks of hair. He soon made to exit the forest.

"What can we do? We must go back. The resistance must know, and Daice is still alive, we can rescue him also?" suggested a hopeful Xana.

"No. We do not go back. We have what we came here for. Daice decided his fate – almost at the expense of our own lives and it was only a matter of time before the resistance were to be finished off; they were naturally far more subordinate to the Dincans," Xander was stern.

"Are you kidding me, Xander?" Xander refused to look Xana directly in the eye. She adjusted her angle in an attempt to lock-in eye contact, but he continued to avoid it.

"Daice I can understand, but the resistance? Those very same warriors who are fighting for our cause? They welcomed us like heroes. Xander, they are depending on us… they are expecting us to save them." Her pleading was futile.

"We are not going back, and that's final. You have fallen slave and allowed your emotions to override your sense of rationality. Xanthari *Septimo principium*, do not let emotion cloud your senses."

"What? This is nothing to do with emotions. These people are the reason why we managed to complete our mission. That is what I call rationality, what do you call it… master?" Xana watched the expression on Xander's face turn to frustration.

"What's wrong? Do you not like being referred to as *master*? That's exactly what you're becoming. All the authority is going to your head. Don't forget that I was appointed head of the Elites also. So don't you ever, ever try and teach me about the Xanthari truths."

Xander walked up to Xana's face, their noses millimetres apart. "We need to go home; we can call for a message to be sent to warn the resistance."

"By then it will be too late, and you know it."

"Do as you wish, I am returning. I will inform Xanthe of your new mission."

Xander turned and walk deeper into the forest towards the river; hoping his harsh words would make a disciple of her. Xana stood for a few moments watching Xander's distinct gait fade into the trees. She made her way back to The Pars.

Walking back to the horses Xander felt uneasy, should he have acted so assertively? He soon came to the rather grim understanding that he had not quite weighed up the probabilities correctly. To him there was a 70% chance she would finally agree with him, a 20% chance she would convince him to go back with her, and a 10% chance she would say nothing and go back without him. Totalling a 90% chance that no matter what they would do, they would be together. But he had made the gamble, and lost.

Almost at the village, Xana realised she lacked weaponry; she tore a limb from a tree and used her bare teeth to strip away the bark, producing a blunt stake. From the same tree she pulled down a long, thick vine and used the stake to cut it from the root.

She arrived back at the entrance of the village. Unlike earlier, there were a multitude of soldiers surrounding the village gates; their intrusion had clearly sparked alarm. She crept over the mound and squatted beside the main gate; she could hear two Dincans talking on the other side.

She began to climb up the wall; the power and thrust of her biceps sufficient to drag her whole body up. Pull by strenuous pull, she made her way to the top. Hanging momentarily, she listened out for guards on the inside wall. The coast was clear. She threw her arms over the barrier.

Avoiding immediate detection, she decided against taking the stairs. Tying the vine to the barrier she wrapped the long end around her until it was tight on her waist. She shuffled herself to the edge of the barrier and allowed herself to fall. As she swivelled down the inside of the village wall, she felt an overwhelming sensation of loneliness; in practice Xander was usually by her side…

Behind the walls of The Pars the number of Dincan militants was overwhelming. Xana began to regret her decision to return. Her mission could no longer be one of stealth but one of discrete mass murder. She shadowed the corners of buildings with her arms spread breadth wise, molesting the walls. To her surprise and relief she arrived at the entrance to the resistance hideout. She imitated the five quick taps with genuine accuracy.

As expected, the wall disintegrated. Unexpectedly, a rather awestruck Hatch greeted her. Xana's face was also surprised, however, her eyes dimmed as she tried to hide the motive of her return. She jumped down into the secluded system. Once inside the subversive network Xana didn't waste any time, she quickly sent two sets of fingers to his temples and he collapsed down to the floor like timber, his eyes open. From this point, Hatch was dragged back to the main quarters, where somebody had every desire to expose his deceitful nature.

They arrived at the second barrier with the image of the fat man painted on it. As before, the eyes were live, but quickly grew wild and vivacious at the sight of Xana. The watchman ran back into the cavern leaving the image eyeless. Soon he returned and drew the picture up. He ushered Xana and the soulless body into the anti-establishment.

In the general's office stood Xana with Hatch's porky body curled around her feet. The general sat at his desk with five resistance members placed strategically around the room. Xana felt a sense of apprehension; the general and his men stared at her awkwardly.

"It is nice to meet your acquaintance again, Xana, many of us thought you would have been killed. So, would you like to tell me what happened?" the

General created a triangular prism with his fingertips and fanned through them pair by pair.

"You have a mole. Xander and I caught him and a Dincan talking about the weaknesses of the resistance and how they plan to ambush by tomorrow. He was a rat, and needs to be dealt with accordingly." Xana was unflinching in her bravado.

"Really? Such a trusted comrade of ours – how dare he take us for fools!" The general assumed a rather mocking tone that caught Xana off-guard. One of the guards cringed and snorted as he attempted to conceal his laughter.

"Could you please, er, un-paralyse him so we can give this worm his just deserts?" Xana connected with the same pressure points. Immediately, Hatch was resurrected, gasping for breath and arms excited like a fish out of water. The general reached into his boot sheath and drew a double-edged blade and slid it over the table to Xana. Without a second thought Xana did what had to be done.

"Where is Xander?" demanded the general.

"He has returned to the Fortress to tell them the news – we have found the parchment." The general's eyes lit up in astonishment.

"You managed to gain the parchment? Where was it?"

"It was embedded inside a wall cavity. Besides the parchment we have other pressing issues. The Dincans are planning to ambush the underground location, we must figure a way to evacuate and counter if possible. Now, if my expectations are correct, Hatch would have shown them all the entries and exits into this chamber –" the general cut Xana off mid-flow.

"Can I see it?"

"What?"

"The parchment…"

Xana could sense something dubious about the general's disposition. Slowly, she placed her hand onto her waist and ran her hand around the side to her spine where the parchment was lodged between it and the belt of the cloak. She handed it over the table to the general who rudely snatched it out of her grasp and looked at it with incredulity. The surrounding resistance soldiers stepped in closer, as if in defence.

"Well, I have returned your traitor to you, my job here is done. I must return to the Xanthari Fortress to bring reinforcements in order to keep the resistance alive… When you asked about Xander… why didn't you ask about Daena or Daice?" Xana naively placed her hand out in order to retrieve the parchment.

The general ignored her gesture and placed the parchment inside the cabinet of his table, turning the lock. It was at this point Xana realised that she had made a mistake. The general's men surrounded her.

"I'm afraid your return to the Fortress will not be necessary. The parchment is now in a safe place, and it is with the people who can get the most benefit from it. And in response to your question, I already know about the other two."

"You are allied with the Dincans," confirmed Xana.

"Bingo! Ding, ding, ding! There lads, we have a winner!" the resistance chuckled a chorus of animalistic joy.

"We have officially been Dincans since they entered The Pars and killed all the people who refused to see the bigger picture. You see, Xana, you fail to see the big-ger pic-ture – in fact you Dahlias and Xantharis are so immersed in your pride and honour that you would rather die than join an army of thousands who have the same aims – may it be for good or evil. Ever heard of utilitarianism? That's our ethos – the greater good."

Xana looked on in disgust, helpless and foolish.

"So why didn't you stop us entering and leaving with the parchment?"

"That was not the plan!" anger infested the general, his face grew a devilish red and spit fired out from his mouth, raining onto the table.

"Hatch fucked up. You were all meant to die tonight – you, Daena, Xander and Daice. But he just couldn't get things right! That is why he is lying breathless on the floor, a weak, useless liability. Your agility was underestimated... I suppose three out of four is quite an achievement."

The general had now crossed the table and was walking around Xana, talking directly into her ear and fondling her legs and waist, searching for any weapons.

"Tell me, you ever been with a man with a bit more meat on his bones than muscle?" he grinned from ear-to-ear, displaying his half empty set of teeth, stained yellow and green, ornamented with black tar. He walked up behind Xana and rested his hands on her waist. Pushing his face into her hair and smelling it. "Innocence," he whispered.

He kissed her on the cheek with his wet, sloppy lips and chuckled once again; with a signal of the hand the soldiers took hold of her and escorted her out of the hideout and marched her towards the enemy war camp. On arrival, she could see Daice sitting up – he had been battered and was covered in cuts and bruises.

Her captors threw her sharply to the floor next to her companion, binding her ankles and wrists with thick cords. She struggled furiously against them but their brawn proved no match for her weaponless, exhausted attack. They completed the knots and studied her writhing, a useless attempt to wriggle free. Resignation hit her and she watched her hands turn a delicate shade of blue. Satisfied, the men headed out of the small canvas tent, aiming a sharp kick at Daice on the way out. There was no reaction.

His eyes were sullen, empty and fixated blankly on his knees. His nose was bleeding; a steady stream of redness stained his lips.

"Daice," her voice trembled in the stuffy air. He did not look up, but instead remained immobile and stony.

"Daice! Please. Look at me. We have to get out of here." Nothing.

"Daice! Listen to me, I am so sorry about Daena, I cannot begin to imagine what you are experiencing but you have to put that aside, for now." No reaction.

Frustrated, Xana struggled against her bonds, succeeding only in rupturing the skin about her wrists. Angry tears gathered in her eyes as she realised the hopelessness of their predicament. The silence that engulfed the two prisoners seemed to purge any sense of time. The only hint of time passing was the gentle change of hue just visible through the tent walls.

After what seemed like an age, harsh voices punctured the stillness, penetrating through the canvas material walls. "He says get the girl; we are no longer getting a reaction out of the boy. It has gotten boring."

There was a derisive laugh.

Two silhouettes appeared like inkblots on canvas. Their distinct bulk gave an air of definite threat. Xana's heart rate accelerated. The two men entered the tent and leered unpleasantly at her.

They reached down and seized her by the elbows, undoing the bindings at her ankles. She began to kick at them furiously and they laughed at the futility of her attempts. She stopped struggling. One of the guards bent over so he could look at her face-to-face. He sniggered nastily, running his fingers through her hair. "You're quite a pretty little thing, aren't you?" he teased. "This is going to be enjoyable." Xana aimed a very hard and well-aimed kick at his crotch. The guard doubled over, cursing profusely.

The other guard threw her angrily to the floor. Unable to use her arms to break the fall her skull bounced off the grass with a damp thud. Stars blinked before her eyes and she stared up at her captors. "I am afraid, my dear, we can't have you repeating anything like that." He placed a heavily booted foot on her kneecap. Xana held her breath, her eyes fixated on his huge foot. He lifted it, and brought it crashing down onto her patella. Xana screamed as the impact splintered the bones in her leg. Tears rushed to her eyes as he twisted his boot. "Another repeat of that little episode," he spat, jerking his head towards his watery eyed companion, "and I'll break the other one."

Xana closed her eyes against the howl of pain that threatened to escape her. The guard directed his attention toward Daice.

"We're taking your little girlfriend. I'd take a good look at her if I were you, she won't look like this when you next clamp those beady eyes on her."

Xana glanced desperately at Daice, who did not move. Then slowly he lifted his chin and stared at Xana, their eyes met – hers pleading, his glazed, impenetrable and dark. The guards chuckled and dragged her out of the little tent, her broken leg dragging uselessly at her side.

She was hauled through a crowd of people; the putrid smell of acrid smoke stung her nostrils as they approached the central part of the camp where a glamorous, jet-black tent loomed. They entered.

The air was filled with the sickly scent of charred incense and alcohol. The general was looming over her from a high-backed chair at a table, strewn with paperwork. A twisted leer played upon his face as he saw his new captive. Dropped to the ground, her knees buckled and bent awkwardly as she descended.

Defiant, she pushed herself up, squaring up to the Dincan general, determined to keep her dignity. He stood before her, extending a hand and caressing her face, the touch of his fingertips sent unpleasant shivers down her spine and she jerked her face out from under his touch. Angrily he seized her again, his thumb and fingers clenching her cheeks tightly, forcing her to look at him.

He pouted his lips and kissed the air. Xana trembled as she realised how utterly powerless she was against these people. She forced her face to remain passive and detached, it was her only means of defence.

Xander sprinted through the darkness. His mind churned over what he had done. He regretted leaving Xana and had decided to return for her. The forest seemed to envelop him like a miniature man trapped in a snow globe. For the time of night, the jungle was curiously noisy. The birds fluttered through the branches and bats were hunting in numbers to feast on one lonely, stricken mammal.

Despite the forest watching him, he trekked through with only one thing on his mind – Xana. He still thought he was in the right. Which, arguably he was. But he knew that if anything happened to her, he would never forgive himself. First he lost Xianni, now he might be about to lose Xana.

He finally reached the river where they had left the horses. It was a shame he would have to leave three of them behind. He launched himself onto his black stallion and started on the route back to the Fortress. He reached the Xanthari gates by the delicate light of dawn; it stood proud and familiar. He crossed the bridge and entered the Fortress, resigned to duty before he could consider sleep.

Exhausted, he dragged his sore feet to find Xanthe and recount their turbulent experiences. He was apprehensive, wondering how Xanthe would react to find one absent, one missing, and one dead. He reached the door to the office and heard two voices echoing from the inside, there was sense of urgency and panic. He knocked and they faltered instantly, "Enter."

Inside were Xanthe and Daveer, who both looked very anxious and sleep deprived, hinted at by the deep bags under their eyes. "Ah Xander, thank goodness! Sit down, sit down."

Xander dragged his feet to the remaining chair and sunk into it.

"We completed the mission, master. However, it has come at a price."

"What's this? Xander, where are Xana, Daice and Daena? Did you obtain the parchment?"

"We managed to procure the parchment. Xana discovered it concealed within a wall cavity in the house."

"Excellent –"

"But," Xander looked at his feet, unable to make eye contact with Daveer, "Daena was murdered in the attempt."

"No!" Daveer jumped to his feet sharply, punctuating his outcry by slamming his hands on the oak desk. He stared imploringly at Xander, "Please, are you certain?"

"I saw it happen."

Daveer's chair absorbed him as he sat back down; Xanthe laid a sympathetic hand on his shoulder. Daveer composed himself to ask, "And what of Daice?"

"He did not accept the fall of his companion lightly. Xana and I were forced to leave him, last we saw of him he was wreaking his vengeance on the inhabitants of the house."

"So you walked away? Allowed him to sign his own death warrant?" Daveer's voice gained momentum and volume.

"I had no choice, it was my duty to protect my companion and preserve the parchment or else Daena would have died in vain!"

Xanthe chimed in, his voice calm, 'And what of Xana, is she here?'

There was an awkward pause.

"No," Xander admitted somewhat guiltily. "She was unconvinced of Daice's demise. And she wanted to relay to the resistance that Hatch, their comrade, was a traitor." Xanthe's face, instead of relaxing, turned ashen and distressed.

"Xander, we have reason to believe that the resistance have turned against us. We were discussing this prior to your arrival."

A sense of dread seized Xander as he realised the implications behind Xanthe's words. Xana had returned to the resistance with the parchment. He had allowed her to go. "And the failure of your task reinforces our suspicion…" before Xanthe could finish Xander had already made his way towards the door.

He sprinted along the corridors until he reached the weaponry store. The startled guard was taken aback by his flat urgency. Once inside, he seized as much as he could carry and hurtled out of the building. He revisited the stables where he obtained a new, well-rested horse and made leave from the fortress; urging the beast to travel as fast as its legs would carry them, acutely aware of Xana's life hanging in the balance. He reached The Pars within a few hours. He bound as many weapons as he could to his body, concealing them from view, and entered the domain of the so-called resistance.

He located the entrance to their lair, where he demanded consultation with the general. He was shown to a small, dark office and instructed to wait, his troubled mind clouded by images of Xana.

His worrying was interrupted by the arrival of the general, who greeted him with a forced grin. Determined to remain pleasant and wheedle information out of him, Xander grasped his hands in a firm handshake, smiling warmly. They took seats.

"Now, what is it that I can do for you, sir?" the General questioned, his voice laced with suspicion.

"I was under the impression that a companion of mine returned to Pars a few hours ago to speak to you after I left?"

"Yes she did… but she left very shortly after. Now, will that be all?"

"Not quite, I was wondering if you could inform me of her whereabouts?"

The general's face hardened as he stood up, "I could not give that information. If you would like to follow me…"

"Oh, General, anything would be of help. Did she mention anything? You must have some clue at least. She didn't return back to the Fortress."

"OK Xander, I've had enough of the endless games… I do know where she is. What I know I shall not tell you. However," the general leaned forward, a nasty glint in his eyes, "I think you should know that her visit to us had been most…pleasurable."

Xander seized the knife concealed in his belt and drove it deep into the general's abdomen, who doubled over, wheezing and taken aback.

"Where is she?"

The general staggered towards the door. Xander followed and dragged the blade under the general's chin, applying pressure into his neck. "Tell me or I swear I will do it," he spat.

The general's selfish little eyes were wide with panic and he stuttered, "The camp, a mile north of here."

Xander smiled, and the general returned the grin hopefully.

The camp was easy to locate. Having donned a disguise from an adversary at the gate, Xander was able to slip through unnoticed.

Xana lay face down with her cheek pressed to the woven mat that covered the floor of the tent. She was trying to sleep, savouring the notion that with unconsciousness she would be free of pain, and unable think about her traumatic experiences. Every nerve in her body cried out, aching relentlessly; the pain was mind numbing and absolute. She heard the tent open but did not move. She had stopped caring; she knew her death was imminent.

Her reverie was broken as two hands seized her shoulders and turned her over onto her back. She stared blankly at a hooded figure, cloaked in the guard's uniform… The face cast in shadow was undoubtedly here to torment her again. She opened her chapped lips in feeble protest. The figure then extended a hand and cupped her face, not in the usual threatening manner but carefully, with reassurance. Such a feeling of tenderness confused her.

A low and familiar voice whispered, "Xana? Can you stand up?"

She shook her head in wonder, perturbed by the stranger.

"Xana, it's me."

The figure drew the hood back exposing a face that was all too familiar. He smiled at her, though the happiness did not reach his eyes. He looked at her with anguish.

"Xander!"

She sat up and threw her arms tightly around his neck, burying her face in his shoulder. He hid his overwhelming feeling of happiness, uncomfortably aware that any witnesses to this display could expose their motive. She felt cold and delicate through her clothes. They drew apart. She delivered one, clean slap across his cheek. Xander accepted his punishment.

"We need to get you out of here, now."

Xana nodded fervently, "Daice is alive, he's here too. We need to get him."

"Xana, we cannot take him with us, it will be too difficult. I can't look after the both of you."

"We have to."

"No, it will jeopardise our escape, I have to get you out."

He stared at her intently.

"No."

Xander ignored this and scooped her up, despite her feeble protest. Finally, he succumbed to a compromise.

"Look, I'll unbind him, and if he can keep up he can come."

He set her down gently and crossed over to the other side of the tent. He severed Daice's bindings.

"Daice, come on, come with us." There was no reply. Xander's patience was lost. He left a knife next to Daice and returned to the task.

He turned and lifted Xana into his arms; she winced as the contact agitated her wounds. They set off out of the tent, keeping to the shadows, thankful for the cover of darkness and the absence of the general.

They reached the gate to find it under the surveillance of five men. He had only one plan. Xander lowered his head and muttered in Xana's ear, "Act dead."

She stared at him then closed her eyes and relaxed into his arms. Her limp limbs hung loose. Xander stared at her horrified; her pale complexion made the phenomena seem far too realistic.

"Stop! Where are you taking the girl?" the first guard demanded.

"I would have thought that was obvious," Xander replied contemptuously. "She's dead. And I have been told to burn the remains. The Xantharis cannot know of this or else they will seek revenge before we are strong enough to defeat them."

"We heard nothing of this."

"Well, why would you? It's only just happened! The general sends me to act in haste before word gets out."

"Well…"

"Listen to me! Do you dare to question the general's orders?" Xander barked.

The guards eyed him warily and after exchanging nervous glances, gave in somewhat resentfully. Xander went forward and they passed through the gates. On the other side and out of sight, Xander broke into a run.

It didn't take too long before the warning bells tolled. He apologised profusely to Xana as the vigorous nature of escape had caused her excruciating pain. She clutched at her leg, tears streaming down her face. He assumed from its awkward angle it was broken.

They reached the sanctuary of the clearing where the horse was tethered. Xander helped Xana onto the saddle. Her breathing was shallow now and her eyes hollow and eerily wide.

Xander sat behind her lace, his arms around her to grip the reigns and hold her in place. He sensed she was slipping away from him, even now.

"Hold on," he pleaded. They departed hastily into the night.

The horse ploughed the dirt with its formidable hooves. Xander and Xana gyrated at the pattern of movement. Xana was slowly slipping into the deep murky world of the unknown.

"Sight!" screamed a distant voice – they had been located. Xander whipped the horse violently with every ounce of energy left in his muscles. The chase was on. A chorus of aggressive hooves could be heard manoeuvring through the trees. They were getting closer.

He looked down to see how Xana was coping. She wasn't there. Xander's heart plummeted and fell into his stomach, acid burned in him all over. He tore the reigns across the face of the horse, dragging it to an abrupt halt. He violently threw himself off the stallion's spine and slapped its rump, making it run deeper into the forest. He listened for vibrations to determine the direction of the search party. He darted in the direction of which he had come, hoping that the Dincans hadn't found an abandoned Xana lying on the floor – or even worse, that she hadn't been trampled over. The pounding of the horses' hooves had stopped, signalling that the chase was over. Which meant either: i) they had lost him and had chosen to carry on the search by foot ii) they had found her. Xander closed in to where a group of Dincans had circled something and seemed to be taunting it. The figure was motionless, lying hopelessly on the ground...

"Has your saviour dropped you off, forgetting that you're kaput?" the grizzly voices chuckled joyfully. Once again, Xander had left Xana in a vulnerable position. He took to the trees for a better scope of the scene. He reached the lower canopy and settled himself in full view of the act. Xana lay shivering belligerently on the forest floor whilst the Dincans used long sticks to prod her.

One of them used his stick to lift up the bottom of her gown; exposing her legs. Xander was buzzing, perched on the edge of a branch. He reached into his bag and unclipped three arrows. Just as he poised the three arrows ready for attack he saw Xana use her able limb to curl over the stick and gain control. She propelled the stick perfectly between the Dincan's legs. Three more men stepped forward. Xander interfered by releasing the succession of arrows into the sky.

The remaining soldiers looked into the sky in amazement, searching for the source of the attack. Xander remained hidden by the vegetation. Suddenly, the soldiers gained on Xana, attempting a quick execution. Xander tried to keep up with the closing warriors, but there were just too many and he did not have enough ammunition. One soldier attempted to behead Xana, but just in time she rolled into safety giving Xander enough time to fire an arrow.

Xander soon ran out of arrows and began to throw daggers, which was much riskier. Xana was forced to roll and dodge the flying daggers more and more desperately. Unexpectedly, another wave of warriors came filing into the forest.

Xander had now officially run out of ammunition. He dropped down to ground level where he saw no option but to carry on the rescue by foot and fist. Like a martyr, he causally walked over to Xana in full view of the opposing militants and picked her up, along with the nearest dagger he could see. Bravely turning his back on the search party, he carried Xana to a safer place. As he walked back, he felt an arrow enter his shoulder blade making him jerk forward, almost dropping his charge. Another arrow soon followed; he gritted his teeth.

He lay her down and kissed her gently on the forehead. He left the golden dagger by her side in the event that he would not return; she could either choose to fight with whatever she had left, or she could decide to make her ordeal a lot less painful. He walked back to face his end.

Xana outstretched her arm and began to weep. Her ailing body attempted to drag herself after Xander, but it was of no use. She collapsed, and her face dropped onto the grass. She punched the dirt and cried out one last time. Back out into the opening, Xana could hear the unsheathing of swords – the same swords that would be used to kill Xander. If only she had not been so stubborn and returned, none of this would have happened. Soon, swords began cutting the air and slicing the ground. This had all gone terribly wrong. "What have I done?" she questioned herself. As she opened her mouth, her tears dripped into the gap between her lips. The sound of dropping limbs, squeals and clangs filled the air. Every sound gave her an ounce of hope; it showed that Xander was still fighting. She eyed the dagger that he had left her. She took one breath and gently but firmly pressed the blade into her torso. "I'm sorry, Xander," she muttered.

As she lay there, rustling sounds came from behind her. Instantaneously, the sky grew black and was covered in a sheet of arrows. The screeches were deafening. The arrows pierced the sky and then descended into the opening.

"Xana!" whispered a hoarse voice. She recognised the tone – it was Daice. He reached for her wrist and pried the golden knife out of her trembling grasp. He tossed the weapon aside and stared at her angrily but she remained oblivious, cocooned in her despair. She was aware of him talking at her, she could sense from his tone that he was fuming, however the broken words lacked clarity and failed to have meaning.

He lifted her up and supported her into the clearing. She did not object. She was too numb to care. In the little battlefield laid a macabre mass of dead bodies. The Dincan carcasses littered the ground. Amongst the thicket of trees, Xana was aware of forms, standing still and alert now having completed the arduous task of eliminating the threat. The clearing was silent with death. It pressed on their eardrums like water and masked any natural sounds, creating a surreal detachment.

Xana's eyes wracked the remains, searching for one face amongst the many twisted visages, all bearing a similar, agonised expression. As she looked, she was simultaneously petrified but compelled to find it. It did not take long.

Xander's form lay slightly apart from the rest, not immediately recognisable due to his Dincan guise. He was crumpled and still hidden under a carcass. Her last hope of finding him alive was vanquished at the sight of him. Forgetting about her broken leg, Xana let go of Daice, wrenching her hand out of his lingering clasp. She hopped awkwardly across the mass of unimportant deceased to Xander, tripping and staggering with the aches of her useless leg. She dropped to the ground next to his head and turned his face towards her, brushing the dirt from his blood-starved skin. Under her palms, his cheeks were cold and damp, coated with blood and sweat. His eyes were shut, concealed by feathery lids.

She quietly whispered in his ear, "Xander?" but there was nothing. She repeated his name over and over, louder and louder. Hysteria overcame her at his terrible lack of response. She dashed the tears from her eyes as she attempted to revive him. She clung to his chest. She felt Daice drop to his knees beside her and lay a hand on her shoulder but she shrugged him off angrily. Daice sighed and instead took Xander's hand, pressing two bony fingers into his wrist. "There is a pulse. He is not dead, but we need to get him back. Now."

Exhaustion and relief washed over Xana in a great tide of emotion. She felt someone lift her off of Xander and carry her to a horse where she was strapped firmly in place. The last thing she was aware of was the gentle lulling rhythm of hooves.

***

The General's beady eyes leering down at her; Deana screaming as life flowed out of her in rivets; Xander's face, stony, cold, dead… Xana's eyes snapped open as a series of disturbing images raced through her mind. She blinked. She was acutely aware of the overwhelming white all around her and squinted against the offensive brightness. Her mind felt lethargic; her thoughts flowed thick like molasses.

A hand clamped against her forehead and her eyes flew open in shock. The matron was looming over her, a clipboard in one hand and a shrewd expression on her face.

"Oh, you've returned to the world of the living I see," she declared, amused by her own dry humour. Xana nodded but the movement aggravated an aching in her head. The awareness of this ailment brought other pains to her attention and she grimaced.

"Where's Xander?" she demanded feebly. The nurse eyed her suspiciously.

"Are you in pain?"

"No."

"Hmm."

"Where is he? Is he alive?"

"First things first, I need you to swallow these."

"But–"

The nurse shoved a small cup of coloured, bead like pills into her hand, and then a chalice of water was hastily introduced to her lips. Xana sighed and consented. The nurse beamed at her patronisingly.

"Where's Xander?"

The nurse ignored her question; she was filling a syringe with an amber coloured liquid. Xana observed as she tapped the instrument, removing any buds of air. Carefully, she seized Xana's hand and plunged the point into her arm. Xana gasped as the sap-like substance entered her bloodstream. Almost instantly a placated sense of well-being consumed her and she sunk back into the downy pillows. She mumbled, "Wheresxander?" and was dragged back to sleep's warm embrace.

Chapter XII

When she next came around she felt different, invigorated. The room was dim and colourless with the feeble light of evening seeping through one small window. She sat up, rubbed her eyes to adjust to the hue of the room and attempted to clamber out of the iron bed, which creaked in protest. Casting back the covers she found her leg strapped to a splint, her knee looked swollen under the bandages. The matron returning with a tray of food easily averted her attention. She set it down on the table next to Xana's bed and took Xana's temperature; the little vein of mercury remained almost stationary. Satisfied, the nurse nodded and offered Xana the tray, whose sudden sense of hunger drove her to inhale her food.

The nurse settled herself in an armchair and took advantage of Xana's silence. "You will be relieved to hear that your friend is alive, although only just. Miracle – I tell you. Nearly a week ago now, you both turned up covered in blood and so damaged it's a wonder you were still breathing –" she paused. "It's been very hard work."

"Where's Xander? What's wrong with him?"

"He's next door. Sit down; I'll take you through in a moment. He's suffered severe blood loss, which has had many difficult implications. He is in a somewhat comatose state at current."

"But he'll wake up?"

"Finish your food."

Xana impatiently scooped up the remaining spoonful of her meal and stood up on her crutches, unsteady yet determined on her broken leg. She followed the nurse out of the room. The nurse opened the door to another gloomy room and allowed Xana to enter alone.

Xander's form was still and pale against the white sheets, his face serene and peaceful. The last of the evening sun shone through a single window, allowing one ray of light to rest directly on his cheek. His breathing was steady but barely visible. Xana sat next to him and took one of his hands in both of hers, resting her chin against his fingertips. She studied his face carefully, expectant. Tears glazed her eyes and spilled onto her cheeks as she peered imploringly.

"Hey…" Xana attempted to reconnect with him. The maid peered through in the doorway, making her feel a little stupid.

"He can't hear you, you know… he's in a coma, a co-ma." Xana shot her a morbid look. The maid sensed her redundant position and made for the kitchen. Rolling her eyes, she refocused on his expressionless face, and continued…

"Yeah… I'm guessing I should have listened – perhaps. But don't get all egotistical on me, look where it got you." She sniggered and glanced down at the floor before returning to the lopsided conversation, tears forming in her eyes.

"Xander… There is something you must know… I saw Xianni. I saw her blindfolded and strapped down to a table." At this point, Xana expected Xander's eyes to fling open and for him to leap out of the bed, but he remained inert.

"I need to go back there to get her. We were clearly right; that body wasn't hers but a decoy for us to think she was dead so they could probably have longer to interrogate her before we launched an attack on them. I just hope that they haven't sacrificed her already, but I don't think they would… she is far too precious." She paused again, this time for a longer period. Tears were now spilling onto their clasped hands.

"I need you, Xander. Please don't leave me. I am clueless without you; you have become my everything – see what happens when I don't have you near me? Things go wrong – terribly wrong. It's true what they say, you never know what you've got until it's gone. Please don't go… I was afraid to say it before but now with you all unconscious I can say it without any reservations. No witty remark for you to reply with." She sniggered through her tears, watching his serene face.

"I am in love with you. There, I've said it. I know you knew it before but just in case I lose you I need you to know it. I love you." Smiling, Xana floated out of the room on her tiptoes… well almost, one of her legs was still broken; but she was smiling uncontrollably in relief.

Outside, Daice reformed, his lip upturned on one side of his mouth in a cruel smirk. He entered the recovery room where Xander's lifeless body had been a point of confession. He stalked the body; circling it and peering down on it like a savage eagle. His eyes grew green with envy. He soon stopped and hung over the lifeless body. "Xander, I love you," he mimicked in a high-pitched voice.

"Hero." His head jerked forward like an eagle pecking the flesh off a grubby carcass.

"All hail the mighty Xander! Who risked his own life to save his woman, but for some reason couldn't just quite manage to save an ally in the same way. Well, that's just swell."

Daice had now bent down and had his lips touching the comatose ear, "I'm sure you and your mistress will run away and get married… if you wake up. But say if by chance you failed to wake up? Or… I don't know – died, perhaps. Then that would mean Xana and I would be in the same boat – right? I must admit she is a pretty little number isn't she?" he smirked again.

Doing another lap, Daice began to disband and reform at will, his grand cloak swishing around his legs. "Daena and I had intended to marry after the entire furore had died down – we had a shared future. Do you, Xander, have any idea what it must feel like to watch as your bride is killed before your very eyes; to watch as the blade is forced into her and twisted – to hear her scream? And there's nothing you can do about it. I find it fair that if not both, then at least one of you should feel my agony… so who should it be?" Daice held onto the last syllable of the sentence and stood at the head of the bed. He offered out his palm and slowly a dagger slithered into it. He stood contemplating with his legs apart and the dagger in both hands held high above his head… "Ah, what am I doing? This is not the right way… it is too obvious. Poison! Ha, don't worry – I have come prepared." From the inside of his sleeve, he took out a small crucible wrapped in cloth. Looking around to make sure he was completely alone, he pulled Xander's bottom lip down slightly, pouring the contents of the crucible in and disbanded before exiting the room.

Chapter XIII

Xianni lay pinned to a circular offering table. All four limbs were tied around stakes nailed in by thick, rusty iron nails. Her limbs were aching and her body felt bare. The fireplace lit in front of her made her sweat profusely. As her sweat dripped, she could hear the deadly sizzles as the fluid was quickly evaporated.

She stank. She was coated in a cocktail of blood, sweat and urine. Her dark brown hair damp on her forehead and frizzy around her neck locked in the heat even more. Her face was unrecognisable. It had been exactly six months (to the day) that she had been held captive. Every night she replayed the scene of her apparent death in her mind. She understood what had to happen, but just never thought it would. She could only imagine the pain and torture that Xander had experienced. To him, she was dead. But to her he was more alive now than ever – she lived for him, to see his face once again.

The door flung open and a mature man entered. His fragile and crooked back curved like a shrimp. He had flamboyant, patchy blond hair and a skeletal physique. His cranium was outlined through his thin skin and his eye sockets were deeply embedded into his head. His nose was bent in the exact same crookedness as his spine. He danced across the room to where Xianni lay, assuming a waltz like posture with an imaginary partner, swerving in and out of the furniture.

"Did your lot have to learn how to waltz before you were taught the art of combat? I've seen your kind in action." He waltzed around her table, making flamboyant hand gestures and twinkling his fingertips, his laugh echoing against the stone walls. Her blindfold kept her senses heightened – but in vain, as the ropes had caused her to be, in effect, harmless.

"Oh how ungentlemanly of me!" the old man stepped in further and went to place his hand on her head. Xianni thrashed from side to side. Finally, he removed the blindfold by force.

"Now, isn't that much better? Unfortunately you missed my little performance but I'll do it again if you really want." He cackled. Xianni realised he reminded her a lot of her uncle – a man of whom she had many exuberant childhood memories of.

"How are you? Keeping up well with the intense torture?" the man sniggered curiously.

It's not funny, she thought to herself, and pictured ways of capturing the pathetic old man and tearing him apart.

"You look slightly tense. I will not pose you any harm. I will be your new physician. The old one got caught with his trousers down alongside the one of the general's concubines. And you can guess the rest of that story aye! I'm here to run tests on you and to make sure that you survive the visit with us before things get rough and there is a full-blown war. I'll be back in a few moments with the necessary equipment. Don't miss me too much!" he exited the room with a soft patter as his slippers brushed the ground.

Not soon after he left another man entered. This one was much more youthful. In fact, if they had met under any other circumstances she may have possibly deemed him attractive. His hair was unusually white, but he had dark facial hair. His features were sharp and precise, which complimented his deep honey eyes.

Xianni attempted to look at him entering the room by shifting her eyes to the corner of her sockets. Pulses of pain shot from her eyes to her temples. Such time without light and movement had stiffened her ocular muscles.

The figure walked slowly over to Xianni. For some reason, Xianni felt more comfortable in his presence (probably because he looked more respectable than the rest of the clan). He stopped at the edge of the table… raised his arm and slapped her repeatedly across the face. Xianni remained silent, taking it blow for blow. She could feel her cheekbones beginning to bruise. In an act of defence she managed to trap his hand in-between her jaws. She bit through his glove, making him yelp in pain. With his free hand, he clenched his fist and delivered a hefty blow to her forehead, her head bounced back on to the table and her vision swirled.

He paused, "Got a bit of fight in you, I love that." He replaced the blindfold carelessly back around her battered head, pulling her hair as he did so. Xianni could hear him beginning to undress himself. First his armoured jacket crashed to the floor, followed by the slight pop of his trouser button, then the unzipping of the fly and descent of the trousers.

"We all learn from our mistakes," the man whispered into her ear and gruesomely licked the side of her face; for a moment Xianni thought to shred out his tongue with her teeth, but contemplated the consequences.

He abruptly mounted her and spreads his legs over hers. She could feel him hard against the inside of her thigh. He shuffled up slightly and began to caress her body. Intentionally bypassing the breasts – he'd come to that later. Xianni left her body behind as she meditated. Sending her to a virtual, emotionless realm where pain and vulnerability were non-existent.

The awful creature arched his spine and poised his pelvis, his breath heavy down her neck. He ran his hands up the side of her leg, starting at the shin and working his way up to the buttock. After yanking her leg up he slapped her thigh. He threw his head down kissing and slobbering all over her neck and face. Barbarically, he tore off the first layer of her clothing but stopped abruptly just before entering her and looked at her vacant face.

He wondered why she was not resisting or terrified. His megalomaniacal quest was in vain if she was consenting. From the doorway, a trolley full of instruments rolled in unaccompanied. The rapist failed to hear it, but Xianni picked up on the rattling of the wheels. She contemplated raising alarm but thought, "For what? They're all the same." She felt him getting nearer and nearer, she couldn't help but cringe and feel the adrenaline pulsating through her veins.

In one last attempt of self-preservation, she thrust her knees up to his groin. He lost stability and fell off the table and toppled onto the floor. Instantaneously, the old man waltzed back into the room. He stopped in his tracks.

"What on earth is going on here? Adlom, just what do you think you're doing you repugnant, malevolent creature. Pull up your trousers right now and conceal what dignity you have left. From what I can see you have little to be proud of!" he glanced down at the red erect genital and shook his head. "Very, very little." Adlom stood up and pulled his trousers to waist level. He was full of embarrassment and anger.

"Old man, is that so? Care to show us what you're made of? You shrivelled maggot."

"No. I have dignity and respect. But if I didn't, like you don't, then I would strangle you with it, just ask your aunt Adera. Now get out; you can be sure that the commander will be hearing about this little happening." Adlom made for the door and confronted the elderly man.

"No wonder you bear no children," the older man sneered. Adlom violently tipped the trolley over, sending all the instruments flying across the room and smashing against the walls; one of the pots and its contents was propelled into the fireplace and created a mini inferno, Xianni could feel the thermal energy rubbing against her skin.

For an exit, Adlom attempted to barge the old man on his way out, but he was surprisingly swift and twisted just before impact, causing Adlom to stumble through the doorway. Just before Adlom was given room to retaliate the door was slammed shut in his face.

"I don't know what to say, but... I'm sorry. Did he actually...?"

"No." Xianni saw no reason to thank the man for saving her; just because he had a sense of sanity in him, unlike his counterparts, didn't mean he should be glorified for it.

"Good. Well, next time – although I doubt there will be one – just raise alarm, I'm always in the room down the corridor to the left. I'm Admeyer." There was something amazingly familiar about this man but Xianni just couldn't quite put her finger on it. All the same, she felt just a fraction more comfortable in his presence – a feeling she almost cherished in her state of despair.

Chapter XIV

Back at the Fortress the day ran past and it was night almost as soon as it was morning. The stars littered the sky, balls of foil floating around the crescent moon.

It had been two painstaking weeks in the Fortress for Xana, with Xander showing no signs of recovery. The once homey house now felt uncomfortable and inhospitable without his presence.

She missed him dearly. She would often lie on the bed where he once lay beside her after her night attack in the ally. Replaying the night where they almost unveiled their love. The very night in which everything fell apart. Regret flushed Xana and she swore that if he ever woke up, she would admit her feelings to him right there and then. The fragility of human life dawned on her.

More weeks rolled by and Xana kept to herself. She lived in a portable cocoon that she immersed herself in whenever she left the house, which tended to be either late at night or at ludicrous times of the morning.

After informing Xanthe of her discovery, she could sense that a huge burden had been lifted from his shoulders. She did not tell him the sorry state Xianni was in as he had tried to save her from the very fate. They both decided that no rescue missions would be attempted for the time being; careful consideration and hindsight proved that single-handed missions were not her forte. She awaited the return of Xander from his "Interval with the gods" as Xanthe called it. Xander's comatose body had been shifted from the rather open hall in the prep room to the underground chamber (which was only known to Xanthe, Xana, and the rather intrusive nurse branded Xaid).

Two days before Xana had first visited Xander, the nurse had placed a wad of cotton wool into Xander's mouth to protect his oesophagus from invasive creatures and insects. It was only when the nurse returned to the chamber to change the cotton wool that she noticed it was soaked in purple liquid. Fortunately, he was still breathing and the cotton wool had absorbed almost all of the poison. The tricky part came when removing it from his mouth to ensure a drop didn't ricochet into his throat.

From this decisive point onwards, Xander was falsely declared dead to the public, specifically to the Dahlias. Daice and Daveer were primary suspects. Already, Xanthe had begun to regret his agreement with them; separation and distrust was brewing in their relationship, even though the war was due to reach them in under a month's time.

Nevertheless, joint training continued. The two ranks learnt how to complement each other's techniques in a collaborative style. The army was at their peak and when working together in unison they were brutal and relentless. The raw malevolence and strategic accuracy proved an infallible combination. Their training sessions soon became lunch matinees as the Fortress' villagers would come and watch their sons, daughters, nephews, nieces, husbands, and wives practice the art of Xanthari and Dahlia warfare, newly branded as Xahlia warfare. It was exhilarating to watch, quite rightly like a performance.

Similarly to Xana, Daice also remained secluded. The loss of Daena had had a much greater effect on him than he anticipated. He thought that with Xander 'dead' and Daena buried, Xana and himself could comfort each other. Little did he know, Xana was holding onto something more precious to her than anything else in the world.

With the war now around the corner, the majority of the time was spent preparing the forest to care for the Xahlias and to entrap the Dincans. The Xanthari labyrinth had now been fully completed and trimmed to perfection. The Fortress lay at its centre, protected by a network of intricate pathways and cul-de-sacs. Both ranks were now comfortable and trained to memorise the way back to the heart of the labyrinth from any point, in pitch darkness.

Chapter XV

Admeyer gently nudged Xianni back to life. To her relief, she was no longer tied up. Broken and bloodstained skin surrounded her wrists like bracelets. She had not been in this chamber before; the room was filled with water – almost knee high. It was disgusting. The walls were damp and mossy brown.

A foul stench burned her sinuses. For a second, she wished she had not been brought to. The ceiling was dripping with a malodorous liquid that fell into the water with a xylophonic melody. There was no light save for a few feeble rays provided by the corridor that cross-sectioned the gated doorway. She attempted to stand, but soon realised that her feet had been kindly clamped to the legs of the chair in which she sat.

"Evening, are you OK? I'm afraid it's time for… Well, you know what… Can I just ask, why don't you just tell them what they want to hear?" Admeyer loomed over her, and then lowered himself down to her level. She did not answer. Carelessly, he shook his head and looked down sharply into the water, mumbling, "When will you realise that I am not the threat?" he continued, "I have a remedy ready for you if you wish. It will stop you feeling the pain so much, although it will not eradicate it completely. You will feel a slight numbing sensation for a ten-minute period, then slowly you will begin to regain your full sensory capabilities. Would you like it?" Xianni looked at him suspiciously and mentally questioned, *why is he doing this? What does he want?*

A part of her felt she could trust the old man, but couldn't bring herself to admit it, and surely didn't want him to take advantage of his position, even if he did rescue her from sexual violation. Thus she remained silent, but shook her head in refusal. "Sure, but I must warn you, today in this room will be a special means of torture that you will *definitely* not have experienced before. Excruciating." He picked up his utensils and waded through the water in his black, knee-high boots. Before exiting he stopped in the doorway – "Sure?"

Xianni nodded, and Admeyer smiled reassuringly, "Good luck." He rang the bell hanging down from the clammy ceiling, and in the next moment he was gone.

On his departure, two giant men filed in. The first gentleman was larger and seemed to be in charge; he was carrying a large plastic bucket. The latter was a little smaller and appeared to be the sidekick. He held a toolbox that clanged and chinked.

As they walked past, they smiled sarcastically at Xianni. For a moment, she wondered why they hadn't placed a blindfold around her head as usual. Then she reasoned that it was probably because seeing the threat would be more unnerving – making her more likely to crack. But for the life of her she could not fathom why her hands were not bound.

The first figure plumped the bucket onto the mossy wooden table and waded back through the water over towards her. As he approached she could see a circular ring of keys hooked onto his belt. One of these must be able to unlock the clamp, which bound her to the chair. She must obtain them. As he approached, she eyed the belt slyly. Waiting until he got close enough to disconnect them.

He crouched over and wrapped his sausage-like fingers around her wrist to secure it to the chair cuff. Xianni took the chance to use her only free arm to discretely obtain the keys; periodically glancing at him and his companion to make sure they were both oblivious to her movements. She continued steadily. In one last leap of faith she grabbed the circular frame and unhooked the keys from the belt. Now the challenge was to hide them within seconds without making a significant rumpus.

"Hey! 'Ow much longah we got till dinnah?" shouted the other man. Xianni remained frozen with her hand halfway between his waist and her chest and the keys dangling from her fingertips. Luckily, he swung around the opposite way and spoke in a deep enough tone giving her cover to set the keys in between her legs, under her dress. She relaxed and allowed him to continue to clamp her other hand.

"Shit, forgot the wrenches. Where did ya say it was agen?"

"It's back in the weaponry chambah; with all da ova bits 'n' bobz."

"Aint that locked? I'm gonna need the keys."

"Yeah sure." The larger fellow tapped his waist, awaiting the jingle. He looked down and saw nothing. Xianni looked him directly in the eye, then at his waist, the façade of bewilderment was convincing.

"Fuck, I've left 'em in the lock; either there or in the cutlery room." He stormed out of the chamber followed by his minion. Xianni breathed a sigh of relief, perspiring slightly. She could hear their footsteps ploughing down the corridor. It was now or never.

Doubling over, she gripped her skirt with her teeth and pulled it back. Using her tongue to curl around the key ring she sieved through suitably shaped keys… One-by-one she set each key between her jaws and tried to fit them. If unsuccessful, she dropped the keys onto her lap and shuffled to the next using her nose: drop, shuffle and clasp; drop, shuffle and clasp. She reached the last key and inserted it into the lock; she twisted her neck and waited for a click. It worked; one down, three to go.

She set about unlocking the other hand and then it was time for her feet. Xianni fingered the leg clamps but struggled to find the lock. As a last resort, she dipped her head into the murky water to get a better look. A burning sensation covered her eyes and her vision became blurrier by the second. Feeling desperate for air she brought her head up. Her hair flung up around her head and water sprayed everywhere. She slumped back into the chair, panting belligerently.

Back in the weaponry room the torturers began to argue:

"Where are the keys then? They're not in either place. And ya couldn't 'ave left them I remember ya walkin' inta the chamber with 'em."

"D'ya reckon… she coulda… you know?" they stared blankly for a moment.

"Shit!" they chorused, rushing to the door and down the corridors.

Xianni had now sat up once again in another failed attempt. From the distance, she could hear frantic feet powering down the hallways. In desperation, she drowned herself once again. She found it. This time there was no time to bring her head up for breath; adrenaline worked its way around her body. She needed to get out of here. The final relieving rotation of the key was made. The stampede was just down the hallway and Xianni realised she could not leave now; too much alarm would be raised.

The two men stumbled into the room and stopped on the staircase leading down into the water-infested chamber. Their prisoner was no longer bound to the chair.

"I told ya, yew knob."

"Shhh…"

They descended the steps warily. The larger of the two signalled for the minion to stand at the base of the steps whilst he slowly waded through the water over to the bucket and toolbox. Xianni remained submerged in the middle of the flooded room with nowhere to go. She was trapped, with no way out; even worse, no way of breathing. Under the water her face looked serene and simple, her lips sealed. Two minutes gradually became five. She was cracking, her eyes were now wide and her lips tight; her face was grey and pallid.

She could feel herself passing out; her heart had slowed down to a faint *lub-dub thud*. Her head was aching and she could feel her lungs slowly tugging against her chest. Six minutes. The two men remained certain she was still in the vicinity. Xianni could see a bubble forming at her nostril; the hoax was over, if the bubble made it to the surface they would certainly have her.

The bubble was now fully formed and surfacing slowly, Xianni watched as it went past her nose, then her eyes, and above her head. It was time, give up of your own accord, Xanthe had taught her. Xianni rose out of the water with her hair covering her face; she was soaked and dripping wet with the toxic fluid. First attempt: failed. The two men smiled.

"About time." The man with the toolbox had a wrench in his hand and repeatedly beat it into his palm; the other at the foot of the stairs watched her in amazement. He continued,

"I was almost 'bout to give up there. 'Tis a shame that ya so pwetty. Now I'm gonna to have to wreck ya face… these are the re-per-cushions of disobedience."

Illiterate fool, Xianni thought to herself.

He drudged closer to Xianni. He was now two paces behind her. She had still not turned around to face him. The man shrugged his shoulders and raised the wrench above his head. Leaning forward, he aimed for Xianni's skull. Lazily, she sidestepped the attack and watched the man fumble forward. It was clear that she was still suffering as her body attempted to pay back the oxygen debt. She was shaking and her lips were purple-grey. Weariness coated her eyes as they flickered from side-to-side… The larger of the two men stepped forward again, but instead of attempting to club her, he launched the iron wrench directly at her face.

To create an illusion, she waited until the wrench almost made contact and used her arm to cower under as she took a large breath and fell into the water. On the surface she could hear the men laughing, as they mistakenly believed she was fatally injured.

"Well, she's not coming up anytime soon!" the minion suggested, hoping to gain recognition from his superior. They both chuckled like hyenas.

Submerged, she crawled outspread on the floor using her toes and fingertips to manoeuvre around the two men. Her splash had created enough tide for her to move underwater without being noticed. Behind the two men now she arose casually, like a grim reaper. Her dress hung black and baggy around her body. Her hair was wet and curly, covering most of her face. She used these moments to catch her breath. The men also waited for her corpse to bob up to the surface. The colour was returning to her face and her lips now assumed a slightly creamier colour, although her breathing was still erratic.

There was only one exit in the room and it was blocked. Still waiting for their prisoner's corpse to float to the surface, the two lads walked to the centre of the room where her body should have been. She waded from under the staircase and round to the front. She climbed the first step. The second. Then the third. The fourth…creak. The torturers jumped and twisted around, the minion holding his hand to his chest as if to keep his heart from leaping out.

"Will ya stop doing that!" shouted the minion experiencing some mixed emotions.

"Listen, lady, you can either have it cool, or hard. Your choice…" Xianni foolishly weighed up the proposal: give in and be mercilessly tortured for another four months or fight and be tortured but kill at least one of the men, or maybe even escape. Fighting seemed the only optimistic option left, so she descended the steps. She assumed a posture of defence. The men looked at her in annoyance and stepped forward slightly, assuming a posture of attack. They both mirrored each other's stance, and Xianni realised that she had made the wrong choice: they were complimentary fighters, each one's skill made to accentuate the skill and power of the other. They spliced apart; she had one on her left and one on her right. Simultaneously, they launched the attack.

Her movements were rash and half-hearted; she was in no condition to fight them, not now. Together, their power and force were too great. All of a sudden, Xianni felt a sharp cold sensation start at the back of her head and trickle down to the bottom of her spine… Second attempt: failed.

Chapter XVI

Xana was sat in Xanthe's office, awaiting his arrival. He had sent for a message to be passed onto her regarding 'urgent matters'. She hoped it was news about Xander, whose unconscious body remained in a new, secret location. Xana began to reminisce about the day outside the auditorium when they first decided something must be done about Xianni's situation. She smiled to herself and a faint tear accumulated at the corner of her eye, slowly descending down her cheek. Suddenly, the door was flung open and Xanthe hastily entered.

"Sorry to keep you waiting, Xana, I'm just going to get straight to the point. The Dincans still have the parchment and although they do not know its full potential, every day they are getting closer to figuring out how to use it. When they do, then what we have strived to keep hidden and secret for the past generations will have been in vain. However, if this is done incorrectly or if any damage comes to the parchment, then the Lost Empire is truly *lost*... forever."

"I respect your candour, but how can we retrieve the parchment? Now that they know we are after it, they will have placed it under top security. I cannot obtain it alone – I need Xander. Or maybe even a whole army!" Xana moved to the edge of her chair.

"Xander is getting better; his muscles are twitching slightly which is a very promising sign. Xaid has gone to the woods to fetch some herbs and oral stimulants. Time, time will tell, and he should be back with us in weeks if the Xanthari gods will grant it."

Xana interrupted, "Oh this is wonderful! Where has Xaid gone? I will accompany her right this very moment! I'm sure he will make it, he's strong, stronger than you give him credit you know, Xanthe. He took arrows in the back for me; he faced a whole army for my protection!" Xanthe slowly reclined into his chair.

"Yes, very strong. But was that physical strength, or emotional weakness? I am not asking you to go back there, I am sure you have suffered enough. I will make the journey alone. I have put my faith in you and Xander a little too much and for this I apologise. Look at what has happened, you have had to recover from a disintegrated kneecap and my son is in a coma. It is time for me to take the torch and carry out what needs to be done."

"It was not your fault. The plan was fine; it was the combination of warriors and egos that got the whole operation tangled into an indistinct web of motives. Not to mention the betrayal of the resistance. I do not… we do not blame you for what happened." Xana reached over the desk and grabbed Xanthe's hand and held it reassuringly. Xanthe looked up and nodded, gripping her hand tightly.

"Thank you, but the feeling I have will not change until I have the chance to break the people that have caused such turmoil within my Fortress walls. The reason I have called you here today, Xana, is because I am well aware that operations can go very wrong…"

"No! Don't you dare think like that, Xanthe. Nothing will go wrong. You are the most skilled man this place has seen or even had the privilege to know. You are from the long line of Xanthari fathers – the chosen ones, the gods chose you for a reason. Are you doubting the authority of the gods?" Xana knew her comments were falling on deaf ears. She wasn't entirely sure if even she believed her own words anymore.

"No, I do not dare, but things happen, my child, you cannot say because the gods are on our side that the people you love will live forever. All I ask of you is to give my wife this, and for you and Xander to help raise my son and daughter, just as you were." The atmosphere grew scarily quite, Xana's heart felt heavy in her chest.

"So, Xana, will you do me this one favour?"

"You have my word."

"I knew I could trust in you. If I am not back in two days from this hour, you shall deliver the letter. You are dismissed." Just before she left, she walked over to him and slipped her arms through his and linked her arms around his back; he kissed her gently on the top of her head. "I'm sorry for what I have put you through, my child," he mumbled softly.

***

Xanthe lay awake in his bed with his wife, Xari, lying serenely beside him. He turned to look at her and smiled, running his hand through her frizzy black hair. Before he left the room, he smelt her hair and kissed her on the cheek. Stealthily, he clambered out of bed and walked out of their bedroom into the corridor. In the next room his two children slept cuddled up to each other, shrouded in a silky blanket Xari had knitted.

From the doorway, he admired his beloved children as they slept – so innocent, so pure. He didn't want to leave. Despite Xanthe's detached outward personality, within the four walls of his home he was still human. He still felt the same emotions as anyone else. It was just his choice not to display it. As he walked through the quad, he felt a sensation of release, yet remorse. On his way to the stables he could see that Xi was on guard. He gave a gentle nod, and Xi opened the gate. He was oblivious to the night's events but he could sense it was something sacrificial.

"Best of luck, Xanthe." Xanthe didn't look back.

Rattling could be heard from inside the stable. Suddenly, there was a cry from inside the cabin. Xanthe kicked the door open slightly and looked in. It was Daveer.

"Goodnight Daveer, what was that terrible cry for?"

"I got my hand caught in the saddle because this stupid horse won't stay still!"

"Where are you making your journey to?" questioned a puzzled Xanthe.

"Well, erm, I'm going back to the Dahlia Fort to make sure everything back there is still in order." Xanthe smelt a note of dishonesty, but played along.

"And where might you be heading off to?" Xanthe had prepared an alibi whilst Daveer was talking his rubbish.

"I'm to time test myself in this night to further familiarise myself with the Xanthari labyrinth. It is not fair only the soldiers are given such requirements. It's much harder than it appears to find your way through – I find it difficult even though I have it scribed on my bel– ceremonial gown!" Xanthe chuckled uneasily as he came dangerously close to revealing one of the best kept Xanthari secrets.

There was an awkward silence for a few moments. They were blatantly both aware of the dishonesty that filled the barn's atmosphere. Soon, Xanthe was ready to leave the barn with his horse fully prepped and ready.

"Well, I'll see you then, my warm greetings to your people."

"Of course."

Xanthe left the stable quickly and rode at full speed. He was not entirely lying; this was a time trial – two days maximum – before he would be dead to his family. Soon afterwards Daveer also left. However, as suspected he did not ride in the direction of the Dahlia Fort. He rode paces behind Xanthe.

Just over midway between the Xanthari Fortress and the The Pars, Xanthe dismounted. From this point he was to continue the journey by foot. He left his horse by the river, so it had a plentiful supply of water and grass in case his adventure took longer than anticipated.

The horse grunted and wearily shook its head. The beast's sixth sense warned Xanthe about some undesirable activity about to take place. Nevertheless, he took all the necessary equipment needed with him to carry out the infiltration. Soon he was in the heart of the dense, humid forest.

Not long after he had begun trudging through the vegetation did he hear splashing by the river. The noise was coming in his direction. He crouched down and watched as the rider slowed down to a halt. A few yards from where his horse stood nibbling on a patch of vegetation stood another horse.

A hooded man alighted and patted his creature gently on the side. He drew a hip flask from his attire and tilted his head back to flush down a pint of water. It was Daveer, again. Could it be that Daveer was following him? Or was Daveer in collaboration with the Dincans? Thoughts raced through Xanthe's mind. He stepped out and walked over to Daveer who was resting.

"What brings you to enemy camp, brother?" Daveer was startled, and began coughing and spluttering on his drink. Drenched, he replied.

"Xanthe? What? What happened to your time-trail?"

"Ah, but I asked first!" Xanthe replied sharply, with a hint of condemnation.

"Alright, alright. I'm going to The Pars to go and obtain the parchment. In all honesty, it was a serious task – we shouldn't have sent a group of infants to do a man's job! And now half the party we sent are dead."

"I too am going to The Pars with the same motive… and as for that, I really think you are underestimating our Elites…" Xanthe felt a lecture coming on and stopped himself before he was in full swing.

"What happened to your horse?"

"I left her at the river. It is likely that they have Dincan watchmen weaving the forest. Horses are a little unsubtle."

"I guess you're right. We shall continue the journey together." Daveer spanked his beast and clicked with his tongue. Hastily, his horse went to join Xanthe's.

"We'll show them how it's done, won't we, *friend?*" Xanthe ignored Daveer's immaturity and waded into the forest ahead. Daveer trailed behind him, attempting small talk.

Chapter XVII

Xianni's eyes were agape. Her wrists were back in the cuffs. The location hadn't changed. Still, she sat bound to a chair in a room filled with water up to her knees. Blood dripped down her neck and her hands had been stained a vivid cherry. Over at the table, she could see the subordinate drawing up liquid into a syringe. Forcing her head to the side he stabbed the needle into her neck.

"This oughta to make ya a likkle more…co-op-er-ative," he laughed shrilly, and clapped his hands with satisfaction.

Suddenly, she felt woozy and began to find it hard to hold her head upright. The first man rummaged through the toolbox and pulled out a pair of metal forceps with spiked tips. "Let us begin," he said, pinching the forceps. The assistant used his two hands to pull open Xianni's mouth, whilst the first used two fingers to uncurl her tongue and lay it flat, pulling it so that it hung from her mouth. Her tongue was placed between the forceps. Slowly and painfully, he brought the two ends of the forceps together. Screams could be heard the whole way down the corridor. Her mouth filled with blood, which spilled over and dribbled down her chin.

"Tell me…" cajoled the perpetrator as he separated the forceps and removed them from inside her mouth. Tears rolled down Xianni's cheeks like heavy boulders down a steep hill. She closed her eyes to try and compose herself, her tongue still drooping from her bloodied, quivering lips. She was not broken – yet. Her captor looked down at her hand and glanced at her fingernails.

The forceps were placed back into the box and replaced with a pair of pliers. It wasn't difficult to figure out his next teasing method. She reclined back further into her chair chanting, "No, no… No!" her voice became increasingly desperate with each cry.

She clenched her fist, tucking her thumb underneath the other fingers. The torturer bent over and looked at her pinching the pliers. *Ting ting.* "This doesn't 'av to happen. Just tell me what I wanna 'ear and we'll let ya go. 'Tis very, very simple, ya see. There is no need to struggle over nothin' – you're a very pwetty, pwetty woman. I don't wanna 'av to turn ya into somethin' ya were not born to be. Is there somebody that ya 'av waiting for ya at home, a husband or partner maybe? Could ya really think he would take ya back lookin' like... a monster? You will lose everything: ya looks, ya love, ya confidence. Why lose everythin' when you can just tell us a few simple words? All we are asking is: Where is the final piece of the *parchment? And how* can we use it? That is all." Xander popped straight into her mind.

She could feel the injection working, her mind was buzzing; colourful random words flashed into her thoughts. Book. Envelope. Library. Heavy. Painting. Xander. Escape. Home. Love. Xana. The image of a disgusted Xander pushing her off his doorstep sprang into mind.

"Focus your thoughts on the parchment." She tried not to, but she was no longer in full control of her mind. She had been trained to rebuke the powers of truth serums but this strain was something unusual. Sweat dripped from her head profusely; her face felt swollen, hot, red. Her clothes were sticking to her; the room spun clockwise, then anti-clockwise.

"The parchment itself is nothing special! Just looking at it gets you nowhere in life! What you have to do is – The parchment itself is nothing special! Just looking at it gets you nowhere in life! And then what you have to do is – The parchment itself is nothing special! Just looking at it gets you nowhere in life! After, what you have to do is..." she repeated the same phrase over and over.

"Damn it! She can fight it." On receiving a sharp slap across the face she stopped. Closing and opening certain doors in the psyche at will proved to be a key skill, strategically taught to her by none other than Xanthe. The urge to come clean grew and grew. Needing to take her mind off her predicament, she began to laugh hysterically.

"She az been adequately taught to bypass the effeks of the truth serum. We must try and break her, da sooner da better, before it wearz off. Continue for me whilst I prepare." His subordinate took the pliers and grinned at her. Xianni was now violently hysterical: "You bastards! Are you that thick you can't figure it out for yourselves? Get away from me! Right noowwwww!" her voice took on a demonic, commanding howl of desperation. The second man began to uncurl her fingertips. "No, no, no!" waterfalls poured from her eyes and lubricated her face. Her head thrashed from side-to-side. Her voice dampened. The resistance was no longer. It was time to accept the hopelessness of her situation. Either tell them what they wished to know, or become disfigured.

Swiftly, without recoil, he tore the fingernail from her thumb. She screamed in deep agony. Her breathing was heavy, and her chest rebounded at the same frequency as her heartbeat.

"Telling yet?" demonic eyes met his gaze, and he received nothing but a mouthful of bloody saliva in his face... Roaring, she tried to tear her limbs away from the chair. The next nails to go were the index and middle finger. Again, the hysterics kicked in as she laughed sadistically and vehemently; a feeble, disturbing endeavour to turn pain into joy.

"Funny, iz it?" questioned the lead man from across the room where he was prodding the contents of the bucket. Without even a glance at her, he said, "Break them." And so his subordinate did, wrapping his hand around the same two fingers and forcing them back on themselves. The tendons snapped one after the other.

"You 'av your rubber boots on?"

"Yes."

"I'm lettin' them out."

The chief tipped over the large bucket that had been sitting patiently on the table. It was filled with water, and Xianni watched it as it emptied. Two electric eels slid quickly out of the bucket into the water-filled chamber. Now all the water made sense, as did the old man's warning that this was a 'special' manner of torture. Each eel was six feet long and swam deep below the water. Their long, meandering bodies zigzagged distressfully. The eels sensed what was left of her body heat and manoeuvred towards her.

They weaved around her feet and between her legs. One of them swam directly into her shin and nibbled angrily; and she felt faint sizzles as the eels charged up. Xianni began to screech and jostle in her chair. Meticulously, one eel wrapped itself around her legs in a figure of eight. She knew what it was planning. She braced herself, squinting her eyes and clenching her fists.

Shock.

A dark figure blocked the doorway and cast a shadow into the room.

"Everyone has gone. It is only a few of us that remain. We must leave and join them now – all men will be required for the infiltration of the Dahlia Fort. Camp has been set up in the woods."

"God, what is all this commotion? We 'ave so much more to do 'ere; she will crack any moment now. My friends are just getting started." Her main assailant pointed to the eels.

"Well you will have to either leave her in the village with a few others that will continue the extraction, or carry on in the prisoners' camp. Now come on." The two men reluctantly replaced their equipment into their toolbox and used large rubber clubs to direct the eels back into the bucket.

***

Xanthe and Daveer had now been walking in the forest for thirty silent minutes. The tension had grown between the two ranks greatly since the failure of the first mission. They had both been subjected to the conflicting views of their own men. The night was humid and claustrophobic. Leaves scratched and irritated their skin as they fought their way through the lush vegetation.

"I do not blame your Elites for the death of Daena. I can see that the past events have distanced us, and this is not what is best for us – especially at a time like this." Daveer was the first to shatter the ice. There was a slight tinge of alcohol on his breath.

"This is true, and neither do I blame yours for the state of Xander. It was a team effort and they all failed to act accordingly. And obviously let us not forget the betrayal…" Xanthe chose his words meticulously, not declaring Xander as dead but insinuating all the same.

"I concur."

They both stopped and peered through a layer of yellow ribbon shrubbery. Beyond their hiding place was a mass area of setup camp. The tents were vast and green for camouflage. A guarded site had been allocated solely to the armour and artillery. It was obvious that the Dincans had set a perimeter for their preparation ground, and were making the final arrangements for war. Xanthe and Daveer fell back and sat on the crisp grass.

"It has begun," declared Xanthe in a rather surprised tone.

"Yes, my brother. Next stop: Dahlia Fort."

"There is no way we can gain the parchment now, their numbers are way more than we had anticipated and we would have no idea where to begin the search."

"Yes, we can. If we split up, I take clockwise and you anti, we will arrive at twelve o'clock at approximately the same time." Daveer carried a determined look.

Xanthe looked at him in shock: "No offence, my brother, but are you crazy? We have no idea how many numbers there are in these tents. We would have to kill everybody in these tents quietly, one-by-one. We're talking thousands. And then we would have to strip and search every tent! I do not have that sort of time, I'm getting older!"

"I was only pulling your chain, Xanthe," they both chuckled and cackled.

"I was beginning to worry about you. Let's get back to the Fortress and do the final preparations for the defence of Dahlia Fort." Xanthe got up first and offered Daveer a helping hand. As they walked away, Daveer looked back and became conscious of the fact that in the days and weeks to come, many would suffer, but even more would die.

Chapter XVIII

Xana was pacing barefoot about the small house. Of late, the house was impeccably clean. She turned her hand to any simple distraction to relieve her mind of the things she thought it best not to occupy her imagination with. The watery moonlight filtered through the drawn curtains, casting a cold mood into the little house. As she walked, her feet made a muted patting sound against the cold flagstones, particularly noticeable due to heavy silence that consumed the place in Xander's absence.

Her mind was troubled, saturated by a tangle of pessimistic thoughts. She could not settle down to any activity. Instead she adopted a circuit, which she had followed for the last few hours with religious devotion. It consisted of a pilgrimage from the living room to the kitchen and back, before plumping onto the sofa. Discontent within mere minutes she would stoke the fire, then pace back to the kitchen, where, agitated by the drip of the tap, she would rally into the hall and seat herself in the living room to stoke the fire, and so forth.

The reason for her anxiety was Xanthe. His solemn parting had left her feeling misguided and abandoned. To her, Xanthe was a paternal figure. She now doubted she would ever set eyes upon him again. At this morbid assertion she was flooded with a sickly depression. The feeling of emptiness was alien and unsettling.

This self-reflective train of thought cast her mind back to Xianni. An image stirred in her memory; a limp form strapped mercilessly to the sacrificial table. Her toes curled as her mind repelled the picture. Compared to Xianni, what she had gone through was nothing. It was difficult to fathom the dreadful ordeal that had been inflicted upon her friend. However, stronger than both of these thoughts combined was her nagging desperation to see Xander again. As her mind turned back to this already exhausted topic she broke her rhythm and made towards the bathroom.

She entered the small, tiled bathroom and lit the paraffin lamp. It flickered merrily; a comfortable glow lit the oblong room. The concept of a warm bath appealed to her. Turning on the twin jets of water, one icy and one boiling, she plugged the drain. The homely sound of the liquid hitting the copper tub was comforting. Noise made her feel less alone. The rising steam passively lifted the weight of her emotional burden.

Xana crossed to the mirror and wiped the sheen of condensation away, exposing her pale face. Her eyes looked tired and dull, her features haggard by recent events. She sighed and began to peel off layers of clothing, tossing them carelessly onto the floor. She shivered as the steam coated her bare skin like light perspiration. The water was inches away from spilling over the rim.

The steaming water was inviting. Deep inhalation of the vapour cleared her lungs, purifying her. Cautiously, she extended one foot into the water, breaking the glassy surface. She climbed into the bath and slowly sunk into its comforting depths, listening to the rush of water in her ears and watching the bubbles of air escape through her nose.

She felt the tension in her muscles alleviate in the hot water and her pulse slowed right down to mimic the relaxed nature of her being. She laid submerged until her lungs started to burn from oxygen starvation and she was compelled to surface.

Reaching for the soap, she meticulously scrubbed herself, as if hoping to purge herself of the dark mood she had recently immersed herself in. The scent of lavender that issued from the bar was soothing at first. Again she deluged herself, her eyes wide open. For a moment she questioned whether there was a point of resurfacing. Her hair floated freely in a medusa-like entwine around her face. The dreadful silence returned. She was lonesome once again.

The Xanthari 'brand' on her stomach began to blur and disseminate under the water, little inky spirals of creamy powder diffused into the clear water. Suddenly, she grew tense and unsettled. The water was now too hot, and the floral soap issued a sickly scent that made her head spin. The stillness now irritated her. She removed the plug and observed the coloured powder spiral down with the water gurgling into the plughole.

Blanketed in a towel she made for the bedroom, leaving a trail of damp footprints on the wooden floor. The cupboard door was flung open as the hunt for clean clothes began; she cursed herself for neglecting such chores as laundry. An assortment of mismatched attire had to suffice. She dressed before the mirror, scrutinising herself. Analysing her body, she began to find every fault she could, "I've lost weight… But I've still got some tub on my midriff" and "I wish my breasts were slightly rounder". On further analysis she came across her knee that was still slightly misshaped but almost fully functional nonetheless.

Her eyes were drawn compulsively to her darkest and most concealed secret. She stared avidly at her stomach. The smooth contour of skin was unmarked and bare; devoid of the very signature that gave her the right to dwell in the Xanthari domain. She tugged a threadbare jumper over her torso and smiled coldly at herself. She turned and clambered into bed, burying her head into the sheets and revelling at the familiar smell. She closed her eyes, a pointless action: she knew she would not sleep.

Chapter XIX

Dahlia Fort was in disarray. Both ranks had congregated for the first war tactics and approach oration, led by the two leaders. Daice stood beside his chief and absorbed every word of the glorious and meticulous style that they would use to combat the Dincans. Xana was nowhere to be found. Nothing else now stood between peace and war – the latter seemed the only option and would be brought to their grounds within a matter of days. The oration ended with a patriotic roar. The warriors divided into allocated sections and carried out the transformation. This involved turning a fort full of inhabitants into one that held a fake 'nobody's home' milieu. The trap doors with which all houses were equipped, that led to the underground Dahlia network, had been covered in rugs and hay. The buildings were transformed into death traps; shrapnel and solid jagged material had been implanted into their structures. Great, long spikes covered all the front doors, with a secret mechanism relating to one single spike to allow entry. The forest surrounding the fort had also been littered and infested with booby traps and self-destructive devices as a tactic of psychological warfare. Unlike the Xanthari Fortress, there was no labyrinth structure surrounding Dahlia Fort, thus once the enemy made it through the forest to the main gate, it was all or nothing.

The Elites were exempt from the early stages of the war and would remain in training in order to analyse the enemy's tactics and hone their skills to perfection. The remaining ranks set up their artillery in the trees and hollow stumps in designated sectors of the forest. The underground network between the cabins stretched as far as the river Morten and led directly to the mountain range leading to the Chantrierian Empire – a safe haven for the Dahlias.

The Chantris and the Dahlias were allies in such times as these. However, the Chantrierian leader refused to immerse herself in this war. Firstly, her alliance with the Dahlias stemmed from history rather than any common ground. She also knew the risk she would be putting her people in. But most of all, she knew that if the Dincans even thought about trying to attack her Empire it would be months before they could ever break through her four Black Marble Walls, let alone face her army.

Chantrierian warfare was different to say the least. Far more ruthless than even the Dahlias, they relied on the brute force and strength of its warriors. What set the Chantris apart from their rivals was their astounding ability to communicate with and utilise animals for warfare. The Chantris were often referred to as the Black Jaguar Army, but their ranks also included primates, elephantidae and odd-toed ungulates.

The Chantris had allowed their land to be a place of refuge for the Xahlia families and injured soldiers. Both Daveer's and Xanthe's families had been allocated a map of how to locate the Chantrierian Empire via a prestigious route consisting of a series of detours to catch tails.

Daice had now regained a part of his old self and was back in training with his counterparts. He was doing it for Daena, and nobody else.

Xana had just climbed out of bed and into the bathroom. For a long time, she stared at herself in the mirror; glancing back down at her stomach where the mark had been washed off. She sighed in frustration and pulled out a pouch tied under the sink basin. She walked over to the bathtub and sat on the rim, unravelling the package. Inside it was a circular mirror with an outline of the Xanthari labyrinth drawn onto it. Next, she drew out an inkpot and quill and retraced over the fainted outline on the mirror. She then pressed the cold mirror onto her bellybutton. A counterfeit Xanthari.

Thoughts ran through her mind regarding her birth mission and her emotional endeavour with Xander. Why did they have to use her? The aim of her covert operation was not to grow emotionally attached to these people, but at this moment, with the war closing in by the day, she had never felt more Xanthari. She calculated how much more time her assignment required her to remain within the Xanthari walls; it wasn't long now, although it had been for as long as she could remember. She felt a sudden rush of guilt and regret wash over her. She could not betray them, especially not Xander, not at this pivotal moment in time. Even Xianni – not only had she lied and betrayed her, but she had also taken her love. What could she say to justify her actions should Xianni return?

There were no legitimate excuses to her actions, and she realised she could not stay for much longer. However, she threw these thoughts out of her mind and prepared herself for another hectic day in the Fortress. As she left the house, she spotted Xanthe coming back through the gates and leaped into the air with joy to see his face again.

"Xanthe!" she ran over to him and threw her arms around his neck.

"Xana, how I am glad to see you again…where were you this morning? Had you not heard of my return and the tactical discourse? I had sent Daice to deliver the message to you."

"No, I did not get any message. I have kept myself to myself lately and haven't spoken to anybody since you left. But seeing who you left it with makes me understand why I didn't receive it!" they giggled and smiled.

"Now, may I ask you to keep the letter? It is just that we cannot tell what tomorrow has in store for us. And with the battle nearing our gates I would like my family to know what is in that letter."

"Yes, of course." The guilt re-established itself as she wondered why he put so much trust in her.

"What is the matter, my child?"

"Oh nothing it's just… Xander. I miss him dearly."

"So do we all, my love. The best thing now is to just wait and be patient."

"I know. I still haven't asked… did you get the parchment? How difficult was it for you, if at all?" she forced a laugh.

"We didn't get it. All this preparation you are oblivious to due to your self-seclusion is because the Dincans are in the forest preparing for attack on Dahlia Fort."

"It has begun already? How far are they? And how long until they reach our fortress?"

"Yes, it has begun. They are just beyond the river Morten, and depending how long we fend them off for at Dahlia Fort depends on how long it will take them to reach us."

"Wow, this is actually happening. I shall head over now and help the preparation. I must do my part."

"Good, I will be over in the afternoon to help. I will be bringing Xari and the children also so they can familiarise themselves with the escape route should it be necessary."

Chapter XX

Xianni resisted the tug of consciousness, mentally battling the current of awareness and wanting to retreat into the dizzy oblivion of sleep. The attempt was futile. The discomfort inflicted by her innumerable lacerations proved impossible to ignore. She opened her eyes. She was lying on her back, the vaulted ceiling of a dingy chamber floated into focus. She could feel no restrictions binding her to the slab on which she lay. Meaning that theoretically, she was free.

She tried to sit up but her bones screamed in protest. She was trapped by pain, another form of torment. Tears of frustration blossomed in her eyes but she blinked them away impatiently with a flutter of dark eyelashes. She closed her eyes and summoned her will power, separating her mind from her physical state.

She decided to start small, concentrating on craning her neck to survey the rest of the room. As expected, the door was closed. However, on a plinth to her right was a heavy silver key, a perfect match to the lock on the door. She tried to extend a hand, and although it resisted, she persevered. The mind willed her mutilated hand the command of flexion. Her fingers did not respond to the instruction, they instead remained limp and useless. Frustrated, she dropped her hand and began to whimper. After so many months of resistance she finally felt as if her spirit was broken.

She allowed herself to think of Xander, an activity she had forbidden herself against. Retreating into the comfort of memory, she tried to recall his face but couldn't piece together the refracted impression. Dismayed, she changed her focus to their last meeting, drilling it into her consciousness. They had met at dawn in the high arched lobby of the fortress, prior to her mission with Xanthe. A secluded area at such a time, the lobby seemed cavernous and devoid of warmth. A sense of foreboding had compelled them to meet and there was an inexplicable sense of urgency that conducted their every word and touch, as if they somehow suspected it was their parting. She remembered their last embrace and he was almost tangible to her. She opened her eyes and the façade shattered alongside her fleeting sense of comfort.

She was urged by the desire to see Xander again. A furious determination seized her being and she devised a plan:

1) Sit Up

She screwed up her face in concentration, her brow furrowed with the effort as she fought the jolting pain that rippled outwardly from her spine across the plane of her ribcage. Minutes passed, the battle was strenuous yet she continued, and finally sat with her back at a right angle to her legs. "OK, well done Xianni. The hard bit is over," she said to herself.

2) Legs Over the Side of The Table

Slowly, she heaved her legs right, they slid lethargically over the edge of the bench, her feet swung limply like a rag doll's. She paused, savouring the tiny victory. Her head was swimming as she attempted to block out the excruciating waves of pain that consumed her. As she sat gathering motivation, there was a click at the door. Her heart sunk as the door opened and a chink of watery light crept into the dingy chamber. She had failed. They had come to taunt her. She looked down at her feet.

"Ahh, well done!" the voice was warm and devoid of the expected sarcasm. It was Admeyer – the little shrimp man. A feeling of relief washed over her. He was bearing a tray laden with medical paraphernalia. Every day she felt herself becoming more at ease with this one particular captor. He crossed the room and placed the tray on a surface with a clatter. He then extracted a syringe and concentrated on filling it with a clear, violet liquid.

"I didn't expect you to make so much progress. You're quite the trooper." He flicked the syringe with the musical ping of nail on glass; air bubbles blossomed and diffused, purifying the liquid. Satisfied, he approached.

"This will relieve the pain."

He took her wrist gently; his fingers were dry and papery as he palpated the delicate blue vein. He bound a tourniquet around her arm and she watched the vessels in her flesh bulge under her pale skin like meandering snakes. Without warning, Admeyer plunged the point of the needle neatly into her skin and administered the liquid into her bloodstream. She felt the icy fluid infuse her blood with a comfortable numbness. She sighed and relaxed, watching as if from a distance as Admeyer withdrew the needle gently and wiped away the little bead of blood from the small puncture in her skin.

He turned away from her and consulted his tray again. She stared at his bustling form, confused, "Why are you helping me?"

Admeyer did not respond, instead he returned with several splints and a white reel of gauze. He tenderly took one of her ruined hands and set about realigning and bandaging it.

"Admeyer?" she stared at him, her eyes wide and questioning. He sighed.

"I… I am a doctor. I do not like to see people suffer." He bent his head low to the task but Xianni was not satisfied. Something about his disposition suggested falsity in his response. But the drug had blanketed her mind in a comfortable sense of contentment. Admeyer's outline was hazy, the room dipped in and out of focus and she felt unable to ponder any issue seriously. Nothing seemed to matter. A voice broke her reverie, "Xianni, my dear?"

She looked at Admeyer, angry for the interruption.

"Try to drink this; it will clear your head." He offered her a small tumbler and she gulped down the fluid. It burned her parched throat and she coughed. Almost immediately her head cleared.

"Were you planning to use this key to quit this chamber?" Admeyer asked, with a troubled expression.

"Yes," Xianni replied defiantly.

"Did it not cross your mind that that would be a pointless endeavour? There are armed guards outside the door. They only intend to torment you."

"Of course it did," snapped Xianni, "But I am not the kind to lay here until one of you decides to break my other hand or rape me."

"I didn't mean it like that, I am sorry. But I am not one of them." They exchanged looks at each other.

"Can I see my reflection?" asked Xianni after a pause. Admeyer's features fell.

"I – I do not have a mirror," he spluttered.

"No matter, that tray is reflective," said Xianni coolly.

"I really…"

"Please."

"Xianni, you were… are undoubtedly a very beautiful woman, however, your ordeal has been traumatic, you cannot expect…"

Xianni laughed humourlessly: "I won't cry. Vanity has long escaped me."

Admeyer turned, resigned, and unloaded the tray. He stood before her and with an elegant flourish of his chorded wrists rotated it to face her. The tray rattled to a halt before her.

In it, framed by the gilded handles, was a pale, oval shaped face. Her eyes were sunken and dull, devoid of the sparkle of life, almost satanic. Her lips were pale, chapped and cracked, their lustre long diminished. Her cheekbones were prominent, the skin stretched over them like waxy paper. One side of her face was purple and swollen; an offensive yellow-green tint shadowed her left eye, which had been reduced to a slit. Her skin was coated in dry blood and congealed sweat. Her hair was lank and lifeless, limply framing her gaunt face. Xianni would never have connected this despairing visage with herself if it did not mimic her every blink and follow her every movement. She twitched her mouth in a disgruntled grimace, the face imitated. Admeyer looked on fearfully. He withdrew the mirror.

Xianni was not disheartened. She sat considering her outlook. Admeyer hovered in her peripheral vision, apprehensive to intrude on her thoughts. Purposefully, Xianni heaved herself unsteadily onto her feet. She tested her delicate ankles and extended a foot, crossing to the plinth where she picked up the key, clamping it tightly between her bandaged hands. The metal imprinted into her flesh, as was the intensity of her grip.

She crossed the room and inserted it into the keyhole with great difficulty and frustration. The set dropped repeatedly from her weak, damaged limbs. Finally, it rattled into position. She could feel Admeyer approaching, his nervousness was irritating to her now.

"Xianni, please, don't."

He was behind her now, pleading, "I beg of you, it will not aid your situation."

Xianni got a perverse sense of satisfaction from ignoring his protest. A compulsive feeling of rebellion against instinctual self-preservation had consumed her. The lock clicked metallically and the door swung open. Admeyer seized the handle and slammed the door shut. Xianni smiled at the floor.

"Please." His face was tortured, torn between duty and morality. He turned, muttering to himself, "You will not be hurt by them anymore, you're a good person, you do not deserve this." Perplexed, Xianni swung around to face him. Admeyer had bent to the floor, his figure tensed with obvious effort. There was a scraping sound. When he stepped aside a gaping hole was visible in the ground. A passage, concealed before by an ornate flagstone, which Xianni had assumed to be decorative, was now open to her. The slippery rungs of a ladder extended into velvety blackness.

She stared at Admeyer in disbelief, and a warm rush of gratitude washed over her. Admeyer returned her gaze with a humble expression. Xianni staggered to him, her thanks unexplainable. "Admeyer, I…" her voice was low and sincere, devoid of her previous arrogance.

"I only judge myself for having permitted your suffering to extend this far."

Xianni shook her head in disbelief.

"This passage leads out directly adjacent to the Camillia Nile just a few miles east of Dahlia Fort. Just follow the current."

Xianni nodded curtly and hastened to the entrance. "I cannot thank you enough."

She stepped down into the claustrophobic confines of the passage. Her bandaged hands made her actions clumsy yet she managed, using her one good hand to lower herself. She heaved herself down the ladder until the rungs expired and she stood knee deep in icy water. Flashbacks of the water-filled chamber tumbled back. The orb of light was the sole light source. Admeyer's silhouette stared down: "Quick, I am going to lock you in. Good luck."

There was a sound of stone rubbing against stone as the circle was hidden. Like an eclipse, the darkness was absolute. Xianni blinked for her eyes to adjust. She could feel the icy liquid rippling northwards; she followed the rapids as directed.

The black liquid burned her legs as the salt came into contact with her wounds. She used her numb fingers to feel the wall as a sense of direction – the only way now was forward.

Her eyes were of no use to her in this blackness so she closed them and relied on her faithful hearing ability. The tunnel was circular; it felt to her that she was walking through a pipeline. A putrid scent clogged her nostrils and burned her sinuses, so she decided to mouth-breathe. But even then the moist air had an offensive taste.

The water was contaminated. She could feel objects brushing past her feet and wrapping around her vulnerable legs, and a memory of the eels flashed back into her mind. The torturer was right, how could Xander possibly take her back looking like this? For a moment, she contemplated going back to the chamber, as Admeyer did say that the torment would stop; this would have given her valuable time to recover her beauty and return to her love as he once remembered her. Nevertheless, reasoning that this could be a true test of his love for her, she traipsed ahead.

Up above, she could hear the boisterous banter of men with thundering laughter. She opened her eyes and saw that another similar opening to the one she had been let down into was open. A thick, circular beam of light created a spotlight on the surface of the water. On approach, she kept her distance, listening to their useless chitchat.

Above her, she heard footsteps walking towards the opening. A stream of urine descended and pitter-pattered into the water where her legs stood submerged. A few more short squirts were flung into the water, finished by a flourish of droplets. She waited for him to piss off, and then edged forward.

Xianni's body was quivering quietly; the torture had given her some shell shock symptoms. Her broken and nail-less fingers were immobile and oddly shaped. Her confidence was slowly being chiselled away; the once almighty Xianni, chosen student of Xanthe, had now been condensed to a trembling, fearful wreck.

Back in the chamber, Admeyer began to reseal the opening he had created for his fugitive to escape. Just as he held the grate over the opening to seal it, the perverted Adlom and another soldier marched in.

"Where is she?" Adlom didn't speak; the other soldier's voice was deep and commanding, quietly threatening.

"I thought you guys had already taken her?" Admeyer played along.

"No, we are sure she was here – with you," he assumed a slightly curious pitch.

"Yes she was, but not for a long period. I had left to fetch bandages and a splint. I told the guards outside to look out for her if she tried anything. She was in a terrible way, could hardly even move her limbs before I quit." Admeyer's excuse was believable, and actually quite true.

"What are you doing with that grate, was that unfastened when you came back?"

"Err… to be honest I couldn't remember for the life of me."

"The old man's lying; she's escaping through the system." Adlom interrupted and by stroke of luck exposed Admeyer's agenda. Admeyer was speechless; his quick answering had come to an end.

"Adlom, why do you hate yourself so much? Is it my fault that you attempted to rape her and failed?" the other soldier looked at Adlom in surprise but sharply got back to the matter at hand.

"Is it possible that she could have escaped through the underground passage system?" the mutual soldier now became the voice of reason.

"Well… I suppose it could be a possibility; however, I am ninety-nine-point-seven percent certain that she has been taken elsewhere."

"That is not the case. Adlom, send for the system to be flushed out immediately."

"That is so unnecessary! Give me a few minutes to talk to the guards; they're bound to know of Xianni's whereabouts." Admeyer attempted to stall the soldiers.

"Since when do we refer to prisoners by name?" the third soldier's scepticism grew, his eyes narrowing.

"She is often unconscious and the only way she answers is by name, it is the only familiar thing that she responds to. Her face and everything else about her is unrecognisable." Defiant glee shone in Admeyer's eyes.

"Fine, you've got five minutes from now to find out where she is. And if we find out she has escaped through the system, you're dead, old man." His face was stern and serious. Admeyer smiled and squeezed past the two men.

He was lost for ideas. He could only hope she had made it far enough to be washed out of the village and into Camillia Nile. Realistically, he knew that at least one of them would have to suffer the consequences. He wandered aimlessly in and out of rooms avoiding the guards, thinking of any excuse or alibi. Two minutes slipped away quicker than anticipated, three to go.

"Give us a sec – I'm just going to go the toilet." Adlom left the room and charged down the corridor. He didn't need to go to the bathroom at all. Despite his Machiavellian nature, he was good at his job and could tell a lie from half-truth or truth. He made his way up the long staircase that led to the boiler cabin…

He reached the top of the staircase and climbed up a ladder to reach the loft area of the building. He lit the lanterns with a bundle of matches and walked over to a series of large water tanks.

Admeyer returned to the chamber to face his judgement.

"Where has Adlom got to?" Admeyer knew what the possibilities were.

"He has gone to relieve himself. Have you spoken to the guards? Do they know of her whereabouts?"

"The guard had also gone to the bathroom, I was just about to go up and talk to him, please bear with me." Admeyer left and sprinted to the pipe room, almost losing his footing on the steps. He burst through the door and witnessed Adlom turning the last wheel on the fifth water tank – flooding all the pipes and passages. He turned abruptly.

"Did you just knock the door off the hinges, old man?"

"What have you done?"

"I've flushed out the whole system, just in case she escaped through the pipework. Our task was not to care for her or help her escape – it was to retain and torture. Whose side are you on?"

"I am on the side of justice."

"You know what happens to traitors don't you?" Adlom relieved his sword from his sheath and brandished it. "They are dealt with accordingly." Adlom pointed the tip of his weapon at Admeyer.

"Don't be so foolish, child. Put that away. You have no respect, for anybody."

"Ooh, is Lord Justice frightened of somebody an eighth of his age?"

Adlom playfully plunged in with his weapon but Admeyer caught the blade by clamping it between his palms. Adlom drew back his sword and swiped to behead. Without adjusting his bodily locus Admeyer rotated his head about his neck; the sword was so close to his head that strands of hair were trimmed off and wafted to the ground. After the sword had cleared his head he popped it back up to its usual position.

His attacker was in disbelief and temporarily stopped his assault, realising that this seemingly old wimpy gentleman was no ordinary doctor. He sharply resumed the attack, now with all his effort, jabbing the air hopelessly. The greying man continued bending, folding, propelling his limbs, and delivering major blows that shook Adlom's bones.

Admeyer now began his own vicious assault, consisting of a multitude of belligerent slaps and punches to his stomach and head. The sword was now useless and bore no utility against the vigorous counterattack. Unexpectedly, Admeyer broke from his aggression and stared eye-to-eye with Adlom. Suddenly, Admeyer's form began to disperse and he was gone. Moments later, he reappeared behind Adlom.

"What… you're Dahlia…?" Adlom swung for Admeyer, his blade slashing a hole through his jagged jumper, exposing his bare flesh. Behind the lacerated attire, Adlom saw something strange on Admeyer's skin, a mark of some sort.

"Why… that's the same mark that the captured girl has on her stomach! You're both working together!" Admeyer looked down onto his stomach and could see his Xanthari Labyrinth brand wide and visible.

"You're a Xanthari!" cried Adlom.

"Xantharis cannot disband." He stated starkly.

His intention now was to end Adlom. Too much had been exposed. "I didn't want to have to do this… well, perhaps you deserved it anyway, aye sonny?" Before the last blow, Adlom pleaded for his life.

"Please stop, I will not tell anybody – you have my word."

His feeble plea did not change a thing.

Adlom's body lay there motionless and broken. Admeyer then punctured one of the steam pipes and dragged the carcass over the pipe to make it appear as if Adlom was the victim of a burst steam pipe. He held Adlom's face and body in front of the steam. Now boils and lacerations lined his face. Then he paced over to the taps and began to turn them off hastily, one-by-one.

Xianni soon came across another spotlight and looked up into the chamber above her head, only to be greeted by a face staring right back down at her. The face called down to her.

"Hey, what are you doing down there?" she dashed off, wading through the water desperately. There was something behind her. She could hear it. It was gaining on her, and fast. She turned around and looked far back down the route she had come from, the first spotlight she had encountered was still alight in the distance, but the light was soon blocked out.

The sound of metal expanding and bolts popping out of place sent reverberations down the passageway. The water was coming directly for her. Up ahead, another grate had been uncovered and a tumbler of light fell through and hit the surface of the water. If she could make it there before the water did, she would be safe. She began to splash and jump her way through the tunnel. It was gradually becoming more difficult as the water rose to her waist level. She glanced behind and was horrified by what she saw – a wall of water was heading straight towards her.

Desperation seized her; her tongue felt thick and tingly in her mouth and her throat began to clog up as she struggled to breathe. The first wave of water hit her like a floating brick wall, knocking her off her feet and throwing her with the current.

Her arms and legs were flailing around as she attempted to raise her head above the rampant flow. She managed to paddle her way to a ladder. Soon, she had a mouth full of invisible liquid and she swallowed gulps of it. Choking and gurgling, using the last ounce of energy in her, she threw her arm onto the ladder rung and clung on for dear life. The water was now above head height, and Xianni floated slightly, taking infrequent steps off the ground to keep her head above the water.

The next wave belonging to the second water tank followed close behind. The power and force immediately dragged Xianni away from the ladder and she was carried further into the passage. The roaring cacophony consumed her head, eradicating lucid thought. The current swept her along the slimy pipeline and then, irrevocably pulled her beneath the surface.

There was a sudden silence as the water blanketed her, insulating her eardrums. The air was knocked out of her lungs in great plumes of sparkling bubbles as the current buffeted her limp and defenceless form with ruthless vigour. Her chest burned as it filled with water, weighing her down, drowning her.

She clawed desperately at the pipe walls, hunting frantically for something, anything that could provide hope of escape from her gloomy predicament. The slippery walls offered no sign of rescue. The pipework was smooth and free of any crevices that she could hope to cling to.

Miraculously, her hand hit something on the wall, finally a chance. She scrambled at the object and came into contact with a metallic rung set in the wall. She managed to communicate to her lethargic mind the instruction to hold on. She seized the iron circle with a new bout of strength at the possibility of an escape. Using the rung as a makeshift anchor, she pulled herself to the upper rim of the pipeline where an inch of airspace remained.

Her face penetrated the surface and she inhaled several deep gulps of the damp air. Composing herself, she sunk again, back to the rung. As she had hoped, she could feel a circular indentation around the circumference of the rung. This was a plug to another pipeline – a way out. She seized the rung with both hands, ignoring any ounce of pain that her mind tried to relay to her. She pulled, and pulled. The structure did not give.

Unperturbed, Xianni returned for another air ration and delved yet again beneath the surface. She braced her foot against the wall and tugged the iron towards her but her strength was cruelly swept away by the sheer force of the water. Heart sinking, she propelled herself to the surface and again filled her lungs with air.

Once more she descended into the inky depths and tugged at the handle, leaning with the current and using its force as a lever. She resisted the urge to surface and persevered at her task. Her lungs screamed in protest yet she further declined the urge to reach up to the air. With her side pressed against the wall she felt something metallic prodding into her. It was a latch, stopping the plug from coming undone. She flipped the latch. Her sacrifice was rewarded.

The outlet jutted out a few inches then tumbled out of sight, a victim to the merciless current. Water started to rush into the new pipeline and Xianni found herself sucked into the narrower passage. The journey was brief, after mere seconds the confines of the pipe disappeared and she dropped several feet into a small, naturally formed cavern.

The pipe from which she fell was visible as a circular dark hole in the shadowy rock face. There she was in the shallow water, coughing, spluttering, gulping air. The cave was illuminated by sunlight, filtering through a grate that covered the cave entrance. She was relieved to find it unguarded. Exhausted, she waded through the pool of water that had filled the cave as a result of her escapade. A thick sheen of rust had encrusted the iron bars, weakening the once strong metal. She raised a foot and kicked a bar. It gave easily, clattering to the ground with a tinny resonance. She stooped and crawled through the hole. Tall trees surrounded her, pine needles lay thick underfoot, and the sound of chirruping birdsong was loud in her ears.

It was dawn. She was in a forest. Exultation filled her. She was free. Free at long last. She laughed, the very opposite emotion she'd anticipated. But it was the overwhelming relief more than anything; success through perseverance and hardship. Then she wept, wept at the thought of returning home. She disappeared into the well-known woodland, in search of a secluded space to sleep and rejuvenate.

Chapter XXI

Xander found himself in free fall. Twisting and turning as if a change in landing position would better his chance of survival. His arms were waving in the hope that by some spontaneous way of divine intervention he would grow wings and fly to safety. His internal organs felt as if they too were floating inside his abdomen. The gravitational forces were increasing his velocity, forcing his breath back into his mouth as he struggled to exhale.

Closing his eyes, he gave up the struggle and let the elements have their way with him. The crescendo of the ocean waves below gave him comfort. He landed into the sea not with a splash, but with a bounce. He opened his eyes cautiously. And found himself in a room.

The room was an octagonal chamber, one that Xander could not pin any sense of familiarity to. The walls were clear and flawless. A bright yellow colour illuminated the space, giving the illusion that the sun was hanging from the ceiling. The boundaries of the room merged seamlessly into one another, creating a depthless quality. After a few moments, the sun began to dim, and the room started to take on a whole new milieu. An intensely macabre atmosphere consumed him.

Something was moving in the room. Silhouettes lined the eight walls. One figure stood against each straight. Xander found himself shifting to the centre of the chamber, making him the centripetal point. One of the silhouetted figures stepped forward. A rose gold light illuminated her face from below. She continued to gravitate towards him. As she did so, her face became progressively familiar. He seemed comfortable yet some inherent aspect of his being told him to quit this room.

He attempted to make sense of the face, but for some reason could not focus on the trivial details. Everything seemed to make sense, but simultaneously baffle him.

He blinked. The action was slow and purposeful. His eyelids descended downwards and masked his vision. The room vanished momentarily. On reopening, the room came back, but now the woman was standing in front of him, their faces almost touching. The light source from the room did not seem to reflect off her, she remained opaque.

The figure had long dark hair cascading to her elbows forming dark curtains around her face. A sense of imminent threat resonated with her presence. Xander drew back instinctively yet the room appeared to move with him, he could not make any distance between the figure and himself. The woman threw back her head and laughed loudly at the ceiling, casting her features into light. Her face was terrifying, evil, satanic; her features were sharp and angular, strangely familiar yet totally foreign.

He stared. The laughter halted suddenly. She flicked her head back down to face him in a swift little movement and returned his stare with her head tilted to the side. As she did so her features shifted slightly, the evil eyes softened, the leer diminished as if it never occurred. He was staring at Xana. Xander relaxed, apprehension dissolving with the absence of the threatening woman.

The room was unnaturally silent. They stared at each other. Xander was aware that they had not met in a long time yet he could not recall the reason behind such separation. This seemed unimportant. Eager to be close to her he stepped forward relieved that the room permitted this movement, she mimicked his action and they embraced. He closed his eyes and wrapped his arms tightly around her. The contact was empty. Despite being able to see her in his arms, he couldn't tangibly feel the action. There was none of the usual warmth, no familiarity. The room shifted again in the brief moment of their embrace.

The intensity of the atmosphere seemed to be mounting; the dark of Xander's closed eyelids were turning red. Alarmed, he opened his eyes. There was no heat source but the room was now filled with smouldering warmth. So much so that he could feel his skin beginning to boil and tear as the hydration was sucked from him. He blanched and shied away, but there was nowhere to shy away from, there was no visible place of origin. Xana stood looking at him with a bemused expression, apparently unperturbed by the ignited chamber.

She observed him through wide eyes, apparently amused by his panic. Impatient, Xander scanned the room for an escape. He became aware of a small door, a black rectangle of wood, immune to the heat. He seized Xana's hand. In contrast to his sweaty palm her hand was cold and void of life. He made to drag her to the door but halted. She would not move. She was restraining him with a vice like grip, prohibiting any movement. He tried to jerk his hand out of hers but he could not let go.

He stared at their entwined hands, only to find that they had merged into a single form, a mess of ten fingers; they were inseparable. He glared at her angrily. He tugged at her but her feet were securely anchored to the Earth.

Beads of perspiration gathered on his brow from the heat and effort, the smell of smoke and burning flesh was making him dizzy and flummoxed. The heat of the phantom fire was searing his skin, his eyes stung at the temperature. His situation intensified by his panic.

He tried to shout at Xana, demanding her to follow him. His voice was lost, almost as though it was being snatched from his throat. She seemed to understand. She smiled lazily and shook her head indicating that they were staying; her skin was still stony cold. Xander could feel himself slipping. The smoke was clouding his vision. Then randomly the figurines combusted and the whole room was consumed by absolute blackness. He existed as nothing in the pitch black.

This was his state of mind. It was intangible and inescapable. The battle back from purgatory was strenuous.

Two nurses entered the room where Xander's body rested. One stepped forward and lifted his eyelid exposing marginally icteric sclera. She pressed her fingers routinely into his wrist, "Pulse is unusually high." She extended a hand to his forehead, "As is his temperature, he's running a fever."

"This could suggest he is near to coming around. We should concentrate on locating a particular external stimuli to wake him up."

"Hmm, send for the girl."

Chapter XXII

The rejuvenation interlude was soon interrupted. Leaves and branches were now clawing at Xianni's face as she pummelled through the dense thick vegetation. The wounds on her feet had reopened, agitated by her vigorous movement.

Behind her, she could hear piercing whistles and thuds of arrows. She was gradually getting further and further away from the search party. She trusted Admeyer and his safe route, but knew that it would only be of benefit if she could create enough distance between herself and these men.

She used her speed and momentum to spring off a tree trunk and leap into its branches; gracefully she clambered up out of sight. Below, she could see her search party trample through the forest like a riot. After a few moments she lowered herself to the ground and walked towards the Fortress, home.

Xianni approached Dahlia Fort. As she walked past, she saw Xantharis – her people – dashing in and out of the fort carrying materials and weapons. It didn't take long before she figured out that some sort of preparation was taking place.

She noticed Xi and Xofia, two of her old friends, walking amongst a crowd of Dahlias. For a moment she thought they were prisoners, yet there was a lack of hostility, in fact they seemed happy in the presence of the Dahlia community. Xianni wondered if what Xanthe and herself had discussed all that time ago had come to pass. At the entrance to Dahlia fort were two large wooden gates. One gate had the Dahlia crest imprinted on it, and the other had the Xanthari crest.

Many months ago, before Xianni's abduction and before the Dincans had reached their shores, Xanthe had heard about happenings overseas. He had forewarned the Elders, as well as his chosen pupil, Xianni. He had also been unfortunate enough to know that it was a matter of time before the Dincans brought their campaign to their lands. And as wise leaders do, he envisaged what would need to be done in order to resist such an invasion. Accumulate enough forces to work with them, in other words, *re-join* what used to be The Pars.

She questioned if the re-unification had already taken place. Had so much changed since she had been away? She decided to go in for a closer look.

Slyly, she crossed the moat and slipped through the side entrance of the fortress walls. She removed her hood in surprise as she witnessed Xantharis and Dahlias training together, so much so that she wished to ask somebody what wizardry had influenced this new unification. The Dahlia fortress was dark and gloomy. Lines of poisonous plants lined the fortress walls. The atmosphere was dingy, almost as if there was a veil hanging over the sky. Chills ran through her making her spine quiver. Objects seemed to shimmer in the distance. Nothing felt tangible. An overwhelming sense of emptiness filled the air. Xantharis wearing their native attire roamed the streets and alleys as if it were their home. She watched as Dahlias would shift and disband alongside her people, who seemed unfazed by it. The Dahlia emblem hung tall in the sky like a black sun. The points of the Dahlia flower sharp and crisp, yet dull and lifeless. She was overwhelmed by the unification and fearful for what it meant.

Just outside the Xanthari Fortress, she stumbled across the tree house she and Xander had built as children; she was not far from home now. Unexpectedly, she came to an open patch of land, where a barrier of tall shrubbery shielded the entrance to the Fortress. According to her internal compass, she was certain that she had reached her destination, but for some inexplicable reason it seemed to be hidden.

She could still feel its presence; the ambiance remained welcoming to her. Following the circular structure, she came across a nifty slit, and swiftly she sidestepped in. She was in a maze. She followed the path through and ended up back where she had started – outside. She giggled at the situation, how ridiculous: she had finally escaped from imprisonment only to be found in a maze preventing her from returning home. She continued to walk around, weariness encompassing her but determination her only source of energy. She missed the first slit made in the shrubbery and took the second opening.

This time she could feel herself getting closer to the centre, and the sense of belonging amplified, her determination growing. The path then split into two: left or right. She looked both ways contemplating for a few seconds. She took right. She walked along the path, using the power of her senses for any hints to guide her. As she began to lose hope, suddenly she could hear voices – familiar voices.

She quickened her pace towards the voices, careful to remain as silent as possible. As she turned a corner, she came to a halt. In the distance, she could see Xeth wondering alone cautiously, as if he was being hunted. She made to walk towards him but out of nowhere a Dahlia emerged from the walls of the shrubbery and disbanded just before Xeth had time to restrain him. Xianni stood silently watching.

"Damn you!" he shouted and continued to walk feebly. Again the Dahlia reappeared and knocked Xeth off his feet, holding a wooden club over his head. Xianni silently ran towards them in order to protect her kind. In a spur of the moment Xeth managed to overturn the Dahlia and pin him to the ground.

"That's enough practice for today, let's go back and get something to eat, I'm starving." Xeth held his hand out to the Dahlia, pulling him to his feet. The unlikely duo made their way through the labyrinth to its centre, where the fortress was hidden. Xianni discretely followed.

After weaving in, out, side-to-side, they penetrated through a false wall of thin hedging made to look like a thick, unyielding barrier. They emerged towards the back of the fortress. Xianni silently thanked them for their guidance and branched off. She was finally home.

Xanthe sat in his dimly lit office making marks on a map and using his pointed fingers to trail possible routes. He soon arose and walked over to his window to observe the training sessions taking place in the courtyard below. He was secretly quite impressed by how both sides had come together so fluidly. He watched as one of his younger Xanthari soldiers managed to tackle a Dahlia twice his size onto the ground. The weight in his chest grew heavier. A sudden knock at his door startled him. Subconsciously he said, "Enter," as he remained transfixed by the duels. He heard the door open and close softly but did not turn around.

Still intrigued by the training session he said, "This is one very impressive training session. We will win this war, I am sure of it." Silence. Xanthe turned and looked unfazed by his hooded guest.

"How can I help you?" the curiosity was live in his eyes.

Xianni stood rooted to the floor, unable to move a muscle. Questions ran through her mind. War? What war? Xanthe had aged considerably since she last saw him, but his presence alone comforted her in an old familiar way she had almost forgotten. She had not really prepared a homecoming speech. He continued,

"Why have you come? Have I sent for you?" still, she remained unvoiced. Xanthe stepped closer, his eyes narrowing. As he did so Xianni also took a step backwards.

She could sense Xanthe was growing weary and defensive, so she untied her belt and revealed her Xanthari brand. Almost immediately, his temperament calmed but he continued to stare at her stomach. Xianni was aware of her immensely frail figure. Her stomach had become inwardly domed, bones visible beneath her thin pale skin. Her waist only centimetres thick.

"It is I, Xanthe…" Her voice was hoarse and masculine with a bewitched pitch.

Xanthe's jaw dropped down to his collarbones, his eyes twinkling at the recognition of her voice, a grin spread across his face.

"Xianni? Can it be?" without thought, Xanthe pounced forward towards the figure and went to remove her hood, she cowered behind her arms, but he successfully removed it. She turned quickly and doubled over covering her face with her arms.

"But what is wrong with you? It has been so long all I wish for is to see your face again, my daughter! Is that so much for a father to ask?" he said gaily.

"You do not want to see what they have done to me," she whimpered, continuing to hide her face.

"Xianni, show me your face." Xanthe spoke affectionately. He walked over to her and placed his arms around her carefully and easily removed her arms from around her face. She stared at the ground with her hair hanging messily about her face like a wild, bewildered creature.

Placing one hand under her chin he raised her head. At first, Xianni avoided eye contact and removed his hand from her chin. Sharply he locked her face into both his palms and stared at her in the eyes. This was not Xianni. Her eyes were like two macabre cauldrons filled to the brim with pain, guilt and sorrow. The vibrant deep hypnotic blue that pigmented her irises was no longer vivacious, the colour seemed condemning and ghostly. Her complexion was no longer desirable, but stained with blood, sweat and tears. Lacerations and bruises decorated her face, the tip of her nose bent to an awkward angle. Xanthe soon realised that her croaky voice must have been a result of the endless screams of agony.

"I am so proud of you. It is an honour to have you back with us." Xanthe pulled her forward into a hug and tightly embraced her, "So proud." Instantly, she broke down in a heap of emotion. The first ounce of affection she had felt since her capture. She wailed and bawled, occasionally crying out inaudible words. All this time, Xanthe's eyes were wide with rage. He would seek revenge, but first he needed answers.

"…Xi, I am sorry – for what I did, for what I had to do. I knew you were strong. I couldn't take the risk. I couldn't let you go through that. I am so…"

"I forgive you. I would have done the same, but somehow they knew your plan. As soon as we left the house I was replaced with a decoy, we stood in the shadow and I watched you kill that girl."

Xanthe listened to Xianni's ordeal. A blow-by-blow account of what happened from the moment she arrived at the enemy gates. Xanthe's heart grew heavier and heavier. They had ruined her. They had crushed her spirit and stamped repeatedly on her identity. She kept the worst of the physical and psychological afflictions to herself, but Xanthe was not oblivious to the ways of wicked men on the hunt for power. She spilled all the inside secrets she had managed to piece together. He was surprised by her ability to compose herself when recounting the gruesome anecdotes. She was stronger than he had given her credit for, but one important question remained.

"Xianni, I did not choose you by chance and what you have endured has reinforced my faith and trust in you. But I must ask, did you tell them anything to do with the parchments? Its uses, its purpose, its decoding anything at all?"

"Xanthe, I don't think so. They gave me a strong serum, something from the solanaceae family by the look of it, but from what I remember I was able to resist…"

Chapter XXIII

Xana approached the infirmary, her heart beating like an African drum. She had been bluntly summoned to meet the matron a mere fifteen minutes ago and had hastened immediately to fulfil it.

She entered the infirmary; the chilly air that filled the entrance to the hall was hostile in contrast to the pleasant heat of the day. Agitated, she approached a large, mahogany desk, behind which a young girl sat, methodically completing forms with calligraphic spirals and flourishes, entirely intent on the task.

Xana cleared her throat pointedly, but the bespectacled girl did not look up. Xana continued to stare at the top of the girl's neatly parted chestnut hair. The girl extended a slender finger to a small neatly carved notice on the desk, bearing the slogan, "Ring for assistance."

Xana scoffed at the girl's pomposity, "Is that really necessary?" the girl ignored her. "Miss?" exasperated, Xana slammed her hand down onto the brass bell; it created a sickly '*ping*' that reverberated about the empty room.

The girl's head snapped up and she greeted Xana with a poisonously false smile, she had two rows of perfect, pearly white teeth. "Good morning, how may I be of assistance?" her voice was thick and a snide undertone was present beneath the polite pretence.

Xana gazed dumbfounded at the girl for a moment; her pale, oval shaped face was lightly dusted with freckles across the nose and maxilla. A pair of round spectacles, which balanced precariously upon her long nose, freakishly magnified her grey eyes. "Madam?"

Xana blinked, coming back to the present, "Yes… Yes, I'm here because I received this note," she thrust the parchment bearing her summons at the girl. The girl pinched the corner of the paper between thumb and index finger, lifting the crumpled note up tentatively as if it personally offended her.

She compulsively attempted to iron out the wrinkles with her fingertips as she deciphered the smudged handwriting. "This seems to be in order, please take a seat, someone will be through in a moment to fetch you."

"Thank you so much for your help," hissed Xana, her voice dripping with sarcasm.

She walked about and set herself down in one of the faded leather seats that lined the waiting room. The chair was uncomfortable and smelled clinical. Xana could just about see the receptionist's head bobbing over the rim of the desk as she scrawled. The silence was loaded and unbearable, broken only by the rhythmic scratching of the girl's quill on parchment. Xana drummed her fingers impatiently on the arm of the chair and awaited the correspondent who would lead her to Xander.

After what seemed like an age, an elderly woman trundled into the chamber and conducted a whispered conversation with the receptionist. She was plump and silver haired, dressed in robes of deep navy, significant of the healing Elders. Xana felt hopeful, not only did she want to see Xander; she was now desperate to be away from this waiting room and its stuffy sentiment.

The woman turned to face her and Xana rose quickly from her chair to greet her. Her wrinkled face crumpled into a podgy smile as they grasped hands.

"Ahh, you must be Miss Xana? I am Xaid, I have been monitoring your friend Xander these long weeks. If you'd like to come with me?"

Xana followed the woman down a narrow passage and was led, to her intense disappointment, not to Xander, but to a small and rather shabby office. Xaid beckoned her inside and Xana admitted herself with some reluctance. She paused in the doorframe.

"Where is Xander? Is he… OK?"

"He is in a confidential location, and yes he has made excellent progress. If you would take a seat."

Disgruntled at the incessant seat offering, Xana plumped into a chair and watched with mounting irritation as the nurse languidly lowered herself into the opposite seat.

"Xander is in a delicate state of mind. His body is completely healed but his consciousness is in a state of flux. His reticular formation seems to be operating avidly, which is good. We suspect from his high pulse rate that he has been experiencing lucid dreams. Mostly influenced by a cocktail of thoughts and external stimuli. This is a very promising sign. We feel that the correct stimulation could bring him back to full consciousness. We need you to talk to him, to sit with him and such things. We believe this could help. Now, would you please blindfold yourself and pop in the ear plugs, his location is a secret only we healers may know; we cannot take the risk of divulgence."

Xana seized the velvet length of material Xaid offered her and bound it tightly around her eyes, pinning her eyelids shut. The nurse took her arm and led her out of the office.

They stopped in what Xana supposed, from the reverberations, must be the cellars. "You may remove the blindfold now," Xaid instructed. Xana did so; her eyes took a moment to adjust to the bright surroundings after the darkness. She blinked. They were standing in a hallway with vaulted ceilings; there was a single door. The matron nodded. Xana stepped forward, her feet heavy. She placed a hand onto the cold, metallic handle and pushed the door ajar. She hesitated and crossed the threshold.

The room was sparsely furnished. In the absence of windows, light came from the several paraffin lanterns set on the whitewashed walls. A dreary, iron-framed bed stood in the centre of the room; the sheets were drawn tightly over a small and docile figure. Xana approached tentatively. Only his face and hands were exposed, his arms were encased in paisley pyjamas and the rest of him was blanketed in sheets, supposedly to combat the low temperature of the basement room.

His hands and face were pale in complexion; the lack of sunlight exposure had given him a chalky, almost translucent tinge. Eyes tightly shut. Unlike before, he did not look as if he were merely sleeping, he looked closer to death. Perching in the high-backed chair next to his bed, she gloomily observed him. She took his hand in hers. The hand was cold and unresponsive.

"Xander?" her voice was quiet and stupid in the silent room. She tried again, her voice stronger, "Xander, it's me, Xana…" Her mind was blank. The task suddenly seemed helpless. An emotional shift inside her caused a sudden flare-up of inspiration, "Xander. I need you to listen to me. If you can hear me, squeeze my hand now."

She waited. Nothing. "OK, never mind that, we'll get there, right?" she started to talk to him, pouring out almost a month's worth of repressed information. Nothing. Casting her mind around for stimuli she began reciting random words, each one a potential stimulus, "Xanthari, Dahlia, Home, Xianni, Xanthe…"

Not one of these nouns ignited any spark of life in him.

"Your name is Xander. You were born on the outskirts of this, the Xanthari Fortress, and spent your childhood years watching the warriors in training. Aspiring to be the best Xanthari warrior that ever lived." She paused; there were massive gaps in her knowledge of his past. "You are one of Xanthe's most learned students, to him you're a son." She changed tack, "And then you met me." Her voice was quieter as she retreated into the confines of her memory; she set about describing their short history together and was dismayed at the lack of result. Then there was a soft knock at the door; the nurse peered into the chamber.

"Xana? You've been here almost two hours. I feel you should leave for today."

Xana agreed but requested a moment longer. She stood up and leaned over his passive form, pressed one hand tenderly to his cheek and laid a kiss on his head. Speaking in a low voice so as to preserve the intimacy of their exchange she whispered, "Xander, I miss you. Come back to me."

She then walked away and closed the door softly. Xander's hand twitched, the action was quick and unnoticed by anybody, as if it might not even have happened.

The next few days proceeded as a hectic whirlwind of activity for Xana. She had adopted a new haphazard routine, which she again followed avidly. Mornings would be spent with Xander, desperately trying to coax him out of the confines of his deep, impenetrable sleep. Progress had definitely been made, especially in the latter days, however the lack of real result was frustrating. She would then spend her afternoons aiding the war effort and training with furious intensity. The last few hours of the day would be spent pouring over library books, researching Xanthari history and famous stories to nourish Xander's mind with.

One day, whilst performing her morning ritual of reading to Xander, she decided to read him a book with a rather ambiguous title, a word Xana had never heard of before, yet the blurb sparked interest. It was entitled Wua hu. It appeared to be nothing but a story tale or a myth. It was about a family that lived in Morten at the time of its unification. This particular family was Chantrierian by blood. They were popular among the locals for their gift of fortune-telling. A couple of pages into the book, a wad of pages had been roughly torn out. Xana attempted to continue her narration, but it now seemed disjointed and nonsensical. She flicked through the remainder of the book to see if the pages had been replaced elsewhere. To her surprise, hidden in the book were some more of Xianni's scrawlings:

$$L.E \times 4.\ 5^{th}\ element = All\ Wua\ hus.$$

As with all of Xianni's other cryptic messages, Xana was lost for words. This made no sense at all. The only thing she could have taken from this was that Wua hus were not make-believe fortune tellers but had some levy in the grand scheme of things – whatever that might be. She was getting warmer and warmer, yet she had no idea how many pieces to this puzzle there were. And even once all the pieces were obtained, she had no idea how to align them.

Daice and Xana had been leading the elites in training and battle. Daice had become increasingly tactile and his pursuit of Xana had escalated. At first, she allowed his comments and actions to wash over her, after all he was grieving; and he had saved her life on multiple occasions. But his persistence became a nuisance. He would make unnecessary comments about her appearance and would make physical contact at any possible chance.

Daice's mind was unsettled. He had no genuine emotion towards Xana. Yes, he thought she was beautiful, but she was not Daena. Images of that night tormented him. He could not fathom how his two allies watched in silence as his fiancée was murdered in cold blood. A part of him was pleased that Xander had *died*, but as expected it did not fill the hole that he felt. An eye for an eye.

Daice walked across the courtyard to the wrestling halo. He entered Xana's halo and offered her a duel. She reluctantly accepted his proposal. They warmed up with a light spar. Daice's movements became playful. He disbanded and reformed behind Xana wrapping his arms around her holding her tightly; he breathed in her ear and commented on her smell. He smiled cheekily, she could hear the smile. She forced herself out his grasp and elbowed him in the sternum winding him. He doubled over gasping for air. She smiled unapologetically. Before he had time to recover she attacked him, forcing him into submission. He tapped her arm signalling defeat. She did not let up.

"Will you stop your inappropriate behaviour?" she asked, tightening her grip around his throat. He nodded his head.

"Me and you will never happen. Get that into your thick skull, you sick bastard. Daena would be turning in her grave." She relinquished her hold, and left the halo.

Daice was shell-shocked, his heart fell into his boots. He took a moment of deep introspection as he walked back to his quarters. Xana's words had penetrated his soul. His heart ached for Daena, he missed her immeasurably. He took a cold shower to take his mind off the negative thoughts. He opened the drawer to find a fresh towel, only to be greeted by Daena's nighty neatly tucked away. Tears welled up in his eyes; he felt a deep sense of shame and loneliness. Bitterness remained, yet his anger ebbed. After Xana's display of strength, he knew there was nothing left he could take from their relationship. Deep down he knew Daena's death was not their fault – and the more he thought about it, her blood was on Daveer's and Xanthe's hands for sending them into the Pars.

Chapter XXIV

It was noon; the midday sunlight filtered gently through the delicate net curtains. Of late, Xianni's sleeping pattern had been very inconsistent. What sleep she did manage to obtain was often invaded by perverse nightmares, from which she awoke at the least in a cold sweat and at worst in terrifying screams. Xanthe had been very hospitable to her during this time, for which she was extremely grateful. He had kept her presence within his household confidential, only he and his family knew of her return to the fortress and it was to remain that way until Xianni decided otherwise.

Xari in particular proved to be a pillar she could rely on during this difficult period, gently extracting her from her tortured memories with patience and understanding. Her motherly presence was soothing to Xianni and she had taken to falling asleep in her embrace. Sometimes when she awoke in distress, Xari would still be next to her, comforting her until she was able to fall back into sleep.

Xianni entered the kitchen where Xari was preparing food, presumably for lunch.

Greeting her in between yawns, she settled at the counter and poured herself some water from a jug on the side. Xari smiled pleasantly, "How did you sleep? You were very quiet last night," she asked in her cool soothing voice, lilted with a hint of musicality.

"Yeah, thank you. It's definitely getting easier."

"I'm glad to hear it."

Xari and Xanthe's youngest child, a six-year-old girl named Xain, interrupted them. She had porcelain skin and tightly ringleted hair of the same shade as her mother's. Even at such a young age, it was evident she would be very beautiful. Xianni sighed, glimpsing her improved, but still disfigured visage in the window.

The young girl protested to her mother, demanding food, for which Xari chided her. Xianni intervened, reaching down and hooking the child up onto her hip, carrying her to the dining room and placing her gently in her seat. She winked at the child and offered her a biscuit, then returned to help Xari with the preparation.

The dining room, like the rest of Xanthe's home, was modestly furnished though still retained an air of elegance and wealth. Xianni admired Xanthe's character; he did not permit any air of his leadership qualities to intrude upon his family life. They were happy. The family (with the addition of Xianni) ate lunch, allowing the children to lead the discussion. Xianni participated with enthusiasm, telling them of the mythical deep woods and the supposed mystical creatures that lived there. When they had finished eating, the children alighted from the table to act out their new game, Xianni grinned as Xain dropped to the ground mimicking the stance of a ferocious beast, growling with vivacity. Xari, too, left the dining area, leaving Xianni and Xanthe alone. They sat in companionable silence. After a pause, Xianni summoned the courage to broach a topic of delicacy she had previously abstained from discussing.

"Xanthe?"

"Yes, my dear."

"I have refrained from asking until now, but what of Xander and Xana? Are they well?"

Xanthe shifted in his chair uncomfortably. After a few minutes' silence, he put down the letter he was reading and looked directly at her, his expression neutral: "Xana is in excellent health. I'm sure she would be delighted to know of your news. Xander, on the other hand, is in a severe condition after an unfortunate accident. He remains… comatose."

"What happened? Will he recover?"

"I am afraid I do not know. We remain optimistic."

"Can I see him?"

"I –"

"Please Xanthe, it may help him. I don't know how, but it might. Besides, I need to see him. I haven't seen him in months… You know how much he meant – means to me…" She stared at Xanthe imploringly, tears beginning to form at the corners of her eyes. The old man sighed empathetically.

"If you wish it, but I must warn you not to raise your hopes too high, or else you'll only have farther to fall." Baffled by his strange sentiments, Xianni touched Xanthe thankfully on the shoulder and exited the room.

At the top of the stairs she glimpsed herself in the gilded mirror that decorated the landing. Her face had healed well, yet there was still startling evidence of her ordeal which seemed somewhat irreversible. Xanthe's hospitality had nourished her skin back to its usual rosiness and helped to fill in her starved features. Yet, the scars interrupted the plains of her cheekbones. Her eyes still looked dull and blunt, her nose misshapen.

Cross-legged, she sat on the bed, caught in deep thought. She ran her fingers stiffly through her hair, it had been cropped short, a seemingly more hygienic solution. Boredom consumed her. Over the next few days, Xianni remained patient and did not broach the subject again. She had imagined her request would have been answered immediately but Xanthe continued as normal. She wondered on several occasions whether she should remind him of the urgency; she was desperate to see Xander. She felt that somehow this meeting would help remedy him of whatever ailment had befallen him. She began to dream of him, the same dream every night. She would find herself strapped to a wooden table in an empty dark room and Xander standing by the door looking at her but not responding. She would scream out his name and he would continue observing her blankly, eyes not blinking, cold and indifferent.

Several days later, Xianni lay in her bedchamber; books lay strewn around her, unopened. As she fell into the initial lull of a mid-afternoon sleep, a soft knock at her door jolted her. It was Xanthe, "Be downstairs in ten minutes," he hissed through the wood.

Xianni and Xanthe reached the infirmary. Her face was shrouded in a hood. They hurried up the steps, quickly and carefully. Once inside, Xianni relaxed and stood in the background as Xanthe discussed the situation with the receptionist, a meek looking girl of about seventeen. Sweating in her thick cloak, Xianni dropped the hood away from her face, forgetting her unsightly condition. The girl stared at her through her rectangular spectacles. Disgust immediately swept across her face but she attempted to conceal it, looking away quickly and shuffling papers on her tidy desk. Xianni, feeling awkward, replaced her hood over her head and followed the matron into the basement.

Excitement pumped through her. She savoured the anticipation of the reunion she never thought would come. They descended an old staircase that echoed with every step they took, leading directly into an intersection of corridors. They turned right into a long narrow corridor, dimly lit by oil lanterns, which hung symmetrically in equidistant intervals along the bare grey wall. There appeared to be only one door right at the end of the corridor, the torch that hung above it unlit. Xanthe stood still and motioned his head towards the end of the corridor, signalling to Xianni she should continue alone. She gave him a feeble smile and nodded back in gratitude before continuing. When she reached the door she looked back for support but he was no longer standing there. The door was already slightly ajar and she peered through the chink of exposure, finding it to be occupied not only by Xander but Xana also. A fresh surge of anticipation infused her body at the sight of her friend and eager to reunite she pushed the door, but halted abruptly as Xana's words reached her ears.

"Xander, I am sorry, my love, I have to go for today, they need me but I'll come back soon. I love you." Xana leaned over and kissed his cheek, obscuring his face from view momentarily. She then stood with his hand in hers, apparently studying his face. Then, quite suddenly, she stooped and swept up her belongings. Xianni withdrew quickly from the doorway and slipped into the shadows, her back against the wall as she watched Xana exit the room and hasten down the corridor she had just come from; a sense of betrayal, mortification and heartbreak overwhelmed her. A moment was necessary to compose herself, arguing with her rational thought and irrational desires and expectations. It could have easily just been a friendly gesture, she thought to herself.

Dread filled her and her chest constricted within its cage. Had she seriously expected him to wait for her when she had been presumed dead all this time? Even if he had, did she seriously expect him to take her back? After so much time, when she looked like this? A searing stab of pain came with the quiet, honest answer... no. She tried to reason with herself, she should not despise Xana. The action was not malevolent. But despite this attempted reasoning, the overwhelming betrayal was too pronounced. She needed to see his face in order to assess how she felt.

Taking a deep breath, she entered the chamber, crossing it slowly and purposefully. She dropped next to Xander, into the chair Xana had so often occupied. She stared avidly at her beloved. His face was gloriously unchanged; she pressed her lips together, fighting the waves of emotion as she reached forward and brushed the hair off his face. His hair was longer than she had remembered, a few greys appearing amidst the thickness of brown. Tears bled down her cheeks. She clasped a hand to her mouth to prevent the sob of emotion escaping. She sniffed.

"Xander…" Her voice was thick with tears and rough from her ordeal. She wondered if he would recognise it. "It's me, Xianni, I came back, after all this time. I came back… just for you…" her voice broke, and unable to bear it she made to leave the room, rising from the wooden chair. To her amazement, he shifted under her hands, stretching sleepily, eyes still shut. His face was relaxed; his mouth stretched in a slack smile as his eyes scrunched with the movement. Panicked, she turned and bolted out of the room without a backwards glance. He could not see her, not now, not like this.

***

Xana crossed the reception, ignoring the receptionist's angry objection and down the narrow passage. She pelted down the staircase and hurtled into the room. It was easy to find without a blindfold, her senses knew the way; she had completed the journey so many times now. At his room, she slowed to a walk and gradually peered inside, suddenly, unaccountably nervous. Xander was sitting up, though was largely concealed from view by a woman bending over him apparently examining him. Xana slammed the door noisily and they both looked up. The nurse beamed at Xana whose eyes were now transfixed on Xander. They stared at each other momentarily, drinking in each other's presence. Then Xana broke the pause, bounding forwards, closing the short distance between them, "Hi, long time…" The nurse was almost forced off her feet as the two of them connected in a strong embrace. Xana could hear Xander gently laughing into her hair as they danced on the spot – the exuberance of a long-awaited reunion filling the room.

Hours later, Xana was still there. She sat comfortably against Xander's chest as she explained all that had happened during his time of unconsciousness. They finally lapsed into companionable silence. After a pause Xander braved the topic:

"Xana?"

"Hm?"

"Was Xianni here?"

Xana looked up, astonished, "No… Why?"

"It's funny, I could have sworn she was here."

"Sure it wasn't a dream?"

"Yeah… I'm almost certain it wasn't. I'm sure she was here, I saw her leave, it was her, she woke me up."

A distinct feeling of hurt punctured Xana's confidence. There was a very awkward silence.

"Xander, Xianni is alive but she remains in captivity. No one has heard any news of her."

"I'm sure she was here."

"Right." Xana stared at him, and then dismissed the issue, recalling what Xaid had said about lucid dreams. "Are you allowed to come home? Tonight?"

Xander grinned, "Of course."

***

Xana approached the frustrating receptionist to arrange Xander's release. She prodded the bell pointedly and girl looked up, "Yes?"

"I am here to organise a release. It has been agreed that he can stay with me in our house until he is quite recovered." She could not suppress her grin. The girl rifled through the neatly stacked towers of paper on her desk. She extracted a hefty amount of documentation and shoved the wad of paperwork at Xana.

"Do you have a quill?"

The receptionist begrudgingly offered, "Please don't chew the top again."

Xana smiled sarcastically, and turned away as she made to complete the forms, being deliberately messy with her handwriting to annoy the receptionist. It was laborious, but for every page Xana turned, the closer she was to being back at home with Xander. After a half an hour of solid work she was done.

The receptionist patted them into a neat rectangle and stamped the cover with a thick black mark bearing the word 'approved'. Xana smiled. The receptionist adopted her false politeness.

"I appreciate that this is a confidential transaction, however, would you like me to contact Xanthe? I'm sure he would like to know of Xander's new whereabouts."

"Thank you, I'd be grateful if you would."

"Fine. And what about the other lady? I suppose she would like to know where he's gone, after all it appears she had a profound effect on your friend's recovery."

Xana stared at her incredulously.

"What other girl?"

"Um she didn't leave a name, Xanthe organised her visit."

"When was she here?"

"This morning, after you left."

Xana gawked at the receptionist, whose stupid, simpering face was now fraught with fear. A sense of deep betrayal consumed her in entirety.

"What did she look like?"

"T-t-tall, dark hair," the receptionist dropped her voice significantly, "she looked brutally beaten up, actually."

"Oh… Thanks. That won't be necessary," Xana felt numb as she forced herself to leave the office and go to meet Xander. The sweetness of their reunion had now been ruined.

***

Xanthe, Xianni and the rest of the family were gracefully awaiting Xari to transport the food from the stove to the table. The two children told Xianni about their day at school and the training they had endured; Xianni listened with wild eyes.

At long last, the food was brought to the table bringing smiles to the faces of the eaters. Xari settled herself next to Xanthe and they began to remove the lids from the pots allowing the aroma to fill the room and, more importantly, their nostrils. They began to dish out the food. Xean, Xanthe's son, grabbed a handful of sliced sausages but before he had time to gobble them down, the food was slapped violently from his hand.

"You know the rules, Xean… Xianni, would you care to say grace?" Xari asked.

"Erm, yes, if you wish." Xianni cleared her throat and began, "Dear lords, where you have provided nourishment and fuel, we beseech you, care for us and help us grow in strength, ability and wisdom."

In chorus, they said, "Strength, ability, and wisdom." They opened their eyes and began to assault the innocent table.

After a few moments of stuffing, there was a heavy pounding on the front door, startling them. Surprised looks were exchanged across the table. From the head of the table, Xanthe arose and made his way to the door, wiping his greasy hands onto his cloak. He opened the door and was greeted by a furious Xana.

"Where is she?"

"Xana, what a pleasant surprise. Who do you speak of? Xari is in the dining hall if that is whom you mean."

"You know who I speak of – Xianni. Where is she? She visited Xander today and was reported to have been in the room with him moments after I visited – with you! What is it with you? Just when I bridge the gap you so easily created, there you go shaking the foundations once again! I know she's here."

"Please be quiet. My family is trying to enjoy dinner…"

"Oh really, is she in there with them?" Xana pushed past him and hastily made for the dining room. She burst through the door and all the heads in the room turned sharply. Xianni was not present. Instead, the wild eyes of Xanthe's children met her, food spilling from their mouths. Xari stood up and smiled at her, one eyebrow raised.

"Apologies, Xari, children. I am looking for Xianni, have you seen her?"

"No, my dear," Xari replied apologetically, focusing her efforts now on wiping the mouth of her youngest.

"OK, I am indeed sorry." Xana inspected the room before she left with sharp eyes. She walked back to the door in utter embarrassment.

"I'm sorry, Xanthe. Xander was certain she was there today, and that it was she who woke him up. And then the receptionist too… I shouldn't have acted so irrationally… So whom did you visit him with then?"

"One of the new trainee nurses escorted me down as Xaid has been a little under the weather." He was cool and calm in his dishonesty.

"Oh right, well I'm sorry, I feel a total fool. I mean after seeing her captive, I guess I thought… maybe she had escaped or you had got her back somehow."

"It's OK, you're forgiven. Now get some rest, along with Xander; you will be training partners from now, he needs to regain his skills as quickly as possible. Good night."

Chapter XXV

Xander remained fixed in front of the fireplace as he had the previous few days. The heat kept him in concentration. Xana had stayed by his side the entire time, silently watching him, as he remained lost in thought. Every now and again they would fall back into comfortable conversation, laughing heartily and momentarily forgetting the anxiety of what was to come. As Xana spent hours by his side, drawing up plans for the upcoming war, Xander observed her solemnly. Xianni was on his mind; she was back and he knew it. Questions had consumed him since his return. Why didn't she want to see him? Maybe she had moved on and didn't want to revisit the past. So why had she come to the infirmary? Where was she now?

The fire began to crackle and dislodge blocks of wood. Xana walked around the chair and joined him by his side. She stared at him, waiting for him to acknowledge her presence, but she did not get a reaction. Unexpectedly he started,

"I'm sure it was her. I could recognise her voice from a million others, and her touch. She was with me, and then she just left. I wish she would show herself to me, before all this we meant everything to each other. Why would she not come to see me?" Xana closed her eyes, they had had this conversation several times. He soon realised he was speaking out loud, and to the wrong audience.

His predicament was now illuminated before him, he must choose: Xianni or Xana. He knew where his heart lay, yet he would give his life for both of them. He was irresolute; something it took years to build with Xianni was equal to something he and Xana were able to build in a matter of months. He stood up and made for the door.

"I just need to go out and get some fresh air. My head is swirling."

"I'll come with you! You're obviously not fully recovered."

"I need some time alone; I'll be back before you go to bed," Xander was adamant.

"OK, you know the Fortress is in the design of the Xanthari labyrinth?"

"Yes, I know. I'll take the underground route instead." He rose slowly, put on a layer of sheepskin and left. Xana followed him with her eyes, hoping he would return. Her stomach grew heavy with regret and passion, of all the people to fall in love with, why him – her best friend's lover? She could not compete, where was the loyalty in that?

Xander wandered the forest alone. Thoughts buzzed through his weak, newly awoken mind. After careful deliberation he chose Xianni. A few moments later, he chose Xana, and next Xianni. Maybe his deliberation wasn't so careful after all. He found himself stood at the spot he and Xianni used to reside in when they were young – the tree house. Climbing up absentmindedly, he reached the entrance and realised that he could no longer fit into the small frame his juvenile body could once easily waltz into. Determined, he crouched down and crawled inside, grazing the backs of his arms on the edges of the opening. To his surprise, he could just about make a figure sitting in the shadowy corner of the treehouse – it was she.

"Xianni!" he shouted so loud that the birds emigrated from the trees. "I knew it was you! Xana didn't believe me. Oh thank God you have returned. All this time we thought you were… Oh how I have missed you. Well, come here, what are you waiting for!" Xianni remained silent in the shadows, unmoving. His heart began to beat at a considerable pace, his eyes transfixed on the figure. Was he imagining her? It was impossible. He had to touch her. He began to walk slowly towards the crouched figure, one arm outstretched in front of him.

"Please don't come any closer. I am in no position to see you, I have… changed." Her familiar voice sent a wave of comfort over him. He waited for her to continue. There was an awkward pause before she muttered almost inaudibly, "I hear that you and Xana have made something of yourselves. And I wish you two the best of luck in all your endeavours."

"What do you mean by endeavours?" Xander asked blindly.

"I have been informed you and Xana are now together. You have moved in together, haven't you? She lives with you?" Xianni's tone was bland and unexcited.

He stood rooted to the ground. This was not how they were supposed to re-unite. The excitement that had encompassed him just a few minutes ago was replaced with dread.

"No, we are not an item. Wait a second, who is telling you this?"

"Never mind, either choice you make, you have my blessing." She continued to look away, towards the corner of the treehouse, where they had once as children engraved their initials into the wood with a blunt tool.

"Why can't I see your face?" asked Xander. He longed to hold her, to smell her, to see the smile that used to lighten up his day.

"It is not how you remember it. I need time to heal. Physically." Slowly, he approached her.

"What did they do to you, Xi? You can't hide it from me forever. No matter what, you will always be my Xianni Xivait. Nothing will change that." She smiled, hidden under the cover of darkness. The only time they ever referred to each other by their full names was when they used to play families as children. She allowed him to edge closer to her. He outstretched his shaking arm and placed his palm softly across her face and stroked it. He pulled her up onto her feet and out of the shadow of the room. She attempted to keep her head bowed, but with gentle force he pulled her face towards him. Her face was now fully visible; scars, swellings, all sorts. Her deep blue eyes told him that many things happened to her, terrible things. Where they once twinkled at him, they now seemed glazed, a deep sadness embedded in them. Xander smiled, and tilted his head endearingly, "Oh how glad I am to see your face again." Involuntary tears rolled down her cheeks. With her face now exposed, nothing else could be hidden. He began to wipe away her tears and pulled her into an embrace. As his head rested upon hers, rage began to swell within him. How dare somebody do this to her? What gave them the right to ruin such a precious life? An image of the new Xianni remained transfixed in his head as her silent sobs wet his robe. She was no longer whom he had hoped would return. Guilt overcame him, he could not see himself coming to love somebody who was so physically different to the person he had previously fallen for. He found himself thinking of Xana.

Pulling her face back up towards him, Xander focused in on her eyes, trying to disregard her swollen and broken features.

"Don't you want to see Xana?"

"No… Err, I mean, not right now. I am not ready to see her yet." Despite all else, he was glad to hear that her voice hadn't changed as drastically as her face. He thought to question what happened to her and what did they do to her. The worst kept flashing through his mind; had they taken her innocence, her virginity? There was a prickly, expectant silence.

Xianni's emotions came rushing back to her. She loved him, and no matter what happened she always would. She searched his eyes, looking for the part of Xander that used to love her. His expression was distant – he didn't know her anymore. She stepped closer to reduce the distance between them and arched her head up to look directly into his eyes, their lips just centimetres away; Xander automatically took one step back. Xianni frowned, it seemed as if after all this time he was only attracted to the physical aspect of her being.

"It's still me…" she sensed his disinclination towards her. She understood it was too soon for them to see each other, and walked back into the corner of the airborne cabin, plumping herself down into the same spot she was in before.

"It's not that, Xianni, it's just, you have to know…"

"Just get out, Xander. Just go," she interrupted his futile explanation.

"I am sorry, Xianni, really, but the reason is not because of you, it's me. I have to tell you something before…"

"Stop it, Xander! Stop the lying. I don't blame you, OK? I mean look at me, I'm a wreck. And you've moved on. I was gone and you moved on. So please just leave before you make it worse than it already is!" her speech was cracking under the immense emotion, her broken voice was heavy with passion and pain.

"Listen, please!" Xander was unable to get a word in.

"Leave."

"Wait, Xana and…"

"I don't want your explanations!"

They bickered back and forth, each one's voice getting gradually more and more violent, "JUST LEAVE!" screamed Xianni, anguish spewing from her lips. She began to wheeze and pant. Finally, he did as he was told and left the treehouse; as he descended the tree he stopped and listened to Xianni's sore cries of regret.

***

The night had come and was slowly slithering away as day dawned. In Xanthe's household, Xianni lay awake on the family room floor, her vision still clouded by tears. She got up and walked into the ground floor bathroom. She plugged the basin and allowed the water to half fill it. She splashed water freely onto her face, the mirror waited patiently in front of her.

She hated herself. Forced to become something she was not had truly been the worst thing that had ever happened to her, and the one thing she had held onto that could make the situation better had released his grip a long time ago.

Staring into the mirror, which gave her an unwelcoming reflection, she quickly turned away and looked down into the basin, where her face was yet again reflected in the water. She removed the plug and watched her image swirl away.

Across the Fortress, Xander was sitting in his kitchen whilst Xana lay awake in the bedroom. She had heard him come in late at night but did not get up to see him, nor had he entered the bedroom to sleep. She could hear him intermittently pacing around the house, knocking things over. He was restless. Every so often she sat up, considering going out to see him, comfort him, but then a sense of dread would fill her and she would fall back into the comfort of the bed, burying her head into the soft pillows to stifle her pain. She knew that Xianni had been consuming his thoughts. She could see the pain in his eyes throughout the days when he would be lost in thought.

She had tried on several occasions to temper his conviction about Xianni's return, but he would become frustrated and leave the room. A part of Xana believed him; after all, the receptionist had described someone very similar to her. But how would she have escaped from the Dincans? And if she had why would she not have shown herself by now? Even worse, why would Xanthe have lied?

Xana knew that Xianni's return would mean the end of her and Xander – a thought that pained her deeply. Never had she anticipated that her emotions towards him would have grown to the extent that she would feel betrayed for being treacherous herself. But then something within her would rise as she fought back her own feelings of guilt. They had thought Xianni died, everyone believed her to be dead. She had not betrayed her. Feelings had developed out of shared comfort and companionship – surely that wasn't a crime? As she fought back and forth within herself, one thought remained at the forefront of her mind – if Xianni's return indeed was true – Xander would be leaving her.

Xander knew Xianni was alive – he had seen her. He spent the next few days unable to contain his desire to find her again. A part of him regretted his obstinacy. Their reunion was far from what he had anticipated. Guilt consumed him as his mind traced the scars and disfigurements of his once beloved. How could he have hurt her so, after all she had endured? He thought to Xana sleeping in the next room and wondered whether his hesitancy towards Xianni was primarily the result of his true feelings towards Xana, rather than Xianni's defacement. The taste of salt at the corner of his mouth awakened him to the presence of the tears that were silently streaming his face. Xianni had been, as long as he could remember, the only object of his affections. He had spent the last few months stifling thoughts of her, repressing memories and ignoring the pain, where he had believed she was dead. And now she returned, broken and fragile, awaiting their reunion and all he had done was demolish her last glimmers of hope. A sudden urge to find her again caused him to stand up in haste, knocking over the stool that had been providing him a footrest. He made to head for the door again before he realised he had no idea of her whereabouts. Surely she wouldn't have returned home. Did she stay in the tree house? Did she stay at Xanthe's? Was he aware of her return? Questions swam across his tired mind and as he looked towards the door that separated him from Xana, another wave of guilt overcame him. Xana. They had been through so much together. Their bond had become nearly unbreakable. He loved her and she him. Fatigue overwhelmed him as he sunk back into the chair and closed his eyes to shut out his mind.

Chapter XXVI

Xianni remained hidden. Her confidence was shattered, the rejection she faced that night had made her question everything she had and highlighted what she didn't have, and that was a partner and a best friend.

The morning came as normal, but with it, came detrimental news. A Dincan traipsed through the woodland, headed for Dahlia Fort. He reached the moat and sauntered over it arrogantly. The guard watched his approach, in full knowledge of the motive for his arrival. She ran as fast as her legs would carry her to fetch Daveer. The intruder stopped just outside the gates and bellowed:

"Daveer. Daveer. Daveer. By the alliance of Dincan – a collaboration of the Dinnoxia and Acanthus tribes – we summon you to forfeit your land.

"For we have travelled far and wide to accumulate land enough to serve our emergent population. War is not imminent if you choose to be kind enough to share your land with us and allow us to rule with you. Do not reject this kind offer; for if you do, you leave us no alternative but to slaughter your army, bed your women, and kill your children.

"Collectively we are three hundred thousand strong, and know with your land you can only have a few thousand soldiers to defend your territory, leaving you with a 300:1 man ratio. Daveer, defence is pointless. I am here as a messenger to you and await your response.

"I will give you one hour to deliberate. Your time starts now."

Daveer was not fooled by his false calculations: he had seen their camp, and it was far from three hundred thousand. He knew that to answer him now would mean the Dincans would start their attack sooner, but killing the messenger would give them at least another day to prepare. Daveer signalled to the guard who recoiled and launched a spear. They shot the messenger and all they had prepared for was now underway.

The war was here.

Chapter XXVII

Daice knocked on Daveer's office door and entered without waiting for approval. He approached the desk, his face stone cold and placed a piece of parchment down on the deep mahogany table. One finger remained rooted onto the parchment.

Daveer looked up quizzically, his irritation at the sudden intrusion replaced by curiosity.

"What is this?"

"The parchment," Daice replied, a small smirk making its way across his indifferent face.

"The parchment?" Daveer's eyes widened.

"Yes. I obtained it a while ago on the mission, I have been studying it for the past few weeks, trying to understand its significance – it bears no use whatsoever. So I've come to you with a counter-proposal – Let us give it to the Dincans and fulfil their futile desire. Maybe this will stop the needless bloodshed which will occur." Daice had practised his speech in his head many times. Daveer paused for a few minutes first studying Daice's face before looking down at the worn out parchment before him.

"Why are you coming to me now?" he was angered.

"I come to provide an alternative to a war."

Daveer stood up suddenly, his chair screeching in protest against the wooden floor.

"Are you stupid? Do you think your selfishness and arrogance has saved your people from this war? We sent four of you and only one came back walking. And you now come to me months later and tell me that the mission was a success? You want to be a hero, is that it? Xanthe and I even risked our lives to go to their camp after your return in an attempt to retrieve this parchment… And you had it all along! And now you want us to trust the Dincans? After what they did to Daena? They would have taken our land anyway and what is more we have now shot the messenger, war is imminent. So thanks for telling me, but now it is too late; your people thank you plenty." Daice's face reddened with embarrassment.

"I never knew… I apologise. But no harm has been done as the parchment is useless!" he tried to redeem himself and his egotistical actions.

"The parchment is not useless. You need to be able to know how to use it. Your eyes alone cannot show you want to want to see – only a selected few have been taught how to harness its capability. Xanthe being the only one alive, and Xianni his trusted student was in the process of learning before her abduction and murder." Daveer now had the parchment in his hands and was fingering the contours.

"But what does it actually do?"

"Held within it are the directions to something of utmost value and virtue. In the wrong hands, there is no telling how the parchment would change the dynamics of this world; but in the right hands – granted that they deserve it – the parchment will increase their power and territory exponentially. Do you remember the folksong that you were told as an infant?"

"Yes, we were all made to learn it off by heart," answered Daice, puzzled.

"Yes, do me a favour, and recite it to me." Daice's face was full of questions, but he thought that his recital might make things clearer.

We run around and find place a to hide
Fighting tough and being snide
We run around and find a place to hide
They all fall, to hail our side!

In the forest we find our home
Where we can survive alone
In the forest we aren't alone
Far away we also meet

To an empty land
Over the mountains and across the sand
Seek, what is Dahlia,
With a giant X marked on our 2nd home,
remember the bones…

Off we go to find it! (Off we go to find it!)
Nix quit, by X we sit!
Leave the X below this
And leave the X homeless…

"Now, do you have any more questions? Or will that suffice?" Daveer reclined in his chair, running his hands through his hair.

"Yes, one more: will you betray Xanthe?"

"Just because it is what we have been instructed for generations, doesn't mean that is what we shall do. Sometimes things change. However, if necessary, often original plans are best kept unaltered, it is not out of the question."

Daveer had been battling with thoughts of how the truce would pan out. Although he had grown fond of his new allies, with so many years of malicious propaganda between the two ranks it was nearly impossible to rid the bad gut feeling they had for one another. Within Dahlia Folktale it was alleged that their inheritance was in the wrongful possession of the Xantharis – the Lost Empire. In order to regain what was rightfully theirs they needed to acquire all four pieces of parchment. Daveer was between two minds. But at this stage in the war, there was no time to divert his attention. First, he needed to focus on keeping the Xahlias alive. Stealing the Lost Empire from beneath the Xantharis would soon be on his agenda.

Chapter XXVIII

Word reached the Xanthari Fortress that the war had been brought to the Dahlias. They patiently awaited their own messenger to grace them with the generic speech. At first sight of his emergence from the bushes, he was shot directly in the leg. Two soldiers fetched and dragged him inside the confines of the Fortress, where he was placed in a chair with a woven bag tied around his head. Xanthe entered with Xander and Xana by his side, just like old times.

Xanthe took a much more Machiavellian approach, "You know I prefer it this way, it makes matters much more… personal; whereby you actually meet the people you desire to kill. And then realise, in actual fact they are a lot more dangerous than you initially thought…" He paused for a moment.

"So I guess you are here to tell us that the Dincans have decided that they want to share land with us, and rule alongside us, am I right?" the messenger nodded his head.

"And you're probably going to duly inform us that the Dahlias have already pledged their allegiance to you, so we are all alone, am I right?" this time, the messenger shook his head vigorously.

"Tell me, what's your name, man?"

"Admeyer."

"Well, 'Admeyer', thank you for bringing us such beneficial news. Let me just ask, before the Dinnoxias and Acanthus merged to become the troublesome Dincans, which one were you?" Xanthe was now becoming needlessly inquisitive.

"I was neither, Xanthe," he replied quietly, his voice mellow.

Xanthe turned sharply and made towards him like an angry bear. He tore the bag from his head, "Don't you ever, ever refer to me by name. The man who is dragged in, and will be killed any moment now for telling me to give up my land for the sake of two foreign regiments, shall not be deemed worthy to refer to any Xanthari by name," he scorned, spittle flickering from between his lips.

"You see these two?" he pointed towards Xander and Xana. "Your men have made my life and theirs hell and the war has not even begun." Xana and Admeyer clocked eyes and locked in on each other. Xana's eyes widened and her mouth dropped open. Her hands began to shake. Admeyer blinked with both eyes twice and winked with the left eye then the right; subconsciously, Xana did the same – recognition. Their code went unnoticed, but Xander quickly picked up on her stupor.

"Hey, are you OK?" she raised her arm to her forehead, wiping away the beads of sweat that had congregated quietly upon her brow.

"How many men do you have?" Xanthe continued the interrogation.

Admeyer refocused, "Approximately just under one hundred thousand."

"But how many of them are prepared for war?"

"At this moment in time, just over a third are kitted and ready for combat."

"Why the cooperation?"

"I told you, I am not a Dincan. I was a part of The Pars resistance but was forced into joining them – otherwise I would have been killed." The first lie to leave his mouth was a believable one.

"Well, we have no more use of you now, it is not that we do not trust you, but I suppose who can you trust of late… Kill him." The same two guards that dragged him in outstretched their bows to his head. Xana could not watch and fidgeted around, looking for a red herring to rescue her familiar.

"Hold your bows; Xanthe, may I speak with you briefly?" Xana's courage was dubious. "We can't kill this man so hastily. Yes, fine he will die, but not now. I have a feeling that he may be able to tell us where they are keeping Xianni."

"There is not much more information we need, we cannot prepare forever. And as for Xianni, if she is alive, this war will see to her release, we cannot solely trust the information of a Dincan."

"But he is not a Dincan, as he said. And how can you give up so easily on her? He will be able to direct us to her whereabouts. Just give me a few minutes with him in a less hostile environment, that is all I ask, and then I'll kill him myself."

Xanthe saw the desperation leaking from her eyes and relented, "Thirty minutes, then he dies." Short and simple. He could sense something peculiar in her sudden sympathy for the enemy.

Admeyer was held in a metal cell. He was sitting up with his back against the wall, legs bent slightly upwards. He could have easily escaped but remained in order to be reunited with his comrade.

Xana scurried into the prison, asking the guards for a few moments of privacy. As expected, there he was, sitting on the floor; she smiled from ear-to-ear. Both sets of her glistening white teeth were glowing like pearls. He jumped to his feet.

"Iilera, Iilera Asherdimer! How wonderful it is to see you again after all these years! How long has it been? Ten years since we have spoken like this?" his wrinkled eyes illuminated with glee.

"And you too, Fasherii! How I have longed to see a familiar face since my childhood! I am still shocked that after all these years I can still remember a face from back home." *Xana* felt a lump in her throat; the emotion was boiling up inside her.

"How is it here? You should be excited; your assignment is almost over! Then you can return home with me and see everybody!" Xana failed to show the same level of thrill as Fasherii.

"Yes, but everybody will be different. I mean it's been fifteen years. Come on, is everybody still… interested in my well being over there? Surely they have forgotten about me by now?" she employed a slight laughter to reduce the solemnity of the topic.

"Not a single person! Believe me. Your family has been waiting for that long to see you again. And I've been watching over you for that long to make sure of your wellbeing. Now I suppose you have acquired what was required of you?"

"Yes."

"Do you have the parchment itself or a trace?"

"Trace."

"Just as good."

"You wouldn't happen to bear any information on the Dincans and their attack, would you? Anything to give us the upper hand would be useful."

"But Iilera, you are talking like one of them! Let us not forget you do not bear that brand on your stomach, and you can therefore never be deemed one of them. This is not your war; if you fight you are only putting yourself at risk! In fact, your mission is virtually over; you could leave now if you wanted to. Do not forget your roots." He looked deep into her eyes.

"How can you just expect me to leave them like this? I have grown up with them, I have been taught all they know. Xander has risked his life for me, almost died for me! How can I abandon them when they need me most? I am one of their commanders. This is my war." Xana found her patriotic streak.

Fasherii now saw where her heart belonged, "OK Iilera, I can see where your loyalty lies, and it sure is not with us…"

"No I never said that. I will return, but not like this, not just before the war; probably after it's over, if not before."

"I have lived to see what happens when the Xantharis and Dahlias come together. It is always bad news. I know, look at me, born of Xanthari mother and Dahlia father. After the Great Xanthari Dahlia War, I was banished to a foreign land – our home, whilst my parents fought each other on the battlefield. This may seem like an infallible combination now but I can assure you this will not end well for everybody."

"That is a chance I am willing to take," Xana shrugged.

"OK, the Dincans have sent messengers to both you and the Dahlias simultaneously and intend to attack Dahlia Fort first. The strength of Dahlia's defences shall determine how quickly they will reach you. If their plan is successful, they will be with you in a matter of days. They reason that they pose a greater threat in numbers. They are coming through facing the Fortress, as is tradition. I have not had time to fully study their approach on the Dahlias, but I suppose it will be a much more complex invasion. Your best choice is to defeat them before they get within a half-mile radius of the Xanthari Fortress. Twice the amount of men are coming to you than the Dahlias; they are hoping to sweep through Dahlia and flank the Xantharis immediately afterwards. So get the woman and children out of here and probably out of Dahlia Fort too to a safe house somewhere – anywhere. As you can see, they are not of the knowledge that you have both races divided equally into both forts. Oh, and their attack begins in exactly three days at dawn."

Xana took a moment to absorb all the information, "Thank you for helping us. One last question, did you meet a girl called Xianni who was in captivity? Is she still alive? And if so, where is she?"

"Yes, she was the one who raised you. She had a terrible ordeal: torture, rape, nail removals and broken bones – just inhumane. I did what I could to protect her and reduce the suffering, but there was only so much I could do without being caught. I did help her escape, has she not returned yet? This was quite a while ago – she couldn't have been recaptured, as I would have known about this. If she did not return I have no clue where she could be."

"So she is no longer in captivity… I knew it. They lied to me all this time. Thank you, Fasherii, I know I can always rely on you. Shall you stay and endure the war or return back home?" Xana began to unlock the cell.

"Home is calling. I shall tell them of your new assignment and wish you the best of luck, take care." With one last smile, Admeyer's form dissolved into thin air.

Chapter XXIX

War

The newly found intelligence had made battle preparations occur more swiftly. The mothers and children from both ranks were rounded up and escorted to Dahlia Fort, where a safe house was allocated to them, knowing that if it came down to it, it would take at least weeks for the Dincans to penetrate their defences. And in the event of a breach of their defences, motions had been set in place the for the vulnerable to follow the underground tunnel running alongside the River Morten to the Chantrieri Empire, a trustworthy ally of the Xahlia people.

Areas surrounding Dahlia Fort had been divided into three zones. Zone Three was the outermost circumference, located 500m away from the gates and covering north, east, south and west borders. Zone Two began at 150m, and Zone One just 100m from the fort.

Once the enemy had breached Zone One, they were now in the so-called Red Zone. If the enemy were to advance here, they would then be able to ram the gates and find their way into the fort; the first sign of defeat.

Similar to the Xanthari Fortress, every inch of soil and forestation within a 500m radius was decorated with ingenious traps. Trees were also hollowed out to encase warriors; the enemy wouldn't know what hit them. It was as if nature fought alongside the Xahlias.

Combatants allocated to the front line trained non-stop, with just an hour's respite between eight-hour sessions. Fluidity between the fighters was now near perfect. The once oil and water relationship had finally emulsified, and was somewhat complementary in nature.

After the initial discontent, they were now confident; never had they seen a side as well-equipped and as skilful as the one they had become. There were even some whispers that after the war they would continue to be one. Of course, these were just rumours, but who was to say that it would not be possible?

Already, relationships had been blooming between the Xantharis and Dahlias. Xi had fallen for a young, fiery-eyed Dahlia called Dahine. Thoughts of the Great Dahlia War were long left behind. Seemingly friendly, Daveer and Xanthe spent more and more time together. Darcie and Xari did almost everything together. As the last few days of peace swiftly ran by, their existence was beginning to resemble what life would have been like as a singular nation.

The Elite warriors were not to participate in the war fully yet. They would fight for the first two days, to plough the fields (as they called it). In other words, to eliminate the first few thousand warriors; then they were to remain in training until after the second week of attack.

Tactics and maps of the forest were reviewed and revised multiple times a day to ensure absolute familiarity.

After the most difficult and strenuous days of any villagers' life, it was nearly time. Come dawn, the war would finally be upon them. That night, not one soul rested.

Chapter XXX

Horns blared throughout the forest.

Birds flocked away from the trees to safer lands. The enemy was assembling. Xahlia Elites had spent their night invisibly immersed in the forest, spotting and detailing the positions of the Dincans. Before the attack had even begun, they had conjured a mental image of their opponents' numbers and stations.

The klaxon was sounded in five sharp staccatos outside Dahlia fort, signalling the beginning of the attack. The custom was for the leaders of the armies to meet at the centre of the grounds in an attempt to give the opposition a final chance to withdraw from battle. Daveer mounted his horse and made his way towards the sounding horn to confront the Dincan army. Alongside him rode Daice and Daphne (Daena's successor), as well as his allies Xanthe and Xana – A united front.

The journey to the battle-line was heavy and silent, filled with anticipation. None of them dared to break the respectful hush. There was no sound except the stomping of twenty hooves on crisp grass. As they emerged into the clearing, ten thousand men greeted them, with the front line seated on their horses. Unfazed by this intimidating scene, the Xahlias rode to address their opposition.

The Dincan general, Adham, broke the silence: "Emperor Daveer, let us skip all the preliminary nonsense and get to the point. Your chances of winning this war are thin if not impossible. So stop being selfish and join us, and you will spare the lives of your people."

"Nice offer, Adham, but I think I'll pass. You may have the multitude of men, but they look like a bunch of pussycats. Good luck. Start the attack whenever you're ready."

"It sure was brave of you to come out here, just the five of you. We could kill you all now and leave your army in disarray."

"Oh believe me, my friend, we are not alone. We have the Xanthari gods and Dahlia demons watching over us too…"

And with that, the five allies turned around and rode back across the clearing to the forest wall. Just before they reached the trees they stopped and turned to face Adham and his men, who looked on in confusion. What were they planning? Xantharis began to emerge from the forest, not that the army could tell the difference between the two forces.

Only three hundred warriors appeared against a dense crowd of Dincans. Adham and his men began to laugh. Foolishly so. Another hundred emerged from the forest, sparsely scattered. Between each Xanthari warrior and the next was a significant distance. Hidden from the viewpoint of the Dincans, Xanthari archers were perched in the tree canopies. Ready to turn the sky black with arrows…

"This doesn't seem like much of a resistance, Daveer!" Adham mocked. "Nonetheless, I say we get this defeat underway!"

Adham's right hand man raised his arm, and signalled to the soldiers to unsheathe their swords.

"Let the festivities begin!" shouted Daveer. The Dincan general looked on slightly puzzled. Daveer raised his double-edged sword. Suddenly, thousands of Dahlia warriors appeared from nothing. They had been there all along, just in their disbanded form. Wasting no time, the archers released their first shower.

"Shields!" cried a warrior from the front line.

The Xahlia soldiers had definitely dressed for the occasion. Across the field was a grand spectrum of attire. The first half of the Xahlia army wore dark, velvety cloaks that signified their status as Elites. A few rows behind, the secondary Elites wore lighter, reddish cloaks. The main army wore blood red cloaks, while the younger fighters at the back wore golden attire.

It was time for the Elites to *plough the fields*. A second succession of arrows was fired, killing far more this time. The enemy forces' horsemen galloped into attack. However, as they approached the Dahlias disbanded, making it easy for the remaining Xantharis to pick the men off their horses one-by-one.

Soon coming to the realisation that the Xahlia forces were far more strategically powerful, the Dincan generals ordered for an all-man attack. After all, their strength was in numbers. They would overwhelm their opponents to the point where they would be forced to fight dirty.

The Elites continued to plough. The men fell from their horses as the Xahlia forces went about them; weaving and waltzing in and around them. It was a beautifully choreographed performance. Gruesome – yet fixating to watch. Despite the multitude of Dincan soldiers, the Xahlia warfare was overwhelming.

The Dahlia's incessant disbanding made the war both physically and mentally strenuous for the enemy. Strategically placed traps underneath the Dincan army also proved effective, as far cries resonated away from the front line. After hours of fighting, the allied forces managed to push the enemy back.

But this was only the beginning.

Mounds of bodies piled up on the grass, as black crows circled the sky, waiting for their dinner. Someway through the battle, the Elites pulled back, using their shields to hide themselves from the numerous objects being hurled at them. The Dincan forces cheered and jested, thinking that they had won the battle. Again, how wrong they were. Once a large enough gap had been created, the Xahlia Elites stopped their retreat. The Dincans grew uneasy as it became clear this was not a retreat, but a new form of attack. From an invisible source, the scent of kerosene arose, and the ground underneath the Dincan forces began to warm and steam up.

Suddenly, the land below their very feet gave way, and they were thrown into a trench ten feet deep. The open ground ate hundreds of them, who were then subjected to a vicious attack of arrows. The hole in the ground was now so filled with bodies that it had clogged full to the brim.

The Dahlias disbanded once again, leaving a few warriors sparsely scattered in visible sight. Expertly, the Xantharis dodged the arrows and used their shields as covers while they waited for the Dahlias to get within range of the enemy. Which did not take long. The horizon was looking bright for the Xahlia alliance, who were losing minimal warriors and leaving the ground messy with thousands of Dincan soldiers. The day's battle was over, and spelled success.

That night, the alliance drank and ate bountifully. If the war was going to carry on like this then they were assured a quick and easy win.

However, little did they know of the hundreds and thousands of soldiers approaching by sea, nor the conflict that would soon brew within their own coalition.

Tired and dreary from the previous night's events, Xander and Xana were abruptly awoken by the sound of drums that indicated war preparation time. Xander arose first, and Xana watched his bare, muscular behind as he made his way over to the washroom. She followed shortly after, also naked. The last few days of preparation and anxiety had driven them towards each other into new levels of intimacy. Tired as they may be, they ended each night in each other's arms.

In the army barracks, Xana began to gear up for another day of mass murder. She came back to the house to help Xander out of bed and to prepare him for training. His body had deconditioned given the time he spent comatose. Only a few people knew he had regained consciousness and had been preparing to join the war effort. For the next three weeks, the light of war shone in favour of the Xahlias.

Chapter XXXI

It wasn't long before the war was brought to the Xanthari Fortress. The same five warriors rode out to the opposition, exchanged their empty words, and returned, establishing the onset of battle. Outside the Fortress, heavily muted by the stone walls, Xana heard strangled orders, shouting and metallic clatters – the heavy melody of war. She reached the doors and slipped outside. The sky was stained smoky black; a bloody glow was visible on the horizon, threatening to dwindle out of sight with nightfall. When it did, war was upon them.

The Xanthari Fortress seemed a far more likely arena to defeat the enemy in. Once the war had begun, it took several months for the enemy to even reach the Xanthari labyrinth, even with the arrival of allies by sea. And once they did make it in, they were quickly picked off within its intricate structure.

Xana ascended the steps, hewn roughly in the stone wall, until she reached the summit of the eastern turret. A line of archers crouched in position, awaiting orders. In typical Xanthari style they wore dark cloaks so that to an onlooker they could pass as mere shadows. Xana took position at the head of the line and crouched with them. She knocked an arrow into place and pulled it back against the bowstring, testing the elasticity. Next to her, a ripple of shadowy movement mimicked her actions silently.

The archers waited, poised for action. Below them, the dark mass of the Dincans once broken, would give way to uproar and devastation. In typical Xanthari style, the drummers began to beat their drums and the choruses began their song. She glanced backwards and glimpsed the silhouette of her house, a furl of smoke issued pleasantly from the chimney. She smiled wryly and gave the signal. As one body, the archers released their deadly weapons into the sky, where they whistled, hidden against the blackness. It was not until they hit the first line of Dincan marchers, causing them to collapse, did the net trap enemy soldiers. Further quick firing saw to the end of them.

To Xana it seemed that Xander's mind was only focused on her. He focused his every thought and action to her. It helped that Xianni played no active part in the war and she continued to stay with Xanthe. Her psyche was not in the correct state for warfare.

Xana was at ease. But still couldn't help but feel a sense of sadness about the matter. She felt sorry and embarrassed for Xianni, who expectantly came back to continue where she and Xander had left off, only to be confined to solitude away from everyone she cared for and everything she had once so proudly led.

Xana watched as Xander joined her on the front line for the first time since the start of the war. She knew that in the back of his head he still felt a certain way about Daice. He was number one on his suspect list of people that were likely to have poisoned him. Xana shared his sentiment. She had not told Xander about Daice's many advances whilst he was recovering from his near death ordeal. Xana tried to mask her disgust for him, especially in Xander's presence.

"Well it's good to be back," exclaimed Xander as he approached the front line. Daice was caught off-guard. He did not know that Xander was alive.

"What's the matter, Daice, surprised to see me alive and well?" Xander looked him square in the face. Daice's feet shuffled beneath him.

"It's good to see you well. We all thought you were dead…" He tried to act calmly although beads of sweat gathered on his brow.

"I was poisoned."

"Oh, who by?" Xander ignored him, smirking. He drew Xana close to him and planted a gentle heartfelt kiss onto her lips, making sure he made direct eye contact with Daice as he did so.

After a long day's battle, Xana thought back to her more investigative period where she spent a great deal of time searching for clues to find Xianni. A picture of the grand mural popped back into her mind. She wondered if the mysterious artist had added to his or her masterpiece. Another flash back of Xiannis scrawlings swam through her mind: $L.E \times 4.\ 5^{th}\ element = all\ Wua\ hus$. It then dawned on Xana that these clues were not to help her in the retrieval of Xianni, but these were key clues of something much greater than her, Xander or Xianni. For the next few days, the mural continued to play on her mind. She was eager to see if further depictions had been made. One evening, when enemy forces had retreated she made her way back to the old shrine. She approached with caution; the royal detail was canvassing the area. She noticed the secret passageway was already open, as if they were protecting something. Xana patiently waited for the guards to divert attention and entered the underground cavern.

Candles lit the entirety of the walkway. As she descended the steps she could hear voices at the bottom. She paused for a moment listening. Deep in the cavern, she heard the voices of Xianni and Xari.

"You are truly gifted, your work is beyond anything I could ever imagine," said Xianni.

"When I was younger, figuring out my abilities and how to manage my visions – my mother would always say to me 'to endure, you must combine a gift you hate with one you love' and painting my visions is really what got me through some of the toughest times." Xari blushed.

'I am honoured that you have chosen to share this with me, I presume Xanthe doesn't know…'

'No, he does not. And it shall remain so – this gift would only torment a man in his position,' Xari said defiantly.

Xana rested her back against the staircase imbibing the revelations. The omniscient artistic genius was in her midst all this time. Her mind was buzzing with questions. She stepped forth from the shadows. The three of them locked eyes. Xari caught like a rabbit in the headlights. She knew there was nothing she could do about the situation. Xana now knew all. Xianni shot Xana with a cold stare, their first interaction since her return. Xana dropped her gaze, all the questions she had escaped her. She turned to exit, just as she did so Xari said, 'Not a word of this to anyone, Xana, or there will be hell to pay.'

Xianni followed Xana to the surface of the tunnel, taking this as an opportunity to de-ice the tension. She called out to her, "Xana, wait!"

Their eyes met intimately for the first time since before Xianni's capture. They were both lost for words. Xana's face began to quiver, and her arm flopped to her sides. She began to whimper and fell into Xianni, who accepted her embrace. The moment seemed to air all of their thoughts and feelings simultaneously. They spent the rest of the day together, catching up on lost time. Xana spent much of this time apologising for how things panned out with Xander. Xianni seemed to understand and did not hold this against her. Her real qualm was with Xander. Xana took the plunge and invited her over for dinner the next day.

Back at the house, Xander was milling around. Xana wanted to tell him everything. But the gravity of what she had discovered was beyond her, and no longer had relevance. Xari was a Wua hu. She knew the beginning and the end. Xana thought back to the picture, and realised that Xari knew there would be a love triangle. Xana's heart lurched as she remembered the small child that stood between her and Xander. Her child. She smiled uncontrollably at the thought. Was she already pregnant? All she was sure of was that she and Xander would live through the war and start at family together…

It was evening and Xari had spent the past hour beautifying Xianni in preparation for the dinner. She was anxious to see Xander again. She was anxious to see Xander and Xana together as a couple. She had accepted her place as second best. Xana saw her through the window as she approached the door. She welcomed her in warmly. Xander stood up and half ran across the room to give her a hug. His touch warmed her heart. Her head rested briefly onto his chest and butterflies fluttered inside her. She wrapped her arms around his neck. Xander breathed deeply, inhaling her familiar scent, locking his arms around her waist. Xana tried to disengage from the scene. The embrace lingered, and lingered. And then lingered some more. Xianni wished it were just the two of them.

Xianni helped Xana lay the table. She could feel Xander's eyes on her, as if he wanted to say something to her. He awkwardly blurted out, "Xi, I'm sorry for the treehouse!" she accepted his apology. Despite all this time there was something magnetic about their eye contact. Their souls somehow still felt connected. Even at distance they felt millimetres apart.

She was happy to have the two most important people to her back in her life. Although the dynamics had changed significantly, something between her and Xander had remained the same. They gravitated towards each other. No matter where they were, they found themselves in close proximity or making direct eye contact; she was sure that Xana had noticed.

After dinner, as they sat down to warm themselves with a cup of tea, Xianni informed them both that she was going to join the war effort and take her place as commander. Initially, they both tried to talk her out of it, worried that she wouldn't be strong enough, but she was adamant that her decision was final. They spent the next few hours telling her all she needed to know, including everything about Daice and his suspect activity. They were relieved to find out this was not news to her, and that Xanthe had been keeping her informed during the war.

***

Two, slow, merciless years passed. Neither nation had ever seen so much death and violence. As a people, they changed, as expected following two years of genocide. They were still a skilled people, yet the longevity of the war, it's never-ending nature and the unlimited resources of the enemy dampened their will to succeed.

The Xahlia wives and children had been confined within the walls of the Dahlia camp ever since the war began. Every so often, a soldier would bring them food and water, if the Dincan spies didn't manage to intercept.

On one very lonely day, at dusk, a Dincan attack was launched. The unprecedented advance threw the Xahlia warriors off-guard. The enemy attacked the Fort from the north and the south, forcing the Xahlias to split their troops.

The south entrance had been breached, and Dincan soldiers were now inside Dahlia Fort. The Red Zone. The elderly, mothers and children were given a safe house – the 'Vulnerable Location' as they called it – where all the vulnerable people of their society could seek refuge in such events as these. The attack was so sudden that they only just made it safely into the Vulnerable Location when the sound of piercing arrows and cries of agony filled the atmosphere.

One of the Dincan soldiers that had managed to breach the walls witnessed the Vulnerables entering the place of refuge. Peering through the window, they spotted the families scattered around the room. The women and children remained silent, thinking they had gone unnoticed. Outside, the warriors marched, their armour jingling. They halted just outside the cabin and spent a few moments plotting.

An object was then thrown onto the roof and the house began to fill with smoke and fog. Next, the windows were smashed open and liquid poured into the house. Gallons of the gasoline seeped through the ceiling, dripping onto those inside. Soon, the furniture was alight and the house was raging with fire. The mothers and children shuffled away and scurried to the far corner of the cabin. Crackles and snaps filled the air, the roof began to collapse, the fire was spreading furiously. Xari parted from the huddle and instructed her children to stay with Darcie, Daveer's wife. She scrambled into the centre of the room, narrowly missed by a blazing beam. She peered at a large tapestry and began to dislodge the woodwork beneath.

Metres above her, a stake-shaped structure swung like a pendulum, waiting for its final support to be loosened by the fire…

She continued to remove the boards and could now see the staircase leading to the underground tunnel.

"Xari, watch out!" the beam was now in free fall and was heading directly for the back of Xari's head. Instinctively, she sensed the danger and with great effort rolled over to her side; the beam plunged into the opening she had created, expanding it. The impact was so great that the surrounding floorboards buckled inwards, flipping her into the orifice. The families looked on in shock. Darcie ran over to the hole, dodging airborne debris. Xari lay at the bottom of the underground staircase, apparently lifeless.

"Xari! Are you OK?" a few onlookers gathered around the hole looking down in anguish. Darcie was on her knees trying to look for any signs of life in her friend.

After a few moments, Xari's arms twitched and she pushed herself up and stood, shaking the dust off her garments.

"The tunnel is down here! Come on!" Darcie called the rest of the group over and the children were ushered down one-by-one as the building continued to disintegrate, their task becoming more and more dangerous by the second.

The last child to be ushered down was a little boy. He was the first and only born of two young Xantharis. Both of his parents were fighting in the war, and thus it was a possibility that come the end of the war he would be orphaned. Too afraid to make the short distance in fear of being caught by burning fragments he stood there, stupefied.

Darcie screamed at the little boy to hurry over to her; he began to cry, his face taking on the shape of a prune. In a flash, a beam fell from the ceiling and crushed the youngster under the weight. The sound of the wood crashing and his shocked gasp echoed around the building.

"No!" Darcie cried. He was either dead or unconscious. She attempted to flip the log over but her strength was insufficient. The building was now heavily collapsing and it was raining debris. She knew she had to leave, but her maternal instinct did not allow her.

"Where is Darcie?" asked Xari after counting all the children.

"She was upstairs still, I think… all the children aren't here… We're missing one," a random voice answered.

"Goddess Xena give me strength," Xari climbed out of the orifice and back onto the ground floor of the disintegrating building. Darcie was still trying to free the little boy.

"There's a boy trapped under!" she gave up in frustration, slapping her hands down onto the beam. Together they tried, but their efforts were not enough. Darcie gave up, and tried to pull Xari along with her, signalling to return to the escape route. But Xari was stubborn and remained trying to lift the log in vain, "Where are you going? He is still trapped! We can't leave him here!" it soon became difficult for the women to hear each other due to the cacophony caused by all the falling objects. Alone, Xari continued to shift the log; the heat beginning to burn her skin. It was hopeless. For all she knew, the boy could already be dead. Angered by Darcie, she made her way back to the orifice climbing over fallen debris.

Darcie reasoned with her: "I tried. We couldn't have saved him. Don't beat yourself up about it, just be grateful it wasn't your child." But Xari ignored her. Hastily, they proceeded down the tunnel. It was dark and damp, the humid air sticking to their skin uncomfortably. They kept close to avoid children straying.

It was a long, winding tunnel, but soon they came to the opening; an area away from war, where the tranquil air brought joy to their faces despite the sorrow in their minds where thoughts of their dying loved ones remained.

***

The enemy forces overtook Dahlia Fort briefly after it had been breached. Dincan forces were frequently being supplemented with more men. New, revitalised men with nothing to lose but their expendable lives. The Xahlias continued their best efforts, which were effective, and often brought their alliance out on top of many battles, but the sheer force of numbers had begun to take its toll. The soldiers began to feel that they were fighting a war that would never end – a tenet destined for failure.

An impromptu meeting was called. The remaining Xahlia soldiers were slumped and scattered around the dishevelled Xanthari auditorium. Weapons lay beside them on the ground, permanently stained with flesh and blood, their owner's handprint dented into the metalwork. Xander stood amongst them observing his fatigued comrades. He, too, had begun to feel hopeless. Over two years of warfare had aged him considerably. His hair now visibly greying on the sides and permanent wrinkles etched around his eyes. He had sustained several injuries, most markedly a deep scar across his chest that still twinged with every deep breath. He had therefore trained himself to breathe as shallow as he could.

He observed as Daveer stood valiantly on the stage, his beady black eyes twinkling – a starkly contrasting image to his audience, who were worn and disconsolate.

Xanthe stood by his side, a sympathetic expression imprinted on his face. The sleepless nights caused by the war and the longing to see his family had left a pattern of ridges on his face, leading from his eyes to the corners of his mouth. His eyes were an exotic blend of hot colours, pain vibrant within them as if he was reliving every day in his mind, so vivid that if you peered through his irises, today's battles could be watched, again and again and again.

Xander couldn't help but notice how weak and feeble Xanthe had become. He looked cachectic, his robes hung loosely over the skeleton that carried him. His back was hunched over and his colour was dun. His gaze was transfixed onto the ground every now and again; he would raise a hand to his mouth and press against it as if attempting to stifle vomitus from projecting out onto the floor.

Daveer's voice projected across the auditorium, bringing Xander's attention back to him. "Brave warriors – each and every one of you. Take a look at yourselves, and those around you – it is by your will that we are still alive. Not too long from now, your children and grandchildren will be retelling our tale to their children and grandchildren; this is how legends are born.

"We, an army of a few thousand men stood up to an army of hundreds of thousands and gave it our all – and a superb job we did of it. Our gallantry and altruism will be recognised, from now to the end of this war, and after our peace. Do not let your courage falter now – continue to fight with everything you have. Dismissed."

Short and sweet is the discourse of defeat.

As the warriors exchanged weary, defeated glances with each other, an understanding of their leader's subliminal message was clear: "We are all going to die in this war, but how valiantly we die is at our discretion."

Xander watched as Xanthe promptly left the stage through the back door, exiting the auditorium. He followed him hurriedly. Along the path, Xanthe's gait was unsteady, veered off diagonally as he struggled in his attempts to redirect himself. He turned the corner, glancing behind as he disappeared. Xander followed the bend, and saw Xanthe sprawled out on the ground attempting to get up, but collapsing every time. He ran over and grabbed him by the shoulder, pulling him up and stabilising him. They said no words to each other; every question Xander was thinking was quickly answered by the sharp glare in his master's eyes: he was suffering.

With their arms locked, they made their way hastily towards Xander and Xana's home. As soon as they entered, Xanthe released himself and held onto the furniture for stability. He began to cough and splutter vigorously into his hands, specks of green phlegm dotted with fresh blood splattering into the air. He stumbled again, resting his hand on the wall, panting like a greyhound. Taking a few deep breaths, he gained enough energy to move over to the chair, leaving a handprint of blood on the wall.

"What's wrong, Xander?" asked Xanthe grimly, with the faintest trace of a smirk.

"Well, seeing as we're being witty, it seems to me you're dying." Xander's tone was flat and sarcastic.

Xanthe chuckled, which immediately turned into another bout of coughing; releasing more blood onto the carpet beneath him. "Yes. It appears that way... I think I have been poisoned. And you'll need to redecorate."

Xander moved closer, perching on one knee in front of him to gain eye contact.

"Who did this?" he asked, desperation and anger reverberating in his voice. "A Dincan? But how? How could they have breached the Fortress and poisoned you without our knowledge? Why not just kill you there and then?"

Xanthe closed his eyes for a few seconds before responding, "Perhaps. Or perhaps not a Dincan but someone from within our own."

"A Dahlia you mean? But why? For what motive?"

"Daveer... Or Daice. But again, I search for a motive. Perhaps because we have lost fewer men than them?" the coughing restarted, more specks of blood decorating the once cream carpet. Some flecks landed directly on Xander's robes but he took no notice.

"When did your symptoms start?"

"About a week ago."

"Have you seen the nurse? What did she say?"

"I can't spend my last days on a hospital bed recovering from a silly toxin; I must be out there with my men fighting to preserve our race, 'til my very end."

"What good are you on the battlefield, and more importantly to Xari, dead? Come, we will get something to neutralise the poison or decelerate its spread. Then, we can try and determine the culprit." Xander took a deep breath and immediately constricted his shoulders as the pain searing through his scar burned through his entire chest.

Chapter XXXII

It had been four days and three nights since Xari, Darcie, and the rest of the Xahlia vulnerables had left on their journey to the Chantrieri Empire. They could finally see the mountain range in which the empire securely nestled. The range was beautiful; dips, crevices, all covered in silky beige carpet.

The children were growing restless, wild and hungry. The sun greedily stole what energy they had remaining in their feeble structures. Xari's mind was still occupied by the death of the infant in the fire, whilst Darcie was determined to block it from her memory, and continued to fixate herself with what lay ahead.

Menacing grey clouds floated across the sun, transforming the bright day into darkness. The river beside them disappeared.

The mothers led the children away from the riverside into the forest for shelter – rain was inevitable. Gathering what materials they could for shelter, they produced three tipi-like frames with large leaves intertwined between logs.

Bullets of water shot down from the heavens, hammering belligerently onto the makeshift cover. How long it would last was up to the gods, all they knew was that they couldn't progress in such conditions, particularly with children to guide. As they cowered from the torrent, Darcie detected a faint rustling through the cacophony of raindrops outside the shelter, but she took no notice and played it down to falling branches.

Hours later, the downpour was stronger than ever and had started to leak through the pitiable structures. Xari emerged reluctantly from her refuge and made a dash for Darcie's shelter.

"Ours isn't going to hold for much longer, is there anywhere else we can go? If necessary, we will probably have to continue the journey in these conditions, at least then we're still making progress." Water was flowing from Xari's face as if she was still being inundated with rainfall.

"We cannot continue in these conditions, the children will catch illnesses, and ascending mountains would be sheer madness. Divide your group between mine and Delorah's and we'll just hope that it gives up soon."

Xari dashed back to her cover and ducked down to enter through the small opening at the base.

She gathered the children and dispatched the plan. She gave them each a number, either one or two (ensuring both her children were number ones) and sent them over in two divisions.

The rain died down and the atmosphere inside the shelters was now jovial as the refugees waited for the sun to show its smiling face again. Then, the rustling was heard again, clearer now there was less rain to mask it. Xari told the children to hush. The familiar sound of a bow being stretched taut was audible in the distance. Frantically and silently, she instructed the children to lay down flat as she shuffled to the entrance, extracting Xanthe's dagger from the sheath wrapped around her thigh.

The arrow was released and pierced the cover with a quiet thud. Xari threw the dagger through the hole created by the arrow; a gasp was heard, then a loud thump.

Slyly, she edged her head through the entrance. Suddenly, something grabbed her and dragged her out by the locks of her hair. She rolled over, kicking the person in the face, using her other leg to trip him up.

She jumped up explosively and scanned her surroundings. The rain was still falling, dulling her perception slightly. Soon, Darcie emerged, and they flipped the body over and analysed it. He was a Dincan. Further rustling was heard from the thick shrubs, and two more arrows were sent piercing through the raindrops. Xari expertly dodged them, whilst Darcie's form dissolved.

Like a two-pack of wolves they ran in opposite directions and dove into the surrounding forest. Together, they fanned through the wood in a semi-circular motion to the source of the arrow. They gained closure, and noticed three Dincans perched on a low branch, ready to fire another round.

Quickly, Xari sprinted and grabbed the dangling feet of one of them, sending him face first onto the mire. Simultaneously, Darcie used the arrow obtained from the first soldier to deal with the other. One remained. He looked at them both and sniggered.

"What a b-e-a-utiful display! So the mothers and children know how to defend themselves too… how, awe-inspiring." A middle-aged man emerged from the red-berry bush. He was the first of many. Xari and Darcie lost all hope, but stood side-by-side in defiance.

"Tie them up and then get the children. Seems like psychological warfare has just begun!"

The women, ignoring the blatant futility of their actions, shifted slightly, blocking the small huddle of children from the advancing men. The sky above turned a steely grey, the dark clouds shifted fluidly miles above their heads like mercury, and sheets of rain began to fall again. It was the kind of rain that permeated consciousness.

One child cried out in dismay, a small, frightened wail; barely distinguishable above the water drumming on their surroundings. The water created a surreal scene of suspended animation; movements appeared lethargic and silent in the downpour. The panic was contagious amongst the group.

The men advanced, seizing Xari and Darcie first. They were thrown to the ground and bound, their cheeks pressed into the sodden earth. Xari craned her neck upwards, blinking water and mud out of her eyes as she watched the men round up the children.

Hopelessly, she watched as her daughter was lifted and cast over the shoulder of a surly looking figure, who turned and carried her away, oblivious to the furious pounding of tiny fists against his shoulder blades.

Chapter XXXIII

Xanthe, Xander, Xianni and Xana sat in the small kitchen of their home, the whistle of the kettle the only sound penetrating the silence. The tumult within their minds was not heard in the little room but the air was tense and morose. Each stared into space, lost in their own thoughts. Soon, their city would be destroyed. The clock was ticking, marking the seconds of their stolen moment of time. Waiting. A sharp, staccato pounding upon the door alerted them to reality. All four started at the sound, staring around suspiciously before they realised it was the door. Xander stood up and answered. Their conversation was inaudible over the uproar of the outside.

In the kitchen, the intrusion of the real world had sparked conversation.

"Xanthe? Are our attempts futile? Do we stand a chance?" Xana looked imploringly at her master, a supposed figure of inspiration and courage.

He did not return her gaze, but breathed steadily with huge effort, as he battled with the poison that had infected his bloodstream. He closed his eyes, his chest rising and falling rhythmically. Xana thumped her fist upon the table. Xanthe ignored her.

Xander appeared in the doorway. Xanthe opened his eyes but remained silent. Xana's eyes remained locked at her master in the aftermath of their non-conversation. After a pause, they felt a sense of awkwardness. Their heads turned up, intrigued by Xander's silence, terrified by what it might mean. Xander's face was pale, his eyes troubled.

"What is it?" snapped Xana, already sounding defeated. "Xander?"

Xander opened his mouth, and then shut it. His mouth was inexplicably dry. He raised a palm to his face. Beads of sweat had appeared around his thinning hairline.

"What?" irritation spewed from Xana's voice, inflicted by obvious anxiety and fear. Xander shook his head, eyes fixated upon Xanthe who returned his gaze. Knowingly, Xanthe lowered his head. He opened his mouth and whispered hoarsely,

"Tell me."

Xander cleared his throat and swallowed a few times. In a dull and lifeless tone he declared, "They have our women and children. They have shown us their intentions via a loss… on your part. Xanthe… I am so sorry."

Xanthe surveyed Xander with apparent calm, "My son or my daughter?"

Xander paused, gauging his master. Then he uttered bluntly.

"Your daughter."

Xana's eyes widened, horror filling her. She instinctively clutched at her swollen abdomen. "Xanthe…" she whispered, her eyes filling with tears. Xianni shuddered as if somebody had walked over her grave. She had grown to love Xain like a sister after returning to the fortress. She laid one hand on Xanthe's shoulder.

Xanthe arose sharply, knocking his chair backwards with a clatter against the flagstones. Unaware of his companions, of his movements, of his very thoughts, he left the little house and followed the contour of the streets until he reached the infirmary, a gravitational pull directing him, where his weakened body screamed in protest. On entering the building, heads turned his way; he ignored them and followed the voices, shouting, distorted.

He was within a vacuum of his own despair. He could sense Xander and Xana behind him moving their lips, but couldn't hear their voices. He burst into the room. It was full of people: the war advisories, the Elites and the generals. They fell silent as they saw him, parting in his wake, their eyes mirrored with melancholy. The movement was slow, painfully so. Tears blossomed in the old man's eyes as a small bed was revealed. He stepped forward, raising his hand to his mouth to muffle his anguish.

There, lying small and cold on the white sheets was Xain. His daughter. Her cherub like face was stained with dirt and blood; her skin was snowy-white beneath the gore. A rough cut across her throat offered the cause of death.

He dropped to his knees and dry, wracking sobs consumed his entire form. He seized her tiny shoulders and clutched the child to his chest, burying his face in her curly hair as he sobbed, "My baby girl," over and over, half expecting the tiny hands to reach up and hug him back like they once used to.

The figures in the room watched as silently as statues. They were waiting. After a time, Xanthe gained composure. He lowered Xain gently to the bed and tucked her under the sheet with the tenderness and expertise only a parent could know. The illusion of slumber was immediately vanquished as he drew a second sheet over her face, hiding her from view. He turned around.

"We will announce our surrender immediately."

Desperate faces looked around at each other. Out of the corner of his eye, Xanthe saw Xander and Xana's blank expressions.

"Sir, we cannot relent, think of what we will lose," a desperate voice spoke.

"Do not argue with me." Xanthe was glaring dangerously at the chief of war.

"Xanthe, I mean no disrespect. I cannot begin to comprehend the pain of your loss; I have two sons myself who I presume are also captured. We are all stricken with grief and worry since the news of the capture of our families. But we cannot surrender, we have no proof that the Dincans will keep their word; have we lost the lives of so many of our men in vain?"

Xanthe was glaring at the man with a look of utter disgust; this man was the product of his teachings. In a surge of vengeance and emotion he reached for his dagger and drew it. The man faltered in his petty arguments and stared, eyes wide with fear, at the weapon. In one swift motion, Xanthe plunged it deep into the man's chest. He watched as the man fell and then left the room to reclaim his family. No one spoke a word.

Xander dragged Xana from the room where chaos ensued following Xanthe's departure. It had happened. The effect of the war was seismic. They were falling apart, disintegrating. There was nothing left to fight for.

Chapter XXXIV

"Daveer, may I speak with you?" Daice's voice was affirmative and cold. Daveer did not answer.

"I hear they have captured the families… and killed Xanthe's youngest." Daveer looked up despondently. Daice continued:

"Is it true that plans have been drawn up to surrender this war? Surely, after all the men that have fought for us and the valuable lives lost, we cannot tell their children that it was all in vain?"

"If we do not surrender soon, then there will be nothing left of either the Xantharis or Dahlias. We must try and give something for the surviving mothers and children to come back to. How can we live on without any mothers or children? They are the next generation."

"Yes, this is true. But have you forgotten the Dahlia folksong? It is written in our prophecy that we are to succeed our ally, and take what is rightfully ours. Let us join the Dincans for now and separate ourselves after, then at least we will have our families and security." Despite Daice's Machiavellian nature, he made a valid argument.

"No. The days of the heartless and reckless Dahlia institution are over. Let us not forget that the Dincans came to us for war first and the Xantharis agreed to help protect us, they didn't have to do anything. Even if we did join the Dincans, what is to say that they would not kill us anyway?"

"Moreover, Daice… how could you even suggest joining the regime, which had your fiancée killed before your very eyes? Daena would not stand for this." Daveer watched as Daice's jaw clenched and unclenched several times, his disposition tentative and his eyes mixed with grief and anger.

"Yes I know, you do not need to remind me what they did to…to her. I will never forget that. As your second in command, I think it is important that you listen to my side here, Daveer. Your judgement is clouded by the news of

Xanthe's child. We must think of our people and our people only. It's the last thing you can do to keep the Dahlias alive…"

"I see your position on the matter, but I fail to agree. My child, one thing that the Elders and I myself have failed to teach our people is honesty and loyalty, which I now regret. How can a people fail to teach the skills that will keep the bond between the people within it strong? I'm surprised that we have survived this long. We have learned a lot from the Xantharis; much more than they have learned from us." Daveer travelled over to the window directly behind his chair and stared out into the forest.

"I have to say, master, that I regret that you feel this way." As he watched his master's back, Daice untied the rope binding his robe closed at the waist.

"You may be unaware of this but I have heard that Xanthe has been poisoned, and does not have too long to live… some hybrid form of hemlock…"

"So, soon it seems that it may be only you to control our defences, as it was always meant to be. Wouldn't you agree? Master, I must ask you once more… to consider joining forces with the Dincans – it is the best option… for us all." His hand fell to the hilt of his sword. He disbanded.

Daveer suddenly felt the discs between his vertebrae sever; his bones crunching as the tip of the sword penetrated his rib cage and pierced his lungs. He began to drown in his own blood as his lungs filled up with fluid. The sword continued to pinpoint major organs inside him, like an internal dissection. The final destination was the heart, which was sliced at the left ventricle, ensuring the blood escaped with high pressure.

Daveer's eyes turned yellow, and then red, and crimson tears trickled down his humble newly learned cheeks. Blood rushed up his throat and merged with the foam at his mouth, flowing like a fountain. Daice reformed behind his master with one hand still clutching at his sword, and the other around Daveer's neck, their faces touching.

"Daice, my son," Daveer gasped in agony. He coughed and spluttered, leaving an abstract painting of red dots upon the window. While Daice whispered, "It was not I, Master. It was you. I made sure yours is less painful than Xanthe's."

Daice withdrew the sword from Daveer and placed it neatly into his lifeless, open palm. Suicide. Looking at his reflection in the window, Daice ran his treacherous hands through his snaky hair, composed himself, and slowly approached the entrance of the room.

"Quick! Quick! Somebody, anybody! Master is Dead, Dead I say! Help."

News of Daveer's *suicide* spread quickly to the Xanthari fortress. Xanthe was shocked at the news. Their pact was no longer; it was now one dying leader and a few hundred withered men against several thousand militants. Having spent the days following the news of his daughter weak in bed, comforted by Xana, his resolution to surrender to the enemy had been temporarily suspended. Guilt had consumed him as he wept over the death of his daughter, the chief of war he had killed with his own hands, the state of his people and the loss of this war. Xana had comforted him, bringing him the antidote to the poison the matron concocted for him every day, gently forcing him to drink it, whilst offering words of support. At first, the antidote had worked marvellously but Xanthe knew that its effects were now wearing off. He could feel the poison spread throughout his body, weakening every bone and muscle. He had become inured to the background pain that stabbed at his entire body day and night.

The memorial was held days before the surrender. The Dincans agreed to a ceasefire on the condition that the Xahlias surrendered immediately after Daveer's ceremony, which Xanthe respectfully accepted on the condition that no more Xahlias were executed.

By this time, Xana was due to give birth to her secret child. She had kept her growing abdomen a secret from all but three – Xander, Xanthe and Xianni. Their presence on the front line was no longer necessary – the war was over, and there was nothing more that could be done about it.

Xianni comforted Xanthe, especially at the time of his loss. But she refused to accompany him to peace talks, she could not stand in the same room with the very same creatures who had taken so much from her.

Xianni left her quarters just before midnight, and was now approaching the infirmary. She knocked three powerful staccatos and awaited a reply. Shortly after, the three short knocks were mimicked on the other side of the door; Xianni replied with melody: two semi-quavers, semi-quaver rest, and single semi-quaver.

The bolts were unlocked and the large metallic door croaked open.

Xana sat squarely on the edge of her bed, her feet placed firmly upon the floor. An air of contemplation consumed her. Closing her eyes and feeling the air enter and exit her lungs with each painful contraction.

She remained in this meditative state for several moments, breathing her way through the intensity of labour. It was like swimming against a tide. She could feel the child inside her; it had quite changed from the peaceful sleeping entity to one of distress and urgency.

It wriggled again and she felt a sudden desperate desire to rid herself of it, it was parasitic, dangerous. The pain washed out of her and there was a shimmering moment of relief. She held her breath then doubled over as a sickening agony lashed her lower abdomen signalling another contraction commencing, as was the relentless nature of childbirth.

She had been confined to this hospital room for days and the child still had not been born. A fresh wash of pain consumed her and she cried out.

Three women filed into the room. They examined her clinically, void of emotion. Their sentiments like the grey room that had adopted a cell like relationship with Xana. Xana sobbed at them, begging them to do something. The women told her to wait out the night and instructed her to drink water.

They left her to rest fitfully. She thrashed about in the sheets. The task at hand had consumed her. She was at the mercy of her child. A figure entered the room; she hoped Xander had somehow managed to sneak in. Through a feverish haze, Xana made out Xianni's face in the gloom. Elated, she sat up shaking. Xianni closed the distance between them and the two women cuddled tightly over Xana's swollen stomach. Xana slumped backwards, smiling weakly at Xianni, and uttered, "Help me."

Xianni heeded Xana's feeble command. Her hands were cool as they stroked the hair stuck to her sister's forehead. She soothed Xana and promised not to leave her to complete the task alone.

The darkness bled out of the room until the steely cold air of morning arrived. Still there had been no alteration. The same woman entered and examined her again. Their faces were solemn as it was announced that the child had become, "distressed" and must be born immediately by caesarean.

Before the instruction had time to settle, the room was full of people. Cloths and rags were thrown over and around Xana. She was undressed, and masks and ominous sets of blades were lined up beside her. Terrified, her fear for the child paramount, Xana wailed.

Xianni soothed her forehead, quickly whispering a stream of reassuring words as the people bustled about. The path of the blade made a crude line that dissected the Xanthari brand on Xana's stomach. None of this was hidden from her. The life of the child had taken precedence above hers and Xana complied without protest.

A nurse to her left dipped a wad of material into a salty solution, soaking the cloth. She coated the bulge that was Xana's stomach in the brown fluid, which smelt like a concoction of wine and vinegar. Xana tensed, staring at the ceiling; she was not prepared but events were set in motion, the momentum was such that they could not be interrupted.

She was in a state of panic, intense surges of adrenaline periodically dulled the pain, the child too seemed to be distressed: she could almost feel its tiny heartbeat buzzing alongside her own thumping allegro. Then the child stopped moving, she could sense its heart rate decelerating. She was injected with a painkiller. The relief was tiny as the morphine infused her bloodstream. The numbness was not complete. She closed her eyes as burning, tugging and pressure indicated her abdominal cavity had now been opened. She opened her mouth and screamed as she was crudely exposed.

Xianni, far from squeamish, was transfixed on the process, admiring the skill behind the procedure. Seeing Xana's stomach bare under the surgical lighting she suddenly noticed the brand was beginning to blur with blood and sweat. The black ink of the 'tattoo' had smudged and started to run, becoming congealed with the blood and iodine. Xianni watched as the nurses periodically wiped Xana's abdomen of the blood and fluid for better access. The tattoo was gone. It was a fake. Xana was a fraud. Xianni stared at her younger sister in utter shock, her feet rooted to the ground. Questions screamed at her but she remained transfixed on the procedure.

Hands plunged inhumanely into the depths of Xana's abdominal region. Their disregard for the sanctity of her body was almost repellent. Xianni watched as a further incision was made, this time through the uterus.

Two hands delved deeper into the bloody mess, pulling the baby out by its head; purple, alien, and inanimate. Its umbilical cord was severed, spelling its independency. No longer connected intimately with its mother, it was whisked away. The baby's silence struck everybody in the room. "Where is my baby going? Why isn't it crying? Is my baby OK? Oh God it's dead..." Xana began to weep.

Mustering the energy to soothe Xana with one hand, Xianni watched as two figures carefully removed the placenta and started to stitch up Xana's stomach, sewing the flesh roughly together as if she had been a mere rag doll. A nurse wiped her stomach clean one more time before bandaging the crescent moon incision, the child's portal to the world. Xianni stared as the clean, white flesh bearing its ugly scar disappeared beneath the gauze. In the mayhem of the birth, no one else seemed to have noticed the absence of the tattoo and its grisly implications.

A burly woman offered the child to Xana with surprising tenderness. Xana's face was radiant, though her bloodshot eyes hinted at her exhaustion. She was pale, almost chalky in her complexion, her hands shook as she clutched the baby to her chest, her lips dry and chapped as she welcomed her son. She half laughed, half sobbed as the child squinted at her, its face raw pink with new life.

Xianni smiled at Xana, and gently planted a kiss upon her forehead and turned with a promise to return soon. Besotted with her baby, Xana did not protest as Xianni exited the room, carrying the burden of her discovery.

Chapter XXXV

Xianni couldn't think of anywhere else to go except the tree house – her designated place of deliberation. The revelation was astounding to her. For over seventeen years, Xana had been a fraud. A non-Xanthari. A stranger, an imposter who had now given birth to a Xanthari child. At first she had been adamant that telling Xander was the right thing to do. But after considering the implications, she thought it wasn't her place to say. She climbed the staircase and shuffled into the tree house, muttering to herself. To her surprise, somebody had beaten her to it.

"Xander?" she enquired. Groggily, he sat up. He looked worn out.

"Oh, hey… Xi… Sorry, this is the only place I can come to when things get a bit heavy for me you know. I guess it's the same with you, right?" a lot had happened since their first encounter and the furore had died down somewhat.

"Yeah, tell me about it. Anyway, I'll leave you to it, night. It's a boy by the way, congratulations." Her voice was emotionless.

"Really? That's great news – the newest addition to the Xanthari family." He smiled at her but his eyes remained grave. As she turned around to head back home, he called out to her. "Please don't go; stay. Just for a little while? I don't want there to be an awkward air around us anymore."

"Erm… OK sure." Xianni turned back and settled herself across the cabin from Xander; getting too close made her uneasy. She continued, "Just so we're clear, my feelings for you are long gone, so if you feel like you can't be open with some things, that shouldn't be the case. I consider you a friend and nothing more Xan, OK?" she felt empowered by her matter-of-fact tone.

"Of course, I understand. I'm glad we can finally put all that behind us." They exchanged glances and smiled at each other for a moment. They both felt as if a weight had been lifted.

They sat and chatted for a while. The conversation started politely as they discussed the surrender, Xanthe and all that had happened over the last three years. Before long, it was almost as if they were back in their special place. Their chemistry was blatant. The air filled with pheromones. They found themselves sitting side-by-side, their shoulders barely touching but the electricity between them tangible. Every now and again, their gaze would meet and silence would become them as they communicated in silence through their eyes, before one of them would look away, the reminder of the past paining them. In an attempt to focus, Xander broke out into soliloquy about his new son, and how this was one step in rebuilding the Xanthari nation. Xianni looked at him in despair.

"What is wrong?" Xander saw the look of regret in her face. Xianni gave him one long look. She was torn. Sitting there beside him as he gushed about his newborn and praised Xana's bravery, her heart broke for him. He had been cheated. They all had. His eyes softened as he raised an eyebrow at her, questioningly waiting for her to answer. She touched him lightly on the hand and warmth spread through her like a fire. She had to tell him.

"Xander, I know you're happy and the last thing I would want to do is ruin that. I still care for you and just want you to be happy. But I feel I must tell you something. And what you choose to do with this information is solely down to you. I will not tell Xanthe."

"Wow, what on earth is it?"

"Xana… is… not one of us… What I mean by that is she is not a Xanthari. She is of another lineage. I don't know which. Look, all I know is that I was in the infirmary with her, and she was not branded… And yes, I'm sure it was her –" before she could get another word, in Xander was gone.

Chapter XXXVI

"Who are you?"

"Pardon me? Xander what's wrong?" Xana was perplexed.

"Who are you? It's a simple fucking question. Look, I will show you. Ask me the question." There was a slight pause; she couldn't believe what was happening. How had he found out? Or was she just overthinking the situation?

"OK, Xander I'll play along, but please calm down, you're scaring me. OK, who are you?"

"Xander Xictorus. Born of Xanthari father and mother Xasteria and Xani Xictorus. Now it's your turn. Who are you?"

"Xander, what is going on baby? I don't understand this game and I'm not in the mood for games so can you just tell me what's wrong." She attempted to caress his face but he pushed her hand away.

"Seriously? You bore my child. You shared my bed. I almost had myself killed for you, and you won't answer me this one fucking question and for what? To save face? Your face is already tainted! Now answer me. Or if you really don't want to answer this simple question, you can show me your Xanthari birthmark and we can settle this that way."

It was over. Her double life had now come to a bitter, confrontational end. Her mouth quivered as her eyes searched his face for any sign of warmth. Her chest felt so tight within her ribcage it became difficult to breathe. Within seconds, she was reduced to tears.

"Xander… I'm so, so sorry…" her words merged into one as she drowned in her emotions. "I didn't know how to tell you. I don't know where to start." Xander was as cold as ice, immune to her pleas.

"How about your name?"

"My birth name is Iilera Asherdimer." Saying her name out loud sounded foreign to her after all this time.

Iilera Asherdimer approached Xander with caution, at this very moment in time, in all the time she had known him he had never seemed so volatile.

"Xander, I never intended things to turn out this way, you know what we feel for each other is genuine, I love you and I know you still love me… I hope." Xander stared unhinged. His face was illegible, she couldn't read his emotions or tell if he was even feeling any. She was unable to think, all she could do was continue speaking. Iilera continued,

"Yes, I am not a Xanthari by birth, but I am a Xanthari by heart, that is why I am still here, that is why I have risked my life for you and for this Xanthari war!" sadness flushed Iilera's system – her voice became a diapason of crying, screaming and shouting.

Xander looked away, "Xander! Look at me!" she was paradoxically angry with him for not believing how she felt and for the fact that it seemed as if he was questioning her intentions. He followed her command and looked up – his eyes a monstrous red, the veins in his temples pulsating like he was trying to cage his inner beast.

"I love you!" her voice now resembled a mourning widow. "Do you believe me when I say that? You bloody Xanthari!" His head flicked up at the word. Xander broke his silence after what felt like an hour of emotional warfare.

"*Iilera* – any other names you go by, huh? You deceitful, manipulative, evil, scheming, cantankerous, homeless… alien!" he pressed his knuckles against his temples to stop his head from exploding. "You tricked me, you made me fall for you, you made me forsake my first love for you. I told you everything! You made me feel sorry for you and your imaginary story! 'After the war I ran out to the battlefield and spent hours crawling over dead Xanthari carcasses searching for my parents.' You made a mockery of my history. And now you tell me you love me and expect me to believe you when you say that? Has anything you have told me actually been true and not some fabrication conjured in your sick twisted mind?"

"Yes."

"What?"

"That I'm sorry, and I wish that I was truly one of you, this life is all I know I don't have a real life anywhere except here, with you."

"Oh really?"

"Really."

"Were you ever going to tell me? I mean honestly if I had never found out like this, would you have told me ever?"

Xana bit down on her lip. She had asked herself this question countless times, the answer to it becoming more and more uncertain the deeper she had fallen. When she had fallen pregnant with his child, a part of her knew that telling him the truth would be out of the question.

"I don't know, Xander. I mean life like this has been so perfect I don't think I would have wanted to have done something... anything to jeopardise that."

"So no?"

She was speechless. Of course the easy way out would have been to say she would have come clean one day but after all this time she had had enough of lies and deceit.

"So what happens now, do you seriously think that things can go back to the way they were? Christ, Iilera, you bore my child! Don't you think before that would have been a better time to tell me? I mean just something like 'Oh Xander, just before we decide to start a family together, there's something you should know, I'm not really who I say I am and everything we have – has been built – on a lie. But hey, at least I told you and now we can start fresh!' You are crazy!"

"I am sorry."

"Well, guess what sorry isn't enough this time. So I guess I'm the one that's sorry."

"So what happens now, do we say goodbye? If you want me to leave the Fortress, I will. But I'll be damned if I leave without my child."

"*Our child is a Xanthari* – you are not. If you leave, our child stays with his kind. And for you, you will go to your kind."

"No, if I leave, he leaves with me." She stared at him defiantly.

It seemed as if they had hit a brick wall in the conversation.

The arguing duo froze for a moment, thinking of what should come next in this deep meaningful conversation. But both of them were flabbergasted and fatigued by the intensity of it. Xander was panting heavily with his hands upon his head and Iilera was hunched over, sweaty and clammy after all the heart-wrenching prose expelled from her lover's lips.

"Look, Iilera, this isn't the time to discuss this."

"God, Xander, will there ever be a good time? This isn't one of those let's wait and let things blow over, this has to be sorted now."

"I know, I know, I just need time. If I decide now I think my decision would be too rash."

"I just really don't want to lose this, or us."

The conversation's tempo slowed and the argument became less heated.

"I need to go for a walk, clear my head, mull things over." Xander left, leaving a heart broken, fragile, emotionally distraught Iilera to counsel herself and the baby who was now wailing frantically. She picked up her son and sat on the chair, rocking back and forth, holding her baby tightly to her chest as she wept into the night.

***

Out of the blue, there were three loud knocks on Xianni's door. To her surprise and delight it was Xander. Her eyes illuminated like fireworks on a dark night. At this moment Xander was now a desperate man: desperate for answers, desperate for reassurance, desperate for closure. Vengeance was his merciless fuel, where wrongs suddenly began to feel right. Even the most humble of hearts seeks revenge of some sort, as subtle as it may be. And this was Xander's plight, his turn for creating some form of mental and emotional stability.

They both sat quietly in the living area, looking at each other, Xander trying his hardest to piece back the features of the woman he used to admire.

"Drink?" suggested Xianni in a ploy to shatter the icy tension.

"Sure."

"I haven't got your favourite 'Noire D'afrique' but I have your second, I hope that will do – you look like you need something a bit stronger anyway."

Xianni ran her fingers through her hair and shook her head seductively like a lion fluttering its mane. She exaggerated the movements of her hips as she cruised over to the kitchen. Xander watched his first love with fascination, granted time had healed the majority of blemishes and battle-scars, but something was missing. It just wasn't the same...

They sat and enjoyed each other's company. Often recalling anecdotes of a happier history. The pair had an extensive past and Xander drew upon these in order to re-establish the flame he had once allowed to die out.

Before they knew it, they had drunk three bottles of wine and were laughing hysterically about a particular memory. It was about fifteen years ago and they were both in a training session. During the spar, Xander's trousers had slowly loosened and eventually fell down to his ankles – unfortunately the day was cold and not at all flattering. Xander promised her that it had grown a lot since then and that it was no longer afraid of the cold.

Before long, it began to feel like they had never parted. Although one thing stayed at the forefront of both their minds – Iilera. His thoughts were unsteady. He felt the only way to regain what he had lost in Iilera was to give Xianni a chance, at least one try.

"Just going to get freshened up." Xianni left the room and made her way up the croaky wooden staircase. For some reason she felt whole again, a feeling she had long missed. It had fallen upon her that tonight was the night; the night she had waited for all those months. The one person she lived for had come back to her, her tolerance was no longer in vain. His previous relationship was no longer of importance. What mattered was that he had finally chosen her. Her jigsaw was now complete, and the picture was a happy one.

As she was away, Xander checked himself in the glass mirror on the kitchen top, running his fingers through his hair and washing his face and neck in the sink. He hurriedly went to sit down when he heard the staircase begin to creak, alerting him of her descent, so to her he never got up and went over to the sink to check himself out; he was sitting there all along.

Xianni entered not as she had left. For one, she was no longer wearing her cloak, which hid her beautiful hourglass figure. She had also rosied her cheeks and let her hair fall sexily over her shoulders. She felt seductive, an enjoyment that had been stripped from her until now. She felt sexy. She felt wanted. Xander ogled her, almost having to wipe the dribble from the corners of his mouth.

"Sorry I took so long; I figured I'd just get ready for bed. But you can stay as long as you like, that wasn't a ploy to get you out." She decided to shut her mouth before her tongue became even more knotted. She floated over to the sofa where Xander was sitting, forgetting that the alcohol had complete control over her being.

"Oh that's fine, it's been so long since I've seen you in your nightgown, I guess I was slightly too naive or young to appreciate how lucky I was!"

Enough talk. Xander placed his glass onto the table ahead of him and turned to face her. Pheromones surrounded them like an invisible magnet pulling them closer and closer… They connected. Their lips gently pressed against each other's. Their humble noses side by side, gradually the kiss became more passionate.

Hands were thrust to their faces, tongues swirling.

Xianni willingly reclined further into the chair, almost supine. Xander removed his garments one by one.

Xianni watched him strip, she was moistening at the labia. Her nipples were red hot and hard. Xander began to help her undress, kissing and caressing every part of her body.

With her back bare, all the scars from the torture she had endured were visible and covered the entirety of her dorsum. The extent of the damage was severe; her back resembled a Jackson Pollock canvas. At long last, what Xianni had waited for and clung on to had finally happened. She was happier than she could have ever imagined. She was finally fulfilled. Her life now had meaning.

There they lay, bare on the couch with a strip of cloth covering them both. She stared imploringly at him, but couldn't help realising the fact that his mind seemed to be elsewhere. She raised her hand and stroked his face delicately. He looked down at her and smiled.

"I've waited for this moment from even before I left the Fortress. For me, Xander my love, it has always been you, and always will be as long as I live." Guilt took hold of Xander and shook him vigorously. He had been no different to those men who had taken advantage of her and stolen her innocence. He smiled awkwardly –

"I have missed you, Xianni." He chose his words carefully. After all, he did miss her.

A great wave of regret washed over him, how could he have been so heartless and foolish?

"I'm sorry, this shouldn't have happened. Not like this." Her face changed instantly.

"What do you mean, why?"

"It just shouldn't have been like this, it should have never happened, I should go." He began to dress himself.

"What was it? My body? My face? My hands? I know they have done a lot to me. But I thought what we had was deeper than that… Xander. I loved you even before I knew what love was… even before I could spell the word! Please don't do this to me."

"Forgive me, I truly am sorry. But I can't help that my heart lies elsewhere. As much as I wish that it lay here with you, it doesn't; it lies with the mother of my son."

"So why did you just sleep with me?" Xander knew this question was coming but had no immediate justification other than malevolence.

"I was hurting, I needed somebody with me, you were the one person that I knew I could come to, to clear my mind and get my head straight. I never meant for it to go this far."

"Oh that's great, Xander. I'm the one person you can come to, fuck, and then go home with a clear head back to your woman."

"No, ahh, I didn't mean it like that, Xi, please. I thought that Iilera and I were done for good and I thought that I could move on and come back to you, my first love. But I still can't help feeling guilty."

"Get out. You are no different to those Dincans who just used me as a relief. You are the last person in the world I would have expected to use me like a whore." Her voice was cracking. A deep, hoarse, demonic tone had possessed her.

"Xander, God damn you. May the Xanthari gods forsake you! Now get out. I don't ever want to see you again." Her cry was now weak and feeble. Xander no longer had a reason or the will to justify his actions. He was violently shoved, poked and kicked to the door. Which also hit him on the way out. Xander's quest for truth and security had failed. Xianni collapsed behind the door and wept, like a used, betrayed mistress. The one thing she lived for had abused, used and left her.

She didn't know what to do with herself. Surely things couldn't get any worse? But on the other hand they couldn't get any better. The worst thing fathomable had just happened. Who was she living for now? The simple answer to that was nobody.

She cried until her eyes were red and sore. She was dehydrated and had lost her voice. There was no more cry left inside her. She lay unmoving, sprawled out on the wooden floor; eyes peeled back like something had taken control of her physical being.

Every now and again she would scream, shout, cry her tearless sobs. She began to regret her decision to live through the torture in order to return home. She wished that she had just told the Dincans what they wanted or that they had just killed her. She had endured so much pain, clinging onto dear life for something that had now become nothing.

She remained on the floor in the very same spot for days, motionless. She replayed that night in her mind continuously, and as she did her emotions fluctuated with each scene. She had long lost hope of any kind; she wanted to die, to be free of pain, disappointment and thought. Free, like the gods had made them to be.

Chapter XXXVII

Then came the day. She never thought she would do it, but she did. One long, deadly piece of rope tangled around her neck and a kick of chair beneath her.

Her corpse wasn't found until days later. It had begun to rot, and the stench of faeces and urine had filled the room with a putrid aroma. But there was one distinct feature of her body that nobody could deny: not once since her return had she looked so calm and serene. It was paradoxically heart breaking yet relieving to see her finally at peace. In some ways, in death she was beautiful again.

Her funeral was held a few days prior to the signing of the armistice agreement. Xander did not attend. He had told nobody about the events of that night as of yet. He let it dwell in him like a parasite, eating away at him from the inside out. *He had killed her. He had tied the rope around her neck and he had removed the chair from beneath her*. The last ounce of strength she had in her broken, beaten down body was raped from her when he used her as an emotional blanket. He had often gone back to her house to apologise and beg forgiveness but every time he had made it to the door he failed to knock and had turned and walked away. The guilt that his cowardice had caused consumed him entirely.

One day, it became too much for him to bear. Every day he would imagine what it would be like to be free from guilt, free from confusion. The only person he could confide in was Xanthe, who didn't know what could be said to lessen the hurt that Xander was feeling, it would be pointless convincing him that he was not to blame when he was. That evening, Xander wept on Xanthe's lap like a child.

Soon enough, Iilera also began to suffer. He wasn't there for her or their baby. He began to spend most nights away from home. She had no idea where he was going or who he was seeing. Her own feelings of grief were dampened by her loneliness and utter confusion. Her mind was so consumed by thoughts of Xander, she barely had time to think of Xianni.

Her mind ran wild with adulterous thoughts. The main one being that he had gone and found himself a true Xanthari to bear a real Xanthari family. After some time, she decided to pack her things and leave the Fortress to finally return to her homeland – the Dimer Empire. The morning of the signing over of land to the Dincan forces she was gone, as surreptitiously as she had infiltrated the Fortress all those years ago.

Chapter XXXVIII

Later that day, what remained of the Xahlia forces met for the very last time in the auditorium along with the Dincans to settle the armistice agreement. As an act of good faith, the Dincans had returned the wives and children to the Fortress with no further casualties. As an act of precaution, Xanthe sent them directly back en route to the Chantrieri Empire, with the exclusion of his own family – he felt it was important that in such pivotal times they remained close to him and that a strong and unified front was portrayed in the face of the enemy.

Xanthe and Xander attended the meeting, knowing full well that it was likely that it would not pan out as they hoped. Both sides knew that the Dincans were not interested in any agreement. Their only interest was the land and army, and the only two people that could stand in the way of that were Xanthe and Xander. They stood at the forefront of the auditorium, side by side facing the judge who sat alone on a long wooden table facing the crowd. Xanthe's family stood directly behind them and the rest of the Xahlia force sat behind, worn and sombre. Parallel to them, the Dincan leaders also stood facing the judge, smiles plastered across their arrogant faces. They had brought a large number of their force, all of whom sat directly behind their leaders, self-satisfied and buoyant. Between the two forces, a narrow walk way separated them, splitting them in half, the contrast in emotions almost tangible along the divide.

Daice stood apart from his people and looked far more comfortable than the rest of them. It was clear that he had been a key iota to the demise of their establishment. Xanthari decorations had already been stripped from the walls and the auditorium was now a blank canvas; ready to be redesigned by its next leader.

As the judge banged his gavel to indicate silence, Xanthe staggered ever so slightly, leaning his elbow discretely on Xander for support. He maintained a stoic façade but his brittle bones were no longer able to stand tall as they once had. Behind him, Xari touched his shoulder lightly in support.

"We are gathered here today to discuss the terms of the armistice agreement," claimed the newly appointed judge. He was a young man, the sort that had been given too much power too soon – toying with authority. He continued, "Unofficial talks indicate that we have come to a settlement, resulting in the merging of the Dincans and Xahlias. We will henceforth reside in peace as one nation." There was a premature sigh of relief. Xanthe gripped Xander's arm, and shook his head, as if to say, "Do not get your hopes up." An anonymous man in Dincan robes approached the bench, "Before we claim ourselves as one nation I would like to ask the judge what he thinks of the horrific, inhumane war crimes committed by the Xahlias on our people under the orders of Xanthe, and his second – Xander?" Xanthe lowered his gaze.

The judge looked directly at them, his eyes narrowing. "Yes, you are right. It would be an atrocity to leave these atrocities unaccounted for. I hereby sentence these two leaders and the Xahlia Elders to one hundred years imprisonment – or death. They can decide which they prefer." There was a loud cheer from the Dincan half of the auditorium. Xari wailed for her husband. In the corner, Daice stood smirking. He nodded curtly at one of the Dincan leaders before returning his gaze to the judge. Xander and Xanthe both saw. He had betrayed them.

"Now, by the power invested in me by this establishment, I hereby claim our peoples as one nation…"

Xanthe was reduced to his knees. Xari and Xean were screaming and crying as pandemonium arose. Xander cried out,

"This is not the terms of the surrender! Stop this." He looked at Xanthe, their empty eyes met; the end had come unexpectedly. Xander shifted his glance to the stalls behind him searching for Iilera and his son. They were nowhere to be seen. He was going to die and they would not be there to witness it; nobody for him to say goodbye to. Beside him, Xari was embracing her husband, both silently sobbing into each other's shoulders, their son sandwiched between them.

For a few seconds, Xari set her distress aside and whispered something so that only Xanthe could hear…

"My dear, I am a Wua Hu, I haven't seen this moment; but I have known from the beginning that this war was not going to end well for us; so I have made sure that we have lived everyday as if it is our last. We have done all we can. I love you now and in the afterlife."

Xanthe nodded curtly at his wife, "My time was coming anyway. I have been dying for weeks, my love. There is poison in my veins. Be strong. I will always be with you."

The Executioner approached like a grim reaper.

"Daddy! Please don't kill my daddy..." Xean whimpered. Xanthe turned his family away and instructed them not to look.

"Take my life, before I take yours," said Xanthe pointing at the judge. In his last act of patriotism he bellowed, "*I audire, ergo I vivere*", in chorus his warriors replied, "*I erit audire, et sequi*". With one smooth slice to the neck it was all over. Xander tried not to look at his master's lifeless form next to him; but he did. This was neither dream nor an act. This was the bitter end.

Xander also welcomed his fate, with a picture of Iilera and his son in mind. He muttered his last words... "Xana, I've been a fool. I am sorry."

Chapter XXXIX

Iilera and her child rode the horse relentlessly through the mountains. She felt uneasy returning to a place called home after leaving the place she considered her real home. How could her father receive her as his daughter after all these years? She turned to her child, who was neatly strapped to her torso with a cloth.

"I know you are too young to fully understand what I am about to tell you, but I want you to try and remember what I am going to say… Lesson one: life is not fair. The more you come to terms with that premise, the less disappointed in life you will become.

"Second: bad things happen to good people, so don't believe in karma because sometimes karma can get it completely wrong. Man is not everything, even after we die, the world will keep spinning, so put your trust in no one. Put your trust and faith in the only one who is infallible – God.

"And lastly: honesty. No relationship can be built on a false foundation; all it will do is collapse. The more you build on it, the greater the fall. Son, it is not your fault that you will grow up without a father, nor is it mine. Your father was a beautiful, brave man who died in a war to protect us, and you should grow to become just like him. It is for this reason that I have named you Xander II Asherdimer. If you can live your life according to these few things, you will live a much more fruitful life than anyone else."

Young Xander stared blankly at her, completely unaware of his mother's soliloquy. He smiled at his mother's soft voice and she smiled back, a single tear rolling down her cheek. They continued to ride for many months taking regular breaks so that she could nurse him, until they finally reached the Dimer Empire, nestled in a secluded area, which sat comfortably in between two cliff heads. At long, long last she had made it 'home', to a place she felt completely estranged from.

Approaching the gates, slowly her heart began to beat faster and her hands felt sweaty. She held tighter onto her child. A guard dressed in their traditional cloaks approached her.

"Who are you and what is your business here?"

"Iilera Asherdimer, daughter of Halaham Asherdimer, returning home from Voyage X."

The guard's eyes lit up as though he had just seen a ghost.

"Iilera!" he jumped on the spot bursting with enthusiasm, "Daughter of Halaham! How your father still speaks of you! Oh, what a joyous day! I cannot wait to see the look on his face when he sees you return home!" she smiled curiously. Memories of her father were far and distant, she could barely remember what he looked like then let alone imagine what he looked like now, almost two decades later. The guard stepped aside and allowed her to enter the Dimer Empire.

Weirdly, she could feel her internal compass navigating her to a familiar place. She could not recognise a single building yet her brain was directing her to a particular location. Soon enough, she found herself knocking at the door of an intricately stone carved building. Her subconscious had taken over and she stood at the door with her eyes glazed. A rather young man opened it.

"Iilera? Is that you?" his eyes widened. His tone was dark and mysterious, as if he knew something but didn't want to share it.

"Yes, it is I. Sorry I do not know who you are. I just knew to come here."

"I am Asher Dimer, the Emperor of the Dimer Empire. Please come in." He extended a welcoming hand. She eyed it cautiously before extending her own.

"Admeyer had told me he saw you at the Fortress and that you held a very high place in the Xanthari council. How we are all very proud of your accomplishments, but of course we didn't expect any less from you, daughter of Halaham. Some doubted you, deeming that the age we enrolled you was too young, but look at what an amazing job you did. Long have your family awaited your arrival, so I see that it is only fair that they get to see you first. But I will need to debrief you tomorrow morning. So go and see Halaham and the rest of your family and we will convene tomorrow! How I wish I could see their faces!" On that note, he got up and escorted her to the door.

"I have a picture in my head of what my house looks like, but could you please point me in the right direction?"

"Your family no longer resides in that house. Follow the path until you get to the garden, then take a right and keep going until you see the home with the high fence and stained glass windows. And perhaps tomorrow we could discuss what you would like to do with him…" he pointed to the back of horse where Xander II hid under a thick cloth. She ignored him and mounted her horse and slowly rode away: homebound.

There it was. Her home. A rather large abode with stained glass windows as promised. A strange feeling overcame her, one that she had not experienced before – the feeling of neglect and rejection. They had left her alone, alone in a different land. With unfamiliar people in a place she was unfamiliar to. They had sent her on a mission alone and forgotten her.

Returning after such a long time and after all that had come to pass just seemed bizarre. She stood ambivalent: should she enter and be reunited with the only family she had left? Or return to the Chantrieri Empire as one of the remaining surviving Xantharis and seek refuge. From inside the house, she could hear the sounds of boys playing and fighting and the intervening shouts of an annoyed mother. A family she had no tangible connection to, just a distant, vague, uncertain memory. She thought back to a hazy memory of her last day at home, where her father had held her by the shoulder and given her a speech about the importance of her mission. He had not hugged her before sending her away.

Turning, Iilera decided to seek shelter at an inn not too far from her family home. She wasn't ready, not just yet, and she wasn't sure if she would ever be.

***

Iilera awoke abruptly, drenched in heavy sweat. Her hair was wiry and positioned haphazardly around her head. She got out of bed and sat on a chair, watching her child peacefully sleep. He was the spitting image of his father. This thought provoked more questions about her own family, what did they look like?

Getting inside their house wasn't a difficult challenge. Before she knew it, she was in their living room in the dead of night. The house was grandiose and spectacular, bedecked with light beech oak boards and intricately stained windows.

The furniture seeped quality and grandeur. She figured that this was their reward for banishing their daughter to a foreign land. Curiosity overcame her;

she went into the kitchen to observe their dietary habits. She invaded every room on the ground floor and even helped herself to a glass of wine to calm her nerves.

As she made her way upstairs to the bedrooms she listened out for any movement, which could signify a conscious inhabitant. She entered the first room. It was a decent size for the two adolescents who lay completely unconscious on the twin beds. On the wall was a photo of the family, and to her surprise there she was, no more than seven or eight years of age, right at the centre of the family portrait.

The next room was her mother and father's. She spent considerably longer in this room. Analysing their faces. All of which suddenly felt more familiar. Memories began to flash back to her, one-by-one.

Iilera cried silent tears as her family slept, completely oblivious to her return. She sat on the floor and wept, the sentiment of neglect weighed on her heavily. How could they do such a thing as to give away their only daughter? She soon realised that weeping at the foot of the bed wasn't going to change a thing. This was not a place that she wanted to stay.

Just as she was leaving, she came across a room that still had its lights on. Intrigued by the possibility that somebody may have woken up, she stalked the door and listened in. She could hear a rapid heartbeat, so small yet so strong. She peered inside and was welcomed by a baby. It was awake and fidgeting like a worm. The baby stopped and stared at her. It reached up and grabbed a handful of her hair. Then it began to smile and babble like it knew it was looking at its sister.

Its big, bold baby blue eyes trapped her. She didn't know what to do with it. The baby giggled. "Shhhh," she hissed. Suddenly, a rather unpleasant thought crossed her mind – they had tried to replace her. She shifted the clothing slightly, yes, it was a girl. They had succeeded in replacing the daughter they had given up. She got up and left, slamming the door behind her as she went. She heard the house awake, as she was lost to the night. She didn't care; she knew she wouldn't be back.

She sat until morning waiting for Xander II to wake up so they could leave. She brushed his teeth and dressed him. Suddenly, there was an unexpected knock at the door. It was the Dimer Emperor.

"What a surprise. How did you know I was here?"

"I know everything that goes on within my walls."

"How can I help you? As you can see, I haven't been to see my family yet, I was just about to go now, actually." She had no intention of telling him anything about the Xantharis or the parchment.

"Oh but you have been to see your family. You have even seen the new addition to the family. Adorable, isn't she?" Iilera looked as if she had just been struck hard across the face, it took her a few moments to compose herself.

"Yes, of course, I had to see them... Before I actually... saw them. But now I really want to see them... that's why I'm going to see them now." The syntax of a confused woman. He looked at her and smiled. There was something dark about him. Something she didn't trust.

"Of course, I understand. OK, that's not a problem. But please do not forget that we will talk this morning – I must debrief you. And I will need the parchment. But I guess that will have to wait. Are you taking Xander II with you to see the family?" another verbal jab in Iilera's face.

"Erm... no, I'm not ready yet." He nodded in response.

"Report to me around eleven hundred." He smiled and backed away from the door.

Iilera sat transfixed on the edge of her bed.

"Xander honey, grab your toy. We are leaving now."

What kind of a people were these? They seemed to know everything she was thinking; what she had done, and what she was about to do. If this were true then he would probably know that she intended to leave. She was trapped in a strange place called home. She tried her luck. At the gate, she asked the guard to let her out.

"Why do you desire to leave, Iilera?" the guard asked plainly.

"Just for a walk, I need some fresh air. I haven't been home in so many years it's just a bit overwhelming, you know?"

"Of course, I see. Well, that will not be possible I'm afraid until you see Dimer himself."

Just as she turned away the guard spoke again, this time his voice was grave. "My sister hasn't come back from her mission yet. You should never have returned."

She was left with no choice but to go and see Dimer. As much as she didn't want to reveal anything to him, she felt she had to. There was no point in lying; obviously he would know because, well, he knew everything.

She entered the emperor's lair alone. Again, Xander II was hidden on the back of the horse outside. He welcomed her warmly, a little too warmly in fact. He positioned her down in his office. They sat on either side of the table, staring squarely at each other.

"I'm glad you came back to talk to me. I was beginning to think that you might not. Before we get started, I must say that this conversation will not be brief by any means, so it may be better if Xander II comes in also; he will not be comfortable on the back of that horse for very long."

"He will be fine."

"OK, Iilera, you have had your time to rest. Now it is time to discuss the revelations you have found in light of your time with the Xantharis. Firstly, talk to me about their way of life and how they are trained from early on. And more importantly how they strengthen their auscultation abilities."

She began hesitantly, only briefly describing their rituals and daily lives. As she continued to look at him, something powerful hit her, as if he was drawing the information from her eyes. She began to say things that were strategically hidden in the back of her mind. She told him about Xianni and the love triangle, the murder of Xanthe's daughter, where the women and children had gone to seek refuge, that she had obtained traces of the parchment.

"OK, tell me more about the parchment. What does it do and how can we Dimers harness its power?" the short interlude allowed Iilera's eyes to break from his and she blinked several times, wondering what had just happened. He literally sucked all the information from her. She began to wonder what other powers this man had. For now, it was safe to say she should never look him directly in the eye.

Staring at the bridge of his nose in order to give the illusion of eye contact, she lied. Profusely. In reality, she didn't know much about the parchment, but what she did know she disguised with falsities.

"So again I ask you, how do we gain access to the Lost Empire?"

"That I don't know. For that information you would need Xanthe, Xianni or maybe even Xander, but I myself am clueless. All I know is that there are four pieces and only once all these are together can one harness its full power."

"But I know this. Where are the parchments?"

"Again, of that I am not sure. After the end of the war, all the people who knew the answers to these questions died or are in refuge."

"Fasherii has already told me that you have prints of the parchment pieces, all four I remember him saying if I am correct?"

"Three of the four," she lied.

"OK, so where is the last one?"

"Again, I cannot tell you; I never obtained it to trace it. Only Xanthe knows of its whereabouts."

The interrogation continued on like this for hours, until Dimer suggested that the interview could last for a while longer still, so she might as well ask Xander to come in and sit down or have something to eat. She was reluctant to let Xander's eyes meet with Dimer's, but all that time on the back of the horse hidden would be too much for any child to handle.

It was clear that Xander was taken aback by the way Dimer looked at him. In his head, he could hear Dimer saying something via some intangible connection. The word 'half-breed' resounded in Xander's head, even though he had never heard the word, or understood its meaning.

Xander soon grew tired and interrupted the debrief, "Mum I'm tired, can we go sleep now?"

"Not until we are done, little one!" replied Dimer.

"I wasn't talking to you... Mum?"

"Dimer, it has been over four hours, I do need a break myself!"

"OK, you may take Xander home and come back in... shall we say an hour or so?"

"OK, perfect." Iilera had no intention of coming back. They had less than an hour to devise an escape route. She was going to leave the Dimer Empire no matter the cost.

They returned to the inn. All their paraphernalia had already been packed. She paced the room, waiting for inspiration to hit her. It never came. So Plan B it was – storm the gate.

The same guard was still at his post. Surveying the area, she was quite certain he was alone. She rode carefully towards him, thinking of how to cause sufficient injury to slip out of the mysterious place unnoticed. As she approached, he walked out towards her as if to block the gate. The plan: step off the horse, give him two bone shattering blows to the head, enough to knock him unconscious and providing her with enough time to clear the area before they began their search.

"So I understand you have had the first part of your talk with Dimer?" exclaimed the guard.

"*How on earth does word travel around here?*" Iilera thought to herself.

"Yes we have, now I really need that fresh air." She was blunt.

"Well, I think you know I can't let you do that."

"I know." Iilera stepped down from her horse.

"You remind me of my sister, you know. You look very much like her. As I mentioned before, she has another few months left of her mission… She has been stationed at the Chantrieri Empire. She was meant to finish a few months ago but things haven't gone as smoothly as planned; you would think with all six of his eyes he could have foreseen that." The guard chuckled and Iilera couldn't help but chuckle too. He was an okay man, with chocolate coloured skin but milky eyes.

"How did you know I had spoken to him?"

"Everybody here, has a connection; if he wants you to see something you will see it. It will simply just appear in your mind." There was a slight pause. "So where do you intend to go from here, Iilera?"

"For some air… Actually, away from here – this is not my home. It is foreign to me. I find it odd that Dimer would –"

The guard held up a finger to silence her, quickly whispering, "Do not mention his name. He can hear it no matter where it is being said."

"Right… I just don't understand how he can exile me for this long and expect me to return faithfully as if nothing happened? I don't even know a thing about this Empire."

"Oh, but you did return faithfully didn't you?" the guard gave a know-it-all look.

"Well, surely you must remember the basics? After the Great War and the divide of Morten, all the races kept to their own people. Everybody segregated. However, before the divide it didn't matter if you were Nanavic, Yaw, Dahlia or whatever – if you found love you just got married. After the divide, everybody forgot about those in this Empire. Nobody wanted anyone of mixed blood – people like us. I guess you were too young to understand, but the point of these missions is to learn the ways of these other tribes so that someone part born of that race can learn to harness their abilities. You-know-who with the six eyes was of the lineages of Yaw, Nanavic and Dahlia, and was one of the first to harness all of their abilities. But I get where you are coming from. This is why I want my sister to never return here, I wish her to remain with the Chantrieris."

"I have people, family at the Chantrieri Empire. I can pass on a message for you, you could even ride with me to see her?"

His face lit up, "Oh how I wish I could. But I cannot leave... The connection – he would find me... But you can before it is too late, Iilera. I will need you to tell her this: that I hope my message meets her in good health. Tell her that the whole family loves her and misses her dearly, but unfortunately Papa passed away a few years ago. Tell her it was a peaceful death in his sleep, and that he did not suffer, even though it was a full on heart attack. Say that as saddening as this is to say, we do not want her to return. She would not recognise anything here, or her family for that matter. Tell her your story; maybe it will help her stay away from this place. Finally, tell her that in my own time I will come and see her and when I come I expect to see a happy family with lots of children! With lots of little nieces and nephews..." The guard began to tear up and his voice became thick.

"Of course I will, what is her name?"

"Her real name is Nadiiya. But her cover name is Akua. Thank you, please keep true to your word. As you have probably figured out I cannot just let you leave. It has to be as if there was a struggle and you won. I will not hit you hard, but you have to damage me. There must be blood and I must fall unconscious at the end. Be sure to tell my sister the measures I went through to get this message to her." The man chuckled again. Gradually, his smile turned to seriousness as he threw an arm at Iilera.

The forest was welcoming to her. After nearly six months of travelling across hills and mountains and riversides, Iilera and Xander II arrived at the Chantrieri Empire. It was immense. A vast, unfathomable black marble structure surrounded the main kingdom. Sculptures of melanic wild cats constructed to look as if they were pouncing out of the walls lined the perimeter. Nothing inside the kingdom could be seen from outside the walls, even at height.

She knocked at the marble gates, bruising her knuckles as she did so. To her surprise, one of the petrified melanic beasts began to move. It prowled towards her. She was frozen. The cat went about sizing her and sniffing her. She had always heard stories about the Chantrieri oneness with nature but didn't think it was quite like this. After sensing her to be harmless, the marble gate was pulled open by what she thought would have taken thirty men, but in fact it took two. The interior was by far the most beautiful thing she had ever seen.

She refused to blink in fear of being away from the paradisal scene. Bamboo shoots and tropical vegetation lined the inner walls. Wild cats roamed the perimeter.

An old man approached her, eyeing her and the child up and down.

"Of which nation do you come?" he asked.

Iilera hesitated. No one but Xander had found out her secret yet. Of course he may have told everyone by now, she could not be sure. But nonetheless, her son was Xanthari and she had to protect him at all costs.

"Xanthari," she replied.

"Name?"

"Xana. Leader of the elites and second to Xanthe."

The old man eyed her up again before turning his gaze to the infant in her arms. She tightened her grip. A few seconds later, she was directed to where the rest of the Xantharis were residing.

It had taken weeks before Xari and Darcie were able to escape the poisoned Fortress. They knew what had to be done before they could leave: they had to regain at least one of the parchment pieces to safeguard the protection of their promised land. It took countless nights and days of meticulous planning, but they finally made it. The Chantrieris were shocked to see them after all they had heard about the collapse of the Xahlias, but gave them refuge nonetheless.

At the sight of Xari and Darcie, her heart warmed for the first time in many months.

Tears rolled gently down their humble cheeks. Iilera heard for the first time how Xanthe and Xander were trialled and punished. How Daice had been the key element in the Xanthari demise. They embraced and talked for hours; spending most of the time soaked in tears. As promised, *Xana* gave Xanthe's letter to Xari. Their loved ones were now dead, deceased, decaying. The Xanthari Empire as they knew it was now dead, deceased, demolished. Their new home was The Chantrieri Empire.

But the Dincans were far from finished. And the Dimers were just about to get started.